Tangled Dreams

A Novel

Delores Lowe Friedman

RED LOTUS RISING

Red Lotus Rising
Queens, New York

Paperback ISBN: 979-8-9948195-0-0
eBook ISBN: 979-8-9948195-1-7

Front cover art and design by The Cover Collection, Inc.
Interior design and typesetting by Mayfly book design

Library of Congress Catalog Number: 2026903276
First Printing: 2026

Dedication

I dedicate this book to my husband, Karl Friedman, whose love has supported my writing for more than fifty-four years. He was my best friend, my muse, and my love, as I was his. In 2020, I read a chapter of *Tangled Dreams* to Karl, a pivotal chapter near the end of the book. He had read this work from its inception. But, as I read this passage to him, he stopped me mid-sentence, asking if there was a comma there just before my pause, editing text in his head. Though his body was failing him, his mind was sharp and clear. I said, of course, and he said, "Go on!" When I finished, we shared a silence that gave gravity to the brewing troubled times ahead, and he said, "Promise me you'll finish it." He was a playwright, always careful with his words.

Here it is, my promise fulfilled.

I also dedicate this book to my son, Ian Friedman. Karl and I were always in awe of his intelligence, and his caring, but during the last few years, since we lost Karl, his quiet strength impresses me most.

Prologue

A few hundred miles off the coast of North Africa, on a clear day in 1845, a sudden storm stirred the sea and lifted the whaling ship high above the churning waters. The captain was sure it was she who wrenched him from his charted course. He could not escape her. He gave his ship her name, Nereida, the Sea Nymph. A Cape Verdean woman; she was a barmaid he took a liking to, a siren who summoned him each voyage. Every time he set sail, he was drawn to her. Now his ship spun around three times, heaved each time in the direction of Brava, her island. Despite his calls to his men to shift the sails, the ship continued on course to her.

As he entered the bar, he anticipated the passion he always saw in her eyes. Today, mixed with her desire, he noticed something else. He leaned to embrace her, but her eyes pushed him back like a fist to his chest. Her dark stare penetrated his skin and chilled his bones. Behind him this time, stood his son and his grandson, the two whom he brought from Portugal. Tired as he was from the journey, he made a joke, "Nereida, why don't you make my son happy."

The glass she was drying broke in her hand, and blood oozed from the wound and blossomed on the towel. Her gaze blackened.

She called out, "Sumadi, come here!" A young man came from behind the bar. "This is our son." The sea captain looked into his face. He saw his own eyes ringed in amber, like the sun. The young man's skin was dark, and his chest was broad and strong like his own, yet he was a full foot taller. His nose was

Roman in shape, like that of his own father. She said, "You will take him to the New World where you go."

"Why did you give him that name?"

"It came to me in my sleep."

"It is a name long time past in my family."

"Then you must do for him as I say."

"I cannot."

The two young men eyed each other. Nereida waved her hand telling Sumadi to return to the bar. Through her clenched teeth, she said, "When do you leave?"

"When I finish hiring a crew."

"You come back here before you go. His eye is sharp, and he does sight the whales better than all in this village. He rides the whale with the skill of a man twice his years at sea. You will take him to the New Land."

"It is not a place for a man of his color. He will forever be in chains."

She spoke again, and this time her voice came from her belly, not her throat. "You will take him, and you will see to it that he never lives in chains. You will see to it that everything the one you call your grandson has, he will have . . . Everything he wishes, mine will wish. Everything he gets, my son will have. Go now, but come back for him, and do not turn against me. I will see that you and your ship will have the blackest fortune if you leave without him. I will see to it. No matter how long it takes. I will see to it."

Part I

I thought I had summoned them, but as they filled themselves in around me, I knew that they were willful beings in control of their own comings and goings. It was the aloneness that made them come.

1

"Professor Jocelyn Kendall, Confidential." The envelope stamped "COPY" rested on the top of the flyers, books, and inter-college mail. The original was probably waiting for me in my mailbox at home. My impulse was to rip it open, but with my hopes on hold for years, I could wait a little longer.

I slid the envelope into my pocketbook and tried to focus on the bare minimum of books I needed to take home with me for the summer. My office was stifling, the windows painted shut years ago. The second week of June, still no air conditioning.

Why I wore this suit jacket, I didn't know. Habit, because of my strict West Indian upbringing combined with my image as a professor, at least according to my mother, whose scolding voice never seemed far from my thoughts.

Someone was at the door. I was sure of it. The longer I lingered in the office, the greater the risk that students would find me, ask how they did on the final—did they pass the course. They were needy at this time, and they made me feel like a mother lion, nursing too many cubs, sucked dry, or so I imagined. I had no children, no husband.

There was a knock. Someone was there! It wasn't a student. I could tell from the darkness of the presence. My students always offered light-ness. Silently, I willed the person away—she clutched at me through the dense hot air. It was a battle of wills. I could feel my strength draining away, my guilt joining her in the battle against me. I opened the door.

"Jocelyn, I knew I saw you go in . . . have a good summer. Any plans?" The department chair's tone belied the words she spoke. Clearly disinterested in my response, I was left speaking to the back of Carol's head.

I answered her anyway, polite as ever. "Remember my grant to study the connections between the whaling peoples of Boston and the Caribbean Island of Bequia?" Carol glanced back at me . . . a momentary puzzlement flashed across her face, her stare unfocussed, dull. Then she fully fixed her piercing gaze on me again. "Right, a travel grant and just before the cutbacks. Enjoy the beach and the sun!"

Just like her to deliberately miss the point and ignore the professionalism.

"No time for that, first I'm headed to Boston . . . What cutbacks?"

She ducked her head back into my office. "Got to rush! By the way, Susan got her Associate. We're planning a congratulatory luncheon for her first thing in the fall."

Her lips curled into a smirk.

"Good for her," I bit my tongue. It was clear now what was in the envelope.

"That article she co-authored with me is what put her over the top." Carol's expression, now a twisted grin, grew broader. "The committee said they wanted to see more collaborations like ours."

When I had asked Carol to work with me on an article last year, she said she didn't do collaborative writing . . . dismissed my request with the comment, "As the Chair, I am busy with other matters." Her deed done, giving me the good news, she left.

My forehead was hot.

Suppressing my desire to slam the door, always the *good girl*, I began stuffing the pastel-colored flyers into the trash without even glancing at them. The mound of paper reached the brim of the can, having nowhere to go—like the storm building in my chest.

"More focus? Are they kidding me?" Mona's voice came back to me from a day earlier.

We had nodded to each other in the building lobby, as we were wont to do when wearing our full doctoral robes after commencement.

"Dr. Hastings," I said.

"Dr. Kendall," she nodded. "Turned me down again," she fixed her jaw so tightly that the muscles pulsated. Her skin looked gray; the light yellow-skinned cast it usually had was gone. One of the most accomplished faculty members in the Sociology Department, publishing no fewer than three articles a year, and now a book.

"You were surprised?"

"Guess not," Mona diverted her eyes, staring off into space. "Said my work needs focus."

She sucked her teeth.

"We know how this works," I said, unhooking the collar of my robe that choked me.

"But this thing has got me stressed. My book got excellent peer reviews . . . nobody has . . . Did you read the Forbes article? This issue about slow advancement for us is nationwide."

"Don't let it get to you. Resubmit next year. After they elevate whoever . . ."

Consoling each other never worked. It was a ritual we went through for lack of any other more active measures, which we knew would make matters worse.

"Can't do this anymore. My hair is falling." She reverted to our shared Caribbean vernacular.

"Have you been to the doctor?"

"Of course," Mona said. "They ruled out everything, but stress. My pressure is through the roof. I'm done with this place." Mona's eyes darted about, searched the air as if grasping for meaning. "Putting my papers in . . . this new early retirement offer is too good to pass up."

The scene flashed before my eyes. It was clear what was in the envelope. I couldn't ignore it anymore, and I stuck my forefinger under the flap, tearing it open.

"Shit!" The thin paper cut stung. I shook my hand and then sucked the blood from it, the salty taste lingered on my tongue. The University's crimson and gold crest was emblazoned on the left-hand corner of the letter. There in crisp black print were the words:

> *We regret to inform you that your request for promotion to full professor has been denied. We suggest that you work with your chairperson to improve your presentation for next year, should you choose to reapply.*

The letters bent and twisted on the page. A curtain of tears draped my eyes. Sure, work with my chairperson! The rules kept shifting and changing like the sands. Sleight of hand, from wanting more papers, to more grants, to more fieldwork, to more theoretical articles. I learned the dance, or so I thought, much in the way the Black folks learned to dance in times gone by. But now the steps were more intricate, more bizarrely contrived. My thoughts were like furies, flying about and shrieking in agony. I ripped the junk mail, thrusting the heaviest textbook on the pile, to stuff the paper into the now full trashcan. Didn't let the tears fall. Made them sit there . . . with the ache. *Twenty-three years—why have I spent my life doing this?*

Somewhere in my consciousness, I heard a tapping sound. I dug around in my bag for my tissues. Then there was knocking, and a voice.

"Professor Kendall? Are you there? I have my paper for you."

"That's okay, leave it in my box," I said through the door.

". . . Just wanted to tell you why it's late."

"It's okay . . . leave it." My voice was now strained. "I won't penalize you," I said, trying to sound as welcoming as I could, poking my finger into the plastic slit of the tissue packet.

"But it says on the syllabus . . ." she persisted.

"I know what the syllabus says, I am telling you . . ." I pinched my nose with the tissue and opened the door, trying to draw in air and square my shoulders.

"Hi Professor . . . Are you all right?" Lisa was one of my wonderful "throwbacks" to the sixties, her blue eyes sharply focused on me, and her blonde dreadlocks stiffly shifted to the side.

"I'm fine. Lisa, I'm telling you, I won't penalize you. Go home . . . have a good summer."

"Okay, thanks Professor. By the way, I'm taking another course in anthropology." She smiled, "Loved your course . . . thinking of Cultural Anthropology as my minor . . . taking your course on gender through the ages." She stood taller and straightened her spine. "Are you sure you're all right?" her stare unwavering.

"I just got some bad news, that's all."

"Can I give you a hug, Dr. Kendall?" She reached out for me. "You're the best. I hope I get into your section in the fall. See you then." I drew her to me. Finally, the girl threw her bag over her shoulder, "Have a good summer, Professor."

Sitting in silence for a minute or two, and placing the letter in my purse, perspiration dripped into my eyes, the salt stinging. My keys were buried in the bottom of my bag. Maybe *I* should retire. My thoughts weighed me down, like a yoke across my shoulders, but there at eye-level to my right, was the photo of my master's students encircling me. I pushed my eyeglasses up on the bridge of my nose to see it better. It was that field trip to Kenya a few years back. The morning we took that photo, I received a "Dear Jocelyn," letter from Paul. First, I laughed at the memory of myself naming it that. Then I recalled the pain. Mumbi, the wise woman of the village, saw the sadness in my eyes, when she snapped the photo. She asked me what the matter was. "Nothing," I said, "just my boyfriend breaking up with me."

"Ya know, sometimes you gotta sweep out da old, to make place for the new."

I laughed. "I'm too old for a new man."

"*Me* older than you. You calling me too old?" She sucked her teeth and shimmied her hips, "Let me see you hand, girl."

She held my opened palm in hers, tracing one line with her finger, studying it, her eyes somber at first then taking on a saucy expression.

Her countenance transformed in that instant into that of a younger woman, caught up in memories she kept private. "Take care child. You don't need my advice on love." She folded my hand up and looked away.

"What did you see, Mumbi?" Her sphinxlike expression puzzled me.

"I see your hands will soon be full, chile. These t'ings you holding so tight, you don't need dem. Just let go."

The universe always answered me. First, Lisa came and brought lightness to my office, now this photo and memories of Mumbi. Four years ago, I had ignored her. I stayed because of my work, my students. I played her words back in my mind again and again. Was it academia I was holding too tightly? Or did Mumbi mean something else?

It was unsettling, thoughts of leaving teaching. I still loved my students' sense of wonder. The essence of my work was finding the connections of peoples in the world. My students were open and receptive to that ethos. And I didn't want to lose them. But Bequia was calling me now, more insistently than I could ignore. I wasn't just grateful for the grant; it felt like a lifeline. The trip would give me a place to focus my writing and publishing interests, yes. But the formal way I described it in the grant didn't hint at all the layers of my journey. There were family secrets I wanted, needed, to uncover. Thoughts of my childhood in Bequia, these last weeks were like a siren's serenade calling me home.

2

---

*W*hen I said marriage is not for you, I had my reasons.

It began with her voice—it haunted me. It felt like a dream, but no, this was a memory replayed, and there was my mother's voice, as if on cue, along with that nagging pain in my lower back. Strange she'd come to this hotel room in Boston to chat. I guess she wanted to catch me early, before I got on with my day. I am sure that's why she showed up in the pale blue of the morning, to mess with my head and remind me that she could. Her voice should have left with her when she died three years ago, but here it was. As usual, she planted herself here on the very day before I would meet with Dr. Gerald Hunter. She never missed an opportunity to ruin my meeting with a man.

You blame me for sending you away to live with your grandmother. I had no choice.

Sure, you did, you could have kept me here with you.

In this loop of conversation repeating in my mind, I was talking back to my mother. I don't ever remember talking back to her in real life. From this distance, I could see that she had a terrible dilemma. I was three and a half when I went to live with my grandmother. Nobody really explained it all to me. The decisions my mother and father made were their secrets. My mother did tell me, "Your father and I didn't get along," but she never said why. Working long hours as a nurse and leaving me with babysitters

9

was her excuse. My grandmother had a home and could care for me. "It would be better for everyone if you go with her."

Over the years, I saw photos of myself in the airport holding my doll when I left, but all I remembered was sitting on a plane, by myself, going to Bequia. I heard stories from my aunt that my grandmother met me in Barbados since Bequia, a very small island didn't have an international airport. We took a small plane from Barbados to St. Vincent, and then a boat to Bequia. I couldn't remember any of those details, but I do recall the plane trip to Barbados. It was a ten-hour flight, and all the strange people on the plane were telling me, "Big girls don't cry!" I kept thinking, *How come they don't know I am not big? Can't they see, I'm little?*

When my mother, whom I had begun calling Rosalie as my grandmother did, came to reclaim me, I was five. She said it was because I had to go to school in the U.S. She and my grandmother, whom I called Mother, argued. There was screaming and yelling. My hands pressed against my ears through it all. Rosalie cried and tried to hug me. I pushed her away, and said to her what Mother said to me, "Why are you crying? That's so foolish!" I remember being pulled in two directions like a prized ragdoll that they both wanted. I still don't know if that tug-of-war was real or just my imagining, trying to make sense of it. Rosalie packed my things, and told me later, she could see in my eyes that I didn't know her. Our closeness was gone. "You were like a little old woman, her child!" she said. Somehow the way she said it, it felt like my fault. But we came home together, back to Brooklyn.

It was a family story that was retold from time to time. And as my mother got older, she told me how sorry she was for sending me away. By the time I was sixteen, and "awkward" as she called me, she recounted the day we left, saying that hearing me call my grandmother "Mother" was the last straw for her, that it hurt her deeply. I made a conscious effort after that to call Rosalie my mother. No matter how many times I told her to let it go, making amends, each time she retold the story she said how sorry she was for sending me away, and I couldn't miss the grief carved in her brow.

The memory always filled me with melancholy, which felt like a crosscurrent in the sea, sweeping my feet from beneath me, always leaving me a little off-kilter. There was more to the story I was sure, but I never got my mother to answer any of my questions. Once we left Bequia, I never saw my grandmother again. Years later, I learned that she died, but my mother refused to tell me exactly when or how.

My hotel room was now blue-yellow, the sun claiming the day and pushing its way inside. The wet hot June morning threatened a sweltering day. I turned on the air conditioner, which I didn't need the night before, and caught sight of Boston Harbor. It was now in motion, a ferry leaving a dock near the hotel. Sailboats, with their masts gently swaying from side to side, tethered to mooring buoys so they wouldn't drift away. An ocean liner seemed to rest atop the indigo waters, gliding toward the horizon. I longed for the sea breezes of Bequia and its aqua, then the turquoise sea. Just a week from now, I'd be stepping onto those shores at last.

My mother's words reached out for me again and shook me.

Don't you blame me! When I said marriage is not for you, I had my reasons.

The first time she said that, when I was a teenager, Bequia was on my mind. I said I'd like to go someday. Out of the blue, my mother said, "Marriage is probably not for you." I was stunned, but I swallowed it whole. Didn't question it. From then on, it became a comment she repeated. Sometimes, she'd follow it with, "Head always in the books," a seeming compliment unless you listened carefully enough to hear the snicker at the end.

Once I was a woman, it was said, "You'll never find a man, always working, studying." I always wondered, could that be why I chose bad boys? You know, the ones with the wandering eye. Eventually, of course, including this last one, I caught him at it. His eye wandered into bed with a girl half my age, and we broke up four years ago.

When I told my mother, she shrugged and gave me the *I told you so* look, and sucked her teeth. "You work ten to twelve hours a day. What do you expect a strapping, healthy man to do?" I finally confronted her, and said, "Why do you always say that to me?" She was cutting carrots to make soup. She stopped, and looked into my eyes, like she was searching for words, with an enigmatic expression masking some truth she did not share. "I have my reasons."

3

"Selena . . . it's you!" I was stuffing my phone into my bag on my way out of my hotel room when it rang. Selena always called when I needed a north star. My thoughts had been on Auntie Grace, along with memories of the scent of orange and lemon peels she kept in the bowl of eucalyptus leaves at the entryway of her apartment. Confounding secrecy about my grandmother came flooding in too.

"You've been on my mind, all morning," she said. "Something's going on? What is it?"

"I know. I know . . . my mother visited me . . . at dawn."

"Banish her!" Selena said, laughing. "You can, you know."

I pushed my glasses fully up on the bridge of my nose and went to turn the AC back on. I laughed. "I wish."

"Let me come cleanse your apartment . . . burn some sage," Selena said, her voice, the soothing, familiar balm it always was.

"I am not at home. She followed me to Boston." The thought drew my attention back out to the harbor that now held only two lonely sailboats.

"A past life regression. That's what you need."

"Past lives, right. You know, ever since you married Luis, your rational mind has been replaced by this para-psychological . . ." I searched for the right word, nothing rude.

Selena was silent for a full minute. "Call it whatever you want, but you need to make a major change, get rid of all the negative energy that's around you . . . starting with whatever his name was. You haven't had a date in what, two years?" Selena chided.

I changed the subject. "I didn't get my promotion."

"Seriously? You've been focused on nothing but this promotion for three years."

Selena was right. "And they're talking cutbacks. God knows if I'll get a promotion next year."

"Why are you still on the fence about leaving this place? Worried about your pension, vest it. Go to another college. But move on!"

"Three years, almost four since I had a date, but who's counting."

"This job has drained you dry." Selena paused, "Pun intended."

Her impish face appeared in my mind's eye. "Stop it." I tried to suppress the laugh in my chest. ". . . I'm thinking about retiring."

"Retiring? No!"

Selena was all of five feet when she stood on her tiptoes, but her persona was six feet tall. "How many times have I . . . Make up your mind to get out of that poisonous place." Her tone reminded me of our first conversation at the Broome Street Bar in the Village. We were at the birthday of a mutual friend. The guy whose party it was introduced us. "Jocelyn Kendall, meet Selena Martinez. You two should chitchat . . . both college instructors."

We made a fast connection that night. Selena spoke passionately about teaching college math, "But I need to build something of my own," she said. She was focused, her tone resolute. She sounded the same today, as she did way back then, "Pursue your own work . . . at a museum, or consulting, or speaking, writing . . . Get away from those hateful people . . . and you will meet someone."

Selena was a series of contradictions, a mathematician, who artfully used logic to debate any topic, who also believed in past lives and karmic influences. We saw each other through my doctorate, and Selena going to work on Wall Street.

"By the way, remember that grant I told you I was applying for . . . I got it!"

"See, that's what I mean . . . Which one?"

"The travel grant to study the whaling communities on that island, just off St. Vincent called Bequia." The tightness in my lower back relaxed for the first time since my mother spoke to me in the wee hours of the morning.

"Where your folks are from?"

"Yes, a small island called Bequia, spelled B-E-Q-U-I-A, but pronounced Beckway . . . I repeated it this time, putting emphasis clearly on the last syllable. "Seriously though, no past life regressions . . . by the way, I booked a trip to St. Vincent for the third week in July . . . setting up a link to the Whaling Museum here in Boston first. I've been corresponding with the curator, and he directed me to some historical records in their library."

"Did you say *he*?"

"Selena, stop it!"

"What does he look like?"

"Selena! He and I email about whaling research. Hardly a romantic topic!"

"Depends. So, tell me some details."

"They have archived records of whaling ships, crew members names, cargo . . ."

"What . . . ?"

Selena made me hungry. Those foil wrapped candies the hotel left on my pillow called me. "Sorry, chewing a chocolate."

"Sugar. Not good," she said. ". . . Have to cleanse your body too. No . . . asking about details on him."

"You made me want this candy. Selena, what was I talking about before you took us off on this tangent?"

"So . . . back to what's important. What does he look like? Young, older?" she said.

"I don't know. He's black, and I'd say about forty-ish from the photo on the website.

Couldn't see . . . It was a group photo. Probably too young for me."

"But you looked, at least. That's a good sign," she paused. "What do you mean too young?"

"Good looking, seemed too young . . ."

"Says who? By the way, they say women should be at least ten to fifteen years older than men, because of when we peak sexually," she argued. "A perfect time for getting guidance from the past," she sang out. ". . . Remove all of your old inhibitions and reconnect with the power of your past lives. I'm telling you, it changed my whole life."

"But you were looking, I'm not."

"Alright, at least, come to our house in Vermont for a week. I'll be there, starting tomorrow for a few weeks. Come to rest. You should float. It will relax you. The floatation tank is all set up. Luis will be sculpting and working on the garden, but he would guide your past life regression. . . . Stay as long as you want just getting . . . grounded."

"Get grounded and float? Selena, you are hysterical. . . . But I'd love to come up to the house to unwind."

A kaleidoscope of memories of her country home filled my mind. Days sitting in their old wicker chair on the porch, reading a good book, or painting with my watercolors, capturing the pinks and pale greens of spring and the crimson and gold of fall on my Leica. Vegetables from the garden. Fireflies lighting up the evening air. The black velvet night sky studded with the brightest gemlike stars.

I slept the deepest, most restful sleep there. It was an escape into myself that Selena's house gave me. I had not been there in so long that I didn't remember myself.

My recollections drew my eyes outside to the docks once more, now filled with passengers departing a ferry, then I caught sight of my watch. "Selena I have to go . . . seeing my aunt. Tomorrow . . . I make personal contact with this curator. Then I will come up to see you. How long a drive is it from Boston to Brattleboro where you are?"

"About three hours I think, you sure you don't want to fly?"

"No, I am going to drive from Boston to you and then back to New York. . . . Time to think. Selena, I just spent more than twenty years of my life at that place. Everything I accomplished amounted to nothing . . . like I was dead there."

"That is simply not true. Think of the kids you turned on to anthropology, your influences in the field . . ." Selena was quiet, but I felt her thinking. "No. Don't let anyone make you think that what you accomplished was not significant. It was. That's why I am talking about a past life regression . . . writing article after article, and not a full professor there? . . . Cleanse yourself of those people."

Selena's comment triggered a memory. "My aunt told me not to take that job when I first applied. . . . Held the ad in her hand and said, 'I feel darkness here . . . a twisting churning darkness.'"

"When did she say that?" Selena asked.

I paused to think, "Twenty-five years ago. . . . Auntie was sensing something way back then."

"Your aunt can see, would she read for me?"

"She doesn't do that all the time . . . it's just when she feels something strongly . . . she might."

Selena's question sparked my memories of conversations with Aunt Grace, snatches of her facial expressions left me with a strong feeling that she knows much more about our family than she's shared. "I became interested in the connections of the whaling people in Boston and Bequia when she said in passing one day, 'Your great-great-grandfather was a whaler, ya know,' and his wife was a Carib Indian . . ." Her silences drew me to her. "I am hoping she might help me with my work in Bequia on the peoples there."

"I also have some questions to ask her about my grandmother's death . . . could never get my mother to give me a straight answer about it. They had some kind of a falling out."

"Who? Your mother and your aunt?" she said.

"No, my mother and my grandmother. My mother always seemed as if she was harboring some secret about her. I stopped asking her about it. There was some mystery about how my grandmother died. . . . Always bothered me . . ."

"Selena, I'll call you when I finalize my travel plans. I'm coming to Vermont."

She laughed, and her voice penetrated my somber mood. "Now we have to work on . . . what's that curator guy's name?" she asked, her throaty giggle was infectious. I laughed, though I didn't want to encourage her.

"Dr. Gerald Hunter. Selena, what am I going to do with you?" My cheeks grew warm. "I'm hanging up."

There was a fleeting instant when I tried to summon the image of the curator I saw online. I could not. Until Selena mentioned it, I didn't even imagine any man's attention. I caught sight of myself in the mirror above the dresser. My hair, which I always kept natural, needed a cut, some shape. My complexion could use some sun. I always looked better when I was darker, coppery. Always a little heavy, with the pounds I put on the past few years, my five-foot-four-inch body just looked "plump," my mother's word.

On a precipice, a sense of vertigo swept me into a mental free fall, my breathing suddenly grew shallow. *Am I doing this too fast?* I can apply for the full professorship again next year. I should have another publication by then, maybe two. How old will I be—forty-six, forty-seven?

Selena's words echoed in my mind. "You need to cleanse yourself of those people . . ." My mind completed her thoughts. ". . . once and for all." She always reminds me of the thoughts that I keep hidden.

4

W e called her Aunt Grace, because she was older than me by about forty years, but I think she was really a third cousin. When I got to her apartment, I was shocked at how time had finally worn away at her. Though we talked on the phone, I hadn't seen her in more than five years. Travel and writing had taken up all my time. My eyes were playing tricks on me, I thought, because the stately, five-foot-six woman I once knew was only a little over five feet, bent, and so frail that I feared hugging her because she might break. Her thick, wavy hair, much like my grandmother's, was as white as snow. It was parted in the middle, in four parts with the two long plaits to the front on either side of her face. The other two dangled down her back.

Sitting side by side with her on her frayed old couch that was crowned with her hand-crocheted doilies, she took me back a hundred years telling me family stories.

"Here he is! Here's the Portugee, your great-great-grandfather, John Matos." She handed me the old sepia photograph, a formal looking portrait of a swarthy-complexioned man with a bushy mustache and light eyes. He was a handsome, burly bear of a man, and he seemed to loom over the diminutive woman seated beside him. He looked straight into the camera as was the practice in portraits of that era, but his gaze was transfixing, making it difficult to look away. I needed to hear his voice.

"That's Aunt Maria, the two of them," she said.

My great-great-grandmother was perhaps in her forties, her husband much older, and his hair gray at the temples. Her long wavy hair was parted in the middle and pulled back. Her face was beautiful, but also an enigma. The photo spurred so many questions in me.

"Maria was her given name?"

"Not her birth name, but Uncle John had her change her Carib name and had her baptized in the Catholic Church."

"What was her Carib name?"

"I don't know. I don't think anyone knows. We just knew her as Aunt Maria."

"Did they love each other?"

"People didn't talk about love back then. Your great-great-grandfather used to bring Maria pretty things when he'd come back from sea. He brought her lovely dresses from America, combs for her hair, and beautiful clothes and things for her home from Portugal."

"But here's two people who were in love, Estela and Rohan, your great-grandparents, your grandmother Luz's parents," Grace said, as she dug through the box looking for a picture. "Here he is, Rohan."

"He had such piercing dark eyes. And so very handsome," I said.

"Yes, he was dark, black as night. And they say, that once he saw your great-grandmother, he didn't stop till he got her. They say his family was against the marriage and did some Obeah spell to pull them apart. And Uncle John and Aunt Maria had a falling out about it too. But he pursued her anyway, like a moth to a flame."

"And here you are with your Granny, Luz. You were just about three then." Aunt Grace had tried to hand me another photo, but I was transfixed by this one. *It must have been taken just before I was sent away.*

"I was there the day they took that picture," Grace said. "Your father snapped it. You were wearing a dress that your mother made. And she said, 'Show Granny the skirt!' And, you spun around and made the skirt flare out. It was one of the few times I saw your mother and your Granny laughing together, and your father too—all of you together." Auntie Grace laughed a belly laugh. I began to laugh too seeing the scene in my mind's eye as she described it. Then without warning, a wave of sorrow washed over me. My heart felt as if it was being crushed in my chest. The innocence and the joy on my face in the photo were painful to behold. My brow now folded as I mourned the child I used to be before they sent me away. Photos I've seen taken a year later were of a sullen child, her happiness stripped away. I breathed in the dramatic change that had come over me. Tears brimmed in my eyes and clung to my eyelashes, and I forced a smile through my grief. Quiet flooded and filled the room.

Auntie Grace patted my knee, "I know. I know," she said. She cleared her throat trying to continue and lighten the mood. "Here's one of your grandmother when she was younger. You see her high stomach, and she had a flat behind, that was the Portuguese in her. She got the long, thick, beautiful Carib hair, and nose and lips, but nothing else. My mother, you know they were really cousins, got the darker complexion." My aunt's comments reminded me of our family's decades-old observations about color and hair and mixed ethnicities voiced in the delight of differences, which I knew sounded like prejudice by those who didn't know them well. The room grew quiet again as she seemed to travel back in time.

Finally, the old woman reached over the photos and gently picked up a small red box. "Jocelyn, if me give ya somet'in' will you take it wit' ya and keep it close?"

"Sure . . ." my words got caught in my throat like a fishbone. Grace's lyrical patois made me wistful. She was almost ninety, and I knew our time together was fleeting and precious. She was my last, close, living relative from Bequia. ". . . What is it? Who do you want me to bring it to?"

She opened the box with great care. Her bent fingers struggled to catch hold of the object inside. Then, she pulled out the woven cord, and hanging from it was a cream-colored pendant about two inches long. It was a polished smooth scrimshaw with inked engravings.

The old woman straightened herself up, and this time spoke in a mélange of her best English delivered with the music of her Vincentian accent punctuating each word. "Your mother gave it to me years ago, but it's yours. It was your grandmother's, your great-gran's, and your great-great gran's. I kept it for safekeeping, and I forgot all about it till I thought about you going to Bequia."

"But if my mother gave it to you . . ."

"Jocelyn, I asked you, if I gave somethin' to you, would you take it? Come here." She was already stretching the cord apart and putting it over my head. The old woman then held the pendant in her hand and placed it over my heart.

The black etching, a figure of a woman and a house surrounded by palm trees, was intricately drawn. "Thanks, Auntie Grace. It's beautiful." The ornament now hung there between my breasts.

"Promise me you won't ever lose it."

"Of course not. I won't take it off."

Clearly, this was a talisman, and though I'm not superstitious, the ceremonial way of her handing it down to me and placing it over my heart was, at first, comforting. And yet, the gesture then set me on edge. The quiet grew between us.

Aunt Grace seemed to visit another place and time, which painted a smile on her lips. "Ya know who you should talk to, my brother, Leland, in Bequia," she said. "I don't know how good his memory is these days. He worked with the men buildin' boats, and he might be able to give you some stories and some jokes from the old days."

Trying to remember if I had heard about him before, and forgotten, I asked, "How old is he?"

"I'm eighty-six, that would make him sixty-seven. He was the baby. Loved the ladies. You'll see. Last time I spoke with him, he hadn't changed. He's pretty, you know with the curly hair."

Auntie Grace giggled, and seemed to relive old times with him, and told me stories about Leland's antics when he was a boy. "He used to go onto the neighbor's land . . ." she whispered as if it were her secret, "and steal the best mangoes from her tree, then take them to all his girlfriends. Each one of them thought he was bringing somet'in' special for dem." The old woman laughed. "Well, my mother's neighbor never tasted a mango for weeks. When she finally caught him, she beat him good with a switch. Then my mother beat him too." Auntie Grace's stomach shook, she laughed so hard.

Then Grace seemed transported in time, her eyes enjoying something private. Then she finally spoke again. "Take care of his chums, they're scamps," she warned, as she covered her lips and giggled out loud. "Vincentian men can chat you up."

Her expression then grew somber and her eyes searched the air in front of her, seeming to rummage through time. "You've been longing to go back to Bequia since you were a young woman. All the questions you brought to me, I could not answer! Grace shook her head. I'm glad you finally going to Bequia. Maybe the confusion clear itself there."

5

"The Whaling Museum on Harbor Road, please." The taxi driver nodded, eyeing me in the rearview mirror. I had fallen back into a deep slumber after my wake-up call at 7:30. It was a strange sleep, more like a stupor. And I was late for my appointment.

My mind was a muddle of questions about the records available in Boston. I knew how the materials were organized, but I wanted to know what historical records were currently available, and the procedures for researching remotely from Bequia. The website mentioned getting permission for remote access from the administration, so I had been corresponding by email with Dr. Gerald Hunter, the director. Now I stood at the front desk with his receptionist, and she ushered me into his office.

It was *déjà vu* when I first saw him. Gerald Hunter was seated behind a large, mahogany hand-carved desk. It wasn't the setting that I recalled. I remembered *him*. I tried dismissing the feeling, thinking about when I saw his photo online, but that was a group shot and I could barely see him. I was certain it wasn't that. As I entered, he was poring over papers in a folder, with several files stacked on the corner of the desk. To his left was a modern steel desk with a computer, a large flat-screen monitor, and an ergonomic keyboard. He seemed at home here in this office, which reflected both antiquity and the state of the art. When he rose as he looked at me, I searched his eyes for some sign that he, too, knew me from some time before today.

"Good morning, Dr. Kendall. This meeting is long overdue. How was your trip to Boston?" I was stunned when he stood up. All six foot, two inches of him towered over me. His skin was dark, the color of rich black coffee, and his features chiseled. Still certain we had met before; I searched his features and my mind for how I knew him. When he spoke, I was taken by the timbre of his voice, a deep bass with vibrations that found their way into my body. I most definitely would have remembered that voice. But it wasn't just that. It was the way he looked at me that seemed to push at my defenses, tumbling them aside.

I lost my breath. His smile then totally disarmed me. If anything about my appearance was totally out of place, his gaze did not reveal it to me, so I tried as hard as I could to regain my sense of purpose. Before I could, he spoke again.

"So, tell me a little more about your work, and I will tell you what we have here that might assist you. Then we will take some information and get you a pass so that you can gain access to the exhibits and the archives." He motioned to the chair facing his desk, pulling it out for me. My thoughts came out in a burst, as I tried to manage the heat that was rising in me, now filling my cheeks.

"It's an interesting story actually. I was presenting a paper on some beginning genealogy work I had been doing on my great-great-grandfather, who was a Portuguese whaler, and my second great-grandmother, his wife, who was a Carib Indian. I had mentioned the name I was tracking, when this woman came up to me after my presentation and said, 'Well you know we may be cousins.' She remarked that my great-great-grandfather's surname was the same as hers. She came from here in Boston. She then laughed and said, 'You look so surprised! You must know that the men on that island got around. They traveled as far south as Venezuela and Brazil. You probably have cousins there too.'"

I lost myself in the story, couldn't stop myself from talking, took a breath and continued. "I was already aware of the route the whalers made that continued from Boston on to Portugal, and then to Cape Verde off the coast of Africa, and then back . . . but her comment piqued my interest and I wanted to begin to focus a study on the connections between the people here in Boston and Bequia. Since my second great-grandfather was a captain on a whaling ship, I figured these archives in Boston would be a good place to start, and then look into the archives in Bequia, and compare notes."

Gerald Hunter's voice insinuated its lilting island musicality. He said something I missed, his voice again affecting me physically before I could respond. It was a tingling sensation in my core I hadn't felt in a long time. The twinkle in his eye and his smile were mesmerizing. My cheeks were on fire!

"I'm sorry, I have been going on and on. I don't think I heard your question," I said, trying to regain my composure.

"I just asked did you find out that you two were actually cousins?" He seemed bemused.

"No actually, I wanted to have dinner with her to compare notes, but she was headed back to Seattle where she lives. You know conferences, I lost track of her card. I don't know if I will ever see her again. But her comment set me on this path, to follow the whalers' stories to find out what drew these men from place to place."

"Well, she is right. There may in fact be many familial ties between the people of Boston and Bequia. I don't know if anyone has done any in-depth study of the connections. But I am more interested in the way you just put that." He leaned back in his chair, his eyes locked with mine.

"Put what?"

"What you said about the men. I would have taken you for a feminist."

"I am, what did you mean by that?" I could feel that annoying crease between my brows deepen.

"You said," he grinned, "you wanted to follow the men's stories. I thought you would be interested in the *women's* stories. The women are the ones who the men pursued." His smile broadened, but seemed to hold back thoughts he was not yet ready to reveal.

"Of course, I will be looking at the women. I didn't think I was minimizing their stories in the way I put that." Bruised, I was busy rewinding my own comment in my mind, thinking about my wording, and miffed that he would challenge my beliefs about who I am as a researcher. My tone must have revealed my anger, and I could feel my arms tightening at my sides. "My plans are most definitely to interview women, the keepers of the stories."

"My bad. Relax, I was just toying with you. I detected that passion in your emails and wanted to see it up close and in person. Why don't you have dinner with me?"

The deep bass tones of his voice struck me in my center. I lost my mental footing. *This is crazy. I am a forty-five-year-old woman. What is the matter with me? I am petrified.* "I don't think I can." I tried holding his gaze, and he paused, as if he knew I would change my mind as soon as the words left my mouth.

"Take some time," he said. "Think about that." He seemed so sure of himself. I clenched my jaws to keep from telling him how arrogant I thought he was. And then he smoothly pivoted back to our business.

"Let me tell you what we have that can assist you. We are the largest repository of artifacts and information on whaling in the country."

Gerald talked about the records that the museum had on Bequia and pulled up some of the online exhibits on the computer, including photos from the in-house collection of artifacts. He told me about the mariners' records I could access, like ship manifests, and crew lists dating back hundreds of years. All the while I couldn't help thinking about how egotistical it was of him to challenge me in that way.

"You need a password and user ID for access to our online archives opened to the academic community, so you can continue your work while you are in Bequia." He turned his monitor around and moved the keyboard over to me, proceeding as if nothing had happened.

My hands hesitated above the keys and sweat beaded my upper lip. "I've got a problem here," I explained, my mind straddling the instructions before me and being sure I rescued my dignity and my ego. "They are asking for the college or university with which I am working. Since I am going on leave from the university, I am an independent researcher now. Am I out of luck?" Although I said this in my Caribbean, "good-girl" polite tone, it irritated me that I needed his help with this and was annoyed at how attracted I was feeling.

"You said that your research is partially supported by a grant in one of your emails. Is that right?"

"Yes. It's a travel grant to focus on cultural connections around the world from the National Endowment for the Humanities."

"Not to worry then, I will do an administrative override, bypass the university affiliation, and enter the funding source." He asked a couple of informational questions, and printed out a visitor's pass for me. Turning the computer monitor around, he stepped behind me to show me the website. After giving me instructions for access, he went back to his desk, letting me put in my password. His presence behind me excited me, so much that I had difficulty typing my name.

When he sat down, he glanced down at my hand, which was now fidgeting, pressing the button on my ballpoint pen. "So, do you already have plans for dinner this evening? I can suggest some places for you to visit in Bequia over dinner." *Is he so presumptuous that he is positive that I will say yes to him?*

"As I said, I don't think so. But I also need to be sure you understand what I meant. . . . My work is important to me . . . I didn't mean . . ."

"I know. My comment was said in jest." He smiled. "I needed to know if I was wrong in my earlier impressions, so I'm glad I was right." He paused, and for the first time studied my face with a serious fixed gaze, which felt as if he were searching my soul. For me, the moment seemed suspended in time, but then there was that smile, and he continued. "And my comments, although irritating, revived your impassioned self."

I didn't know what to make of him. He wasn't attacking me as I first thought, he was probing. As the tightness in my chest relaxed, I was doing all I could to keep my knees pressed together. "My passion is not so easily shaken."

"I see that. An oversight on my part." He sat back in his chair, a broad grin on his face, and he just took me in.

"Just curious, where are you from?" I said, needing a pause.

"My family's from Bequia. And I have family from St. Vincent and Barbados."

"So do I."

"I know," Gerald said with a laugh that startled me for a moment. As he paused, my focus drifted back to his lips crowned with a perfectly trimmed mustache.

"How did you know?" I managed.

"You mentioned it in one of your impassioned emails. Did you change your mind yet . . . about dinner? Do you like seafood?"

"Maybe next time," I blurted, despite everything I now recognized as my desire. I kicked myself later, of course, when I thought about what I had done. It wasn't just interest, I wasn't just interested in the sources he might have. I was fascinated by him.

"Other plans?" He really wasn't going to accept my No.

"I guess I am not a spur-of-the-minute type of a person. I'm driving to Vermont early tomorrow morning. I like to get on the road early to beat the traffic . . ."

He seemed to turn over my words in his mind. "You believe in 'next times'?" he said, as he handed me the file folder and pass he made for me. "When do you leave for Bequia?" He was putting duplicate copies of my paperwork in a folder.

"Next week."

"Have you found a place to stay? I was going to suggest a property I stay in when I'm there. . . . If you want me to." He paused as if he was waiting for me to speak. "In any case, good luck with your research."

He closed the file folder with the copies of the paperwork, put it to the side, and then stood up to usher me out. He had pulled away. No, I had pushed him away.

My hands shook as I put my file folder in my attaché. I felt exposed. "I am sorry I couldn't do dinner tonight. I was going to stop over at my aunt's, to bring her some stuff before I leave Boston." The mess I made with the excuse of not being able to go was unfixable. I didn't know how I did this. *Or did my mother make me do this!* "No, I haven't found a place to stay in Bequia."

"No worries. I'll send you an email."

"I do appreciate your help," I said, trying to rekindle his interest, standing and realizing it was too late.

When he looked at me fully, his expression seemed to lighten. "By the way, that necklace, I was going to ask you about it over dinner if you said yes. Where did you get it?"

"My aunt just gave it to me. She said it was my mother's and my grandmother's, and going back to my great-great-grandmother."

"Do you mind?" Gerald leaned closer to me to examine the carving.

"I don't want to take it off."

"No, I just wanted to see the etching better."

I could feel his breath on my chest. Feeling him so near to me, I feared he might be able to see my heart pounding. "Yes. You said your great-great-grandfather was a captain on a whaling ship? This does seem to be an authentic scrimshaw carving on the tip of a whale's tooth. I wouldn't be surprised if this dated back to his time. Did your aunt say how old it was?"

"She said he gave this to my great-great-grandmother."

"You know these objects were worn as protection," he said.

"Well, I am aware that amulets were worn for that purpose, but I wasn't sure about this piece."

"Yes. Sometimes sailors gave their wives things to wear close to their body to protect them while they were away." He paused, watching my reaction. "They also gave them to their wives to keep them . . . chaste."

I blushed. He smiled. It was his closeness to me, and his deep voice which now had its way with my senses. "I believe I read that."

"The etchings usually tell a story. This one is interesting, the woman standing in front of the home, but turned away from the sea. Sometime in the future I would like to study it, more closely, and compare it with others here in our collections."

"I promised my aunt I wouldn't lose it, and to keep it close. And I don't want to leave it anywhere to be studied. I am not superstitious or anything. It's just that I promised her."

"Then I guess that means you will have to say yes to dinner the 'next time.' I will bring my loupe so that I can see it better. Besides this drawing of the woman, there is a symbol that I can't make out here on the back. This marking is a bit strange. Well, maybe *next time*."

I studied his face. He wasn't mocking me. I laughed.

"I've said something funny," he said with a quizzical expression on his face.

"Just what my aunt said, right before I left yesterday."

"What's that?"

"Be careful of Vincentian men. They'll chat you up."

"So that's why you wouldn't have dinner with me."

I could swear I detected some radiance about him. I wasn't sure if it was simply the fact that it had been so long since any man had shown an interest in me, or the lightness of his wit.

I fingered the amulet, feeling the fine lines that etched themselves into the tooth.

"Take care of yourself down there."

"Of course."

Auntie Grace was surprised to see me again when I brought her some canned goods, soups, and fruits. I told her about the museum and all the resources I could access in Bequia. She asked a few questions about how that was possible and then shook her head. Her *café-au-lait* complexion brightened with her smile when I told her about Dr. Hunter and described how tall and handsome he was.

"He asked me out to dinner," I said before I could stop myself.

"Hmm," she said, smiling and lifting her eyebrows.

"But I said I was coming here, packing, and leaving early in the morning."

"What do you need to pack? You are not getting any younger, Jocelyn."

"Auntie, maybe my mother was right. Marriage is probably not . . . for me."

"I don't know what was wrong with your mother telling you something like that." She shook her head.

"When he asked me, I just wasn't prepared."

"You have to be prepared to go to dinner?"

"Okay, Auntie Grace, I don't want to argue with you."

"Jocelyn, I put those photos I showed you in this envelope. I wanted to give them to your mother, but after she left Bequia she never wanted to talk about it. After your grandmother died, she never even went back." The tightening muscles in my back began to twinge.

"What happened to my grandmother's house, and her things?"

"I don't know. Your mother let the house deteriorate. I think it something 'tween them, your mother and grandmother."

"What was all that about? Did it have anything to do with my grandmother's death?"

"Me . . . me no know." Grace fell into the patois of the island and seemed lost in the memories.

"They said he, your great-great-grandfather, was a jealous man. They said he had the villagers watch Maria when he was off to sea. But she was a free, fierce spirit, and he couldn't tame her. That's what they said."

"Tame her?"

"Those island men are like that." Grace punctuated her comment with a nod of her head. "Possessive. And John, even though he was Portuguese, he was very much like that too. But they say she used her powers from her people. I know you don't believe in this, but they say that your great-great-grandmother took away a woman's power of speech. Some busybody was threatenin' her with saying something to Uncle John, and Aunt Maria told her she better shut her mouth. The woman sassed her in some way, and the next day the woman was struck dumb, and never spoke again."

"Auntie Grace, sometimes people attribute some magical forces to things they don't understand. The woman probably had a stroke, and it was just a coincidence."

The old woman laughed. "You know when you were born your grandmother said she didn't like the way you always had your hands open. She said you would give away your power. She said, 'Me gon' have to train this girl to use the craft, not throw her energies away.' Your mother and she had some fallin' out, and your mother tole her not to be fillin' your head with that old stuff. After that, she packed you up and brought you back here."

"What happened to her after we left, and why did my mother never want to talk about it?"

"I don't know, but the whole town was whispering, and your mother felt that it was connected to how her mother died. Your mother felt shamed, but everyone said all the talk was just gossip, and it started with Aunt Maria. Frankly, I think it changed your mother dealing with the stories, because when she came back to the States, she was never the same."

"What stories?"

"I don't know. I don't know if anyone does. I think the stories are buried with her. I put the portrait of John and Maria, your great-great-grandparents in the envelope. I also put in the pictures of Estela and Rohan, the love birds, your great-grandparents, with a few more of you and Luz."

"I tried to give these photos to your mother, but when she came back, she said she didn't want any reminders of any of them. Never made sense."

The room fell quiet, and Auntie Grace shook her head slightly and seemed to search the air for something to say.

"Well, I am going back. And I will be there the second week in July."

"I wish your mother wasn't so stubborn, would've taught you the ways if just for your protection. . . . When you go to Bequia, just be aware, people there dance a different dance, and their lives are all tangled up in ways that you don' know. Just take care you don't get swept away."

"I won't get swept away, I have too much work to do."

"What I am saying is the energy there can draw you in. It can knock you down and sweep you up like the waves in the sea." Grace's brow furrowed, and the area between her eyebrows creased.

As the quiet grew between us, I put away the groceries and changed the linens on my aunt's bed and dusted the living room tables. "I could do that you know," my aunt said. "I'm not an invalid." Her voice made me smile. Kissing her cheek and neck as I began to leave, maybe it was all the stories and pictures, it all triggered a memory. "Didn't I used to call you Tantie, Tantie Grace? That just came back to me."

"Yes, when you were a little bit of t'ing."

"Just remembered it. I will see you when I get back, Tantie Grace. I put international calling on your line, you can call my number the same way you always do, and you will reach me in Bequia."

Back at the hotel, I had only my toiletries and a couple of things to pack. I bought myself a sandwich and ate it at the desk in my room as I had so many times before when I went to conferences. *What is wrong with me? Why didn't I accept Gerald Hunter's dinner invitation?* He didn't do or say anything that would frighten me. Actually, I found him enticing. And there was something about him that made me feel safe. But I had trouble trusting safety.

It wasn't him. If I was honest, I knew it wasn't him. I was afraid of myself, afraid to be open to him. I could be the researcher, the anthropologist, but I was terrified to be with him simply as a woman. It had been too long.

The drapes were parted, letting a shard of light filter in from the harbor below. So many hotel rooms at so many conferences, I had never learned how to make them feel like home. Always tried to enjoy each one for its own character. This one was modern, blond wood, sleek. The now charcoal-black muted lines of the furniture and their angular blocks of shadowy darkness felt somehow comforting. It was lonely, but familiar.

I closed my eyes and began to doze off. His voice intruded, "You believe in next times." I opened my eyes, and lifted my head. It took me a moment to realize where I was. I expected to see him there.

6

My mind wandered. I couldn't think of anything but his face. I breezed by my turn to Selena's house. Nothing recognizable on this maze-like twisting country road that I could remember, a puzzling tangle with no place to turn around without putting my car in a ditch. I pulled over and called Selena. Luis picked up. My breathing grew shallow. He could hear it, and calmly talked me through getting back to the road I knew, but the panic left me unnerved.

When I finally reached Selena's house, I felt out of sorts, exhausted, and my back was stiff with pain. But climbing the steps to their home, and seeing my friends' faces again, I knew I was where I needed to be.

"How was Boston?" Selena asked.

"I hate to say it, but I think I made a fool of myself," I whispered out of earshot of Luis. ". . . Was thinking about him, Gerald, when I got lost."

Selena glanced into the kitchen at Luis, then mouthed, "What happened?"

"I feel ridiculous. This man was gorgeous, and he asked me out to dinner, and I froze."

"What do you mean?"

"Gerald asked me to go out for seafood. We were just talking about my study, and he set everything up for my research, and when he asked me, I just didn't expect it. So, I said something dumb." I hunted through my bag for my back pain pills.

"That's what I meant when we last spoke. You are always buried in your work."

"No pain pills. Selena, I don't know who the hell I am." I stood up, stretched my arms up and to the side, and down to the floor, trying to relax the muscles in my back.

"That's why I suggested a past life regression. Get rid of all that old baggage. Just sayin.'"

Selena *knew* me. I trusted her completely, even when she gently but lovingly pointed out my "issues".

"Don't scold me, Selena. I've beaten myself up since it happened."

"So, give him a call, say you were tired from the drive from New York, and that you would love to have dinner next time."

"Been there, literally done that. It made me the object of a joke." Selena looked puzzled.

"He said that when I came back *next time*, he would share some places for my research. I think that's what he said. I don't know. The whole thing left me feeling insecure, adolescent."

"Adolescent is good. That means he was hot."

"That's why I couldn't think straight. The guy is six foot two or three. The sparkle in his eyes! This beautiful smile . . . such a turn on."

Selena raised her eyebrows, "Haven't heard that from you in a while. Too bad he's not going to Bequia with you."

"He comes from there! . . . Said he would email me some places to visit and to stay in Bequia this week. . . . Maybe I can try to start over."

"Call him! You don't have to wait to be courted anymore, you know. We're not living in the 1800s, though you seem so. . . . Make the first move."

"I know. I know." I groaned. Selena could make me cringe at myself like nobody else could. "That reminds me of something my aunt said the other day. That my great-great-grandfather tried to 'tame' my great-great-grandmother. She was a Carib Indian and he was Portuguese, and I guess he was attempting to make her act more European or something.

I don't know. But the word angered me. I am studying this, and should be dispassionate, but . . ."

"There's stuff like that in Puerto Rico, where stuffy upper-class Spaniards marry free-spirited women, who have African blood or Taino blood, and try to change them."

"It seems that whenever my great-great-grandfather would go out to sea, he would have the villagers spy on her."

"He was probably afraid she would be unfaithful or something," Selena said with a shrug and then a lascivious smile.

"My aunt said that she put a spell on a woman who was talking about her . . . made the woman mute."

"You're kidding!"

"No. Supposedly, she never spoke again. Told my aunt it had to be a coincidence, but . . ."

"Selena laughed, then continued, "Don't doubt what she said. I believe in trying to attract positive energy from the universe. You can attract negative stuff too. We all have some power . . . we . . ."

"Now you sound like my aunt. I feel I have some intuition . . . but that's it." I stroked the scrimshaw pendant half-consciously until I saw Selena noticing it.

"That's a nice piece. Did you get it at the museum store in Boston?"

"No, my aunt gave it to me. Actually, she placed it on me."

Selena leaned over to look at it more closely. "That etching is lovely."

"When she put it on me, she warned me not to take it off. She said it had belonged to my grandmother and my great-grandmother and my great-great-grandmother. Gerald said that it appeared to date back to that time. But he wanted to study it further."

"Gerald said that?!" Selena put her hands on her hips and said,. "Well, well, well . . . Gerald does want to see you again."

"Selena, stop it. Anyway, I thought my aunt was worried about my work, and my asking questions in Bequia."

"Why?"

"I don't know. She warned me not to get caught up in something there. I remember thinking at first that she was talking about an insular island culture . . . I should be careful of asking questions that offend folk.

But I think she was telling me not to get 'swept away' in the energy there. You know what I mean?"

"Of course! This is a talisman. She put it on you as protection," Selena said.

"Yes, and when Gerald said it could date back to my great-great-grandfather's time . . . and that men protected their women and tried, to keep them safe and . . . never mind."

"What?"

"Nothing . . . just, he said sometimes these are made by husbands to . . ."

"What?"

"He said, sometimes they were made by men to keep their wives . . . chaste."

"He said that? Chaste?" Selena grinned.

"Yes. I wonder if my great-great-grandfather had it made for my great-great-grandmother." My cheeks were aflame, and I think Selena noticed.

"I am liking this straightforward Mr. Hunter more and more."

"Dr. Hunter. And he had the nerve to challenge me on something I said about my research. I said I was interested in why the men were pulled . . . the whalers went from place to place.

"He said he thought I would be interested in the women's stories."

Selena said, "Aren't you . . . interested in the women?"

". . . Of course, but somehow I placed much more emphasis on the whalers' stories than their wives. He called me out on it."

"Okay, Dr. Hunter!" Selena pumped her fist in the air.

"Great, so you're taking his side." I looked at Selena, and she flashed that half-smile grin at me. We laughed so hard we snorted. It felt like the old times, before we were chasing our careers and what we thought of as success.

A yawn rose in my chest and escaped my lips. "Selena, I'm exhausted. The drive took me almost five hours and wiped me out."

"Just sleep as long as you need to. Dream about Dr. Gerald Hunter!" She laughed.

"Selena," I moaned, and headed to my bedroom.

Selena's playful conversation planted Gerald fully in my mind along with his comments about my pendant. The more I thought about my research and my need to unearth my family secrets, both seemed connected. Now even Gerald seemed somehow intimately linked because of his knowledge of the subject and his sensitivity to me, if I didn't push him away for good. When I learned that Gerald was from Bequia, it should have been a clue that he was intertwined in all this, although I could not yet tell how or why.

The *ga-unking* sounds coming from the pond woke me. The first time I heard them years ago, I asked Selena what that noise was. I laughed out loud when she said, green frogs. "They always say frogs croak," I said.

"Yeah. bullfrogs croak, but green frogs say, '*ga-unk*.'" We laughed every time there seemed to be a chorus of them.

Pulling the covers over my head was always my first instinct in the morning, but chattering drew me out. Two cardinals were perched outside my window. That birdhouse was not here last time I came! Lifting my head and craning my neck to search for the crested bright red male who just flew away, I spotted him down at a feeder. The darker female seemed to be nesting, lifting and placing twigs in the birdhouse, and he brought seeds to her! Trying not to disturb them, I sat up slowly, but they startled and began to chatter and cock their heads, then flew away.

In the kitchen, Luis and Selena were sitting at the table, Luis with a cup of coffee, which I was ready to have too, and reading the paper. Selena was seated cross-legged facing him with her Kindle.

"We saved you some coffee," she said. "There's this oatmeal bread Luis baked yesterday, and here's some cheese, and fruit . . . oh and wonderful boysenberry jam I made."

My mouth began to water. "Sounds great!"

"How's your back?" Luis asked as he refilled the bowl of berries and melon.

"So much better. My head's better too. By the way, you have the most beautiful birds outside the window of my room."

"You mean Cardinale and Isabella. They're our lovebirds," Selena said.

"Yes, he was feeding her."

"He takes such good care of her," Selena said. "They say that when you see a cardinal, it means a loved one is visiting you from the past. Cardinale and Isabella are not always there. This is a good sign for a past life regression," she said.

"That's exactly what I was thinking," I said. "If Luis would guide me . . ."

"Really?" Selena said. "After all the times I've suggested it, the cardinals convince you?"

"If you really want to do it today, you shouldn't eat, and don't drink that coffee," Luis said. "You need to be relaxed. . . . It's like a deep meditation."

"Ah man, Luis. I can't have . . . ? Not even coffee? My stomach's growling . . . I need my coffee in the morning."

"You can have something after," Selena said.

"And when this is happening, what am I supposed to . . . feel?"

Luis stood up and had this all-business expression on his face. "You will need to focus on what comes up for you. Sometimes it's a sensation . . . a person; other people feel a place. Just allow your mind its freedom." After a moment, he continued, "There's no script for this Jocelyn."

"'No script,' I get it. Don't know what will happen. What have I got to lose," I said, unable to hide my skepticism.

"What I am saying is," Luis's voice sounded strident, "you may be aware of going back to a time and place and becoming another person. You might not. I cannot predict. You don't have to do this, Jocelyn." He seemed to be losing patience. His words were clipped. "Talk to Selena. She has gone through it a few times."

"I think Luis is pissed with me." I sat on my hands trying not to reach out for a piece of melon.

"No!" Selena said. "No food for you!" We both giggled. She paused and seemed to struggle back to a serious mindset. "Past life regression is different for everyone. We can't predict the details in advance."

". . . What happened to you?"

"At the time, I was wrestling with so many things in my life. My husband, Marcos, was destroying my self-esteem . . . telling me what to do at every turn. And I was listening! In my job, my male colleagues were blocking me, making it hard to advance in the areas I wanted. It was as if everything that was *me* was being squashed." Selena seemed rueful, studying the air in front of her. "I realize now, it wasn't only them doing it to me, *I* was doing it to myself. I didn't have the *cojones* to confront any of it."

I began to tear up. Selena seemed like she was reliving that time in her past, which of course sent me, empath that I am, down that road with her. "You always seem so confident, Selena." It was still a surprise to me that she felt this way. I never thought of Selena as lacking in self-esteem. That was me, not Selena.

"That's how you saw me . . ." Selena opened the jar on the table, and tipped it in my direction, "but inside I was like this jelly. I had just moved to Puerto Rico. He was from an upper-class family, and he thought I was the greatest thing since sliced bread because I had my own career. He then began to systematically take over every decision about everything, while sleeping around."

"I think we lost touch for a while . . ."

She stretched herself up in her seat and squared her shoulders. "Yes, because I was in PR trying to be Doña Marcos Garcia. I didn't know his finances, and here I am, finance is my field. Come to find out, he was deep in debt and had *una puta* on the side. I was devastated." Selena nested her plates and pushed them aside.

"You never told me those things back then." The loss of Selena, at that time, hit me like cold water flung in my face. She didn't invite me to her wedding. She was just gone.

"Shame silenced me. I knew it before we got married. Felt I could fix it . . . make it right," she said, her voice almost in a whisper as if confessing in a cloistered space. "I had left New York behind for him. I felt like a fool."

"You say that like it was your fault." Regret was etched on her brow.

"Because I felt—and still feel—that it was."

Selena appeared to grow visibly smaller as she sank into her chair.

"Don't beat yourself . . ." I started to say, but she put her hand up to stop me from consoling her. We had more in common than I thought, bad choices in men and ownership of our mistakes.

"My mother and my sisters thought I was crazy leaving him. Anyway, told a friend in New York how I screwed up, and she said, 'Time for a past life regression.' She suggested that I see Luis."

"That's how you guys met? When was this again?"

"I can't believe I never told you this story. It was around 2001? Yes, 2001 . . .

"I was doing my doctorate . . . was buried in my doctorate till 2003."

"I was covered in the dregs of that marriage." Selena's face seemed pale, like the blood and the life had left it. "Suffice it to say, I walked in there complaining about how terrible my husband Marcos was, how terrible my first boyfriend Diego was, and how I hated how I was treated by the chauvinistic men at work. He said, 'So why are you punishing yourself?'" Selena stopped speaking, and put her hand up to her mouth. Her eyes welled up.

"'Punishing myself?' I asked him, feeling totally indignant," Selena said, half-laughing.

"Then he said, 'You keep letting these people into your world. You are the one who's allowing them in, why are you punishing yourself?'"

Selena and I exchanged a long, teary-eyed look before she went on. "I told him, 'I don't know why I let them in.' Then Luis said, 'Sometimes people find answers to their repressed feelings in past life regression.' I can hear him now." She smiled even more widely through the tears. "He will explain the details to you, but after, I had a cathartic release of all the hurt." She paused again and bit her lip. "It changed my whole life. I began trusting myself again, got a divorce from Marcos. And that was when I started my business."

Some of my own questions from that time were finally answered. So many questions about what happened between us. Blamed myself at first, wondering what I did to make her not call. But when I heard from her about two years later, she mentioned difficulties in her marriage. Said she didn't want to talk about it. I left it alone. I was glad to at least know I hadn't done anything to cause it. "I don't know if . . ."

"You do not have to do this, Jocelyn. Do it only if you want to."

"I do want to. I just worry about what I'll learn . . ." My fingers were touching the pendant again, a gesture that was becoming almost automatic now. "Okay. Let's just do it."

In my room, I pulled a big T-shirt over my tank top and then went into the den where Luis was waiting. It was dimly lit. I sat on a rattan chair, upright, not letting my back rest.

I exhaled and it was audible. "I'm ready, Luis. I've made up my mind."

"Tell me why you want to do this."

"'Cause Selena said I should." I joked, but then my sadness began to well up before I could control it. "Selena must've told you I decided to take a leave of absence from the college. . . . A lot of professional jealousies there at the college, but it was all I had . . . just feel so alone. I am feeling disconnected from everything."

"How long have you been feeling this way?"

"At least three or four years . . . broke up with a guy four years ago."

"May I ask why you broke up?" Luis asked, his voice gently entering my consciousness.

"He was sleeping with another woman, a girl really. I found him . . . with her. Since then, I feel old, unattractive . . . afraid to meet or become close to anyone." I squeezed the rattan arms of the chair. I wanted to hide behind it.

"Is there anything in your childhood that you relate to this experience, or that you feel opened you up to being with someone who would betray you in this way?"

"Sure. Try my father who left my mother and me. Try my mother who left me with my grandmother, then snatched me away from her, never telling me why. Are you kidding? My life is filled with people leaving me. That's not new!"

". . . Sounds like you are angry at them for hurting you."

"Not anymore. I'm accustomed to it . . . What upsets me the most are the secrets."

"Well," Luis gestured to the mattress covered in a sheet resting on the floor a few feet away, ". . . When human beings suffer any traumatic situation, they might not deal with it at the time, but at some point, they must attend to the injury."

He moved to the window and lowered the shade. "If you suppress your feelings, they will come up eventually. In past lives, often we can find lessons that we can use in this life. It is a meditation, a deep meditation. Once in that state, allow your mind its freedom, see where it takes you."

He began talking me through steps relaxing various parts of my body. I found myself feeling rested. I thought I heard him on the periphery of my consciousness, say, "Keep breathing, breathe."

"Now you are moving back in time. Back, back in time. Back to before you were born. Back, back."

I have no sense of time. But I am . . . on a beach, where I'm walking, searching the horizon for a sign of his ship, longing to see it. The sea, sweeping in around my ankles is pulling the sand from beneath me, making me unsteady. As I hold my arms out to my sides to regain my balance, I notice that I am bare to my waist. My skin is golden brown and taut, and my breasts small.

There was Luis again, his calm voice saying, "Relax. You can move to an important time for you."

I feel a sharp pain first, and a moan grows into a howl that escapes from deep in my gut. My belly is swollen. I scream, unable to stop the pain. Responding to the woman talking to me, I shake my head no. I recognize her voice, but not what she is saying. And then the pain comes again.

My body quakes from the pressure inside me, a burning pain. She, that same woman, is scolding me. Her finger is in my face, and her deep voice is guttural but familiar. Then I feel my heart being ripped from me. I open my mouth to scream, but no sound comes out.

Luis was softly repeating my name. "Jocelyn, tell me who you are." There was a click. I didn't know what that sound was, but it seemed to come from the corner of the room where Luis was. I couldn't lift my head, and I couldn't see him. Gibberish spilled from my lips. Tears rained from my eyes as I tried to tell him who I was, but the sounds ran together.

"Jocelyn, you will open your eyes when I tell you to," Luis continued, "and when you do, you will take from this experience everything that it offers you to move forward in your life. When you open your eyes, you will be refreshed and full of life's energy. Remember the lessons of the past life regression. Five you are beginning to awaken. Four you are feeling more awake. Three, two, one. You may open your eyes and wake up."

I feel my eyes flutter open, rediscovering myself, still lying on the mattress. The room came back into focus, along with Luis in his chair.

"Luis, it was like a strange dream, but more real somehow. I had a swollen belly like I was pregnant, and such pain." My upper lip was speckled with perspiration.

"Do you remember any more of it?" He seemed to be searching my face for clues.

"No details except a strange feeling like I was in pain. And a sadness, like I lost something." For some reason, I didn't tell Luis about the woman. I had no idea who she was.

"I think that's good work to come out of a past life regression. Good, good work."

"But there were so many confusing parts. I was hurting and afraid."

"Just let yourself be. Rest. Maybe that was too much for one session. Do you want something to eat?" Luis said, as he opened the shade.

"No, I am fine, just a little tired." I returned to my room, needing to be alone. At first, I tried to remember more of the dream, but it was blurring. All that was left was the young girl staring out to sea. Then this woman who was pregnant. I wondered if any of it had to do with Bequia, if that's where I would learn more about this place and these people. My head ached. Luis said not to overthink this. I allowed my mind to let it all go, trying not to crowd myself into a conundrum of questions I could not answer.

7

The sun was rising. I knew it. The black sky blotted it from my view, but it was there poised to pierce the darkness. I had to go out and find it. The liquid warm morning draped about me, as I searched the horizon. There, just a whisp of white gold as I stood in the wet grass to wait and welcome it with gratitude that it had come again. Dawn in Vermont was a mystery to me before today, and I was now drawn to the sliver of yellow-orange light peeking through the darkness. Aware of my skin and my nakedness under the T-shirt, I felt a flush of shame. A stronger energy inside me resisted restraining my body, wanting to let myself alone. *Maybe the past life regression?*

I hunted through my room for my watercolors. The sky streaked with so many blues! I tiptoed into the kitchen to fill a paper cup with water and went down to the pond. I dipped my brush and lifted some pigment, and my arm moved with fluidity as I painted, sweeping across the paper, depositing color in ways I had never been able to in the past. I was capturing the gardens, individual wildflowers, and even single blades of grass.

There was a flat stone where I sat near the murky edge of the pond as a small frog climbed on a rock that was resting in the shallow. The sky, just azure now, its blue light washing over the frog's green skin made him look other-worldly. Until now, frogs held little interest for me except for their early morning calls. But here was one climbing out onto a rock, and his neck ballooned with air as he exclaimed his *ga-unk* sound. He made me smile. For some reason I couldn't explain, I looked up the green frog's sounds on the internet yesterday after the past life regression, and they said it sounded like a plucked loose banjo string. The piece said that only the males made that sound, and that *ga-unk* was a mating call. There was indeed a female frog resting nearby on a fallen branch, her rounder body was what distinguished the two. She was quiet, seeming to take little notice of him. He puffed himself up yet again, insistent on being noticed, and boldly exclaimed, "*Ga-unk.*" He clambered onto the same fallen branch resting at the water's edge and climbed onto her back. They rested there together, and he gently and almost imperceptibly squeezed her abdomen, an embrace it seemed. She did not resist his presence there squeezing her belly, rounded I now realized with eggs, a cluster of which emerged. A gelatinous nest rested atop the water until the frogs' feet propelled it, and it slowly drifted away. The tiny larvae would become tadpoles in days. I would be on my way to Bequia by then. The frogs soon swam off, each one taking its own path.

Sunlight began to fill the sky, painting it a milky blue. By noon, I had covered the walls of my room with paintings. Though they called it my room when I was in Vermont, I shared it with another artist in their family. Artwork was always collecting there. Vermont always gave me the time to reflect and create. But this seemed extraordinary. It was the day after the past life regression, and I felt like I was seeing the world with new eyes.

Selena told me how beautiful the paintings were, and admired one watercolor of a green frog that she put up on the wall. Luis asked if I was hungry. He was headed into the garden to see what was ready, good for lunch and dinner later. I followed, but must have startled him because he turned suddenly, eyes wide. "I didn't hear you there," he said.

". . . Just wanted to see the garden," I responded, exploring the small, patterned plot on my own. "This corn looks ripe," I said, peeling the husks back and biting into one. "Sweet!"

". . . Looks good," Luis said, with an odd expression.

The peapods were quite plump, and I pulled off a few and handed them to Luis, who nodded. I plucked and placed more of them in the basket. Squatting to look at the squashes and handle the blossoms, it was then that I realized that investigating the garden like this was new for me.

"Your back must be much better," Luis commented, seeming perplexed.

There was no sign of my stiff back. "Yeah, it *is* better."

We had a salad for lunch and the corn. I saved the husks. Twisting a few together, fashioning a doll, and handing it to Selena who had been working on her laptop. "Thanks, lady," she said, standing the doll up against the pepper mill.

Folding the husks, a pattern came into my head—a little cross, then I bent the pieces and connected them to that shorter piece, constructing a braid of sorts.

"Are you finished with these?" Luis asked, reaching for the strips for the compost bucket.

My hands drew them to me to protect them. "I'm sort of weaving them. Do you mind? Just enjoying . . . Vermont brings out my crafty side." I laughed at myself.

Luis's eyes were fixed on the braid that I was making.

"Where'd you learn that?" he asked.

He must have been intrigued by the intricacy of the pattern.

"I don't know, just made it up." The braid grew as I spoke. My fingers moved deftly, selecting the strips and constructing the long serpentine, coiled braid.

Luis seemed deep in thought, troubled.

"What's the matter Luis?"

"Do you speak any foreign languages?"

"Some Spanish, and a little Swahili. Why do you ask?"

"Just thinking about the past life regression. Do you remember anything more from it?"

"No, very little, but I was wondering earlier if it gave me this new feeling for my painting." Engrossed in weaving the husks, the braid now had begun to reach the floor. "By the way, Luis, I would like to experience that past life regression again before I go. Would you do that with me again?"

"You need to fast, so dinner should be your last meal, and we'll do it tomorrow morning."

"For someone who was so skeptical, I'm amazed that you want to do this twice," Selena said. "What are you doing there?"

"It's a little weird, I know. . . . Just had this pattern in my head. It seemed to work out perfectly. The husks stimulated my mind on this weaving thing."

"About your creative side, there's a craft fair in town today.

"I want to go to that craft store . . . if it's still there?"

"Are you kidding? Brattleboro is the craft Mecca. Anything you want, you name it. if you . . . get yourself together, we can head into town in an hour or so," Selena said.

"I need a needle."

"There's every kind of needle you could want—knitting, crocheting," Selena said.

"I'll know what I want when I see it." I quickly sponged off, washed my face, combed my hair. I brought a cloth tote bag to the table, and carefully coiled the strip into it.

"How much time do you need?" Selena called out to me. "Remember . . . no fashion police in Vermont!"

"No, I'm ready."

When we got in the pickup, Selena whispered, "Are you okay?"

"Sure why?"

"You got ready so fast. It's just that you always had more of a . . . they used to call it a 'preppy look.' . . . And today, no bra?"

"No one in Vermont wears a bra, Selena."

"The hippies in town, maybe . . . never mind."

We drove in silence. My mind was on the scenery we passed, and noticing the trees, the farms with patterned fields of corn, and the apple orchards. Though I had seen them over the years, today my thoughts were focused on the way they were arrayed, the ripeness of the crop, and questions on when they should be harvested.

"Is something wrong? You're . . . so quiet." Selena seemed tentative.

It was too hard to explain all that I was thinking to Selena. "I can't describe it. Resting my mind, I guess . . . enjoying being here."

The park in town was crowded with stalls with artists displaying their jewelry making, tie-dyeing, weaving, and pottery. Veering off on my own, I lost track of Selena, stopping to look at crafts and chat with the artisans. A table filled with handmade clay pots and bowls drew me to it. "What kind of clay did you use making these pieces?" I asked, unable to stop myself from lifting and tilting them, feeling the weight of them in my palms. The surfaces of the pieces were smooth as if sanded before painting.

Selena tapped my arm. The artist, a woman with gray hair, wire-rimmed glasses, and large strong looking hands said, "Just your ordinary red ceramic clay. I have a can of it under the table, if you would like to feel it," she said, pulling out the tin and opening it.

"How much does it cost? Can I buy it from you?"

"I paid twenty-five for it, but I used some. . . . You can get it at the craft store."

"I'll drive you there, then if they don't have . . ." Selena said.

"No, I want this one that you used. I'll give you thirty-five for it . . . for your trouble."

"We have a truck," Selena said, pointing to where it was parked.

"My son will take it over there for you. It's heavy," the woman offered.

"No, I have it." I squatted down and lifted the tin of clay up.

"Your back . . . you better take it easy," Selena said.

"I'm . . . Pain's gone."

"But you wanted a needle, remember."

". . . Got some from a woman in the other tent. My braid reminded her of baskets in Brazil and the Caribbean. She said she was glad to see someone was keeping the craft alive."

Selena drove us home, periodically glancing at me with a bewildered expression. I noticed the looks, but loved losing myself in the trees and the greenery as it passed.

"I am going to take a nap before dinner," Selena said, as we got into the house. "You?"

"No, I am going to work a bit with this clay."

"Use the wooden table out back. Enjoy."

I pried open the can and untwisted the plastic bag, smelling the earthy odor of the clay before I felt it. The cool red-brown clay filled in under my nails, painting my hands a tan-gray color. Rolling beads, fashioning long oval shapes, and a handful became a long snake.

Sweat coated my brow. I went inside to get some water to make slip, a clay and water mixture, I learned about in an art class years ago that was used to make the coiled clay stick together. My research focused on the Carib Indians, described coiling as a technique they used in pottery making. *I couldn't help wondering if being drawn to this clay was Bequia creeping into my thoughts.* Slowly pressing and smoothing the long snakes with the slip, I shaped a bowl. It had a round belly and was built up almost eight inches. Perspiration speckled my upper lip and streamed down the sides of my face.

"You've been working all this time?" Selena said, startling me from my deep concentration. "Luis is cooking. Are you hungry?"

"I guess."

"I made some squash soup and some steamed vegetables. Something light," Luis said, joining us on the porch. "You made that? Where'd you learn that?"

"Just experimenting. That dinner sounds good. But I think I will pass . . ."

Luis's brow furrowed, he stiffened, as he glanced at Selena. She returned a worried look. Seeing the exchange caused a slight tightness in the muscles in my neck, but I was too tired from the work on the clay to question them.

Sunlight faded, and the sky had grown from magenta to turquoise, and as I got to my room, I was calm, peaceful. Something had changed within me. Although I wondered if it was the past life regression, my snatches of memory of the dream had held no clues. All I knew was that I had spent the day exploring and discovering new aspects of my being. I was drained but content.

The next morning, while in my room, I could hear their voices, or could I just sense what they were saying? I wasn't sure. This was the second day I had been up as soon as the dawn sliced the darkness. When I first heard them, I was outside picking flowers. And then in my room, I heard them clearly, their heads together in their bedroom.

"She seems different to me . . . stronger in some ways, but so different," Selena whispered.

"Lifted that big tin of clay. And quiet, so quiet. What happened in that past life regression?"

"Where is she?" Luis asked, then moved into the hallway.

"Still outside, I think."

Luis cupped Selena's ear and whispered so softly, his voice was barely audible, yet I could tell what he was saying. "I'm sure she went back to a past life."

"That's it then . . ." Selena covered her mouth seeming afraid she had spoken too loudly. There they were on the other side of the wall, but I could see them clearly. Selena leaned toward Luis, whispering in his ear.

"No. 'Member I asked her about any foreign lang . . . I taped her," Luis said, gesturing "Shh" with his finger in front of his lips, then pointing into the kitchen, as if he was telling her to move in there so as not to be heard.

That was the click I heard during the past life regression! He was taping me.

"I am sure she was speaking a foreign language close to Spanish; my guess, it was Portuguese, but it was garbled . . . was afraid she would stay there. She fully seemed to inhabit the . . . I think I need to tell her again that the knowledge she gains from past lives must remain focused on this one . . ."

"You want me to talk to her? Never mind," Selena said as I came up behind them. They looked like two children caught at something naughty, both seeming startled by my presence.

"Were you guys talking about me?"

"Just thinking about your past life regression," Luis said, then leaving abruptly.

Selena turned on the light in the kitchen. "I thought you were in the yard." She seemed to be busying herself, straightening the placemats and then filling the coffee pot at the sink.

"You guys were talking about me, weren't you?"

"We're . . . just a little concerned." Selena put a slice of bread on a plate and a butter knife on the table.

"Great!" I knew there was an edge in my voice. "You were right. Being here is just what I needed to clear my mind." My voice was raised. I was irritated that she wouldn't answer me.

"I feel so close to nature here this time. Selena, you are dodging me. What were you saying? Everything I was feeling good about, you have me worrying about now."

"Luis will talk to you about your past life regression. Let me just tell you. Having a past life regression for me was like . . . a movie. You watch it. Then you come out, and just . . . if you learn something you can use it in this life. . . . Don't try and stay there and fix stuff. You can't do that."

"Of course not." She seemed seriously worried.

"By the way, I didn't know you knew how to weave," Selena said.

"I didn't really, it seems to come naturally to me, though. It's almost like I am rediscovering something that I had known all along. It's relaxing."

"You're an early riser all of a sudden," Luis exclaimed, grabbing his mug.

"Yeah, I was up and enjoying the sun, checking on the vegetables. You guys are scrutinizing everything I do. . . . You're making me nervous."

Luis looked at Selena for guidance. "Did Selena tell you about her past life regression?"

"Yes . . . said it was like watching a movie."

". . . Good metaphor," he said. "Keep that in mind. I'm ready if you are. . . . Come, let's go." Luis walked in his usual energetic pace.

Following behind him, then turning back to look at Selena, I said, "We will see what we will see."

"Just listen to Luis. Follow his instructions."

"People say that there are cosmic lessons to be learned from going back to past lives, knowledge we should have learned in the past."

I stiffened my spine. "I heard you say this morning that you think I passed into a former life." I would not let him get away without answering me.

"I didn't want to influence your experience." He settled into the chair, and seemed to be searching his thoughts before he spoke.

"You seemed worried, Luis."

"No, but yes . . ." he paused. "You seemed to have entered a past life last time. I want to see if we can access it again. But . . . anything in a past life, you cannot change it there. You can only use what is learned to better this life, here and now."

"I understand. Selena said that too. Why are you reiterating that? I get it."

"I just want you to be . . . sure to recognize that you . . . I will ask you to describe what you see. Answer and do just what I suggest. Do not get swept away in the vision."

I felt a sense of *déjà vu* as I listened to him. I heard those words before. He then prompted me to relax, naming the parts of my body beginning with my feet. I began to yawn and felt uncomfortable in my skin. "Go back, back in time. Back, back . . . to the time that was important to you."

I was sitting on the beach. My belly was swollen. I rubbed it.

"Describe for me where you are, and who you see."

". . . Sitting on the beach, and everywhere behind me, there are palm trees and other trees. I don't know what they are, but they are very beautiful. I think I know this woman."

"Your hands, what are you doing?"

"I am making a basket to carry my cassava in."

"What is the woman wearing?"

I looked down and said, "I am not wearing anything on my breasts, but a cloth is covering me."

"Is it you, that you are seeing?"

". . . Her face looks . . . it's my great-great-grandmother, but I think it is also me. I see. . . . Is that his ship? No!"

I heard Luis say, "Describe what you see now. What are you doing?"

"It is a ship or a boat . . . from long ago. I am afraid my husband will come."

"What are you doing?"

". . . Putting on a dress . . . he bought me. My husband cannot come now."

"Why? Tell me what is happening?"

"I am hiding. Shhh! Please. Shhh!"

"Jocelyn, step back. . . . You are not of that world. Come back to this one."

I could feel Luis's presence there with me, but . . . as if I was both in the past and here in this time.

"Jocelyn, can you hear me?"

I cowered in the corner, afraid to move . . . afraid he would see me.

"Jocelyn, take from this experience what you feel is to be learned. Bring that knowledge to this world, leave the rest behind."

Luis was quiet. Where did he go?

"Did you hear me, Jocelyn?"

I nodded.

Confused, only snatches of a dream remained, seeing a ship, and running. Feeling afraid of a man was all that was left, but I don't remember why. Tired from all of it, I wanted to stay there and sleep.

"Jocelyn, you will wake as I count backward. Five, four, wake and feel refreshed, three, two, one."

"Luis, did you just tell me not to be swept up in the past or something like that?" I had this nagging tension in my neck from this sense that these words had been repeated, and that it was an important message for me.

"Before the past life regression, I said that, yes."

"I just remembered where I heard that before, my aunt told me the same thing."

"What do you mean?"

"I think she was talking about my research. It was just funny how both of you used the same words. 'Don't be swept away.'" Now it seemed it was not just my aunt telling me about my research, but now Luis was warning me of the same thing. My visit to Bequia and this past life are all tangled together in a powerful mix.

"I was just going to say . . ." Luis paused to think then said, "Let me put it this way, sometimes people have aftershocks of memory of these regression experiences. Remember that *past* life is over, and this is your life." Luis opened the shades as if he were trying to fill the room with the light of the day.

I couldn't help but laugh, "Luis, I won't lose my grip on reality. I am so hungry."

"No, what I mean is, you cannot change anything there, only here."

"Don't worry. I am protected." I pulled out the talisman that I wore around my neck.

"Take what I am saying seriously. What is that?"

"It's a charm, my aunt gave me for protection." I walked into the kitchen, where Selena was seated at the table.

"Well, I only remember snatches of a dream," I told Selena . . . "But Luis just said sometimes you can have aftershocks or flashbacks. We'll see."

That day and the next, my last in Vermont, went all too quickly. After I finished the small basket I made, I worked the rest of the day finishing what became a clay jug. Bequia became the center of our conversations the last day, and I showed Selena the photo of my great-great-grandparents. Selena studied the sepia-toned photo and said, "Your great-grandfather's eyes seem to carry his travels with him." She was then transfixed by my great-great-grandmother. "She was so beautiful, but *her* eyes seem to hold . . . a burden."

I saw it too. The look held a story I had to unearth.

As Luis placed my bags in the car, he said, "Give us a call to let us know how you are."

"Sure, not to worry." I hugged Selena. "I'm going to call Gerald Hunter when I get home," I whispered to Selena. "Maybe I can tempt him to come to Bequia to meet me." As soon as I said it, I thought, where did that thought come from? It felt impulsive, not at all like me. The sensation was new, but freeing. I was all too often boxed in with rules I made for myself. It surprised me that somehow I said something out of character and outside of my quirky self.

"What?" Luis asked.

"Girl talk. Not for your ears." Selena laughed, clasping her hands on his ears and kissing him on the lips.

"Sounds delicious," she said to me. "Call me." Selena winked. "Let me know what happens."

The rearview mirror adjusted, I backed up and turned the car around. My body was alive with an anticipation of . . . I did not know what.

8

The airport was wall-to-wall people, a place of managed turmoil and organized confusion. My purse, sunglasses, keys, and change in two plastic trays were gobbled up by the X-ray machine. Normally, I would be irritated by the chaos, but I was excited about finally leaving for Bequia. The couple in front of me in line seemed unconcerned about the swirling crowd of passengers and airport officials, focused only on each other. He was a bespectacled man in his mid-thirties, and his wife, I learned almost immediately, a chatterbox with a British accent, was a little younger. Her sunglasses crowned her brunette pageboy-cut, hair. They giggled and cuddled each other as they waited. When she asked me where I was going, and I said St. Vincent, she bubbled over with conversation.

"We've been there two, well, this is our *third* honeymoon there. Have you ever been?" she asked, stroking his chest.

When I told them that I hadn't been there since I was a child, she began to volunteer restaurants I should visit. "Dalila's has the best flying fish," she said, "oh and she makes a fish soup with cornmeal dumplings that are so delish." I shared that I was going on to Bequia, a smaller island in the Grenadines.

"Babe, we should check it out," she said, gazing into his eyes.

Her freeness touching him drew my attention. I never engaged in public displays of affection. It was just not something my family ever did. As I moved through the radar scan, the couple disappeared into the crowd. In chatting with them, I lost track of the plastic receptacle holding my sunglasses and change.

"I believe these are yours?" A baritone voice insinuated itself into my consciousness.

"Yes, thank you." I glanced up as I was hopping on one foot, putting on my sandal, and caught sight of a man with deep bronze-colored skin, mixed race I thought, or sunbathed European. He had a British accent, but with a West Indian lilt, and he was quite tanned for a Brit. I lost my balance, and he grabbed my arm, stopping me from falling.

"I've got you. No worries."

He was about five foot ten with lean muscles and strong hands. His eyes, which were a light brown almost gold in color, had charcoal flecks. His gaze drew me in, and I struggled to look away. When he focused his attention on me, his eyes seemed to darken to umber.

"Thanks, I'm fine."

As I steadied myself, he set me free. He looked at me with that second glance that said he had seen me before. I felt I had encountered him previously as well. My attention shifted to the items I was securing in my bag, and when I looked back, he was gone. The mass of people now spilled out into the concourse, where I stopped to buy *Essence* magazine and *O*, and then continued on to the gate. In the waiting area, clusters of people chatting and some sleeping took up every seat, leaving me to stand. Everyone perked up when the ground hostess moved behind the desk, and announced the flight in a beautiful Vincentian accent. I couldn't stop myself from smiling, and caught sight of the man who had handed me my things. He smiled in my direction as if in response to me. I looked away, uneasy with what I might have begun.

My trip was going to be a long one because I had to first fly to St. Vincent and then take the ferry to Bequia. My original plan was to stay a few days in St. Vincent to see a rental agent, but once I saw pictures of the home that Gerald Hunter suggested, I decided to take it. Constrained by the impulsive decision, though it shortened my trip, rather than stay in St. Vincent as planned, I wanted to try and get to the house in Bequia before dark. *How had I let this virtual stranger control where I stayed?*

His effect on me remained intoxicating. It wasn't just the superficial attraction he held, like his height, his voice, and his desperately good looks that drew me to him. There was an energy that attracted me not only to him, but also to the place he suggested, which exuded a sense of protection, a puzzling thought.

Last night, I hadn't slept and was exhausted. Getting on the plane, all I wanted was a pillow so I could go to sleep. With loads of miles accumulated on my card, I had upgraded for the first time to first class. Tugging my carry-on behind me, I was on the plane and opening the overhead compartment doing a happy dance in my head.

"You need a hand with that?"

"No, I've got it." I turned to see those light brown eyes. His curly brown hair was lighter at the tips from the beach and the sea, I thought. I looked away. He did not. I tried to maintain control, pulling the suitcase up and pushing it into the overhead compartment, then pushed my glasses onto my face. His eyes scanned my hair and then moved to my neck and chest. He then seemed to study my arm, then my hair again, and my face. Unmistakably, he scanned every part of me, without seeming to care if I noticed him looking.

Thinking that he would then move further into the plane, I stepped into the window seat—mine. Securing my boarding pass in the elastic pouch on the seat in front of me, I noted that he placed his carry-on in the same compartment as mine, moving into the seat next to me. Struggling not to look in his direction, despite my best efforts, my gaze was drawn to him.

It was strange, even though I had waited to get into my seat to go to sleep, now all I could think about was the man sitting next to me. His speech had either a Bajan or a Vincentian lilt, I thought. He had his laptop open and was scanning images of sailboats. *Sailboats?* I wondered if he owned one, maybe sailed himself. He turned off his computer when asked by the pilot. The flight attendant asked if he wanted a drink after takeoff, and he said no, then quickly said he did want something to drink later. His forearm, the only part of his body I could see without turning all the way around, was muscular, his linen sleeve rolled up over his biceps. His skin was tanned such a deep bronze that it glowed. He reached overhead to turn off the light and adjust the air. Every move he made attracted my eye like an illusionist's misdirection. The air over my own seat jammed.

"Would you like that on?" he said, his voice sounding like a croon.

"Yes, actually."

He twisted the knob, and said, "Light on too?"

"No. No thanks."

"By the way, it is a long flight, let me introduce myself. My name is Derek Reynolds."

"Dr. Jocelyn Kendall." I finally looked at him fully.

His eyebrows lifted, he appeared surprised. "That's always good to hear on a flight."

"What's that?" I asked, perplexed by the look.

"That there is a doctor on the plane."

He had so captured my thoughts that I had missed the import of his comment, though that had been said to me so many times before.

"No, I am not an M.D., I am a Ph.D. in cultural anthropology."

"Interesting," he said, then was silent.

"I can't help but ask, if you don't mind, but your accent sounds as if you are from Barbados or St. Vincent."

The flight attendant came through the plane closing the overhead compartments. The pilot made a comment about taxiing. I fastened my seatbelt.

"Actually, Bequian."

"Are you really? I am headed to Bequia," I said, before I thought to stop myself.

Again, he raised his eyebrows. "Most people from the States don't know our island. We actually prefer it that way." He smiled, putting his finger up to his pursed lips, and mouthed "Shhh."

A smile escaped my lips, though I was not intending it, and I covered my mouth because of my embarrassment. He looked squarely at me, which made me even more self-conscious.

"Why are you headed to my island?"

I thought his question forward, but intriguing. "Research. My family is originally from there too . . . always been interested in some family history, and . . . connections between the families in Bequia and Boston because of whaling."

"So, you are headed to Bequia directly?" A mischievous gleam lit up his eyes.

"Yes, I was going to stay overnight in St. Vincent, but since I am renting a house in Bequia, I'm taking the ferry there. What do you do, if you don't mind my asking?"

The plane was now on the runway, and I could feel it picking up speed. I gripped the armrest.

"I am an artist," he said, appearing unconcerned by the takeoff. Absorbed in my expressions, his gaze was unflinching.

It took me a few minutes to respond, waiting for the plane to finish climbing. After pressing the flesh that blocked my ears to equalize the pressure in my inner ear, I finally asked, "An artist?"

He stroked his chin, raised one brow, and seemed to enjoy the fact that I was still paying close attention. "Yes, a painter . . . and I design and build sailboats and small yachts for my family's business. I take it from your accent you are from the States, my guess . . . your accent . . . New York."

"Yes, New York."

"Well, I am fourth generation Bequian, but my family is a bit of a mix, English, Portuguese, Cape Verdean, and a little Carib Indian in the mix from way back."

"And what else can you tell me about your art?" I tried an open-ended question, much the way I conducted my interviews. He intrigued me.

"I paint, but I have lost my muse," the charcoal-gray flecks seemed to fill his eyes and reflected a darkening of his mood, "so I am working on a new boat." His aspect changed briefly, but when he regained his focus on me, he brightened. "You have the most expressive face," he said. "How are you getting to Bequia from St. Vincent? Have you made plans?"

"The ferry, as I said."

"Sorry, I must have missed that. I still enjoy the ferry, but I've chartered a plane. Would you like to fly with me? It's a little clipper and will get you there in no time, and no waiting for the ferry with your bags and such."

Fly with me? "No, I couldn't. I wanted to experience the ferry and . . . just don't want to get there after dark. . . . Meeting the housekeeper Haynes."

"You will have lots of time later for the ferry, won't you? How long did you say were staying to do your research?"

"A few months, maybe more. I'll see." It was more than a little presumptuous of him, I thought, to suggest his own plans for me.

"You see, plenty of time to enjoy the ferry. On the plane, I can have the pilot take you over La Soufrière. I am sure you are familiar with our volcano, which is visually breathtaking from the sky."

It would be great to see La Soufrière from the air, I thought. There was something irresistible about this man with the light brown eyes. He seemed playful, ready for fun. And the sooner I got settled into the house, the better I would feel. I did not want to arrive after nightfall.

"Let me think about it."

The flight attendant offered us drinks, and Derek ordered a rum punch. "A rum punch for you too?" she asked me solicitously, while gazing at him.

"Just fruit juice. It's a bit early for me. What fruit juices do you have?"

"What about a virgin punch, no rum?" the stewardess asked.

"Okay, that sounds fine."

"I thought you said your family is from Bequia," Derek laughed.

The flight attendant brought the drinks, beautifully mixed in tulip-shaped glasses, and took our order for brunch.

"This is the virgin, right?" I asked, and the flight attendant nodded.

Derek looked at me and raised his eyebrows and gave me an impish smile.

The rum punch loosened his tongue. I learned that his family's boat-building business, now focused on yachts and was several generations old.

I asked about how they started, wondering about his family's connections to Bequia's history.

"Began in the early 1800s with my fourth great. He was a bit of a scoundrel. Had a wife in Portugal, one in the Grenadines on Mustique, and they say one in America. Back then, he had a home on Nevis too. They built larger sailing ships, especially whaling ships. My family says I remind them of stories about him." He smiled as if he enjoyed the comparison.

"So, you have wives in . . ."

"No," he cut me off. "I think my mother likens me to him in his looks from the stories, light eyes, and his gift for invention." He laughed—at himself, it seemed. "He, my fourth great, had a penchant for mischief, which my mother accused me of, and is the reason she said she was likely going to have an early death."

He searched my eyes as if for signs of my passion for his stories, no doubt accustomed to it in women. I guessed he was the baby of his sibling constellation and his mother's favorite. "She used to say I'd be the death of her, but she's still alive, in her seventies." He laughed. "She embellishes the truth where I am concerned. I am her last, and she loves me best." *I was right!*

When he was not painting, he felt lost, he said, and that is why this last year was so difficult for him. He had just been in London, but was glad to be going home. I made a note to ask him more about the founders of the boatbuilding company and whether they were also linked in any way to Boston. He told me he hadn't painted in more than a year. I wondered why.

I, too, revealed far more about myself than I expected to, telling him about my leave, my research, and my desire to talk with people about Bequia's history. By the time we finished brunch, I grew tired. And though I might have chatted on, I excused myself to get some sleep.

"Think about flying with me to Bequia. Contemplate it in your dreams. When you awaken, you will be more predisposed to it." His voice was like velvet. The thought was placed there so gently that I could not protest.

Smothering a yawn with one hand, I tucked my pillow next to my window. The bed of clouds seemed to be cushioning us.

"Would you like that closed?" Derek asked, reaching past me to slide the plastic window shade down. I closed my eyes and slipped off.

The charcoals and blacks of sleep devoured me and seemed boundless. I came to rest in a room, a billowy bed beneath me. There was a tugging sensation on my right foot. I kicked instinctively, trying to open my eyes, but I was laden down with sleep. There it was again. This time a hand had a grip on my right ankle and was pulling it to the side. It felt improper somehow, because the tug of the hand seemed to part my legs. I kicked at it again, this time harder, but my foot simply stroked the air, not making contact. Then there was a strong hard yank of my leg, which woke me. I wrenched myself free of the blanket of sleep.

My eyes fully open, I expected to find someone gripping my leg. Derek was there watching me. I thought, at first, that he had witnessed the act, or perhaps partook in it. It took me a few minutes to discern where I was. My pillow was still resting against the wall of the plane. Derek wore an expression of bewilderment and concern.

"You had a stretch of bad dreams back there," he said.

I felt naked. This stranger had witnessed something that he shouldn't have. As I realized that it had been a dream, I checked the time on my watch. We were less than an hour away from landing. I had slept for almost two hours.

"What did you say?" I wanted to rebuff his intrusion on my privacy.

"You seemed to be struggling with something or someone."

"I am sorry if I disturbed you." Tension tightened my neck and shoulders. I could hear my voice grow strident, unable to hide my irritation. He was being intrusive. *Or was it the dream or the snatches of it?*

"No worries. Your expressions were very interesting, actually," Derek offered. He seemed now focused on exploring my change of mood.

"I am not trying to be rude, but it is uncomfortable being told by a complete stranger about one's sleeping habits," I said, reaching out for the seat in front of me, intending to stand and move past him.

"You are absolutely right. My artistic curiosity! Sorry." His contrition seemed sincere, though his eyes seemed to seek out more intimacy than I cared to share. The expression on his face said he relished it.

Derek stood and stepped into the aisle to let me pass. Closed in the tight bathroom cubicle, I thought about my reactions, trying to ascertain if this was my old self, closed and fearful, or whether I had any real reason to feel offended. It was the dream that left me feeling unsettled. I didn't want my prickliness to mar my arrival in Bequia. I shook the feelings off much the way I shook off bad dreams in the past, though I had never ever had a dream like this one before. Washing my face in cool water helped. That's when I noticed that my cheeks were hot. When I went out into the cabin, I tried to do so with the openness the trip had created in me from the start.

"Sorry if I offended you," Derek began. "As an artist, sometimes my focus is on the visual. Most of my models are women, so I have always been interested in exploring women's thoughts and emotions, because they color my canvases. Your cheeks were a beautiful shade of cinnamon."

Was he always so open with his commentary about women on first meeting? He's a ladies' man, a bad boy. I tried to remind myself what I had learned too many times about bad boys. Did I really need yet another lesson?

"I had a disturbing dream."

"Your work must have brought you in contact with some varying views of dreams," Derek said. "And I'm sure you know that some people back home think bad dreams are really visitations from the spirit world."

"In today's world, we think that we have things on our minds we are working through."

"There is no dichotomy there, if you believe, as many do, that the problems you work out in this life are those not completed in last lives." His eyes danced. "As an anthropologist, you must have studied many cultures that believe . . ."

"I have, but as it relates to me, I am going to a new place, settling into a new house . . . working on a new project." *Why am I telling him all this?*

"So new beginnings."

I began to laugh.

"Did I say something amusing?" Derek smiled reflexively.

"Well, my best friend just had her husband perform a past life regression on me because she said that since I was doing all of these new things, I needed it."

Derek frowned. "I think these modern-day past life regressions are nothing more than the rituals of the elders that put us in contact with our past worlds."

"I don't know if it worked on me. I have little recollection of it."

"Well, you can always give it time to reveal itself to you. Bequia is a very receptive space."

As the flight attendant passed through the cabin, routinely looking down at the passengers and asking if anyone would like some water or something else to drink, Derek smiled at her and then at me, and said, "I am ordering another rum punch to toast the landing." The flight attendant was beaming at him invitingly, and he turned to me. "Will you join me?"

"No, no thank you," I began, then surprised myself an instant later. "What the hell, sure."

"Two rum punches, then," the flight attendant said, returning with them a few moments later.

"By the way, where are you staying in Bequia?" Derek asked.

"It's a home in Friendship Bay, called Sea Breezes Villa. I'm renting it."

"I know the house. It's big, and on the beach. Lovely!" He was suddenly quiet.

"Where do you live?" His silence compelling me to know more.

"An artist community up in Moon Hole. The homes are built into the hill, all-natural stone. Furniture and accoutrements are built from the indigenous trees of the island and whale bones. Exquisitely beautiful views of the sea! Artists and writers live there. . . . You should come visit some time. You would enjoy working there."

"Moon Hole?"

"A somewhat curious name. Moon Hole is named for the volcanic rock which forms a natural arch there, and frames the setting moon." He smiled, clearly knowing he captured my imagination.

"Sounds fascinating. A good friend made the arrangements for the house. I will see how I like it there . . . lots of work to do. So . . ." I found myself once more erecting walls that I did not want to build. There was something too beguiling about him.

"No one would distract you from your work. We are all either working on something or thinking about working on something," he laughed. "By the way, did you make up your mind about flying to Bequia with me?"

I struggled again, trying to sort out his comments and my suppositions about him. After a quick pause, he asked, "A good friend from

Bequia? Anyone I might know? . . . I know almost everyone on Bequia."

I hadn't intended to tell him his name, but the words blurted out anyway. *Maybe it was the rum.* "Dr. Gerald Hunter. His family is from Bequia, but he lives in Boston. I think he vacations in Bequia. . . . A curator at The Whaling Museum in Boston. . . . A friend." I heard myself naming Gerald and his friendship as a protection against Derek's advances.

"I know *of* him . . . you said you were friends?" Now he had the look of someone calculating where all the pieces on the chessboard lay.

"We struck up a friendship by email over the past few months over my research, and I actually just met him. But he was kind enough to tell me about this house."

Derek's expression took on a Cheshire cat grin. I could swear I heard him say, "He shouldn't have sent her my way." Was I reading his mind, or projecting? My sensitivity to the thoughts of others was sometimes helpful to me at the college, but since the past life regression, it had grown intense, acute. "What did you say?"

"I didn't say a thing," he said. He resembled a child caught with his hand in the cookie jar. He was quiet for a long moment, then said abruptly, "Yea or nay. I can call ahead for the pilot to chill a bottle of champagne to toast our arrival."

"I think I will pass on any champagne. . . . Have to keep . . . uh, my wits about me. . . . Don't know my way around in Bequia."

"I can see you to your home, I have . . . a driver is picking me up at the airport."

"Just point me to the taxis, and I will be fine."

What is happening? I spend more than three years totally alone, and in less than a week I have two men interested in me.

Derek was yet again openly studying my hair, my face, my eyes. This time I could not look away. We had finally made sustained eye contact, and it was as if he parted the closed draperies of my soul, and with no hidden spaces, he seemed to feast his eyes on me. His fixed gaze permeated my being. My arms felt weak and they lay on the arms of my seat limp. I felt vulnerable, defenseless.

"You know, I would love to paint you."

Dumbstruck at first, I was just beginning to shake myself loose of this feeling of helplessness. My lessons of the past kicked in and found voice, "That sounds like a pickup line, and not a very good one."

"I'm serious. I would love to paint you, a portrait. No ulterior motive."

I laughed out loud. Finally, I became aware that there were people seated behind us, and on the other side of the aisle. I covered my mouth. Somehow, he had so taken up my attention that I hardly knew they were there.

"I've said something amusing. That's a start."

"I was warned about Vincentian men twice in the States before this trip, you know!"

"Warned? Were you?"

"Yes, once by my aunt, who said take care they will 'chat you up.'"

"And the second time, you said it was twice."

"Yes, you do listen closely don't you? Yes, it was my friend, and he said, to be aware while in Bequia." I had pushed my chess piece out.

"He said that, did he? So, is this your boyfriend?"

"No!" His intrusive question caused my face to flush. His eyes told me the wheels in his head were turning.

The flight attendant passed by to retrieve our empty glasses and asked if everything had been all right with the flight. Her eyes were clearly more focused on Derek. He told her they were fine, and asked her how long her stopover was. She said three days. He asked her had she ever been to Bequia, to which she responded, "No."

"You should come visit," he said.

The conversation was for my benefit. The flight attendant, about forty, with her blond hair pulled back into a twist, and her suntanned skin, turned to walk away. *Oh yes, he was a bad boy.* Paul was a bad boy, and it took me several years to figure out that I was choosing to be with someone who was always a flirt. Paul was a player and never resisted looking at or beginning a conversation with every hostess, waitress, bar-maid, or anyone in a skirt.

Derek seemed to be seeking a window into my thinking. "Your friend said you should be careful in Bequia. And I agree, you should be careful. Which is why I offered to see you home," he pressed his case. "If you want to come along, you let me know."

The proverbial ball was in my court. If I wanted to fly and get a lift, I had to ask. Derek seemed suddenly uninterested in the answer, turning his attention to the flight attendant as she made her sweep through the cabin. She surreptitiously handed Derek a card, which he palmed and placed in his pocket.

There it was, that feeling of inadequacy. I was jealous. *Why?* I hadn't felt that in years. *How did I end up here?*

The landing was gentle. Through the window, I could see the lush undulating green hills of St. Vincent and the aquamarine waters rushing and waning in and around them.

"You know, I think I would like to fly with you." The words spilled from my lips before I could edit them.

"You would? Are you certain?" he asked, teasing me.

"Well, don't say it that way."

He laughed. "Why don't you let me take that bag? It's a bit of a trek, especially in this heat."

As soon as the doors opened, the warm humid air flooded and fogged the cool cabin. Perspiration speckled my face and neck. Derek took hold of our carry-ons. Though I wanted to seem independent and capable, I had to admit it was nice to have the attentive treatment of a man. He took the lead walking just a step ahead of me into the airport.

"Your passport," Derek said, directing me to the official personnel, then heading for the baggage area.

An attractively husky, dark-skinned man in his forties smiled, approached Derek. "This is Cyril, he'll take your bag." He nodded and directed his comments to Derek, asking how the flight from New York was. There was a short wait for our luggage. I pointed mine out, and before I knew it, we were climbing into a small twelve-seater plane and strapping in. We were the only passengers.

The pilot came over to greet us. Derek introduced him and said, "Peter, give us a turn and good view of La Soufrière."

"Of course," the pilot said. He was thirty-something, wearing a white shirt with epaulets, and a blue and red striped tie. I recalled the photos in our family photo album of the uniformed policemen, Black policemen, and here was a young Black pilot and his playful eyes shone. With Black pilots rare in my American experience, I smiled to see him. He responded with a smile to Derek, and a glance and a polite nod in my direction.

Cyril, now in the role of flight attendant, asked Derek if he wanted him to pour the iced champagne. "No, we had rum on the plane, and the lady doesn't want to mix."

"Some rum punch then," Cyril offered.

"For me, yes."

"I'll have a little, for the toast," I said.

Cyril brought us goblets of a beautiful red rum punch with fruity chunks of pineapple and orange slices. He then disappeared into the cockpit and sat with the pilot.

We took off and climbed. The turquoise pools of water framed the densely green island of St. Vincent. The lush hills rose and fell until La Soufrière emerged, growing to the highest point on the island. She was so many greens, and at her summit was her mouth. She seemed stately. The pilot dipped a wing as he made a turn and allowed a view into her center. There was a crater dome of volcanic ash.

"She last erupted in 1979," Derek announced, gesturing with the hand holding the glass. "But one of the most devastating eruptions was in the early 1900s. Many fled the main island then, and came to Bequia." I could tell this wasn't his first time performing this chat. "Scientists believe that she is showing signs of erupting again soon. Let's hope she does not get angry."

Time seemed to telescope, and I heard Derek and the pilot talk about descent. Minutes later, we were on the ground, and Derek said, "Welcome to Bequia!"

Unsure if it was the rum, I was a little lightheaded as we stepped down out of the plane. A wet blanket of heat cloaked me. Cyril took my heavier bag and Derek's, and Derek carried my carry-on and his own. Again, he walked one or two steps in front of me. As we approached the entrance to the airport, he said, "You'll need your passport again."

"You back, man?" the passport agent said. They laughed and spoke in a patois to each other that I didn't understand. The man looked down at my passport, and turned an eye to me, and back to Derek.

"Are you here on business or pleasure, Dr. Kendall?" His officious tone hid a smile that was lurking somewhere beneath his business-like façade.

"I suppose both," I began.

There was an exchange of glances and grins between the two men, who seemed to share a secret understanding.

". . . But business for sure, research," I said, trying to assert the seriousness of my visit.

Derek took the passport and handed it back to me, glancing back at his friend. His chum raised his eyebrows and gave a slight nod of approval to Derek. Uncertain if I was particularly sensitive to cultural cues because of my profession, or if my observation and interpretation would have been obvious to another woman, too. But the men's conversation and furtive glances made me very conscious of my *femaleness*. A heat rose in my chest and up my neck, filling my cheeks and my forehead. My breasts pressed against my bra and blouse.

"My car is this way," Derek said, as Cyril headed across the street. Derek took a pristine white handkerchief out of his back pocket, "Do you mind?" he asked, as he lightly dabbed the perspiration from my upper lip.

I never got the chance to respond, but he seemed more aware of the aesthetic than of my answer. He studied my face with an intensity that I had never experienced before.

"You'll become accustomed to the heat," he said, folding and putting his handkerchief back in his pocket.

As we drove to Friendship Bay, which would be my new home, everywhere I looked Bequia was alive. To my left were the endless hues of green, the deep forests on the sloping hills of Bequia; its palm and coconut trees arched and bowed, contorting themselves in directions defying gravity. On the hilltops, their silhouettes were etched into the sky. Along the roadway, palms with broad trunks squatted like sturdy guardians of the island. Weighted with green and gold fruit at their peaks, the coconut trees were like dancing girls, fronds spread like arms embracing the warm sea breezes, which slipped through their fingers as they swayed wherever the wind swept them. To my right there was the sea, aqua then turquoise, then azure and violet, and the bright blue of the sky, which stretched above us.

Shrubs painted orange, gold, and ruby red, intermingled with floral trees, filled the air with a fragrant perfume; all seemed arrayed for my pleasure. I felt exceptionally alive in anticipation of all the secrets Bequia held. Fields of stalk-like plants with white and pink blossoms stretched into the distance.

"Are those the frangipani blossoms I've read about? And these are oleander flowers, right?" I asked.

"Yes, oleander there! Open the window. Can you smell them?" The fragrant bouquet filled the car.

"They smell lovely! But they have a dark side, don't they? I learned of them in Africa."

"Yes, the plants have a poisonous sap that you should avoid touching. Bequia is intoxicating, but you must always take care." Derek took my hand and held it in his lap, which I permitted accidentally, since I didn't see this gesture coming. It lasted for less than a minute or so. He smiled as he looked at my palm and fingers, then placed my hand back on my own knee.

His touch, his focused attention, and the flush of blood to the surface of my skin all made me feel much warmer than the cumulative effects of the heat and humidity on the island. Bequia's brew had begun to seduce me.

Part II

The first to come brought gifts, the sea and sunshine in his eyes. She would not let that be. Her fury summoned the one who came at night, delivering the cool heat of moonlight. I shook myself to loosen his hold on me.

9

The sounds of gravel hitting the tires and the underside of the car signaled our approach to Sea Breezes Villa. Though I had seen photographs, I couldn't believe how grand it was. Its limestone façade reminded me of photographs of my grandmother's home in Bequia. A heavyset woman with a towel suspended from the waistband of her apron looked out the side door as the car rolled up the driveway. She smiled and waved toward us, then ducked her head trying to see inside the car. When Derek got out and walked in front of the car, as I followed, her expression soured, and a scowl lined her brow.

"Yes, just as you expected, this is Haynes," he said to me.

A skeptical glance was all Haynes offered, then said, "Your bags can be brought in through here, Mum. I will show you the house now, or if you would prefer, I can make a pot of tea." She paused, then added glancing at Derek, "Or I could prepare a full tea service." Though her tone displayed a modicum of discomfort with his presence, I liked her strength of character. She was no pushover.

"No, that won't be necessary. Derek, I really do want to relax and get unpacked and situated."

"Of course. I'll just have the driver take these bags in for you." The chauffeur lifted both suitcases and Haynes turned saying, "The bedroom is this way."

The interior of the house had a tropical old-world feel, which I loved, with its large dining table with two small palm plants on either end of the sideboard and a silver tea service in its center. Gerald had said he stayed here often, and I guess we had the love of this traditional décor in common. Because the chauffeur moved so quickly, I barely saw the living room, but caught up to him just as he was putting down my bags. My picture window gave me a view of the beach and the aquamarine waters with ribbons of turquoise and azure stretching out to the horizon, which took my breath away.

As I began to thank Derek so that he would make his exit, the telephone rang. The cadence of the two-ring pattern was much like the sounds of phones in other countries that I had visited that were part of the United Kingdom. Haynes turned on her heel, glanced at Derek briefly, and picked up the phone next to the bed.

"Yes, Doctor. She has arrived already. Yes, of course, hold on please. Dr. Hunter is on the phone."

I turned my back on Derek, and toward the window. "Dr. Hunter, Gerald? How did you know I'd be here so soon?"

"Actually, I was just checking to see if everything was ready for your arrival. You reached there faster than I imagined. At least I can be certain that you got there safely. Does the house meet your expectations?"

"It exceeds them, I. . . . It's lovely. The view is exquisite."

"I'm glad you like it. By the way, I have arranged for Haynes to prepare as many meals as you would like this first week, while you get acclimated . . . and learn your way around. I hope that is all right with you. And do call me . . . if anything is not to your liking. I will . . . contact the owner."

"I can contact her on my own. . . . Don't want to bother you . . ." His self-assured manner was attractive, even though it left me feeling that he had taken charge of my interactions with the manager of the property.

"It . . . simply would be easier if I did it." There was a click, and Gerald Hunter was gone.

When I turned back to face Derek, he seemed to have been processing every word I said. "I must head home. Enjoy your stay. And of course, if you would like to see Moon Hole, do give me a call. Here is my number on the island." His card simply read, "Derek Reynolds, Artist. Bequia, St. Vincent and the Grenadines," with his number and email address.

"Would you like some refreshments out on the veranda?" Haynes said, reappearing and seeming far more relaxed after seeing Derek to the door. As she led me out to the back of the home, she paused to show me the kitchen, which was spotless, with a rather large, beautiful workspace and overhead ceiling fan. A breakfast area at the far end from the door held red pillows placed into wicker chairs. From the veranda, I could see the lush, green pathway leading down to a gate that opened onto the peach-colored, pristine beach. Coconut and palm trees and a breadfruit tree draped themselves around the veranda. Down the steps near the beach, a flamboyant tree was ablaze, immodestly displaying herself and her red blossoms in full bloom.

"Some orange water and watercress and chicken salad sandwiches, Mum." Haynes placed a tray in front of me. "Will you be taking dinner at home? I have swordfish, or chicken, if you prefer. And if mistress would please tell me her preferences, I can plan meals for the week."

"Thanks so much Haynes. Haynes, is that your last name, or your first? Is that what you prefer to be called?"

"Yes, Mum."

"If I am called on the telephone, you can refer to me as Dr. Jocelyn Kendall, but you may call me Jocelyn." I was already munching on the sandwich, which had been trimmed of its crusts and cut into quarter triangles. "This is delicious, Haynes." I knew I was going against the cultural mores and asserting my American culture in asking to be called by my first name, there was so much formality in our exchange. If I was going to live there for a while, I wanted to be comfortable.

"Yes, Mum. Thank you, Mum. Mistress Jocelyn, about dinner?" I noted the extra "Mistress" tacked onto my name. She was making her point.

"I don't guess I will be all that hungry. Is there any more of this chicken salad?"

"I will prepare a proper salad for you, Mum. Would you be needing any assistance with unpacking?"

"No. I think I can handle that."

In so many ways, I had stepped back into a different time. This culture was an interesting dichotomy. On the one hand, the West Indian class system, influenced by the British, was accommodating in that one always felt served. But on the other hand, it was constricting in dictating how one could interact. Although I had tried to strike a more familiar tone, Haynes had put me in my place and maintained hers.

After sitting and gazing at the glittering sea, the warm tropical air laden with moisture enveloping me, I unpacked and hung up my clothes in the big cedar closet. I stored my personals in the bureau, which held fragrant small soaps in small ceramic saucers that I could swear I had seen before, and scents that I recalled. But though the sea mesmerized me with its many aquas, turquoise and midnight blues, the deep mattress invited me to rest, and I untied the mosquito net just to see it cascade around the bed. It was as if I were revisiting a place that I had once lived, and loved. Before I experienced my routine musings prior to sleep, the bed swallowed me up.

I fell into an abyss, and just as I feared I might hit the bottom, a peaceful calm came over me, and I was walking along the beach.

My walk became a playful romp, chasing the seawater at its edge, enjoying the feel of the tiny bubbles on my toes. Crabs scurrying sideways on the beach then secreting themselves in holes. They then popped up again with their two beady eyes atop their heads, watching me as I walked. The aqua water was clear and revealed sea urchins and sea stars resting in the shallows. As I peered out to the sea, the colors deepened to cobalt until what I saw held me transfixed.

A large ship was anchored there. It had a sail of long ago, and the sight of it jarred my insides. There were men on the bow, and one of them was looking at me through a spyglass. Other men joined him there, and he pointed. It soon became clear he was pointing at me. They began to lower a smaller boat and climb down the side of the larger vessel to board it, and they headed in my direction.

Before I could think, I ran. First, I raced along the beach and then darted into the growth of trees and bush. There was a narrow path that had been worn down, and I followed it. I began to shout in unfamiliar words, and far up ahead I saw a large round hut-like structure with a cone-shaped thatched roof. My bare feet, which I feared would be cut, were not bruised. My soles were thick and tough. That is when I noticed that my breasts were uncovered, and I wore only a woven cloth around my hips. My body was youthful and strong, and my color golden brown. Three muscular men raced out of a larger house carrying knives, and ran in the direction from which I came. Then three more followed them with two more in close pursuit, carrying wooden clubs. A woman, clad as I was, but with larger breasts that hung down to her waist, grabbed me and pulled me into the grass and bamboo-like structure. Other women hid behind a wall holding the hands of young children, who were beginning to cry. They distributed knife-like stone weapons, and the women hid the children in the rear of the longhouse behind a grass-covered false wall. Their flashing eyes told the children to be silent, and they lowered their eyes and covered their lips with their fingers. The woman, who held the whimpering infant, pushed her breast into its mouth. Finally, I saw my mother with her arm around my sister, whose arms were wrapped around my mother's waist. A hush fell over the space. Huddled so closely, my skin pressed against my sister's, and the heat made us perspire.

The stillness grew and I squeezed the knife, preparing for an attack. Instead, a cascade of laughter showered the longhouse. "Mariel!" the men shouted, then they said something I did not understand. The language was foreign to me. Yet, the more I listened, though the individual words had no meaning, the import of what they said made sense.

"Mariel, you have won the eye of the seaman. He's a Portugee. Mariel, where are you?"

By the time the words crept more deeply into my consciousness, I fully realized that they were talking to me. All the women went out to hear what the men were saying, and soon they looked at me and giggled, all except my mother. Then the men laid a gunnysack at my feet, and they pointed to it and gestured to me to open it. My father pushed me and then gestured to me to do as they had bid me. Within that roughly woven material was another bag of the softest silken cloth, the color of magenta.

"Mariel, open that one," my father commanded. In it was a highly polished wooden box with tiny bits of different kinds of wood, and a metal key and lock. I turned the key, and it sang to me.

Some of the children moved closer to it, and I took in the music and felt soothed by it. Now the music from this magical box was connected to the men who came to me from the sea. I looked up to see them collected there.

"Mariel, he wishes to meet you," my father said. The women chattered on in their own language. Somehow, the anthropologist in me knew it to be Arawak, which they kept after being taken by the Carib men. Now they pushed me to accept, and though this was new to me and not fully understood, I nodded yes.

When the men called out something, from the bush, he came. His hair was as dark as the darkest night. It curled and grew not only on his head, but also down the sides of his face and onto his chin and jaw. The hair there grew brown, and then red, and golden around his lips. I found that I wanted to touch it. His skin was dark and swarthy, and his eyes were the color of the sea, with flecks of gold like the setting sun.

My father told me to smile and then said something about my teeth and my hips and children. I soon gathered that they were talking about my bearing them. Then the men said something to me about my Portugee. He laid a larger sack at my father's feet, one larger than the one he had given me. This time, my father opened it, and it contained pieces of gold. My mother had the strangest look on her face. My father said something about a home. He said that his daughter was to be a fine lady, and the Portugee nodded, and said that he would be back when he had built a house.

My mother finally spoke up, "What is there for me, the mother?" My father scowled, but tried to hide his embarrassment by saying, "Our people say that a gift must be given to the mother if her daughter is to be taken from her."

The women in the group looked on in disbelief. But the Portugee nodded to my mother, and said he would bring a suitable gift when he returned. He turned and the men parted, giving him a path, and he left.

All the people treated me differently the next day. The women bathed me and took great care of my hair. My sister was the exception. She hated that my father favored me. The young men looked at me out of the corner of their eyes. My father treated me like a prize possession. I was guarded at all times by one of my brothers. And my mother, with a small group of women, began to talk to me secretively about men and their desires. They would sometimes giggle or laugh, telling stories about how men were weakened by their needs. The women made me to understand that since we did not have physical strength with which to control them, we must use our wit.

The Portugee went out to sea. They said he would come back for me when he had built a proper house. But days went by and the moon turned her back on us. So, from time to time, I held the magic box and opened it to let its captured music fill my ears and bring back the vision of him to my mind.

I struggled to pull myself from this slumber. My body felt laden with stones that held me down. As I began to open my eyes and see the room about me and recognize that I was in Bequia, the cool breeze of the evening wafted in through the open window and cooled my body. The air seemed to envelop me with a sense of peace. As I lay quietly, almost afraid to move and lose track of it, I remembered the dream. It was odd, at first, because my dreams had been lost to me for so long. Since before my last visit to Vermont when the past life regression sparked flashes of scenes, I had not recalled anything of substance when I awoke from sleep. But now I recalled every detail. I remembered the minutia of this dream better than some of the more mundane goings on in my life. The girl, Mariel, was inextricably tied to me in some way beyond my dreamy imaginings. Somehow, she had become me, and I her. As I thought about the Portugee, I longed to see him again. I laughed at myself. I had never had a dream of a man I wished to summon at will.

My window framed the sea and the horizon. The sun had set and the sky, at its highest point, was a deep blue with a peachy sorbet color just below that. I wanted to explore the house. Haynes left the hallway illuminated by nightlights which lit my way. Opening the door near my bedroom, I discovered another bedroom, appointed with brightly colored bedclothes and a tropical painting above an antique washbasin. I now realized that Haynes left each room lit by a small lamp. There in the basin sat a large pitcher that appeared to date back to the 1800s. Selena kidded me that it was the era I loved best, and here were remnants of that time for my delight. Next door was a library-office with a rolltop desk, and a flat workspace, where I decided I would place my laptop. To the rear of the house was a stretch of hallway and another door, but this one was locked. Because of my memory of the blueprint and length and breadth of the room, I imagined it was a sitting room. I added the locked room to my mental list of questions for Haynes.

Wandering into the parlor, I found an old antique curio cabinet with a large conch shell and three scrimshaws similar to the one I wore around my neck. There was a large pearl displayed in what appeared to be an antique jewelry box. The cabinet door was locked tight. The owner of the home must only rent to trustworthy guests, I thought. On the wall behind the cabinet, an old black and white photograph depicted men disembarking from a whaling boat. The photo adjacent to it depicted a whale carcass. I tried to square my feelings of protectiveness for the whales with my respect for the culture that relied on the whale for food, and a way of life. This was clearly a man's space; the slaughtered whale did not seem a decorative touch of a woman.

A museum curator could not have arranged a statelier example of a nineteenth century dining room, with its grand cherry table and chairs and antique credenza topped with a beautiful silver tea set at its center. I wondered if it was used or just there for show. My grandmother used hers every Sunday. As that thought lingered, I remembered that my parents were poor by comparison. We lived in a three-room apartment when I went away. I wonder if that's why they sent me away. At the head of the table, there was a note held in place by a bud vase holding a bright-red flower, a daylily, I thought. The note from Haynes held only one misspelling, my name, and showed her to be quite attentive.

Dear Miss Joselin,
The salad I made is in the fridge. There is also fresh papaya, and mango.
I will be there in the morning to make breakfast. Please tell me
what Mum would like me to make, and what time you rise.

Haynes

It was strangely calming knowing that she would be there in the morning. Dr. Gerald Hunter thought of the very thing that would ensure my smooth transition. Though I struggled against the comfort of having a man make decisions that I might make for myself, I had to admit that I enjoyed his caring thoughtfulness.

A swinging door led to the spacious kitchen, which straddled two worlds—sort of like me. Living in a modern world, I always carried the beauty and the reminder of how it used to be. This space was a blend of both modern and traditional furnishings, a state-of-the-art refrigerator and dishwasher, side by side with a grand old galley stove. The overhead ceiling fan with old-fashioned enamel blades, and the reclaimed wood cabinetry with porcelain tile and brass knobs, decorative touches from the nineteenth century. I swept my hand over the butcher block counter, worn down in places, imagining generations of women cutting and chopping and preparing meals. I felt at home.

On the other side of the kitchen, a door was slightly ajar. No light switch on the wall outside, I pulled the door open to see where it led. The interior was dark, but I made out a large storage space inside, and an overhead pull-string, which I tugged. This was a true cook's pantry that brought back tasty memories of my grandmother's cooking, and even my mother's holiday dinners. Bags of rice and pigeon peas for peas and rice, bags of flour, and ground grains like cornmeal, with which my grandmother made cornmeal dumplings for her fish soup. On the back wall was a roughly hewn wooden cabinet—an antique apothecary cabinet with a glass door, with herbs packaged in boxes and small packets with handwritten ink labels. Its door did not budge. Another question for Haynes in the morning.

Passing back through the kitchen, the veranda, though dark, was inviting. I turned on the outdoor light. The sea breeze kissed my cheeks with a salty mist, and I marveled at how at ease I felt in this new place, moving from room to room, simply curious about what I might discover. The moon was full, and its light painted the surface of the sea with a luminous silver sheen. The single light bulb glowing on the porch invited moths that danced and flitted about. I didn't swat at or try to get away from the flying insects as I might have in the city, but rather delighted in the life that they represented. Bequia tapped into a serenity that I had not felt in some time, if ever at all.

Perhaps it was the darkness and the rushing sound of the sea that permitted my thoughts, fragments really, not full intentions or even desires, just whisps of notions to join in the dance of the moths. The peace here in Bequia felt fraught just beneath the surface. *Could I maintain my serenity with the men who, it seemed by magic, had entered my life?* Gerald came first, and gave me a home. He eased me into it, attending to needs I had not imagined that I had. His attention was like a warm embrace. As his image, his face and smile, took up space in my mind, I could swear I felt the embrace tighten. I worried that I might not be able to breathe. Then there was a sensation of a kiss, his kiss, on my lips. My hand moved up to my mouth as if to stop my lips from parting. Then Derek fascinated me with his invitations to Moon Hole. He dared me to seek out adventure, an inclination that I avoided because it was always punishing. The Portugee then inhabited my dreams. I wanted him to come again so that I could get to know him.

10

Sunlight warmed my cheeks and colored my eyelids crimson. Birds outside my window called, welcomed me. Through the veil of the mosquito net, there was the sea, brim with blues. Enjoying the solitude of the house, I slipped on a long cotton tee and wandered toward the kitchen, heading for the veranda.

"Good morning, Mum. Did you rest well?"

I froze. Haynes's presence jolted me, and I had to breathe deeply to collect myself.

"I didn't know you were here, Haynes." Busy with filling the kettle, she didn't notice my alarm.

"Was here all the night, Mum. You wish to take your breakfast in the dining room or out on the veranda?"

Before I stopped myself, I turned sharply around and glared at her. "Did you say you were here last night?"

"Yes, Mum. Me stay in the servant's quarters downstairs last night." Her head was buried in the refrigerator, and she came out holding a carton of eggs, unaware of my vexed expression. "You rise at nine each day, Mum?" she asked, finally looking squarely at me.

"No, usually at eight, but I was tired from the trip." I did my best to conceal my irritation, and continued, "and that bed is so comfortable. But wait, I was up last night. Are you saying you were here?" Her welcoming smile showed no understanding of my annoyance. "Yes, Mum. Me hear you, but you didn't call out, nor nothing. Me not want to trouble you. I prepare your eggs, and I'll bring some fresh orange juice out on the veranda."

My neck stiffened. "Haynes, do you normally stay the night in the servant's quarters?" The notes I read about the house said nothing of this.

"Dr. Hunter arrange dis. He said I should stay the first couple days, so you have what you need and know how to get around and such."

Unsettled, I blurted out, "Haynes, do you have Dr. Hunter's number nearby." I did not think to mask my irritation. Gerald was making plans for me, plans I always made for myself. His concern held a sensation that could only be described as control.

"Mistress Jocelyn, I hope you are not angry wit' me. I wasn't sure when you want breakfast, and I didn't want to trouble you. . . . Couldn't tell you I would be staying . . . 'cause you went to sleep so suddenly . . ." Haynes's face, so warm and welcoming just a minute ago, was now lined with worry.

She was right. I don't know where all my irritability came from. "No, no. I didn't mean to . . . no everything's fine." I forced a smile onto my lips, and I accepted the woman's explanation with as much grace as I could summon, but I couldn't help feeling restricted by Gerald's *concern*.

"Haynes, I need to contact a Prof. Thomas Bailey. How might I reach him?" I wanted to shift attention away from my displeasure.

"Yes, Mum. Dr. Hunter mentioned that you might be needing his number. Here it is on the board, near the telephone book wit' all St. Vincent and the Grenadines numbers. This book is for Barbados. The professor is here in Bequia, so you don't have to take the ferry dere. Dis is the name of a taxi that can take you anywhere on Bequia. Mum, when you done wit' your breakfast, I will walk you through the house with the keys, so you know where everyt'ing is, and what needs locking if I am not here."

"Speaking of locking things, I noticed a cabinet back there in the back of the pantry. It was locked."

"Yes, Mum."

Haynes made no attempt to explain.

"Is it a spice cabinet?" My curiosity was piqued by Haynes's silence on the matter.

"Some, and some herbs."

She offered no further information. "Why is it locked?" I persisted.

"Since the house is used by friends . . . of . . . the owner on occasion, we keep the herbs under lock and key, and . . ." Haynes paused seeming to search for the proper word, ". . . safe."

The kitchen door out onto the veranda was ajar, and the aquamarine waters drew me to the wooden railing of the porch. I felt a bit dizzy, as the house was built on the hillside. I had to steady myself, feeling a bit of vertigo. It was a sensation I did not feel yesterday or last night. The darkness cloaked the steep incline.

"I'll eat out here, Haynes."

I went into the bathroom to freshen up and get dressed, came back out and the little table was set beautifully. Silver salt and peppershakers, a cloth napkin, all were neatly arranged to the center of the serving table with marmalade and a fruit jam in small ceramic pots. The care and attention Haynes paid to details impressed me. As I opened the small pot of jelly, she said, "The jelly is guava. I hope you enjoy it."

My mouth watered. "I haven't had any since I was last here."

"When was that, Mum?" Haynes gently inquired.

"When I was four."

"Then I hope it is as good or better than you recall. Let me get your eggs."

She brought back the scrambled eggs, which were perfect, with whole-wheat toast.

My favorite teas, Twinings Earl Grey and Twinings English Breakfast tea, were next to a teapot of hot water with a small pitcher of cream. Haynes must have noticed my frown, which I didn't know I revealed. "Is something wrong?" Her expression both questioning and apologetic.

". . . Nothing really. Do you have lemon? I take my tea with lemon, not cream." I never acquired the taste for tea with milk or cream the way the British drank it.

"We have limes," Haynes said with no apology. "Try some coconut bread," she offered, and waited for my reaction.

The bread was delicately sweetened and had a light flaky texture with bits of grated coconut and raisins dispersed through the slice. "It's delicious, Haynes. You remind me of so many treats I had as a child. I actually made coconut bread with my grandmother. She let me grate the coconut."

Haynes's smile brightened. "You have to be careful of your fingers," she said with a warning tone I remembered so well. "The rest of da loaf is wrapped in plastic, on the counter."

". . . So many good memories, you bring back."

The veranda seemed a cloistered space, surrounded by trees and the vines that stretched onto the porch twisting and twining themselves between and around the railings. Once I was alone, the birds seem to find their way onto nearby branches. They cocked their heads and serenaded me, some nearby, and others from far away. I searched for them, and found them hiding in the shaded pockets of the trees. A tiny bright yellow bird, clearly braver than the rest, boldly bounced from an overhanging branch and onto the porch. He then bounded onto the veranda floor, searching it seemed for a morsel, some crumb that tumbled from the table for him. I laughed and hearing me, he retreated a bit then quickly regained his courage and kept me company as I ate. I don't remember ever enjoying nature and its creatures this much, beginning in Vermont and now here in Bequia. *I have to ask Luis if that could be a sign or lesson of the past life regression.*

When I finally finished eating, I called out to Haynes. When she came out, the yellow bird flew up to the railing, hopping along it and eyeing her.

"I think I am going inside to make that call. Look at this little guy!" I said, gesturing toward the bird.

Haynes laughed. "Yes, he's here often, sings for his supper."

"I think he was waiting for me to drop something."

"Take care feeding him, they'll all be here every mornin'! The phone plug is out here if you want me to bring it to you, Mum."

"Thanks, Haynes. You think of everything."

As I dialed the number, out at sea there was a boat close enough for me to make out the form of a man at the bow, looking in my direction. That uncanny sense of having been here before now happened again, but as I tried to remember what specifically this reminded me of, I heard a voice from the phone's earpiece.

"Good morning," the Vincentian lilt was like music.

"Good morning, Prof. Bailey? This is Professor, I mean Dr. Jocelyn Kendall."

"Yes," he said, pausing as if waiting for some clarification.

Hoping to jog his memory, I said, "Dr. Gerald Hunter suggested that I call you."

"Yes . . ." he answered, pausing again.

"He said that you might help me in my research on the men who were involved in whaling between Bequia and Boston."

"Oh yes, of course . . . yes, I recall." He laughed, it seemed at himself. "Well, why don't you tell me what you need and how can I help you?"

"I am trying to explore the familial connections between Bequia and Boston. I am looking at the possibility that the whalers had families in both places."

"So you want to do an historical study?"

"Well, more of an anthropological study. My focus is still fluid. I am beginning with an exploration of my own great-great-grandparents. My twice great-grandfather was a Portuguese whaler, and he married a Carib Indian."

"Oh, your family is from here?"

"Yes, but I'm . . . I want to look more broadly at how many families might share names, and if I can interview folks to find out if families here have bloodline connections, or maybe . . . know stories of related families in Boston. I want to look at birth and death records . . ."

"Well, I can point you in the direction of historical records. We should have tea and chat. . . . Haven't been out to the sea in Bequia in some time, so busy. Dr. Hunter said you are staying at Sea Breezes?"

"Yes." It sounded as if he wanted an invitation to tea. "Should I come to you, or would you be willing to come for tea? Dr. Hunter told me to ask you to look at a scrimshaw I have from my great-great-grandfather."

"I recall him saying something about that. Well, I will bring my glass with me."

"Pardon?"

"My loupe. My magnifier."

"Oh, I see. So, you'd like to come? When might you be . . . ?"

"I'm off to Barbados on Tuesday, for a few days. And I won't be back in St. Vincent until Wednesday next."

"So, you want to come next week?"

"No, I am actually finishing a paper for a presentation that week," he paused and I heard him turning pages in a calendar or date book. ". . . then heading to London."

I always felt tension first in my neck, and there it was. "So, you want to come the week after?" I continued, trying not to have my frustration revealed in my voice, but it had begun to crease my forehead.

"No, I know this is short notice," he mumbled something to himself. ". . . but if we don't do this today or tomorrow, we have to put it off for a while."

I carried the phone into the kitchen and repeated, "So, you would like to come for tea for today or tomorrow?" and looked bewildered at Haynes "Let me ask Haynes if she can prepare tea for today."

She quickly nodded. "Ask him if he will arrive for high tea or low tea," Haynes said.

"Prof. Bailey? will you . . ." I began, shrugging my shoulders, apologetically at Haynes.

"High tea . . ." he answered, before I finished.

"I guess I will see you later today, then." A bit flustered, I continued, "What time should we expect . . . ?" But he had ended the call.

"Haynes, I am so sorry to do . . ."

"No need, Mum."

"Should I call him back? I have no idea when he's arriving."

"He will be here at about four, Mum. That is his practice. He does take the meal in the dining room, and I will set it out. He prefers fish . . . swordfish is his favorite. He takes his tea out on the veranda. Then he takes a constitutional out along the beach."

"So, he's been here often."

"Yes, Dr. Hunter entertains him . . . when he's here."

"Those plans sound fine. I'll leave it to you." Curious, I thought, how this world weaved itself about me so effortlessly. It was comforting and constricting at the same time. It was akin to a good undergarment, as they used to say. On the one hand, one prefers to be without it. On the other hand, it sometimes feels good to be well-supported. I smiled at my musings. This new place was fitting around me in such interesting ways.

The gravel from the driveway rattled to say that Professor Bailey had arrived. My image in the mirror somehow seemed younger; the lines on my forehead and brow seemed less defined, and some had almost disappeared. The sleep I got last night must have done me good. As I hurried to the door, I remembered that Haynes would receive the professor for me, and breathed in the restful rhythm of this place. Sprinkling my hand with the Florida Water I found in the second bedroom, I put it on my neck and wrists. It was a light citrusy-scented cologne; another memory of my childhood stay in Bequia. It was on the bureau with the 4711 Cologne and Bay Rum, which wasn't rum, but a men's cologne used by grandfather. I imagined it was used by Gerald when he stayed here. I didn't recall the fragrance on him the day I met him at the museum, but then I could hardly breathe at all when I was close to him.

The dining room table was beautifully set, and I continued into the kitchen where Haynes was opening the door to the veranda.

Prof. Bailey, so nice to meet . . ." The professor didn't turn in my direction. Haynes pointed to her ear. She tapped his arm, gestured toward me, and spoke crisply, "Prof. Bailey, meet Dr. Jocelyn Kendall." He smiled and put out his hand.

"Good to meet you," I said, at first a bit perplexed.

His face, dark in complexion, imprinted with laugh lines, glowed with a sprightly expression. He had a small frame, and stood only about five feet tall, with gray hair, parted and neatly combed to the side. He was wearing a white short-sleeved cotton shirt and a maroon bowtie, reminding me of a Trinidadian professor I met once at a conference. He reached into his pocket and turned the knob on a small mechanism, his hearing aid. He finally fixed his gaze on me.

"Good to finally meet you, too. Dr. Hunter told me about you a few weeks ago, and I was looking forward to chatting with you." He then tapped his left ear, which held the hearing aid and readjusted the mechanism he had taken from his pocket. Haynes waited and watched him attentively, then said with her voice raised, "Shall I pour you some orange water, or would you prefer some coconut water."

"Coconut water would be fine."

"And you, Mum?"

"For me too, thank you."

"So, your family is from Barbados?" He continued out to the veranda with a jaunty stride and sat in what seemed his favorite chair near the door, where I sat earlier.

"Yes. I was here in Barbados and St. Vincent when I was little. I don't remember much about it."

"And your great-great-grandfather was a Portuguese seaman?" The old man looked at me over the lenses of his half-glasses and nodded as I spoke to him.

"Yes, and my great-great-grandmother was a Carib Indian." I searched his face for some connection to my story.

"That wasn't uncommon."

Haynes brought out a tray with two tall glasses of coconut water over ice. Prof. Bailey took a good long sip. "You know, they call this nature's plasma. Good for everything that ails you."

Smiling to acknowledge his comment, I went on. "All I know about my great-great-grandparents is from family stories. I really would like to document it, the history, and the stories better. But my curiosity has led me to the greater story about the men who traveled between Bequia and Boston. Many of the same Portuguese names were in the ship manifests I researched, also in the telephone books, and I wondered if the bloodlines were from the same men. In essence, I am interested in whether the folk here are cousins, so to speak, with those families in Boston." I paused, catching myself at my phraseology once again. "I should say that I am interested in the stories by women and men on the families' connections. I may have focused on the bloodlines because of the fathers' surnames. And, of course, the women may well be the ones who hold the stories and the history in their hearts and minds."

"Indeed." The old man removed his glasses, rested them on the table in front of him, and closed his eyes. He then took out his handkerchief and wiped his glasses. "I think you should focus on the women. The real meat of your research will come from the women."

"Frankly, Dr. Hunter called me out on my point of view, which I didn't mean to misally with my philosophy."

The old man laughed.

"I made you laugh? Something I said was funny?"

"Gerry is pugnacious, isn't he?" he laughed. "Did he pull you into a philosophical debate?" He laughed again, tilting his head down to study my face over his half lenses, taking another sip of the coconut water.

"Sort of. He tried to. Yes, he did." *Why am I equivocating?*

"That's a compliment. Take it as one. He must have thought you smart and tough enough to engage with." He had a mischievous half-smile that turned up on the right side of his mouth. When he flashed it, he seemed to be sharing a secret insight.

"Yes. He was right, but it was hard to admit."

"Knowing Gerry, he wouldn't need to drive the point, just pepper you with it a bit." He laughed a belly laugh. ". . . But the women drew the men to the places where they made families. The women are the keepers of the power. They maintained the families in both places. They stayed and kept the communities whole." I imagined him lecturing a class, taking them in, weaving a narrative. "And most importantly, the men came back to those women time and time again."

Haynes came out and asked, "Would you like to come into the dining room for tea, now? Everything is nice and hot."

"You see, the women are the ones who run everything!" He laughed. Haynes held the door open, smiling but unsure of the import of what he was saying, but seeming quite accustomed to his playful nature.

Happy for the relative cool of the dining room, I walked in ahead of him.

"Also," he offered, "the women know the stories. Right, Haynes?" He raised his eyebrows to punctuate his comment, and then smiled in a somewhat impish manner. She shrugged and nodded at the same time, pulling the seat out for him.

The table looked like a painting, set with the gleaming silver tea service at its center. It was far more elaborate than I had imagined. Silver napkin rings and the whitest linen napkins and tablecloth over the embroidered beige one. There was a cloche-covered silver platter in the middle of the table, and a smaller covered bowl sat next to a salad bowl with tomatoes, leaf lettuce, and avocado. Once we were seated, Haynes asked if she should serve and looked to me. I nodded, and she dished out an ample swordfish steak for Prof. Bailey.

"Is that my favorite, swordfish?" Prof. Bailey asked. "And the cou-cou looks delicious."

I must have noticeably stretched myself up to look at it, because I hadn't had cou-cou, a West Indian cornmeal dish like polenta, since I was a child.

"Don't tell me you have been in the States so long, you aren't familiar with cou-cou."

"I haven't had it in a long while. Is that okra in it? I remember it." My mother didn't make it, said my grandmother never taught her how to make it without lumps.

Haynes lifted a heaping spoonful of cou-cou and put it on Prof. Bailey's plate, while he chatted on. "You are in for such a treat with Haynes's cooking," the old man said. "Her fried flying fish, delicious. And her fricassee chicken, oh my."

He closed his eyes and silently said grace.

Prof. Bailey devoured his meal with gusto, asking an occasional question, eating, and listening, until he finished his food, leaving only some lettuce and tomato behind. He said he had never been to the States, and inquired of me about the weather in the winter. He told a story of how a relative of his got off the plane in November and when the cold hit her, she was on the plane coming home a week later. He laughed and pushed the lettuce and tomato around on his plate. Haynes cleared the table. She had timed it perfectly.

She brought in a teapot, coconut bread, and fruit salad, and served it up.

"So, let me see this scrimshaw that Dr. Hunter was talking about."

I reached for the cord around my neck. I patted the object and pressed it against my chest.

"I just want to take a look at it under the loupe," he said, seeming to expect me to remove it. "I promised my aunt that I would keep it close, not to lose it." I stretched the cord, extending it to him. He leaned in to look at it. "It does seem to be authentic. I would say it is a sperm whale tooth tip. I would have to use some special equipment for dating, but easily it could date from the mid-1800s."

"I had no doubts about its authenticity."

"This drawing of a whaling ship nearing an island and the house might indicate that the maker was trying to insure his safe return and the safety of his family in his absence. The woman has her back turned to the ship. Odd."

"Why?"

"Because typically women are smiling or waving. But she has her back to the ship, turned away."

"I think the marking on the back was the one that Dr. Hunter said needed interpretation. There are curvilinear lines and they fit into a circular or maybe oval shape."

"This is unusual, and doesn't seem as if it was made by the same carver as the other drawing on the front."

"What do you mean?" I asked.

"It is as if the etching on the front, the rendering of the island, was made by a different artist than this carving on the back. My guess would be that a native person, a Carib, made this carving on the back side of this amulet."

"Why do you say that? Is it a hieroglyph? That's what I thought."

"Of sorts. It is a symbol of a frog woman. It has several meanings. It was used to symbolize the wet season. It could mean that the person was trying to keep the wearer safe during the wet season. You know, during hurricanes and such. . . . Or . . ." he looked up as if he were searching his mind for the answer.

"Yes, or what?"

"This symbol was often used to indicate a sign of fertility. Look at it through the loupe. You see? There is the head of a frog, but on the bottom half it has the female anatomy and displays itself. The Caribs did not place the same taboos or moral judgment on such displays, and used this symbol quite often."

He handed me the loupe, and as I focused my eye on what had seemed to be circles and curves, there was indeed an image of a frog's head and the nude lower body of a woman. It was jolting to my sensibilities at first glance, and I could feel my cheeks flush. I had seen so many artifacts from Asia, Africa, South America, and Europe that represent fertility with women's genitalia exposed, and large breasts, and bellies. Yet, somehow, I blushed. Maybe I was remembering Gerald and the sparkle in his eye as he mentioned that it might have been placed there to keep my great-great-grandmother "chaste." Though he didn't mention her explicitly, it seemed he implied her in his comments about sailors and their wives. Soon, I was mesmerized by it.

"That is why I think this was done by someone other than your great-great-grandfather," he continued.

"Maybe he had it done to help her become fertile," I offered.

"Maybe. But why then was it secreted so, and hidden in these other curvilinear lines? A bit of a mystery! The artist's drawing on this side is quite explicit. I would like to let a Carib look at it."

"I thought virtually all the Carib Indians died out, or had intermarried," I said.

"Well, they say that many Caribs engaged in mass suicide to escape slavery, but rarely do they talk about how they rebelled with Africans and fought wars against the British. After those rebellions, many were exiled to Honduras after they were defeated. But there are a few left on the windward side of the island, some on St. Vincent, and in Barbados. Some say they know the true history of the islands better than the stories in our history books written by the British."

"I really don't want to part with it," I said, reaching for the amulet as it rested on my chest.

"No, you will come with me. I know an old woman who lives up country."

"When do you want to go? Next week?"

"No. I am quite busy next week as I said, preparing for my presentation. What about tomorrow? Sometimes Vivencia goes to the market to sell trinkets, but never on Saturday. She says it's too much for her, and Sunday she may be at church."

Haynes came in and noticed we had not touched our tea. "Is something not to your liking, Mum?" Haynes inquired.

I was still distracted by the image on the back of the pendant, sensitive to it resting between my breasts. Prof. Bailey looked to Haynes and then me to respond.

"No everything is wonderful. Just chatting."

"By the way, I can't help noticing that since we were talking about the scrimshaw you have seemed . . . well, preoccupied," Prof. Bailey said pushing his glasses up on his nose and studying me intently.

"I am. Yes, the carving on it was a . . . puzzlement. Why was it there? What is its meaning?"

"I am sure we will learn more tomorrow, but remember, the markings on these artifacts mean very different things to the people of that time. I am sure you know that as an anthropologist."

"Of course," I said, chiding myself for letting the image trouble me so, and revealing my feelings so openly. "Frankly, I don't know if I am ready to go tomorrow."

"I know it's short notice, but I have a heavy schedule the next few weeks. I must admit that this drawing being on the back of the ornament piques my curiosity. It is very intriguing," Prof. Bailey said.

"I don't know why, but I just find it troubling."

"Do you think this is having this effect upon you because these are family members? It may have been that you have identified too strongly with the information, and its implications for your twice great-grandmother."

Prof. Bailey's sympathetic expression seemed to say that he recognized my dilemma. I was now fully both an observer and participant in this journey. Very often anthropologists choose this dual role. I had chosen it. The closeness I felt to this research embedded me in the role. My family's history was entangled in the amulet, and the marking held a mystery I had to unearth. "I don't know why I feel this way," I said, trying to push the thoughts from my head.

We ate dessert and chitchatted further about my work. Prof. Bailey suggested the offices and the clerks who would be most helpful in looking at birth and death records in St. Vincent and Bequia. After tea, we strolled along the beach and he pointed out the homes with short anecdotes on the owners. Some homes were owned by Americans, some famous movie stars, others were British businessmen, and Caribbean doctors and lawyers whose names I tried to commit to memory in case I met them on walks along the beach. I tried to keep up with the conversation, but I was mentally far away. At one point, I felt I must have blanked out, because Prof. Bailey was heading to the stairway to the house. Haynes called the car, and I had not remembered Prof. Bailey mentioned he was leaving.

On his departure, Prof. Bailey said to me, "Don't trouble yourself so much about the marking. I am sure Vivencia can help us understand its meaning. By the way, wear socks and good walking shoes, as we need to walk a bit when we get out of the car. You may want to wear lightweight trousers. They will protect you from the mosquitoes. I will hire the driver because I have a fellow who will take us and wait for us, and not charge an arm and a leg. If you call and they hear an American accent, well, dare I say . . ."

Before I knew it, the odd, chipper little man was gone. My head was swimming. The different scenarios about the etching were racing about in my mind. My aunt told me that my great-great-grandmother had one child who died, so the theory that made the most sense was the one about fertility. The need to protect her from hurricanes was also a plausible theory. But the glyph's explicit rendering of the female genitalia, and the suggestion Prof. Bailey made that it was secreted on the back within the lines and curves of the drawing on the amulet was troubling. I needed to rest.

As I headed into the bedroom, Haynes stopped me with her voice. "Mum, I will be leaving for the day. Will you be needing me to cook tomorrow?"

"Tomorrow?"

"Yes, tomorrow is Saturday, and I usually take Saturday for my family, and Sunday I go to church in the mornin'. But since Dr. Hunter asked me to stay until Mum was comfortable, I . . . I can serve a supper on Sunday afternoon if Mum wishes."

"No, I will be headed out with Prof. Bailey for a few hours tomorrow. There's plenty of food here for Sunday. Why don't you take the weekend for yourself? I need to go lie down now."

"But Mum, I wanted to show you through the house and point out the keys."

"I know, but I don't know what has come over me, lately when I get tired, I feel as if I can barely hold my head up. I must lie down."

"Was everything to your liking today?"

"Today's meal was excellent, and you have to know that Prof. Bailey enjoyed it. And you brought back memories of my grandmother with your cou-cou. Delicious! But I must go lay my head down." I was now leaning on the armchair at the head of the table.

"Me wrote me number on a piece of paper and put it on the board in the kitchen. If you need anything, you can call me. I have made some salad for later, and there are fruits and breads out on the counter. Oh, and I made some fish soup in there for you, if you will like it."

Haynes tugged at the sash of the apron, and folded it up. She waited, I thought, to hear if there was anything else needed of her. When I noticed that she hesitated, I said, "Haynes, thank you so much for everything. Oh, it is the end of the week, I should be paying you. I am sorry."

"No Mum, Dr. Hunter has taken care of me for this week. Just that you look weak . . . you might not be accustomed to such a heavy meal at this hour. Let me see you to the bedroom. Then the walk on the beach. Perhaps I should stay a while longer."

"No, I'll be fine," I said taking a step, and then holding on to the chair. Haynes grabbed my arm and supported me, as I walked to the bedroom.

"I am going to give you some coconut water. It will bring you back. It could be the sun. You aren't used to it yet." Haynes brought a cup of coconut water and held the cup and supported my head, helping me to sip it. As I drank, I began to feel myself revive. "Haynes, you are a true godsend."

"Should I look in on you tomorrow, Mistress Jocelyn?"

"No that's not necessary, I am sure I will be fine, and Prof. Bailey is coming in the morning."

"I'll call then. . . . You just try and get some rest now."

Knowing that Haynes would be calling was comforting. The woman left the room, and I laid my head on the pillow. The restful place between wakefulness and slumber drew me. I had now come to know it as the space between *now* and *then*.

He is planning to kill me! There was a group of women around me, and I was Mariel yet again. My arms were raised above my head, as the women instructed. They placed this white dress over my head. A thing already bound me 'round my waist, and made it difficult to breathe. I insisted that they loosen it, and they did. I would surely die at the end of this ordeal. White was the color of death, the color of visitors from the spirit world. The dress cloaked me down to my ankles, and I was much too hot in it. The women said that I had to wear it because it was my husband's way. My father approved. I had to accept. They said that once married, he would take the dress off so that he could fasten himself to me as my mother had described. This terrified me. How was I to take him into a space I could not even see? My mother said that it hurt at first, burned like fire, and then would bring me pleasure. I could not understand how that could be. My mother pointed out the animals, dogs, goats, males mounting females, and I feared it even more. Although I had seen such things before, I did not think of them as happening to me. I held on to my mother's arm. The other women all laughed at me and said that I would come to not only enjoy it, but I would crave it, long for it.

We walked, my family and the villagers, to the house the Portugee had built for me. I had never seen it. As we walked along the beach and then into the growth of bushes and trees, the house seemed to rise up amidst the green. The women nodded and exclaimed audibly in the affirmation that it was a big, good dwelling that the Portugee built. It was made from river rock and limestone he brought from Barbados, the doors from wood that was polished until it gleamed in the midday sun. There was a path to the front of the house, which was beaten down by the feet of the workers who built it. It was up a slight incline and built in a clearing that was surrounded by trees. Coconut, palm, mango, breadfruit, banana, star apple, and soursop fruit trees surrounded the house.

One woman whispered, "She will grow fat from all the fruit he grows for her," then laughed out loud, her own round belly bouncing.

I glared at her, thinking it was her jealousy and mean-spiritedness that made her speak so. The women laughed and covered their mouths.

The women told me that some of the trees grew wild there, and some the Portugee brought and had planted on the land. As I approached the front of the house, I looked back, fearing I had lost the sea. Instead, there it was, and I welcomed the sight of it. All I would have of my past life would be this view. The Portugee would soon own me—my body and my soul.

There he stood in front of the house, taller than I remembered. He smiled at me, approving of my looks, I thought. There was a White man with him, who had a stiff white choker 'round his neck and a black jacket. He held beads and moved them about with his fingers. He wore a necklace with a pendant that was in the shape of a cross, which hung down a long way from his neck. Days before, the same man had sprinkled water on my forehead, and he drew that same cross, then calling me Maria. I knew it was significant because the Portugee smiled.

My father pushed me to stand next to the Portugee, my feet settling and stuck in the sandy soil, and my knees trembling beneath the white long skirt that draped them. The other White man spoke. Words said by him and the Portugee that I did not understand flew about my head. My father, mother, and sister all stood beside me, silent until the villagers laughed and sang. The Portugee's crewmen drank rum, danced, and made music with sticks they fingered and blew. The women from the village roasted fish and made crab stew. Full and tired, they eventually packed up the remains of the festivities and disappeared onto the beach and in different directions. The day moved past me like a swarm of butterflies.

Then I was alone with the Portugee. Out of the corner of my eye, I kept my gaze on him, waiting for him to pounce on me. My body was rigid and ready to fight him off, but he did not attack. Instead, when I reached back to try and loosen the fastenings on the dress, he came toward me, his palms open, showing me his hands and the desire to help. And so, he pulled the lacings from the tight band that was squeezing my waist. He placed his hand on my side so gently, I was bewildered. Yet, my muscles tightened and I pulled away, looking down at my hip where my skin had been creased and reddened by the tightly fitting undergarment. He rubbed the flesh with tenderness, and leaned down to look at it, I thought. But instead, he kissed it. I drew away and grabbed the night-shirt hanging on a door, billowing in the sea breezes. Though I wanted to bare my breasts as I was accustomed, I covered myself, remembering that my mother and the village women said that seeing my naked body would make him come for me. When I recoiled, the women who surrounded me laughed and made pawing motions, and growling sounds like large cats, mocking me. Now it seemed they were wrong.

He was nothing as they warned, calmly taking off his jacket and shirt and placing them on the chair next to the bed. Backing away from him and toward the wall, I soon learned that he did not come for me. He said some words which I did not understand, but I felt no fear of him. Then he sat on the bed, took off his boots, peeled his pants down and pulled them off. Unclothed, he seemed comfortable for the first time in the day. For a moment or two, I was transfixed by the sight of him, ex-posed as he was. Though my people did not wear clothes, the men always covered their privates. He lay there bare. There would be no way I could allow him to enter me lest I tear in half. As he sat on the bed, I moved further away near the table in the corner. I stayed as far away as I could.

"Maria," he said, patting the bed and beckoning me as I drew closer to the wall. The room was darkening, and I thought he was going for a lantern in the closet. Only his broad strong back and his bare behind were visible, and his powerful legs were firmly planted on the floor as he reached up. Then there was a clicking sound. Though my eyes were glued to him, his back was to me. Confounded, I could not tell what that click-ing was. The music pierced my watchful silence, and the box that he had given to me many moons ago sang. It had disappeared, and I had accused the women of stealing it. My clenched fists close to my sides, I stamped my foot when I told my father to find out who took it and to punish them. They all laughed at me. Now the music filling the room was as mesmerizing as it was the first day the Portugee laid the music box at my feet. He waved me to him again, but this time he had covered himself with the white cloths on the bed. I looked at him as fiercely as I could, and he turned himself away from me indicating that he was going to sleep. Before long he was snoring. I then waited to see if it was a trick before moving to sit on the edge of the bed. My body was ready to run if he reached for me, but the bed was soft. I grew tired, and felt I would disappear into it, so I rested my head and the darkness filled in around me. My vigilance waned, and I succumbed and let the night spirit me away.

The deep dark slumber surrounded and swaddled me, letting my mind lose itself in the peaceful place where I could feel my shoulders cradled from behind. It was in that magical moment when one knows that one is dreaming that I made a choice to remain asleep, and not jump up in alarm. I knew where I was. It was that place of long ago, and this was my home. My husband had nestled himself in next to me. He had been such a gentle lover, not at all what I had anticipated, fearful as I was about being taken from my home and my people. My sister came to me a few days after the marriage to ask me what it was like to be with him. Words failed to describe the care he took to have me want him, his soft caresses and gentle touches on my stomach and breasts. His whispers were like music, though I did not understand what the words meant. But he left me, chasing whales, and now he had been gone so long. No words for the longing I felt for him, the desire I held for his return.

His hand now stroked my neck, and his finger tracing its way down my back warmed me. Something felt odd, and my belly tightened, but I opened my eyes to look out into the room, and there against the wall was the large basin and pitcher that I used for bathing myself in the morning.

My eyes closed, and I nestled my head back to rest it on John's chest. Such a broad and barrel-like structure, and such a comforting place was his chest! But now it was his hands that I focused on. They played with the tips of my breasts, exciting them. I enjoyed the ways he toyed with them. I well knew the landscape of his chest and its strength and the sensation of his touch. As I sought to ease myself into the space in which I had grown comfortable in the past, and in which I took pleasure in the months before he went to sea, I took note of the height of the form behind me. Had he been gone so long that my memory had betrayed me? This body was longer and leaner than my husband's. There was a different musculature. I could not breathe. I now feared I might not be dreaming. "John?" I whispered his name. I knew the answer before I heard the voice reply.

"No, it is not him."

11

The telephone rang its odd two-ring cadence. My hand met the now-familiar touch of the mosquito net, which I lifted to reach the receiver.

"Morning Dr. Kendall, did I wake you?" he laughed. "We are still on for this morning?"

Dr. Bailey sounded a bit too chipper for me. "Yes, of course. This is the best sleep I have had in weeks." I could have rested there an hour more.

"That's the great sea breeze. Some say it is intoxicating. Just to let you know, I will be there at ten."

I wiped the sleep from my eyes. "What time is it?"

"A little past nine." He was gone.

The clock on the nightstand confirmed it. *Okay, I need to go get myself together.* It took an act of will to raise my body from the bed and move into the hallway, when the phone rang again. *I hope he wants to make it later*, I thought, run-walking back and throwing myself across the bed to grab the phone.

"Mistress Jocelyn, good morning. Did you get a good sleep?" I clenched the phone, wanting to slam it down and race to the shower. It was Haynes!

"I did, thank you."

"How are you feeling this morning?"

"Good, but rushed. I have to meet Prof. Bailey in a half hour." My voice was strident, I could tell. But Haynes did not seem to detect my angst or my being miffed. She continued in her languid chatty manner.

"Well, there is coffee in the coffee maker as you requested the other day. There is fruit as you know, and bread . . ."

"Thank you," I cut her off. "Haynes, I am so late already."

"Don't go out into the sun without eating, mistress!"

"Okay, okay . . . gotta hurry."

I bolted for the bathroom, but my image in the mirror stunned me and held me transfixed there for a full minute or more. The dark circles under my eyes were gone, and my skin looked years younger. After the shower, it happened again. Droplets of water seemed to glisten on my skin, and I could not help admiring my appearance as I passed the full-length mirror on the bathroom door. After dressing, I flipped the switch on the coffee maker and drank some orange juice, which seemed to energize me even more.

The sea pulled me out to the veranda. Breezes of the fragrant trees, lush with fruit and blossoms, embraced me. A hummingbird, gussied up in an iridescent emerald collar, hovered next to a crimson-colored blossom that cascaded over the railing. The symphony of songbirds' calls and insects' trills held me spellbound. And the seawater stretched out to the horizon filled with aqua, turquoise, and cobalt blue, an expanse stretching into forever.

Captivated by Bequia, I had to shake myself from its spell, and rush into the bedroom to grab my straw hat. The coffee was ready. I sliced a piece of coconut bread and washed it down just as the car horn tooted outside. The professor was standing to the side of the car, "So, I woke you," he chuckled, watching as the driver opened the car door for me. "The island breezes act as a soporific!" he laughed. Sporting a straw hat and no bowtie, he seemed more a pixilated scamp, a word used by my Aunt Grace warning me not to let Vincentian men chat me up.

As we set out, I attempted to watch the turns for some later trip I might take on my own, but I quickly surrendered to the circuitous journey, knowing I could never find my way back on my own. The car stopped abruptly, and the driver got out and opened the trunk and produced a long wooden walking stick. No houses in sight, Prof. Bailey deftly wielded the tall knotted staff, and gestured in the direction he began to walk. "This is Goat Hill," he said. "The previous owner of this land had a herd of goats." He laughed. "Vivencia always has one or two. She lives right up at the top of this hill."

A small gray goat bounded up to us, followed by a brown one that pranced in the hoofprints of the other. Playmates, they bounced around me and finally came toward me, studying me with their odd eyes with black horizontal slits for pupils.

"Take care of the gray one, she eats clothing. She'll take a bite out of your shirttail if you are not careful. Shoo her with your hands."

"Why doesn't she bother you?"

"She knows my stick," Bailey laughed.

"Where's the house?" The heat was already becoming oppressive as the trees and shrubbery seemed to fold around us. The mosquitos began to whine, and I slapped my forearm where I felt a stinging bite. Craning my neck, I tried to see the home that we were approaching, but the greenery seemed to grow ever thicker the higher we climbed.

"Just up there a bit more, behind the breadfruit tree," he said.

Finally, as we made our way around the bend in this narrow footpath, there was a wooden house, its boards gray and warped and the gate in front hung askew by a rusted hinge. The veranda had three old, bent wicker rocking chairs.

"Vivencia! Prof. Bailey here. Vivencia!!! I brought someone here to chat with you."

"Is that Dr. Bailey me hear?" The voice came from the dark space outlined by the wood-framed doorway. The screen door creaked, and a sleepy old black dog lumbered out first, looking drowsily up at Bailey, then me. Showing little interest in me except a lift of his jaw and a half-hearted sniff, he headed out to lie down under the broad breadfruit tree in the yard. A rail-thin old woman came out behind him and squinted at me while coming to shake the hand of the professor. Her fingers were gnarled, and her translucent skin was a golden brown with blue veins protruding and mapping themselves across, up, and around her wrist.

Her eyes were somewhat milky. I reached out to her, but she stood back and looked at me, studying me from head to toe.

"This is Dr. Jocelyn Kendall. She is a professor doing some research."

The old woman sucked her teeth and rolled her eyes and started to turn her back and walk over to the porch.

Dr. Bailey slowed his gait, seeming to realize he had started off on the wrong foot with Vivencia, and began again, this time with a more familiar tone. "Her family's from here, ya know, originally from Bequia. Maybe you know them. Can she tell you?"

"She can tell me, but dat don' mean me know nuthin'."

"Well, my great-great-grandfather was a Portugee whaler named Matos, John Matos, and my great-great-grandmother's baptized name was Maria. She was a Carib."

The old woman's eyes darted up at me, raising the hair and goose-bumps on my arms. So transfixing was her gaze that I tried to look away and could not.

"She name was Mariel," she said, as if daring me to doubt her.

"You knew her?" I asked, without realizing the impossibility of that question.

"Vivencia knows all of the history of this island," Professor Bailey said.

I wanted to acknowledge my mistake and thank the old woman for the nugget of knowledge, but I was struck dumb. I had heard that name, Mariel, before. In my dream.

"Come out da sun and sit," the old woman said, waving her frail arm toward the frayed, wicker chairs on the porch. She lowered herself into one and began to rock, keeping her eyes fixed on the air in front of her.

"You know she had two."

"Excuse me," I said.

"She didn't have one, she had two." The woman's eyes were now closed.

I looked to Prof. Bailey for some direction. He put his finger to his lips, gesturing that I simply sit quietly and listen.

"She had the white and the black and energy that was powerful. She did make the magic. She silence one and crippled others. She mudder give her the gift, but she haf no power to stop the one far cross de sea, who put a curse on she. She plagued by the powers again with the white and the black. But the energy twist and turn on her. The poor t'ing. What you know about she end? 'Cause it be terrible," the old woman said, now looking at my face, as if to judge my reactions to the words she had just uttered. "She children cursed, and she children, children."

Her words travelled about in my mind before resting on me—and inside me.

Prof. Bailey's eyes fixed on me too. He seemed loathe to stop Vivencia, since he had explained in the car ride that it was always a tricky thing carrying on a conversation with her, because she runs hot and cold. "Once she ran cold, she refuses to speak to you at all," he had said. My hands spontaneously moved to my lips as if to hold them closed and prevent any questions from escaping my lips.

Tentatively he said, "Vivencia, we wanted to ask you about an amulet."

I lifted the scrimshaw out, as my blouse was covering it. Dr. Bailey reached for it, and for the first time since my great aunt put it around my neck, I freely took it off. Strange, but although all this time I was so reluctant to part with it, now in the presence of this old woman, I relinquished it and was at peace. Prof. Bailey carried it over to Vivencia. She squinted down at the etching, and he took out his loupe. "There is this marking," he said, "which I recognize of course, but I wonder can you shed more light upon it." She looked through the loupe, first studying the front, and then again the back. She smiled and handed the amulet back to Bailey.

"Me tell you she had two."

"What do you mean?" I asked.

"The one who is White and the one who is Black." She seemed to point to the two sides of the scrimshaw. "Two of dem."

"Two . . . ?" I paused, hoping she would fill in the rest of the sentence. But when she did not reply, I said, "Are you saying she had two husbands?"

"Yes, me tell you dat. There is confusion of energy around her." Irritable now, her voice was strained.

I did not know that my great-great-grandmother had married twice. "You mean after Matos died? I mean John Matos the whaler."

"Yes. I know him. John Matos, ya say is your great-great-grandfather. No?"

"You mean before she married him, she married someone else?"

She shut her eyes abruptly. "No. Me tired nuh. Me goin' inside now. The heat's too much for me."

"But can you explain what you meant?" As I put the amulet back on and began to speak, I noticed the old woman turned her back to me.

"Me done talking." She waved her hand at me and continued into the house.

"Can we come back another day, Vivencia?" Prof. Bailey asked.

There was no answer. The woman had disappeared into the dark doorway. Her dog lumbered up the steps and into the screen door that labored to close.

Prof. Bailey picked up his walking stick and beckoned me to follow him. The driver had pulled the car under the shade of a big breadfruit tree and was sitting on the fender. "Back to the mistress house, Professor?"

"Yes."

"What do you think?" I asked Bailey.

"She sounded fairly certain of the family. It seems your great-great-grandmother had a second husband. You appeared upset in hearing that. But what interests me is that she repeated that on looking at the other side of the scrimshaw. I was certain that the other side was etched by another artist, and I thought it was a native person."

"But I couldn't get her to tell me if it was a second husband or first husband."

"It takes a lot out of her going back like that. It's almost as if she is channeling the past rather than just recalling and reciting it. She actually spent a lot of time with you. Some people, she just looks at them, turns her back, and refuses to tell them anything.

"She said, 'One Black and one White.' That's it! I bet a Black Carib did the other etching. That is a Carib marking, so if she is saying he is black, he must be a Black Carib." As Prof. Bailey said these words, I felt a chill move in a wave through my body. Hair rose again on my forearms.

Bailey chattered on, though I couldn't tell about what. His words ran together and seemed to become one murky pool, sounds flowing every which way.

When we arrived at the house, I got out of the car and moved to the doorway.

"Do you want to go look at marriage records . . . maybe the week after next week? You should become familiar with those records anyway," Bailey shouted after me.

I shut him out. The heat hung on me as I walked up the stairs to the kitchen, and pushed the key into the lock. The door seemed heavier than when I left earlier. I went out onto the veranda. As I studied the blue-green expanse, I thought how the sea wrapped around me the same as it did this morning, but my world had shifted. My mind was spinning. My great-great-grandmother had married twice, and I had never heard that. *The dreams which have fascinated me since I arrived, revealed much of this to me before Vivencia, but a second husband?* Though I feared the bed, it drew me. *Who was in my bed?* I knew the voice, but from where? Sleep and its images, along with questions about this second husband, pressed me. I willed myself back there, and though I feared him, I feared not knowing more.

The dream place was now becoming familiar, and though I did not welcome the thought of this man who had invaded my consciousness, I felt I knew him. It was unsettling.

"Do you not know my voice?"

As his words filtered in, I could see the image of the one we called the Black Carib, who had come up onto the beach with my brother. He had smiled at me and elbowed my brother and glanced my way as if he was talking about me. I had gathered fish from the catch and paid little attention because the Portugee was at sea and I was waiting for his return. My brother told me to beware the Black Carib.

"He lives on Petit Nevis Island, speaks many languages, and is fierce. He has enemies, and I think he has a wife," my brother said.

I had no worry because the men would protect me as my father ordered, but he had come back more than once and tried to catch my eye each time. I told my brother that I did not like the way that he looked at me. At first, my brother laughed. The next time he and the Black Carib were with the other men on the beach slaughtering a whale, my brother was more watchful. He wrestled the Black Carib to the ground and held a cutting tool to his throat. With his teeth clenched, my brother seemed to utter something into his ear. I did not see him again.

Now he was in my bed.

"You do know that when I yell and the people come, you are a dead man."

"You have been without a husband long enough to crave my touch."

A chill ran the length of me.

I lurched forward to sit up, and his hands pulled me back. "Who are you?" I whispered, pulling away and feeling his fingers grip my shoulders and pin me to the bed. But though his hands held intention, I did not detect cruelty in his touch. His grip loosened in that instant, that moment which hung there in time as my gaze took in his face, and his scrutiny of me seemed to peel away my fear and fill me with fascination. His dark eyes with golden flecks shone in the darkness. The sea breezes cooled my warm cheeks, and filled and furled the billowing sheer curtain draped at the window in the pool of moonlight. "Leave, or I will scream."

"They cannot hear you. You are in this big house that the Portugee has built. He has taken you so far away from your people that you have no protection."

Fright raced through my body. I was alone.

"So, you can't woo your own woman, you must take from another man," I said, before I stopped my tongue.

"I have a woman," he said, now full throated as he loosened his grip.

"Then why are you in my husband's bed?" I placed John's presence between us so that the Black Carib would not mistake that now there were three of us here.

"I thought I did see your desire."

"You were wrong."

"Then perhaps I smelled it."

"You are rude."

He stood up and towered over me. He stood as tall as a horse. "I could take you," he said.

"And you would have nothing."

"The Portugee travels away for many faces of the moon, you will desire me."

"I will not," I said, though my voice wavered.

"Oh, but you will. I can see that you will." His brown eyes, speckled with gold, surveyed the length of me. Inside, I felt a weakness of spirit that I feared he sensed.

He turned and strode across the room. The power he had excited me. I stood up. The room seemed to fill with the energy of our two wills, circling and testing the strength of the other. It was as if the forces took shape and twisted and turned like a hurricane that swirled about the room. My ability to send him off was empowering. When the space around us became still, he turned his back, climbed out the window, which I realized was how he entered. I wrapped the bedclothes around myself. For a fleeting instant, I wished John were truly there, and that I could have his protective embrace. Being alone, I knew I would have to rely on my wiles to keep me safe. There was something stirring about that knowledge. I trembled, and the tremors incorporated themselves into my dream.

Bolting upright in the bed, I held on to the sheets. *What is this? My dreams are back and now I must manage the players within them?* I sat there a moment or two, looking about the room. There was safety in the space, and yet the dream left a sense of foreboding. I felt a confusing desire to succumb to the dream, to reenter it and to stay there. This dream space held a morass of secrets that drew me like the moths that bounced about in the light on the veranda of this grand old house. They tapped against the bulb seemingly unable to stop themselves from getting as close as they could to the light. Then they'd hit the glass and bounce away, only to fly back and slam themselves into the glass and the light once again.

These men in my dreams—are they my great-great-grandmother's husbands? Have I gone back to her time as it seems, or am I just creating these dreams from my musings?

The questions were an intellectual exercise at first. Then the memory of the Black Carib filled my thoughts. *Suppose I cannot keep him out of my home, my bed.* This dream beckoned me to this strange man's touch again. Our fates were braided together somehow, and despite my connection to the man that I knew as my husband, the three of us were entangled. I needed to find out how our worlds met. It was that time of day where one cannot tell if it is early morning or early evening, the sky slate blue. I did not know how long I had slept. Yet as I gathered my thoughts, I watched the sky darken, and realized night had barely begun.

Part III

He returned to take me. No words of mine would make him go. His caresses captured my being, and my mind had no moorings.

12

I could not sleep. It was either the disturbing day that caused me to ruminate, or my fears about my dreams. At well past midnight, I sat on the veranda and watched the starlight dance on the sea. A boat that was lit from stem to stern moved into the pool of moonlight. The phone rang, and I grabbed the outside receiver fearing that it was ringing for all my neighbors to hear.

"You are awake." A baritone voice crooned at me through the earpiece.

"Who is this?"

"You do not recall my voice."

"I said, who is this?" My mind must be playing tricks on me because I had heard these words or maybe this thought before.

"It's Derek, Derek Reynolds."

"You shouldn't do that!"

"Sorry. Didn't mean to alarm you." He sounded contrite.

"I hadn't a clue, who could . . . it sounded as if you knew that I was awake because you were watching me or something."

"Actually, I am watching you."

"What did you say?" I sat upright.

"I am looking at you right now from my yacht."

"What?" I grabbed at my nightdress, pulling the hem down with one hand and reaching toward the neckline with the other. Having done so, I felt foolish. Surely, he could not see me clearly from such a distance.

"Yes. Mine is the yacht out in the water in front of your house. I have this great spyglass. You are clutching your clothing all too tightly."

"You're kidding me."

"No. I was out and caught sight of you sitting there. Lovely, I might add. I thought maybe you would like to come out for a nightcap." He was silent, seeming to leave the thought there to linger for a moment. Then added, ". . . or perhaps you would like to come to Moon Hole, to see the sunrise and get out of that stodgy old house."

"You think you can come and spirit me away in the darkness onto your boat," I said playfully.

"No, actually I thought I could entice you to come out to my yacht, but if you would rather be spirited away, I can handle it. Some women have told me that I am an old soul, with more than one lifetime of experience."

His confidence was like a flame that drew me toward him, and I was tantalized by the thought of going out to the yacht with him. I couldn't sleep anyway, was actually afraid to sleep. He would be a distraction at the very least. "Okay, a nightcap, but that's it. What should I wear?"

"Something that you don't mind getting wet. Bring a bag with some things for a change just in case."

Never got a chance to reiterate my insistence that I would only stay briefly. In the bedroom, I found some shorts and bathing shoes since I had to wade out into the water to get on a boat. Grabbed a bathing suit, shorts, and a filmy cotton blouse, then tossed underwear, cotton tee, and jeans in a canvas bag. *Am I taking too much? I don't want to give him the wrong idea.* But I was glad to go, because it was better to escape into the night with Derek, the devil I knew, than to be alone with my dreams and the Black Carib. I wondered what his name was. I tried to think back and retrieve any sense of what he was called, but could not. Yet at the same time, I realized I had adopted this world and its inhabitants as my own. There was a knock on the door. For a moment, I froze in mid-stride, questioning my impulsiveness.

"So, you are ready? I've got the bag," he said seeing me, his eyes dancing. I had forgotten his incredible golden eyes. There was the impish glint that I recalled. He always looked as if he was thinking something improper.

He was wearing a black T-shirt, and it was rolled up around his biceps, which bulged as he lifted the bag. His skin was a darker brown, I thought, than when I saw him a few days before. He held a lantern flashlight with a strong beam focused on the stairs and held my hand taking me down. As we got out to the beach, a shadowy form rose up and I soon saw a short, stocky dark-skinned man climb out of the boat and grab the bag from him. "Do you mind getting a little wet, or should I carry you?" Derek said.

"No, of course not, I've got bathing shoes," I said, realizing this was the first I thought about my weight since I left New York. Comfortable in my skin now, the surf, warm and bubbly like champagne, invited me.

"Let me lift you." He reached over and gave me a hand, as did the man in the boat, while they both raised me up and in. Derek sat facing me, and seemed taken with me, while the other man pushed the boat further out into the surf. He then climbed in, rowed us a bit, then started up the motor. Its churning vibrations raced through my body, as we were soon speeding toward the yacht. The house lamp on the porch receded into the distance. Moonlight painted the water silver, and the light spray of the sea caressed my cheeks.

The yacht loomed large, higher in the water than I anticipated. We came along behind it, and a crewman above beckoned me up. The moment I began climbing up onto the larger craft, I became aware of my vulnerability out in the sea with Derek. *Why hadn't I thought of that before I left shore?* Nervous about climbing, I soon sensed Derek had literally stepped on the rung beneath me. Feeling his body resting against mine excited me as I stopped momentarily on each rung. His crewman reached down and pulled me up. Derek came up behind me.

"What will you have to drink? Pick your poison," Derek said.

"You shouldn't say that to a woman alone who just boarded your boat late at night?"

"No worries. We have a fairly well-stocked bar, nothing truly deadly. What would you like? Are you hungry, Emmett can whip you up something?"

"Do you have that rum punch that we had on the plane?"

"Rum punch is Emmett's forté. Someone has ordered your specialty, Emmett. I'll have some too. So, what have you been up to?"

"A little research, but just on family stuff. It's what has kept me up late tonight. Soon I should be a bit more focused. I plan to go into St. Vincent to look at some marriage records. What have *you* been up to?"

"On the beach, and in the sea, but finally drawing. And I think I'm ready to start painting. . . . Haven't painted in over a year." His brow furrowed as if reliving something he would rather avoid.

"That's a good thing that you have your art back." Again, he disarmed me. "I am having a hard time actually concentrating on my work. I keep getting sidetracked onto my own personal history, which seems to attract me so strongly."

"What's sidetracking you?" he asked.

"Just finding out things about my family I didn't know."

"Like what?"

"Like that my great-great-grandmother may have been married twice. And that she met with a terrible end. I spoke with a griot of sorts who told me that today."

"Vivencia?"

"Yes. You know her?"

"Of course. She is very good. She knows the stories, all the goings on here on the island for generations. So, if you don't mind my asking, what is so concerning to you that she was married twice."

"I don't know. When I left Boston having seen a photo of her and her husband, and had envisioned a romantic love story—now it's ruined." I laughed at my own naïveté. "I know how this sounds, especially for an anthropologist. It's ridiculous." Despite the fact that my discipline had taught me that living in a culture can alter one's objectivity, my dreams had enmeshed me in my great-great-grandmother's life in ways I had not anticipated. They were changing who I was. "I actually find it interesting," Derek said.

"Well, it's also the way Vivencia said it. She said *she had two husbands*. It just made me uncomfortable."

"Even better. Remember, you're in the Caribbean, on an island. Lots of mischief making here. It's hot, and people get passionate." Derek's raised eyebrows punctuated his comment.

"We are talking about a hundred years ago." I couldn't help wanting to protect the virtue of my twice great-grandmother.

"It was still an island, and it was still hot, and there was still a great deal of mischief made. You really should have a chat with Cassandra. She is studying the sexual mores here from a psychological perspective. She's down from Yale. She lives here in Moon Hole."

"Let's change the subject," I insisted.

"Let's talk about Moon Hole, then. You really ought to consider moving there. The environment is perfect for research and writing. We do have Wi-Fi, a little spotty at times, but it is a natural setting. And actually, I was going to call you yesterday. I was wondering if you would sit for me. It needn't take up all your time. Maybe an hour or so each day." He stopped speaking, tilted his head to one side, and studied my face yet again.

"No. The first time you said that I was sure it was a pickup line, your ulterior motive. I am not sure what it means now. But no." I hated photos of myself and usually destroyed them.

"I have been drawing pictures of you from memory, trying to capture the bone structure in your face, your upturned nose." He paused briefly, but the comment seemed spontaneous and genuine, reminding me of my father. He'd tap my nose lightly, playfully when I was little. That was all before he left. "If you would sit for a portrait, it would get me painting again, and would give you a memento of Bequia if you like it. And it would just be easier if you lived at Moon Hole." He laughed. "So yes, I have an ulterior motive."

"Interesting *quid pro quo*. I paint you and I will give you the portrait and . . ."

"Yes, that is exactly what I mean. It's been a long time since I have even had the desire to paint, so your gift to me would be getting me to begin once again. I think you've given me back my muse." He seemed ready to disclose something private. Then Emmett came to the table carrying a pitcher of punch that was a rainbow of scarlet and amber at its base. "Emmett, you have saved me once again." The man looked somewhat puzzled, but seemed accustomed to Derek's conversation, and I guessed that he felt it was best to say nothing. He poured two goblets and handed one to me and one to Derek.

"You are in for a treat," Derek said.

I sipped it. "This is delicious, Emmett. Thank you." He smiled and nodded his acceptance of my compliment.

"So does this tack work for you? You offer to paint a woman, give her the portrait, and take her to live in this secluded place. Then she's yours for as long as you want her. I mean, strip it down and it is an offer to paint a woman, then you take her to bed. I get it. Thanks for the window into your art of seduction, but no. I will be far too busy to sit for a 'portrait.'" I didn't know what had loosened my tongue. My words spilled out without a filter. It couldn't be the liquor because I had only taken a few sips.

"American women are so funny. You are all so suspicious." His eyes were no longer playful. "You see sex, your sex, as a prize of some sort."

"We just know a line when we hear it. What other way is there to view it?"

"Actually, in this case, it wasn't a line, as you call it. And one might say that sex between two consenting adults is a shared experience, rather than a prize taken by one from the other. And no, usually it is the other way 'round. Usually, a woman is attracted to me or I her, and we go to bed. If she reveals something interesting in herself to me, then I might ask to paint her."

"So is this boat ride the prelude? Do you expect to get me drunk, bed me, and then ask to paint me?"

"This is a yacht. And no, it is not a prelude to anything, though that might be lovely." He smiled. "And this fire I see in your eyes might be quite interesting to capture on canvas. No, what I started to say before was that there was something about your face that I noticed on the flight to St. Vincent. I can't quite put my finger on it. I tried to capture it from memory, but I couldn't. Never mind. No matter. By the way, I can have Emmett make you the virgin one of these," he said raising his glass, "pun intended."

"No, I prefer my poison tonight. Sorry, I don't know where all that came from. It has been a long, long day." I was tired of sparring, and welcomed the opportunity to relax with a drink and rest my mind. "So why haven't you been painting?" It might have been the rum because I now felt perfectly relaxed.

"I am sure you don't want to hear that sad tale."

"I do, actually."

"The last painting I made was of a woman who left the island last year and went back to England. We corresponded for a while, and I thought she was coming back. She went back to her husband and alas, she broke my heart." He gestured, placing both palms on his chest and his head slumped to the side. He then looked up at me as if judging my reaction.

"So, is this the truth or . . ."

"No, I assure you it is the truth, though it is a bit more complicated than that. I won't bore you with the sad details. Suffice it to say, she took much more than my heart away. My muse went with her too."

I understood. When things got rocky with Paul long before I caught him cheating, I lost my desire to work. My self-esteem suffered. The article that should have taken a few weeks to finish ended up taking months. It slowed my progress to associate professor, and I hated myself for it. I viewed Derek with more empathy.

The conversation began to flow more easily without the battle of wills that I had created at the start. It could have been the rum, or just my need to let down my guard. And the longer we sat and talked the more comfortable I became. The sky was growing a deep royal blue and a lighter blue at the horizon.

"May I entice you to see the sunrise at Moon Hole. We may still catch it." He called out, "Emmett, can we get to my favorite spot for sunrise?"

"I do think we can, sir."

"Then tell Roger to take us home."

The boat's motor began. And as the yacht set out, Derek raised his hand and pointed to a sliver of orange ablaze out on the horizon. The boat raced through the water, as a fiery orange ball rose slowly into the sky, dripping bits of itself, like tears, onto the sea's surface.

Derek moved behind me as if he were presenting this delight to me for my own private pleasure. He draped his arms around my shoulders. I reached up for his hands to steady myself in the moving craft while my eyes feasted on the fountain of golden light billowing up on the horizon. The fiery yellow orb was mesmerizing and making me lightheaded, like I might swoon. The blazing ball, dripping golden light, pooled itself on the water below. I felt fingertips brush across my breasts, and felt him kiss my neck and then my shoulders. It wasn't clear if the yacht was now stopping, my weight shifting from the sudden stop, or the liquor. "I feel a little dizzy," I said. He guided me down the stairs to the space below deck. It was there waiting, and now I could see it. His bed was covered in a silky bronze material, and the pillows were a brighter cinnamon color. My knees were weak. "I am missing . . ."

"No worries, there is time . . ."

My blouse draped open to one buttonhole. He must have opened it so that it wouldn't tear.

My body settled into the bed and was sinking into layers of down with darkness filling in around me. The shadows of the sparse furnishings of my home were there on the wall just past the large pitcher with water. The bent wood clothing rack held my nightdress gently billowing and ballooning with the sea breeze. I was more at ease as the comforts of my home appeared, lit by the moonlight that brightened the windowsill.

His touch was ever so light, as were his caresses, his kisses were artful, arousing. His lips pressed mine, and then he searched for my tongue with his. The intrusion sent a jolt through me, and I gained the will to yell out. He covered my mouth with his, muffling my cry. As he explored my mouth and then kissed my neck and chest, I did not stop him. He toyed with my breasts, exciting me to a pitch that I reached for him. Touching him, I could no longer hide from the truth. I had let this man into my bed and into my mouth. I pulled back my hand, trying to right this wrong. He knew, but was not deterred, kissing my breasts, tracing his finger along my belly and down to my thigh. He found my center, and I did not stop him. He probed, using his fingers, and my insides craved his touch. When I could no longer stand my need, I reached for him again and he climbed upon me. I guided him, and he pierced me. I could barely breathe. At that moment, I recalled the night my husband made me his. It had taken time to make me want him, but when he entered, it was at first a burning sensation, but in time a wonderful joy I welcomed. It had been so long since John had been there with me. He left me so soon for the sea. The thought of him sustained me through the long nights without him.

This time there was a searing heat as I stretched, and then my body offered no further resistance. The passion made me writhe, loving how he stayed with me so long that I remembered myself. As he moved with me, my mind left me. He was delving deep as if he were claiming the inside of me for his own. With no thoughts, I had only sensation. The hunger I felt was more than I could contain. I lost any sense of guard or self-protection. Without warning, my insides quaked. A scream escaped my lips, and he covered my mouth with his hand. I opened my eyes, looked up, and I saw the Black Carib, Sumadi. That was his name. He was there, inside me.

I must have welcomed him somehow. How else could he have known me so? I felt such shame. I pushed him off of me.

"You are finished with me now. You want to send me away." He laughed a booming deep-throated laugh, and lifted off of me. My cheeks burned with disgrace. He stood up, a silhouette, the details of his face and body hidden in shadow. He reached down for his pants, and the moonlight revealed his face with a bemused expression that seemed to mask all that he wanted to say. He climbed onto the window frame. "You know you will want me again. You will remember my touch."

"I won't." As the words left my lips, I knew that they sounded weak. Though I felt shame, I also felt alive and desired.

"The Portugee shouldn't leave you alone so long. Leave the curtains open to one side, and I will come back," he said, his voice now a guttural whisper.

I didn't get a chance to say anything in return. Or maybe I didn't want to.

He laughed again and disappeared into the darkness.

As sleep lifted away, my face warmed with the morning sun. I heard my husband's voice. "Mariel. Where are you? I am home at last."

His voice yanked me from my bed, and sent me stumbling toward the basin to bathe. The smell of the man who had been in my bed was surely still there.

"What are you doing? Come here. You do not have to wash. I wish to taste and smell your skin."

"I am not fresh." Those words slipped out. Now my heart hoped that he did not understand my meaning.

"I do not want you to be anything other than you are. Please come here and let me kiss your face."

The water was cool. I tried to wash my body. He came up behind me and kissed my neck. There he was in the looking glass above the basin. His sea green eyes, with their golden centers, were like sunshine, my body trembling. He cupped my breasts. I felt only fear that he might detect that someone had been there. But he did not. He smelled of fish.

"Let me wash you first," I said.

He stripped off his shirt and laughed, then lay on the bed. I forced a smile through my fear, and wet the cloth one more time, and this time soaped it up and bathed his face and his neck, then his arms. Then I washed his privates, which grew as I handled them. Then I wiped his thighs, and his breathing became deeper, and his eyes closed, and he slept.

"John?" I whispered.

He raised his hands, to reach for me to draw me into him, and I rested my head on his broad chest, finding the safety I always felt with him. Lying with him there, happy for his touch, I was comforted that I did not have to fear a return of Sumadi, for a while at least.

13

Derek was lying beside me. My face was hot with shame. At first, I thought it was from seeing my state of undress. My blouse was unbuttoned, and my breast was exposed—but it felt like something deeper. I pulled the sheet up to cover myself.

"Don't, I was studying the light there," he said, his eyes lit up with an impish gleam. Sunlight filtered in from the windows on two sides of the cabin, which was spacious and seemed like both a bedroom and sitting area.

"I am trying to hold on to my dignity, if there is any left." I searched the air, studying the events of the night before, for whatever details I could remember. The alcohol, as I recalled, was my reason for finally shedding my inhibitions. "It was the rum punch," I said.

Knitting together my memories, I was torn between feeling alive again and that, somehow, I had succumbed to the machinations of a man whom I did not yet trust. *How did I get on this yacht with Derek in the middle of the night?* I had to face it, though, the impulsiveness that made me give in to him was liberating.

"So, you are up. Are you hungry? How about some chilled orange juice to cool those flushed cheeks? Such a beautiful shade of cinnamon!"

He had a disarming way of saying things, which I could not prepare for—throwaways that excited my insides. He handed me a goblet of juice. "I am a little hungry." I was trying to read his reactions to me, to tell what, if anything, happened the night before. Though my blouse was unbuttoned, it didn't seem I had disrobed, though I had this sensation of heat in my center. For all I knew, it could have been another dream.

"We have some of Emmett's banana bread. You want to come up on deck? You can see Moon Hole from here."

"Not just yet. What happened last night? I was tired. I drank a little too much . . . so I think I got . . . drunk. And . . ."

"And . . ." he said lasciviously.

"And never mind."

"I can tell you that last night you were extraordinarily beautiful," he said.

"But I do not normally . . . I was so exhausted from the day."

"That you allowed yourself to come under my spell?"

"Don't ridicule me."

"I am not ridiculing you. I mean it. I know I took advantage of your weakened state, getting you onto my yacht." His eyes twinkled naughtily. "I always take an advantage when it's offered. So, I got you to Moon Hole. Do you want to come out and see it?"

"No, I mean, I don't just sleep with someone until I get to know them." His laughter bounced off the walls in the tiny cabin. "Don't laugh at me. I am trying to salvage a little of my self-respect here."

"Why, because you think I slept with you, and that diminishes you. And that isn't supposed to make me laugh? Look, I don't sleep with inebriated women. My ego can't accept that a woman does not fully engage. So, no, we did not 'sleep together,' as you put it. Trust me, if and when we do, you will be fully involved. You will actively choose to do so. You will ask me to make love to you."

I felt his words before I heard them. "You are too full of yourself Mr. Reynolds."

His eyes grew dark. He seemed to have played his trump card and was through with the game. "Come up on deck," he said, rising from the bed and turning to go upstairs.

The small mirror in the cramped cabin bathroom reflected my nettled expression and lined brow. The claustrophobic space shut me in with my embarrassment.

Derek was on the sun-drenched deck above, looking toward the shore. There was a rocky cliff-like structure rising out of the sea. "So, that is Moon Hole." Derek gestured with his coffee mug. "An architect, who wanted to preserve the natural formations of the caves, built these homes. He used natural materials on the interior spaces. We can go over by motorboat, and you will see it close up."

"I probably should get back home." My thoughts squirted out. "What time is it anyway?"

His head snapped around as his eyes locked with mine. His expression was frigid.

"I'll have my driver drive you back. Emmett, call Trevor. Tell him to pull the car out. He's taking the lady home. And Emmett, can you bring up the tote that we left downstairs, and then lower the motorboat. We are going across." He drained the cup of coffee. He bundled his pencils, wrapped them in a rubber band that snapped each time he pulled, twisted, and looped it around the pencils and released it.

"You're angry at me, aren't you?"

"No, just weary of the back and forth."

"Well, okay. I'll go over to take a look, and then I have to go."

"No!"

He stopped speaking. The sound of the winch sliced through the silence, bringing the motorboat up closer to the rear of the yacht. Derek descended into it, and a crewmember took my hand. Dizzied by his abrupt departure, I missed the first step and clenched the rung of the ladder trying to regain my footing. Derek was silent on the boat ride. As we got across to the beach, he and Emmett helped me out of the boat into the surf where the water was thigh-high. On the beach, we encountered a hilly structure, and a worn footpath that stretched back and away from the shore. Alongside the cave there was a stone stairway. We continued up to the first level of the caves. "We are climbing to Tranquility," Derek said finally, and then laughed, punctuating the irony of the moment. A hand-painted sign, with flowers surrounding the name "Tranquility," was nailed into the tree beside the opening to the structure.

"The tables and chairs and various artifacts inside of the villa are all fashioned from whale bone, natural stones, and indigenous trees." Derek's chat seemed a practiced speech he'd used many times before. "This cavern belongs to a writer, who's a friend. We have to climb to the next one, which is mine."

Trying to continue the conversation, I said, "What is yours called?"

"We're coming to it now."

There was the sign, and it said simply, "Dominion."

As I stepped into his hollowed out living space, I was struck by the fact that it opened out onto a view of the sea that was spectacular. There was no full wall, just a half wall forming a balcony of sorts. "It is wide open!" There was a huge gaping space through which I could see the yacht, and the sea reached out to forever.

"But the car is out this way. Trevor!"

"I don't have to go so soon," I said, making amends.

"It seemed you wanted to do so a few minutes ago. I am tired of the bickering. This is where I do my art. I protect this space."

"Are you asking me to leave?"

"Only if you intend to continue with this . . ." he searched for words and turned his palms up in a gesture toward me, ". . . whatever this is. You saw the name of my space here, Dominion. I named it that for a reason. It is where I live, and where I create. You see the sea," he pointed to the view, "the breeze cleanses this space, and I populate it only with people who understand what this space means to me. Do I want you to go? No. But I show you my home, and the first thing you say is you have to go, and then you ask me the time. You mucked the whole thing up."

My glib banter was thoughtless. The events of the past few days swirled through my mind. My dreams left me uneasy. "A lot on my mind," I tried to explain. "And 'the back and forth' as you call it, is just my manner, I guess." I had been called combative by a man early in our seeing each other. He was Kenyan, and at first, I saw his comment as simply paternalistic. "When do you take off the boxing gloves?" he once asked.

"So then, let's leave it out here." He stood there, at the threshold, waiting for my response. He did not budge. A sea breeze wafted in through his space.

"Okay. . . . Sure." I hung up my boxing gloves.

"Do you want to come in?" he asked, his hand holding on to the door jamb, blocking my entrance.

"I do."

He lifted his eyebrows in a feigned come-hither expression. "Ask me."

"What?" I couldn't restrain my smile as I realized his meaning.

"Ask me to let you in."

I laughed. And I heard myself say, "Derek, may I enter your . . ."

"Dominion?"

"Derek, may I enter your Dominion?"

"Trevor," he shouted.

"Yes, sir." A disembodied voice responded from the pathway to the left of the entrance.

"Never mind, our plans have changed." He wrapped his arm around my waist and guided me into a large living room. "So, this is where I do most of my entertaining." There was a couch with big orange and red pillows and a huge straw ottoman with an aqua cushion, which could easily seat three people. His love of color was on display. The veranda, made out of stone, stretched out in front of the living room.

Then we stepped into another room, "Here's my workroom." There was an easel, racks of canvasses, and paintings up against the walls. Walking and stopping to look more closely at his paintings, Gauguin's work came to mind, partially because of the subject matter of women with golden and burnt sienna complexions. Almost all were nudes, seated, reclining, bathing, combing their hair.

"I can tell you love to paint women."

"I do."

"This work is beautiful. You *should* be painting."

"I know! That's why I asked you to pose."

"I don't think I am the right sort of . . . subject," I said, finding myself blushing and my skin warming at the suggestion that I might pose for a painting like the ones I saw before me. He put his pad up on the easel. He looked at me sheepishly, "So you won't do me the honor?"

"No, I think not," I said, regaining my composure. "And you have obviously had so many more beautiful subjects."

"None more beautiful than you. I was hoping." He opened his pad and turned to a drawing he did of a woman's face.

The drawing was hypnotic. Looking more closely, then stepping back to see it as a whole, there was something familiar about the drawing. It was my face, so at peace. I lifted and turned the page.

"I was studying your hands there."

Then I flipped another page and there was a torso, breasts. A woman was lying languidly on a surface with one arm bent, with her palm cradling her face, the other hand resting on a pillow. I noted a beauty mark on the left breast that I recognized. This, too, was a drawing of me, this one more detailed, so fully realized that it had life. A surge of emotion flowed through me. As I took in the image, the beauty and the freedom in her posture splashed over me like a wave. There was passion mixed with contentment in my likeness that I did not remember feeling in so long, if ever. I covered my mouth lest the sensation be given voice. At that moment, I was angry that he had stolen my presence and crystallized it there on paper. Yet, I felt a kinship to the emotion that he captured, something that I had forgotten, or never known.

He smiled and closed the pad. Then he stepped into the room that held his bed. The bed was oval in shape and there was a lightweight silken coverlet with patches of aqua and turquoise and purple, the sea, all pieced together. "You can guess what happens here." He laughed. I shook my head.

My cell phone rang. It wrenched me from my feelings of being trapped and suspended between serendipity and shame, at being caught in such a moment. *I couldn't be drawn and painted as he captured me—a professor, a researcher and writer. How could my image be captured here in this way?* I turned my back to Derek, scrambled through my bag, and got my cell out, seeing four missed calls. Two from here on the island, and the last one had an area code for Boston with a number I did not recognize. I thought of my aunt and prayed that she was alright.

"Hello?" I said, trying to conceal the fear in my heart.

"Dr. Kendall, Jocelyn," a male voice, deep and enveloping.

"Yes, who's . . . ?" As I asked, I knew. "Gerald . . . Gerald Hunter?"

I was at once relieved and taken by surprise.

"Hope you don't mind my call, but Haynes contacted me and was concerned. She said she did not find you this morning. There was no note. She called you a few times, no answer. I am glad to hear your voice."

There was a moment of irritation, feeling constrained by the notion that I would have to account for my comings and goings. "I'm fine. I probably should have left a note."

I was quiet, so was he. "I don't know if I mentioned Mr. Derek Reynolds to you. He came and asked me out to a ride on his boat . . . yacht. I should have left a note for Haynes. I am so sorry."

"Derek Reynolds, yes of course," Gerald said, and then there was prolonged silence. Finally, he said, "I know the family and am familiar with him."

"I did tell you he had offered me a seat on the plane he hired from St. Vincent to Bequia?"

"I am sure you did." There was another long pause. "Is he there now?"

"Yes, actually he is, I was looking at some of his paintings." I wanted to explain. His voice was like a cloak, so when he did not speak, I felt bare.

"He does have a 'reputation' there in Bequia," he finally said. "By the way, I am planning a trip down within the next week or so."

"You're coming down? Does that mean you will need the house?" This was all so awkward.

"No, I have property where I will be able to stay. No problem. Well, I will call Haynes and tell her that you are all right."

"I can do that." The notion of his being in Bequia, reminded me of what Selena said weeks ago, and without thinking, I said, "I hope you will let me know when you are arriving. Perhaps the dinner you spoke of might be had here in Bequia." I looked around for Derek, hoping he was not listening to my conversation. I didn't see him. I realized I had just asked Gerald for a date.

"I can arrange that. I would love to show you some of the island and perhaps introduce you to some of the people who might help you with your research. Prof. Bailey said he had a good day with you."

It was odd how much he had followed my comings and goings. "You spoke to him?"

"He called after you had tea to tell me he had seen you. I hope he has been helpful."

"Very, we have seen each other again since then," I offered.

"Yes? Well, you can rely on him. I will leave you, and I hope you haven't minded my calling after you, but I was concerned. You cannot be too careful you know. It is not New York or Boston, but as I said, Bequia does have its own intrigue, as I am sure you have gathered by now." His voice was strong, now deep in his bass register, and powerful in its delivery. It wrapped itself around me. "Say good afternoon to Mr. Reynolds, and tell him for me not to count on monopolizing your time in Bequia."

"I can't very well say that," I said, feeling Derek behind me.

"You don't have to say anything, that was a poor joke." And with that, he was gone.

"I take it, that was your gentleman in Boston."

"I wouldn't characterize him in that way."

"Perhaps you wouldn't, but I think he would presume to do so."

The drawing in the pad, opened once again, drew my eye. My mind was spinning. Here were, it seemed, two men vying for my attentions. I felt strangely suspended between abandon and protection. There was this dangerous freedom with Derek, and a sense of security I craved, which I now felt hearing Gerald's voice. It was a curious security, in which I felt bound to him, and he me, in some way. I wanted to feel it all, the freedom and the fold.

14

"Selena," I whispered, "is Luis nearby?" From where I sat under the umbrella at the far end of the veranda, I watched for Haynes, who was late in arriving.

"No. He's in town. Want to talk to him?"

"No, not yet. Just you."

"How's Bequia? Did I say it right?"

"Selena, you're not going to believe this. I met this guy on the flight down. I get the feeling he's a bad boy, but his family's in the boatbuilding industry, and I thought he might be another resource for my research . . . crew lists, sailor's journals, etc."

"How old is he?"

"I don't know. I'd say forty-five."

"Forty-five's good. . . . And a bad boy you think can help with your *research*? Got it!" Selena's lascivious cackle bubbled through the earpiece.

"Don't start, Selena! So, he convinces me to take this flight with him to Bequia. He has his chauffeur drive me to my house down here. I'm thinking he's going to be hard to keep at bay." I lowered my voice to a whisper. "Then who calls the minute, I mean the very minute, I get to the house, but Dr. Gerald Hunter? Derek asks who is he, and if he is my boyfriend, and then backs off."

"Did you want him to back off?"

"I did . . . seems to have a dark side. But it is so weird! No one in my life for almost four years, and now it feels like there are two men . . . competing for my attention."

"Don't fight it, girl . . . enjoy."

"Selena, you know that's not me."

"Maybe it should be. That's why you had a past life regression, sweetheart," she laughed even harder.

"So, here's the rest. . . . The other night, I'm sitting on the veranda, and I see this boat, well this *yacht* out on the water. It's Derek, the guy from the plane. He tells me he's watching me, and I should come out to see this house. He told me about it on the plane, an artists' colony called Moon Hole."

"This guy seems like a piece of work. Come see my *artist colony*?"

"He's an artist."

"Oh. I see. So it was, come see my etchings."

"Stop. He says, 'Come see the sunrise in Moon Hole.'"

Her laughter came out in bursts. I pictured her covering her mouth, her laughter spilling through her fingers. "That's too much."

I tried to breathe and collect myself to tame the giggles I now had. "I told him I would go for a nightcap. Well, the nightcap turned into the night."

"You slept with him?"

"Well, no."

"What's his story? Is he gay?"

"No, he's not gay." I lowered my voice again, suddenly aware that I was outside and neighbors, though not near, might hear me. "I got so drunk that I fell asleep."

"And he didn't try anything? Interesting."

"He said, and get this, that he doesn't sleep with inebriated women, because his ego can't allow him to, and I would have to be fully aware and tell him I want to."

"Oh my, my, my! What have you gotten yourself into?" Selena chuckled, then grew quiet, as if she was going to offer some serious comment, then changed her mind.

"Wait, so I'm leaving in the morning . . . this morning . . ."

"That was last night?"

"Yes, just a couple of hours ago, I said I needed to get home. Who should call on my cell, but Gerald."

"You've got to be kidding."

"Nope, and he tells me he is coming down here in a couple of . . . I don't know . . . weeks."

"This is almost primal, lady. It's like these two guys smell each other."

"I know. Gerald told me to tell Derek not to try and monopolize my time, because he was coming down. But I didn't even tell you the really weird part."

"To me, this part just sounds hot. And you know these island men. This is a who is *mas macho* thing."

"Well, the really strange thing is that I started having these dreams when I got down here." I took a deep breath. "I really should ask Luis about this."

"Speaking of the Devil, he just walked in."

"Don't tell him about the other part. But . . ."

"Who is it?" I heard him say in the background.

"No, of course not. It's Jocelyn," Selena said.

I could hear her passing the phone. "Luis, tell Selena to pick up too."

"How's the island girl? Okay. Selena, pick up in there," Luis shouted.

"Funny you should say that," I said. "I have been having these dreams, and it's like I stepped back in time here on the island. Based on what I am learning about my great-great-grandmother, I think I may have stepped into her life."

Luis appeared to hesitate. "If you're learning stuff about her, you could be incorporating it into your dreams."

"No, I know how that works. I began these dreams the first day here. Could it be the past life regression?" At that moment, my neighbor stepped out through her gate onto the beach and waved to me. I waved back, then took the phone inside. "What do you think? Could it be the past life regression?"

"It could be. . . . What are you dreaming?"

"Long story short, I dreamed of a girl, well *I* was this girl. I think I was my great-great-grandmother, and in the dream her husband is out to sea. This other man comes into her house and tries to seduce her." I would have told Selena the details, but not with Luis on the phone.

"So far, as dreams go, not so bad. I could get into that," Selena laughed. "Sorry Luis, but a dream is a dream."

"I can handle it," he said. "Jocelyn, you knew your great-great-grandfather was a whaler. Maybe . . ."

"But I am *in* that time—with all the details, things I couldn't have devised. And there's a lot of stuff coming up for me in real life too. So . . ."

"Are there any lessons in the past you're gaining for right now? I can't guide you while you are in a dream, so you'll have to trust your own power. Remember, what you learn in that life has to be applied in this one, and not vice versa. You can't change *that* time."

"I find that I don't want to." When I said that, I realized how true it was and how it sounded. I wanted to gather up my words and stuff them back in my mouth. "But I'm afraid something might come up that I cannot handle."

"Just remember that you cannot control it. You can only experience it and learn from it. Okay? Keep us posted."

"Yes, I want to hear more about the two gentlemen suitors," Selena inserted, ". . . especially the good doctor. You need to leave the bad boy alone," Selena said.

"Two gentlemen suitors?" Luis said.

"Girl talk, not for your ears," Selena said. "Bye, girl. Have fun."

They were both gone before I could focus on what I had not said. I had left out my foreboding about not being able to escape from the dreams if I needed to. And I had become impulsive, as if someone else was making decisions, not me.

A knock on the door startled me. I pulled back the gauzy curtain, and there was Haynes holding a cloth tote bag. "Just didn't want to disturb you, Mum."

"No, of course not. Come in. By the way, I am sorry for not calling you back right away. I was . . ." For the moment, I was searching for words to explain where I was the night before.

"No matter, Mum," Haynes cut me off. "Just hope Mum is not upset with me for calling twice. I had concerns about your safety." She began putting a bag of flour and tin of condensed milk in the pantry.

I felt the island culture construct its rules on class around me. Haynes did not want my explanation. She wanted it known plainly that it was not her place or interest to know the details of my evening. She had knocked on the door for the first time, giving me the signal that she knew that I might have been in a compromising position. The complexity of all of that was crystallized in the brief exchange.

"Do you wish for me to cook today, Mum?" she said, as she emerged from the pantry. "And maybe we should go through those keys to the house today."

"Yes, I want you to cook today. Perhaps I can go through the house with you later."

"Then you wish me to come this week? Dr. Hunter said I should raise that issue with you to be certain that those be your wishes."

Dr. Hunter and Haynes discussed my habits and daily activities? Comforted by their concern a few days ago, now I felt scrutinized, exposed. "I wish you to remain as the housekeeper here for me for as long as I am here, if you don't mind. What is your fee?"

"They does pay me one hundred pounds if me come to cook and clean each day as needed, except me Saturdays for me family. I can come after church on Sundays if you have a special occasion if you can tell me in advance, but pay extra."

"How much is that in American dollars?"

"About one hundred twenty-five American dollars, and extra for me Sundays, but I does the wash, and the ironing. I goes to town and does the marketing. If you does want, me can come less days, we can make some other arrangement."

"I am more than happy for you to have Saturdays and Sundays off."

Haynes nodded, finally smiling, which changed the atmosphere in the room. "Would Mum like anything for lunch?"

"Just some of that tuna and a slice of toast, and maybe some of your coconut bread and tea." The exchange with Haynes bound my stomach like a girdle because of what was not said about the night before.

"Shall I serve it in the dining room?"

"That will be fine." She chose the formality of the dining room, but it felt right.

A moment later, when the phone rang, Haynes called out, "It is Prof. Bailey." She brought the phone to me.

"Dr. Kendall, I've been thinking. Was your great-great-grandfather Catholic? We can seek out the Catholic Church records for a marriage here in Bequia."

That was when I remembered the first dream I had and the Catholic priest. "He was. My family told me that my great-grandmother, his daughter, became Protestant when she married my great-grandfather."

"We can check the marriage records and any baptism records for your great-grandmother. The records should reveal a divorce or an annulment as well."

"An annulment?" The muscles in my stomach tensed, and I had a sinking feeling in my chest.

"You remember what Vivencia said about her having two husbands? Maybe there are records . . ." *Why is this affecting me like this?*

"So, when can we go?"

"Tomorrow. I spoke to Father Silva who's a friend of mine. He said he could look up his records. Give me your great-grandfather's name again."

"Matos, John Matos. He was my great-great-grandfather."

"John Matos. Do you know how he spelled it? The Portuguese spell John, J-H-O-N unless they anglicized it."

"No, I haven't seen any written records. And my great-great-grandmother was Maria. I don't know her Carib name or her maiden name. But didn't Vivencia say Mariel? And did you say Father Silva? Gerald suggested in an email that I talk to him too."

"Father Silva is well known here on the island. Next Wednesday, as you know, I am off to Barbados to work on my own research. You will be on your own for a while after that. Tomorrow, same time, the driver and I will be there."

Hanging up the phone, a wave of emotion passed over me, filling me with anxiety. I wanted to look at the records to learn as much as I could, but the image of my twice-great-grandmother felt tarnished. I identified with the young girl who romped on the beach in my dream. I was Mariel. The man who was let into my bed—I did it. Luis's warning that I could not change or control anything in my dreams made me anxious about the players in that time and space. Yet the draw was stronger, even as my fear about what I was learning was more pronounced.

The phone rang again. I jumped, jolted from my ruminations. "Hello, Dr. Bailey?"

"Jocelyn?" My aunt's voice, sounding shaken.

"Tantie Grace? Are you all right?"

"Are you all right? They say you were nowhere to be found last night."

"What?"

"They say you disappeared last night."

"Who? Who said that?"

"Leland. I told you about my brother. He said you disappeared into the night. No one could find you. . . . Called this morning asking if I heard from you."

"You have got to be kidding me. How did he know that?"

"Look I told you, on an island people talk. He knows someone who . . . was looking out for you. Just leave it at dat."

"Tantie Grace, I am a grown woman. I went out. That's all."

"You can't just disappear like that. You have to let people know where you are."

"How did you know I *disappeared*. as you put it . . . ?"

"I just know. People there know. They talk."

Heat rose in my cheeks, and then up into my forehead. Anger deepened the line between my brows, as I fought not to take it out on my aunt.

"Tantie Grace, did you ever hear that my great-great-grandmother had two husbands?"

"No," she paused. "Why are you asking me that?"

"I heard," I began, but was cut off by my aunt whose voice now seemed stronger, strident.

"Don't believe everything you hear there. She had enemies. I told you that."

"But did she get divorced or . . ."

"Jocelyn, you just cannot leave well enough alone. You vex me so." Her voice was now strained and reedy.

No good-bye. Her anger was on full display, filling my chest with bile. Had Haynes said something to someone? Maybe to the people who lived across the way, the young man who climbed the coconut trees? *Who is watching me?*

My coconut bread uneaten, I left the table. Needing to clear my mind, I put on a swimsuit, grabbed a towel, and went down to the sea. Forgot my water shoes but decided to go without them. The bits of shell and coral pricked the soles of my feet. Seeing through the clear sea water, I tried to avoid the dark-brown sea urchins with sharp spines that I recalled from my childhood could puncture me and cause injury. But I wanted to feel the buoyancy of the sea beneath me, determined to continue in despite the sea shells and sea-stars, the seaweed that now wrapped 'round my ankles, all of the debris on the sea floor. *I should have worn my sea shoes.*

My hopes were that the seawater sweeping over me might wash away my feelings of being bound up in this culture, but it only swaddled me in them. I swam underwater as far as I could until I felt my lungs struggle in need of air. Trying to stand, my feet did not touch bottom, but I came up to the surface and gasped, then turned to see the beach and the top of the house behind the trees and swam toward it. My chest tightened trying to hold my breath, and my feet strained to touch the seafloor, yet again it eluded me, so I gasped once more. A yelp escaped my mouth. The house was closer, but I needed to swim some more to save myself. My arms were fatigued, and my legs kicked as hard as they could, but were weak. I lifted my head to take in air and screamed out, but seawater filled my mouth and went into my lungs. My arms seemed disconnected from my body as they now flailed wildly, and I tried to scream, but no sound came out. My body descended and I could see the aquamarine sea's surface overhead. It was burying me beneath its liquid salt, and my ears were stopped. *The sea was swallowing me.*

It was quiet. A swarm of butterflies kissed my eyelashes, tickled my neck and then my breasts. They collected themselves about my belly, my thighs, and then my center. Their delicate dance left sprinkles of golden sun drops that warmed me, making me moist. Then there was music, the lyrical sounds of his voice, "Minha Linda, meu amor, te amo."

The song drifted into my ears and bits of the sun drops collected on my eyelashes. There before me were John's eyes, blue green with golden flecks like the sea dipped in sun. His touch was as gentle as the breeze of a hovering hummingbird's wings. I unfolded ever so slightly showing my crimson center. As he touched, I opened. The petals stretched themselves to feel the delicate probing. The weight of his body pressed mine. The strangeness of the intrusion became welcome with each entrance. He enveloped me. I did not have words in his language, so I simply said his name, "John." Peace rose in me. I felt him say, "Mariel, this is the first time I hear you speak my name and see you smile with your eyes." It was the morning of the third day of our marriage, and we were fastened.

I rose and tried to take the bedclothes from the mattress, seeing they were soiled, stained. My husband stopped me. He kissed my fingertips and spoke to me in his language, and I knew that he did not want me to trouble myself with such things anymore. Shrugging my shoulders and gesturing the question: How then would the cloths be cleaned? I tried to show him I did not want anyone to see my things so stained. He spoke in his language and then called the name, "Leila!" and pointed toward the fresh water catch. I understood that he had hired a woman to do that work, and it was no longer befitting me, the wife of a sea captain.

As I started out to pick fruit for our breakfast, John took hold of my shoulder. His eyes fixed on my breasts, which were uncovered, and he gave me a shirt of his to wear. The sleeves hung down below my fists and the tail of it reached the backs of my knees, but I smelled him in it. It felt good wrapped up in him. As I picked up a ripe mango, an olive-skinned woman with black hair and dark eyes walked toward me, carrying a basket resting on her hip.

"Señora Matos."

"Leila," John said, and handed her the bedclothes. Though I did not understand his words, his tone seemed to be instructive. She lowered her head in his presence, and put the crumpled sheet into the basket, lifted it onto her head, then disappeared into the bush.

Shades of aqua and the water surrounded me, and I felt my descent, succumbing to the water's will. Peaceful liquid rest. My memories now flowing over me with bubbles of life rising 'round me. The sound of nothing, silence clogging my ears.

My arm was yanked, pulled from its socket. My head lifted from the water, sunlight jolting my consciousness. The skin on my legs burning, pounding on my back. Lips covering mine, air forced into my chest, fingers clawing my mouth and throat, I coughed, then heaved. Vomit and spittle flowed from my mouth. As my eyes blinked open, a brightening haze revealed the figures of Haynes and the boy who climbed the coconut trees, kneeling over me.

"Mistress Jocelyn, are you all right?"

Unable to speak, I coughed again to clear my throat of the bits of food and salt water.

"I am going to call the doctor," Haynes said, pushing herself up to stand.

"No," I managed to say, spitting the last of the food and water from my mouth.

"Carry her to the house, boy."

"That isn't necessary," I said, pushing myself up to sit.

"Let him do it." The boy lifted me into the air, dizzying me as he carried me up the steep staircase. I was cold. My body trembled.

"Take her in there," Haynes pointed to the bedroom.

"How is your breathing, Mum?"

"I am fine, just a little chilled . . . fussing too much." Haynes pulled out a coverlet from the cedar chest at the foot of the bed, the scent of lavender wafting about me as it billowed then fell.

"I'm calling the doctor to have him look at you."

"That's not necessary." My voice grew strident, annoyed.

"Mum, Dr. Hunter would not forgive me if I did not make sure Mum was all right." Haynes implored me, asserting her fears such that I could not argue with her.

"Okay. Okay."

"You rest, Mum."

Haynes was talking on the phone, then came back, "He will be here straight away." I drifted off for what I felt was just a few minutes. But the space between *then and now* had grown so thin that I slipped back without warning.

"Mariel," my sister called, seeing me walking along the edge of the sea. She whispered in my ear, "How was it? Do I fear it?"

"No," I giggled and covered my lips. "It was like . . . I have not the words."

"Everyone is proud that you were pure."

"What do you mean?"

"Well, they saw the bedclothes stained with your innocence."

"Who saw the bedclothes?"

"The village. The woman who cleans for the Portugee placed them on the rocks before washing them. It is their custom."

My face did redden, and I turned away.

"Do not feel so. You must grow accustomed to their way, if you will please your husband."

My sister's face was innocent of the consequences that were beginning to form in my mind, and now I felt in my body. With only that brief warning, the sensation of a thunderbolt struck me. Heat rose in me, filling my chest and then my head. Images and thoughts of the intrusive eyes. My strength drained from me. Struggling to keep my shoulders square, I looked for anyone who might have witnessed this spectacle, but there was no one—just this insistent tapping on my shoulder, and the male voice filtering through my unconscious.

"Dr. Kendall. Can you hear me? I am Dr. Manley, here to examine you!"

A smiling round, brown-skinned face, his stethoscope hardly fitting around his neck, he reached out for my hand, saying, "Let me take a listen. Can you sit up please? Sounds good."

"I told them, I'm fine."

"Yes, but it is always good to check after a near drowning. You are very lucky the boy saw you. He's a good swimmer."

"Yes."

"Ah, your lungs sound clear. That's a very good sign. Haynes, give her some coconut water."

"Yes, Doc."

"That should revive you a bit. It is almost teatime. I hear your stomach growling, but eat only something light. I will be by tomorrow to listen to your lungs one more time, just . . . as a precaution."

"I was headed out tomorrow."

"I wouldn't advise it. Take a day to rest."

All this attention was binding. "Are you sure this is all necessary?"

"I wouldn't advise it if it were not. I understand you intend a long stay. I want it to be a healthy one."

Packing his satchel, he stood up, his cream-colored suit creasing at the joint of his hips. He reached for his straw Panama hat and left.

My sense of privacy had been breached, and these people closed themselves around me. I knew I should be grateful that they saved my life, but their protection was suffocating.

15

"You ready to come out and play?" Derek's baritone voice flowed into my ears. Snatches of sensation from a dream still troubled me. No real images, just feelings of disgrace. Torn between the calming aquamarine blues outside my bedroom window and the calls of the birds, which were now more like bickering, I tried to quiet the conversations from yesterday—my comings and goings examined.

"I can't go anywhere. . . . The doctor confined me till tomorrow."

"I can come and spirit you away in the dark of night again." He lowered his voice to a practiced *sotto voce*, which I imagined he used in person too—with women leaning in, his warm breath filling one's ear.

"No, don't do that. I'm serious. Do not do that," I whispered, sounding as emphatic as I could. Haynes was in the kitchen, and I didn't know how much could be heard from room to room in this big old house.

"You know, I tend to do what I am told *not* to do," Derek said.

"That last trip out on your yacht has cost me dearly . . ."

"Cost you dearly in what? Did your gentleman friend scold you?" He laughed out loud.

"No, with some family from here."

"Welcome to island life on Bequia. That's why you should come live in Moon Hole. There you are free to do as you please without the judgmental eyes everywhere."

"No thank you. I actually am quite pleased with this house. I feel safe here."

There was a long silence, which intrigued me. "What are you thinking?" I said, shaking my head at myself, feeling how easily his silences stripped away my defenses and drew me in.

"Just that you choose so called 'safety' over freedom," he asserted.

There was always something jarring about his comments. He had an insidious way of undermining my confidence. "What you call freedom makes me available for you."

"True."

"That is in *your* best interest, not mine."

"I assure you it will be mutually rewarding."

"Being there doesn't seem like freedom, it seems like being controlled by you."

"That might not be so bad, you know."

"Derek, I have to go."

"Want me to come throw pebbles at your window?"

"Good-bye, Derek."

I ventured out to the dining room, where my breakfast was waiting.

Collecting myself, which I always had to do after an encounter with him, I remembered I needed to call Prof. Bailey. Next to the telephone was the scrap of paper scrawled by Haynes with his number. My neck muscles tightened. I dialed Dr. Bailey, though I almost decided not to, just to defy Haynes intrusion. "Bailey here."

"Dr. Bailey, it's me, Jocelyn. I'm afraid I can't go to the church with you today . . . had a bit of a problem . . ."

"I heard," he said. "You should have someone watch out for you when you swim. It was pure luck this time."

"Seems everyone knows what happened to me." Perspiration beaded my upper lip. There was a click, and the overhead fan went on. I looked around and saw Haynes flipping the switch, giving me an acknowledging nod. The fan stirred the air, but I coughed, choking from the scrutiny.

Professor Bailey seemed sympathetic. "Island life. Anyway, you can go on your own on Wednesday, or later in the week if you like. Remember, I will be in Barbados. I will text you the number of the driver. He knows you, won't overcharge, and will wait for you. The priest's name is Father Silva . . . from Portugal, originally, but he has been here more than forty years. You might inquire about other areas of your research. I will tell him that you will call to reschedule."

Just as I finished my eggs, the landline phone rang again, "Dr. Bailey?"

"No, this is St. Mary's Church, the clerk, Ouida Barrows, in charge of the church archives, calling on behalf of Father Silva. Dr. Bailey called with some information from you."

"Yes. We were coming today, but had to cancel. I was wondering if I could come on Wednesday or Thursday."

"Well, that's the thing. Father Silva asked me to call you and get the spelling of your great-grandfather's name."

It is Matos. M-A-T-O-S I think. And it is my great-*great*-grandfather."

"Prof. Bailey gave us that spelling. We just wanted to check that it wasn't Mates, which is a Spanish derivation of Mateo. And do you know if he spelled his first name, John, J-O-H-N or, J-H-O-N in the Portuguese way."

"I am unsure of that . . ."

"Not a problem. So, I have it now. When do you think he was born? I mean approximately," she prompted.

"I mentioned to Professor Bailey, maybe from the early to mid-1800s, maybe as early as the 1820s or 1830s. But I am pretty sure he was born in Portugal."

The woman paused and seemed to be studying something. "That is what Dr. Bailey said.

We do seem to have records for him, but there seem to be a few irregularities that we are looking into. We are searching our archives for any additional documents."

Somehow her comments and the tone of her voice squeezed my temples like a vise. "Are you saying I shouldn't come?"

"No, you are welcome to come on Thursday, and we will share with you what we have. However, these records are not computerized. These are handwritten ledgers, which we must read through carefully to be sure we have identified the proper documents for the person about whom we are researching."

My wrinkled brow now seemed to have preceded a headache that began to throb. "If you prefer that I give you more time . . ."

"No, Father Silva is looking forward to meeting you. It isn't every day that we have a professor from New York with roots in Bequia as a guest on the island." There was a pause. "I believe Father Silva would like to meet you for tea, so you can chat. That will give me a little more time to investigate these issues and meet with him."

My chest tightened even more. "What issues are you speaking of?"

"Father will need to discuss this in person, if you do not mind. He will sit down with you and these documents at about three." The woman's voice dropped almost to a whisper.

Issues to discuss? Out on the veranda, I looked out at the sea hoping to get the feeling of solace it always gave me. Instead, the aquamarine waters that stretched out as far as I could see to the left and to the right just made me feel trapped. *Have to get outside!*

Heading down to the beach, trying to get rid of these sensations of confinement, which clearly I could discard if I simply viewed these circumstances differently. As I got to the bottom of the stairs, a dark shadow swept by me. A large frond from a coconut tree fell at my feet, just missing me by inches.

"Sorry, Mum, I didn't see you dere. Are you all right?" The young fellow up in the tree slid his machete into a leather sleeve on his hip, and began a descent, his tough feet curling about the trunk of the tree.

"I guess. I am . . . glad I ran into you though . . ." My voice thin and wavering betrayed my words as I tried to calm myself. "I was going to thank you for yesterday. You saved my life." I laughed nervously. "I will give Haynes something for you, as thanks."

The boy grinned as he moved the huge frond out of my path. "No worries, Mum. That isn't necessary."

"No swimming for me today!" I wanted to go back into the house because of the jolt of the falling palm stalk but was determined to find some solace on the beach. It was laced with a thick brown seaweed. I imagined the unbroken dark line of vegetation encircled the whole island. As I passed the next home, the middle-aged woman in the garden called out, "Pardon me, Professor! You're the guest who's staying here. I am Greta Hazell. My husband George and I are here from London." Taking off her gardening glove, she reached out her hand.

"Hello. Yes. Dr. Jocelyn Kendall. From the States, New York City."

"Yes, we know."

My brow must have creased.

The woman smiled and nodded. "Yes, everyone here seems to know everything about you before you arrive. We thought it troubling at first too, but now it's rather comforting."

"It can be a bit . . ." I struggled for the right word.

"Intrusive? We thought so, but coming here to live as we have from London, where it's a bit impersonal, it is good to know people are watching out for you . . . an island thing. Just came to say hello. So, cheerio, bye."

The solitude I sought, I could not find. I needed to talk to Selena. Up on the veranda, the phone was where Haynes must have left it for me.

"Selena, got to talk to you."

"Getting ready to go into a teleconference. Luis is home."

"No, I don't want to talk to him. Just, I'm being suffocated by all these people seeming to know everything about me."

"Oh," she said laughing. "You mean the 'bochinche.' That's what they call it there. It's the gossip."

"It's driving me crazy."

"You'll get used to it. How long are you going to be there? You *better* get used to it. Gotta go."

The heat was oppressive. I finally did some work, writing field notes on my first meeting with Prof. Bailey, and my visit with Vivencia. Jotted some questions for Fr. Silva. Haynes said it felt like rain and asked to head home early. She had baked and done the wash. Humidity hung in the air. The island culture was like a tight ring closing in on me.

When I finally showered to cool off and tried to relax the muscles in my neck and back, I headed in to bed, to nap. I undid the mosquito net, and as I draped it around the bed, I noticed a dying mosquito in the netting. My grandmother used to clap her hands on the mosquitoes to kill them. This mosquito was more on the outside of the net than in, but I didn't have the heart to end its life when it had a fighting chance to get away. Instead, I closed my eyes, to shut out the pressing weight of the island, and drifted off to find that familiar space in time.

The blue-gray light had begun to filter into the house. The sweet smell of Sumadi was in my bedclothes and on my person—musk tinged and sweetened with the scent of coconut oil, exciting me. He had been here. As I turned, his taut warm skin brushed against my arm. My body grew rigid with fear as my eyes widened. He was there in my bed! An audible gasp escaped my lips before I could press my hand over my mouth. It was daybreak.

"Get out of here." My voice a frantic whisper as I pulled the bed-clothes around my naked body and pushed him with my fist.

Startled by the blow to his arm, he bolted upright, his hands combatively clenched.

"What are you doing here? It is morning."

"You well know what I am doing here." A smile then filled his face and laughter broke from his belly. "You left the curtain open. I came."

"I did not." The rum, I thought. The night before, thinking it would put me to sleep, I drank a glass of rum. I was certain I had not pushed the curtain to the side. Yet, a blurry recollection of him coming in through the window stirred me. I told him to leave, but I could not recall how strongly I protested him being there, missing my husband and needing his touch. Sumadi had a way of revealing my desires, though I fought to keep them hidden.

The week before, I had fallen on my knees, which burned from the sand and bits of shell that cut into my skin, asked John to stay with me. He seemed to take pity on me and said that he would be back within the year. I wept for five days. My sister stayed two days with me. The women, who had witnessed the scene, came to console me. But then they told me that I must learn to enjoy being alone and made jokes about not having to wash the men's dirty clothes. One taught me an intricate pattern for weaving baskets.

Another taught me how to build the sides of clay pots to great heights and how to make paint. Some of the older women joked about me learning to pleasure myself, and others still told me about their lovers, who visited them when the whaling ships set sail. I tried to enjoy their jokes and merrymaking for my benefit, but I felt an emptiness that I could not contain.

Leila gave me the bottle of rum, said it would help me sleep. It was that seventh night. I had taken the small glass and filled half of it with the amber liquid, which burned my throat and stomach going down. Its warmth spread through me, and as I watched the moonlight dance on the sea, I did not feel so sad. John would be gone for many turns of the moon's face. I wondered where Sumadi was, yearning for his touch.

I didn't recall placing the curtains as he had told me to, but I did remember going to sleep and dreaming that my husband had come home. He was touching me. He touched me until I could not bear it. It was then that I knew he was not my husband, but I could not stop his caresses on my breasts and belly. I begged him not to make me feel so. He asked me if I liked it, and I said yes, but should have said no. He was on top of me when I fully realized what I was doing, and in that moment, I did not have the will to stop. I was so in need of him.

It was not as it had been with my husband. It was an unleashed urge that I could not contain. I had no mind, only my senses. He whispered in my ear, "Do you enjoy so much with the Portugee?" And I wanted to shut him up for throwing my betrayal in my face. "Do not bring my husband into this bed." He laughed and whispered in a guttural bass tone, "I will put him there at the foot of the bed and let him watch." He pointed with his chin lifted in that direction.

Shaking my head "no," the agony of my need filled me with such desire I could not stop him. My mouth clenched and bit the bedclothes, so as not to scream out. The craze of that moment took me, until he collapsed in exhaustion on top of me, and I sank into the bed gasping for the night air, needing to sleep.

Awake now, seeing him here as the sky became more blue than black, I gritted my teeth, "Get out of here!"

"Not until I have you again."

"I said, get out."

"You don't mean that." He looked down at my breasts, which belied the words that I had just spoken. My nipples beaded with desire. He leaned down to kiss them, then took one into his mouth, toying with it with his tongue. I brushed his face away and spoke through clenched jaws. "Stop it!"

"Shhh," he said, parting me, his fingers stoking a fire in me.

"I'll scream," I said, my voice weak with longing.

"Only in the pleasure I give you." His grin was broad, daring me to stop him.

"You need to get out. Someone will see . . ." My words said to leave, but my thin and unconvincing voice begged him to stay.

"Your body wants me. It does not lie." Straddling me, he said, "It is there, take it."

Seeing him in the morning light, ready and fully ripe, made me ache in anticipation. Though I knew I should not, I guided him. The languid, deliberate entrance made me tremble. I enjoyed the fullness of him. He must have known, because he withdrew, teasing me, and repeated that slow, practiced entry. Over and then over again, he breached any resistance I had to him, till I could not recognize the deep guttural tones that came from my throat.

"Yes, I know," he said, totally in control. "Don't worry. I will not stop."

My sense of time dissolved. My insides quivered, and I opened my eyes to look at this man who had taken possession of my body. He seemed an animated sculpture with his chiseled nose and his nostrils flared as he enjoyed his power. His eyes held light as if there was a fire inside of him.

He ignited my womanhood, which had been buried in my loneliness. Behind him, through the window, the sky was growing brighter. I had no voice to tell him to stop because my openness was intoxicating. It was then that his body convulsed and stiffened. He throbbed there within me, and filled me with himself.

We lay there, his weight now pressing on me. He turned and fell onto the bed beside me. He was quiet, except for the sound of his breath. Several minutes passed when he said, "You see, you wanted me, and you will want me again."

I thought about what I had done. I had betrayed my husband and had welcomed this. The truth in his words savaged me.

The light outside was growing. The shame in me overflowed. Tears squirted from my eyes.

"Leave my home before people see you."

My tears annoyed him. I had ruined the moment of his parting. He pulled on his pants, picked up his shirt. He climbed through the window, the blue light of morning sky behind him, and his body was a violet shadow slipping into the dark dawn. I feared the women's eyes, the fishermen going out for their catch. I didn't know who might be watching.

16

St. Mary's Church was a quaint little building that stood tall atop a hill. Sea roses grew just outside the rectory door. Though smaller than the cathedrals in New York and Boston and Europe that I visited, the church had a magnificent stone façade, and a building plate said that its first worshipers gathered on the island in the mid-eighteenth century.

My great-great-grandparents might have attended this church, and I could be walking in their footsteps. Goose bumps raised on my arms as I lifted the large brass knocker on the door, striking the door only once when it opened abruptly, startling me. A heavy-set, yellow-skinned woman greeted me, "Afternoon, Dr. Kendall?" She was a short woman with a round face, framed with large wire-rimmed spectacles; a second pair of glasses hung down and rested on her rather large breasts.

"Welcome to St. Mary's. Father Silva is waiting for you in his office. I am Ouida Barrows." The woman looked down and avoided my gaze. Her voice seemed to drop to a whisper, just as it did on the phone.

"Nice to meet you. I must say that some of the things you said piqued my interest." The woman did not acknowledge my comment, simply turned her back and walked through the small vestibule and down a long, narrow, dim hallway. She had a slight limp, but it did not seem to slow her down much. She made her way to a room where she knocked first, then tilted her head toward it to listen. A soft mellifluous male voice said, "Come. Come in."

"Everything is cleared up. Father will explain." The woman looked away from me and toward the priest as she spoke. "Father Silva, Dr. Kendall. Right this way," she said this time with a full clear-throated voice. She paused long enough to hear the priest say, "Yes, I will explain everything. Ouida told me how she made an error in her research." I felt the woman's reaction, and turned to see her eyes flash, and a scowl line her forehead. She turned on her heel and left the room.

"Dr. Kendall, do sit down. Welcome to Bequia and to St. Mary's." The office walls were lined with books. A few feet away there was a small conference-type table, upon which were two ledger-type, clothbound books. Bookmarks with gold threaded tassels parted pages, and there were two pairs of white cloth gloves resting beside them. Once seated facing Father Silva, the conference table was to my back, but its presence loomed large behind me. I wondered what secrets lay there in the creases of those old logs.

"So, tell me about yourself. How did you come to this research?"

"Well, my great-great-grandparents lived here, as I guess you know. And I have long been interested in the connections between Bequia and Boston, given the whaling trade. I have a fellowship to study families, who have lived in these two places. I am looking at historical records, birth, marriage, baptisms, and I felt that there was no better place to begin than with my own family's story. Prof. Bailey said I should speak to you. Ms. Barrows . . . Ouida . . . certainly got my attention . . . when she said she did find records on my great-great-grandfather."

Father Silva's face was a peaceful, expressionless mask. He nodded from time to time to indicate that he was listening. Unlike Ouida, who while on the phone seemed to be concealing information, Fr. Silva was a blank slate. He was a short man, thin and balding, with an olive complexion; his face, which did not flinch once, was inscrutable. I paused, but he did not speak.

"I was wondering what, if any, records you found on my family," I continued. "You know genealogy has become quite popular in the U.S., and of course, as an anthropologist, this subject matter is very interesting to me." I was talking too much, as usual. I turned my attention to the room and the books, tidily arranged. Remaining quiet, I'd wait him out. Sooner or later, he'd have to speak.

He studied me, as if he knew I had intentions and motivations beyond my anthropological research. I didn't want to tell him anymore and remained mute.

Finally, he spoke. "I have located some documents on your great-great-grandfather. What do you know of him?"

My right hand reflexively clenched and grabbed hold of the arm of the chair, my irritation building, but I drew on my training and responded. "Well, I was told he was a sea captain of a whaling ship. I was told he married my great-great-grandmother, who was a Carib Indian. I saw old photos of them from the late 1800s. I lived with my grandmother who told me about her mother. But my grandmother died when I was young. There seems to be some mystery about that. That's all I know really." I searched his face for any clue as to his findings, and if they coincided at all with what I knew, and if he could add to my knowledge. There was nothing.

"I do think I have found some records on your great-great-grandparents. That's what you were seeking, am I right? There were some documents which seemed to suggest conflicting facts, but I have sorted them out. A case of two different men named Matos. A John and a Joseph, no relation," he asserted.

"Conflicting facts?"

"As I said, that is all sorted out. Why don't we go and take a look at the records we found." He stood and pointed to the conference table, then moved to the head of it.

"We are handling some very old papers so, if you do not mind." He handed me a pair of white cotton gloves.

"Of course."

He put on his gloves and lifted the cover, and then the silk bookmark, opening to a page in the middle of it. He put on his glasses, and bent over it, slowly moving down the page, studying the handwritten notations.

"Ah, here is the first one we found." He shifted the book in my direction and tapped the line he was referring to as he spoke. "We found a record of his marriage here. John Matos married to a Maria, no last name, on August 27, 1866. Our records indicate that he was thirty-five years old and that her age was designated as 'Unknown.'"

"Did they marry here in this church?"

"No. It seems they married at a home elsewhere on the island. But they baptized their child here, two and a half years later." He opened and then parted the pages of the second book, and tapped the line where the christening was noted.

"Estela Matos. That's my great-grandmother." I sat back in my chair, searching the air before me. "Do you show her child, my grandmother, here?"

"No, but we did not search for her. In fact, we show no wedding for Estela. It could be that she left the island, or the church."

"About the other Matos that you mentioned . . ."

"As I said, there is no relation," he said, closing the book, ". . . and he was only on the island briefly."

There was a knock on the door. Ouida came in and stood by the door. The priest went over to her, and she whispered something in his ear. "Dr. Kendall, I am afraid I cannot have tea with you after all. I have a call, an important matter to which I must attend. Ouida will see you out." He removed his gloves and handed them to her.

She stood, holding the door for me with one hand and a manila envelope in the other. Stunned, not expecting such a sudden end to our meeting, I reached for the envelope and Ouida looked me square in the eye for the first time.

"Ouida, what is that?" the priest asked reaching for the envelope.

"Just a few pamphlets on your work with the poor children on the island."

He took the envelope from her. The woman's visage changed. She tensed and her shoulders hunched. Her eyes moved from the envelope to the priest's face and back. He opened it and took out the material inside, made a cursory perusal of the material and stuffed it back in the envelope. He handed it to her, and the woman's shoulders, drawn up to her neck, seemed to relax slightly.

She began walking toward the hallway and the exit. "Ouida!" the priest said, in a rather commanding tone. No words passed between them, but the look on the priest's face held an admonition. She seemed compliant at first, and she nodded in an obeisant manner. Once outside, she looked me in the eye once again, now defiant and said, "Do look at the material in the envelope once you arrive home."

"Of course, I'm interested in the charitable efforts here on the island."

"I have included a source of more information for you." Her gravelly whisper held an edge.

"I will definitely read it when I get home."

The driver, a paunchy man in his fifties, was seated on a stump under a huge breadfruit tree, mopping his brow with his white handkerchief. The drive down the winding road was dizzying. As we reached the coast, I noticed that I was gripping the large envelope that Ouida gave me, as if it held a clue to the woman's secretive demeanor.

17

The kitchen had become a hot box. I opened the door to the veranda, switched on the overhead, and unsealed the envelope Ouida handed me. I shook the pamphlets expecting a note of some kind to fall out. There was none. There were two pamphlets with photos of school children in uniforms, girls' hair in pigtails, boys, their hair closely cropped. Their beautiful bright faces belied the text, which spoke of their impoverished families and the hardship the world economy had wrought on them. I vowed that when this mystery was solved, I would contribute to their cause. Beyond these stories of the needs of these children and the work of the church to clothe, feed, and educate them, at first glance, there was nothing. I made a mental note to send them a check, but I studied the brochures back and front again for some message from Ouida. Well-hidden in the print beneath the address for contributions, there was a handprinted note, which said, "For more information, call me," with Ouida's name and phone number.

The note called no attention to itself. It was directed to me. The woman's behavior when the priest searched the contents of the envelope was now clear. She appeared unsettled, frightened even. Once he secured the materials in the envelope, she had been visibly relieved.

I resolved to call in the evening when she probably reached home. Famished, I searched through the refrigerator for something quick and grabbed the block of cheddar cheese. Uneeda biscuits would be great, I thought, remembering the comforting snacks I had as a child with my grandmother. There were two shelves of teas, chamomile, ginger, hibiscus, jasmine, peppermint, and periwinkle. *I never knew they made tea from periwinkle*, I thought. The door leading from the driveway to the kitchen opened, then closed. "Who's there?" I shouted from inside the pantry, looking for anything I might use as a weapon. No response. There was movement into the kitchen and rustling of papers.

"I said, who's there?" projecting my professorial raised voice I had used in lecture halls, hoping to frighten the intruder.

"Haynes here, Mum. Where are you? Me brought some things from the market."

When I came out of the pantry, Haynes was visibly shaken, clutching a cloth bag filled with groceries.

"Just looking for some tea," I said, placing the box of periwinkle tea on the table.

"So sorry, Mum, if me frighten you." Unpacking her cloth bag, Haynes took out a piece of salted cod fish, a large green bread fruit, and a small brown bag, which held something that I had not seen in a while.

"Are those akees? . . . Haven't seen them in years."

"You know them then. Me bring dem for you to try. You like dem?"

"I was just going to have a late lunch and some tea."

Haynes's gaze fell to the box of tea. "No, Mum, you do not want that tea. That should have been in the other cabinet." Haynes took the box from my hand, searched for a key on her ring, put the box inside the cabinet, and then locked it.

Haynes's action startled me. "Why? Why don't I want to drink that tea?"

"Well, Mum it will make you . . ." she seemed to be searching for the right word, ". . . sleepy. Let me take this on a tray out on the veranda for you." Haynes seemed to be changing the subject; she put the plate on a tray, took out a small cheese knife, cloth napkins, and began to arrange some crackers she took from the cabinet. "Come, you can sit."

"But why did you lock it up? When I have trouble sleeping . . . I could have it instead of the chamomile. It smelled lovely."

"It makes you sleepy, and . . . and it . . . can . . . give you . . . dreams."

"Dreams?"

The woman seemed to search for words. "It open you for receiving . . ."

"Receiving what?"

"It is meant for other purposes. It must be locked up and not taken mistakenly by someone who does not know its powers." Haynes looked annoyed. "I can brew you another tea if you like. Me made you some nice sorrel you mentioned the other day if you does want something cold instead." She took out the tall bottle of dark red liquid. It, too, was a memory from my childhood, although I bought it once in the West Indian market in Flatbush in Brooklyn. It was a fruity, sweet, and tart drink that I loved.

"Actually, the sorrel would be wonderful." Once out on the veranda, the way she changed the subject and misdirected me made me more curious about the periwinkle she didn't want to discuss.

"Haynes, do you know a woman by the name of Ouida Barrows?"

"Yes, she does come to my church."

"Oh, are you Catholic? You attend St. Mary's?"

"No."

"Then this must be another Ouida Barrows. This woman is a Catholic."

"She may say she be Catholic, but she does come to my church," Haynes asserted.

"What church is that?"

Haynes looked away. The woman's eyes seem to search for words. "The meeting hall. It is the church of our people. It's up the hill dere so." She pulled the curtain to the side and pointed to the front of the house.

"I don't see a road."

"No, I was just giving you the direction, you have to walk up . . . dere so to see it. It's called Lowman's Road."

". . . It is not Catholic?"

"No, Mum. Me did the cleaning when you was out. I thought you would be at tea this afternoon. . . . Just brought these t'ings, but me have to get home to my family. Me left some kingfish for later, and rice. Dere's a salad too, unless you want that now . . ."

"Haynes, wait one moment. What kind of church is it?"

"I do not know what you are asking me, Mum. It is our church. You Americans have your churches. We have ours. We does respect the spirits of our ancestors. I don't know what else you want me to call it. Now I have to go." The woman seemed trapped and irritated. "Does Mum want anything else?" She turned and disappeared through the door into the kitchen.

"No, I am fine."

"Den, me see you tomorrow." Her comment seemed to be offered as an afterthought of politeness, forgotten in the awkward exchange. Within minutes, I heard her footsteps on the gravel.

She seemed awfully anxious to get out of here. She never even brought me the sorrel, I thought. I ate a piece of cheese and one of the biscuits. Why was she so reluctant to talk about that church, so defensive? I was well aware of both the Africans and the Caribs having small statues representing family ancestors in their homes. So it wasn't that comment that disturbed me. It was the way the woman bolted from the house on any discussion of the church.

The phone rang, and I thought it was Ouida.

"So, are you finally at home."

"Derek?" The mellow tones of his voice were unmistakable.

"You know my voice."

Given the disturbing day so far, I actually welcomed the banter he offered.

"What have you been up to? Exploring our island? Working hard, nose to the grindstone?"

"A little of both actually. I've been up to St. Mary's. Found some records on my great-great-grandparents."

"So, you should be up for some play tonight. We are having a party at Moon Hole."

"I don't know. I still have some follow-up stuff to do this evening. And I don't think I am in the mood for a party."

"Our parties put you in the mood."

"No, really, I have a few things I am wrestling with. . . . By the way, are you familiar with a church over here near the house I am staying in?"

"No, no more Catholic churches over that way."

"I don't mean a Catholic church. I am not sure of the denomination. Haynes mentioned it and pointed down the road from the house. She said it was a community church or something like that . . . spoke of a connection to ancestors."

There was a long silence.

"You there? Do you know the church I'm speaking of?"

"Yes, I'm here. I think it is a small meeting hall, just a house really, where the people engage in . . . well it is a spirit worship and such. It is definitely not Catholic."

"Is it on Lowman's Road?" I probed.

"Yes. I think they call it the Lowman's Road Church. That is what Haynes may have been talking about."

"I . . . well," I paused, "so there's still a strong belief in magic, spells, and spirits and that sort of thing here in Bequia?"

"Well, for an anthropologist that's an interesting statement."

"What I mean is, is there a large following? Remember my family has been living in the U.S. for most of my life." *My mother kept so much of that from me.*

"A spiritual connection to the ancestors and delving in magic and medicine is woven into the history here in the African and Carib culture."

"I know it is part of the history, here." As I said these words, I realized that the search for information on my family had made me lose sight of the tenets of my training. I had behaved more like a prosecutor with Haynes than an anthropologist.

"People you wouldn't suspect, prominent folks, doctors, lawyers, some Catholics, have their spiritual advisors. Ask your friend the professor. Bailey?"

"I am familiar with the history of the spiritual here. Obeah men and women played an important role in helping defeat slavery by using their potions and spells against plantation owners," I offered.

". . . The British, and the Portuguese and other Europeans . . ." he said.

"I know" I interrupted, ". . . they had their own superstitions and beliefs, too."

"It is a little otherworldly to you Americans. Woooo!"

"Don't do that."

"Just having a bit of a joke with you!"

"I know the history. The African's religious meeting places provided a basis for planning for rebellion. The knowledge of the potions and the medicines from Obeah have been passed down through the years." The locked cabinet and the periwinkle tea in the pantry flashed through my mind. "We have an herb cabinet here with a lock on it."

"They do have guests there, time to time. I guess it is just a safety precaution, locking them up," Derek said. "Come stay in Moon Hole a bit. Come tonight. It will lighten your mood."

"I don't know."

"Maybe I should call my Obeah woman and have her put a spell on you so you can't help yourself but come to me."

"I mean it. Stop it."

"So then, you do have respect for the power they hold over the believers. . . . And for that matter the non-believers," he laughed.

I reached for the amulet I wore around my neck. My aunt's words came back to me. She was quoting my grandmother, "We're gon' haf to teach this girl the craft . . ." I couldn't remember the rest. But I knew it caused part of the falling out between my mother and grandmother. It was at least one reason why my mother packed me up and brought me to the States.

"I'll stop. But I hope that didn't dissuade you from at least considering coming to the party. We work our magic with rum punch, and my intoxicating talk."

My thoughts shifted back to Derek. I wanted to be taken away from this place. Somehow the house, which I had felt so comfortable in, now seemed threatening. I had seen Haynes as my protector—a godsend, that's what I had called her. Suddenly she felt like one more impediment to my understanding of my family's past.

"You there?" he said.

"Huh?"

"I just said, let me take you away. Bring a change of clothes. I should warn you, most of the people here are artists, so they are a little . . . uninhibited."

How did I get roped into staying in this big house anyway? Dr. Gerald Hunter. He had done this.

"Yes, yes. I will come."

"So, I will pick you up at nine."

When I planned this trip, it was supposed to be a freeing experience. Somehow living here has been restricting. Gerald Hunter is running every-thing. It was as if I left my own free will behind when I came to Bequia. That isn't me. I have always been fully in control of my own decisions.

"Hello. You there? Is nine okay? Will it give you the time to finish your work?" Derek asked. His voice insinuated itself into my thoughts again.

"Yes, nine is fine. Frankly, I want to forget all of this for a while."

"Well, Moon Hole is just the place. I will come by car to pick you up."

I checked the time. It was nearly five. I headed through the living room to the bedroom to find something to wear. Heading into the shower, I remembered my call to Ouida Barrows. I went back into the kitchen and fished through the pamphlets and found the one with the woman's number. I didn't want to think or rethink my call. I dialed.

"Good evening. Who may I ask is calling?" The voice on the other end sounded youthful, polite.

"Hello, this is Dr. Jocelyn Kendall. I would like to speak to Ms. Ouida Barrows, please."

"Mummy is not here as yet? May I take your number and a message, please?"

"Perhaps I should call her back. I will not be home later tonight."

"I do expect my mother in rather soon, but if you would like you can call back."

"No, I guess I can leave my number."

"Just a moment then, I need to get a pencil." There was the sound of footsteps, and then a rustle of paper. "Okay then, you said your name was Dr. . . ."

"Dr. Jocelyn Kendall. I think she will know why I am calling."

"Yes, and your number?" There was whispering in the background, and the girl said, "Can you hold please? My mother just got in. She just needs to rest her things." There were muffled voices, and I thought I heard the woman say something about taking the call in the back room. Then I heard a shout to her daughter, "Hyacinth, hang up the receiver. Dr. Kendall I am glad you called."

"Hello, Ouida. I am glad I got you. I think you suggested I call you for more information."

"Well, yes. I think Fr. Silva left you with the wrong impression. What did he tell you, finally?"

"He said that you found two men named Matos, and one was John, and I don't remember the other name, Joseph? He said that the other one was no relation to my great-great-grandfather. And that my great-great-grandfather was wedded in the 1850s and that his child, my great-grand-mother, was christened there at St. Mary's."

"Those things are true, but that's not the whole truth. There are more records. I make no mistakes in my research."

"Don't take the comment by Fr. Silva as criticism, Ms. Barrows. There is no shame in finding two different men with the last name, Matos. If they are not related, you are not to be blamed."

"No, there were not two. There was only the one, your relative."

"I don't understand."

"I want to tell you what I found, but I can't tell you anything unless you promise to keep it secret. You cannot go back and question Father about it." The woman lowered her voice much as she had in the earlier telephone conversations.

"Look, your great-great-grandfather married twice."

"Twice?"

"Yes."

"Who was his first wife?"

"You said your great-great-grandmother was a Carib, right?"

"Yes."

"Well, he married her twice."

"I don't understand."

"I don't either, but a year or so after his first marriage, he had that marriage annulled."

"Annulled?"

"Yes, the priest gave him an annulment. Then the same priest married them again about a year later in the church. And their child Estela was . . . christened there?"

"Yes. Father Silva said she was christened there," I said.

"Yes, but that was only about six months later. She was born two months after the second marriage," she said.

There was silence. I tried to process these facts and make them fit into some understanding of my family. I did not understand why my great-great-grandfather would annul his marriage but then remarry. "I don't understand. But why didn't Father just tell me this?"

"Well, he didn't want to have to explain how the church would do this."

"How did they do this?"

"It seems your great-great-grandfather was a wealthy man. And his money was very powerful with the church.".

Her tone made me summon up the face with the enigmatic expression I had seen in the photo of my great-great-grandmother that my aunt had. Having stepped into her life, I now took on the melancholy I thought I saw in her face, but I did not wish to talk to this woman anymore. "Ms. Barrows, I think I must go."

"Dr. Kendall, please don' tell Father what I have told you."

"No, of course not. But wait. How do you know this?"

"It was all there, not just in the book he showed you. But in the other book, too."

"But he did show me another book with the christening, but nothing else."

"No, Father doesn't want to show you that the priest had his own book of notes, a smaller book, not the big ledger. That little book contained the transactions he had wit' your great-great-grandfather. They don' like folks to know they done such a thing. What can I say?"

"I think Fr. hiding more on you family because he took the book from me once he saw me reading it," she whispered.

"What more?" I asked, realizing my voice was raised.

"Me don' know."

"I need to go. It has been a long day for me."

"Don' trouble yourself about all this. If I find anything, I will tell you. . . . Seen so much of these family secrets in those books."

"Thank you for your time. Ms. Barrows, I need to ask you something unrelated to this."

"Yes?"

"Ms. Barrows, do you know a woman named Haynes?" There was silence on the line.

"Haynes?"

"Yes. Haynes."

"Is that her last name?"

"You know, I'm not sure."

There was a long pause, and the woman started to say something and then stopped.

"She says she knows you from her church up here on Lowman's Road."

"No, she must be mistaken. You know I attend St. Mary's. I must go now. Please do not mention this to Father."

The conversation seemed to present more questions than answers. *What other transactions with my family was the priest hiding?* But the weight of the knowledge about my family pressed on me most of all. I really didn't want to go to Derek's house, but I had to get away from the events of this day. I felt buried in a mournful melancholy that I could not fathom. It was, after all, not my marriage that had been annulled. What must that have done to my great-great-grandmother, and did she even know? My head hurt. In the bathtub, I let the rainwater shower run on my head, to gently wash away my dark thoughts.

Sliding hangers back and forth in my closet, I began to select cloth-ing, choosing deliberately and decidedly to reconnect with the self I had found in Vermont. *Where are my senses? How did I get shut down like this?* My red cotton halter dress and white shell earrings. The dress's material was filmy and somewhat revealing, and I felt it suited my adopted new mood. Refreshed and renewed. I packed my orange swimsuit, a turquoise cotton T-shirt, and white shorts, got made up, combed my hair, and then put on the dress that tied 'round the waist. The full-length mirror behind the closet door framed my image transformed. I spritzed my wrist and neck with Poison perfume. No matter how uninhibited the other guests were, I was ready for an island party.

And once I tossed a couple of toiletries in my bag, I headed out onto the veranda. The last of the sunset had set the floor of the sky's horizon ablaze and left me wondering if my great-great-grandmother had loved the sunset here as much as I did. Or had she been burdened by the power her husband held and her helplessness to control her fate. Perhaps that was the source of the sadness I saw in her eyes in the sepia photograph. Too much time trapped in this house. *I'm not married to anyone. I do not need to be controlled by Gerald Hunter. I can do what I please.* No more sadness for me tonight. I am going to have a nice big glass of rum punch. Hope there is some good music because if there is, I am also going to dance my ass off. I am going to Moon Hole.

Part IV

She has wound it up, caught me in her conjuring. I sense it but have no escape. My will wavers in her wake. These beings she has placed around me do summon me like the siren's song.

18

The phone rang as I was fastening my earrings, and I was expecting to hear Derek's voice. My image, head to toe, came into view as I stepped back from the full-length mirror. The sash on this dress accentuated my waist, and the bodice pushed up my breasts. I looked hot.

"So, how's island life treating you?" Selena's laugh was infectious, and I found myself giggling. "Has it lost its allure? Tied you up?"

"Funny you should say that. Getting out of this house tonight."

"Where to, and with whom? That guy Derek? He's looking for trouble. But then maybe that's what you want."

"Actually, I do . . . can't talk too long. He should be here any minute."

"Where is he taking you? A club? Are there clubs on that little island?"

"A party at his house, that artists' colony I told you about . . . Moon Hole."

"Moon Hole? That's a strange name for a community."

"It's a group of caverns where you can see the moon set through the natural stone archway. All the furniture is made of indigenous trees, whalebones, and shells."

As I shut the overhead fan and lamp, the luminous sea drew my eye. The picture window framed the inky water glittering with moonlight.

The moon was low in the sky and full, a witching moon, its light a shimmering curtain painting the sea's surface with pools of spilled liquid silver.

"Sounds like it will put you in the mood for your work. Whaling and . . . such."

"Right now, I'm actually trying to escape the research about my family tree. Everything I find out is disturbing."

"Disturbing?"

"So hard to explain! It's a long story, and I am feeling trapped in this house."

"Trapped?"

"Yes. I don't know why I let Gerald Hunter make all of my arrangements. That's not like me."

There was a tapping at the door. "Hold on . . . it's Derek." I cupped the receiver and whispered to him, ". . . a friend from New York. . . . Selena, I will get back to you in a day or two."

"Maybe three or four," Derek said in a throaty voice.

"Sounds like he has plans for you." Selena laughed again. "Don't do anything I wouldn't do. Talk about being in trouble. Watch out for that bad boy."

"The car awaits . . . and this is for your hair, beautiful lady," he placed a bright red amaryllis behind my ear.

I took a step back to look at my reflection in the door's windowpane. I did look beautiful.

"Thank you."

I couldn't take my eyes off of Derek. He was only five foot ten or so, but he appeared taller because of his lean, bronze form. His white short-sleeved linen shirt and rolled-up shorts revealed his muscular arms and legs, flexing with each of his movements.

"Who is receiving your guests?" I asked, trying to distract myself from my desire to reach out and touch him.

"My guests? Alex and Cas, good friends, are greeting people. There are folks also going to Alex's dwelling later probably. I had food, drinks, everything set up. This your bag?" Derek grabbed the canvas bag and took my hand, stopping at the top of the stairs. "Careful, it is dark out here." He stopped to look at me, his eyes traveling slowly from my head to my toes. "You look amazing!" He kissed me on the lips, parting them with his tongue.

"Let me put the light on above the door," I said.

"No need. Your eyes will adjust."

"I think I should leave it on."

"I was hoping you wouldn't want to come back here any time soon. Stay a week or so with me in Moon Hole."

Thinking twice about following his suggestion, I decided to go back. *The men here try to control all of my actions as if I have no mind of my own,* I thought. "I don't like to come home to a dark house," I insisted, going back to open the door, turning on the lights to the stairs and the kitchen. "Let's just not get ahead of ourselves!"

"I think that is exactly what we should do, get way ahead of ourselves," he said. The sparring aroused me. I thought he might kiss me again, but he seemed miffed that I didn't follow his directions. Someone was there in the darkness. The embers of a burning cigarette fell to the ground, its sparks flying and then going out. I could see a shadowy movement tamping it out.

"Good evening, Dr. Kendall."

"Cyril! Good evening."

He opened the car door, and we got into the spacious back seat with the bar in front of us.

"Some rum punch?" Derek said, his voice now an aphrodisiac.

"Yes, I could use that."

"At least, you are finally ready for some fun."

"Yes."

"I have begun painting and it's all because of you."

"Really?"

"I have a few sketches that I put on canvas. If you'll stay a few days I can work on one."

"Derek, I don't know if I can stay that long."

"Just sit long enough for me to take some notes and do some plotting."

"Plotting?" I laughed.

"Not that kind of plotting. Though that happens all the time in this mind." He seemed to enjoy my question. "I mean, laying the pose out on the canvas, being sure everything is where I want it."

We drove in silence after that, and I wondered what he was thinking. The car stopped abruptly in the darkness. No sight of caverns there, but as I got out there was music. "That music, is that from your place?"

"Yes, that's Soca. It will get you up and keep you dancing all night long."

Cyril laughed. "Yes, all night long."

We walked down a stone stairway lit by tiki torches, voices bubbling up from below. As we entered his cavern, a golden hue illuminated the room, and the faces of the people were lit with the cast of candlelight. Guests were standing holding drinks, some sitting, heads together chatting, and some sprawled on the floor at the far side of the room, which was covered with red pillows and thick rust-colored rugs. The bar, dining area, and counter were filled with glasses and bottles of alcohol of all shapes. The music was coming from his veranda, where there were folks dancing.

Derek put his hand around my waist and drew me to him as people clustered at the bar seemed to notice him and smile at us both.

"There he is!" one tall, strikingly handsome brown-skinned man bellowed and laughed.

"We wondered when you'd get here." He and Derek embraced.

"Basil, when'd you get back from Jamaica."

"Yesterday. I ran into Alex . . . She said you'd be surprised to see me. Who is this jewel?" he asked, beaming at me.

"Jocelyn, meet Basil. Don't take on anything that he says."

"She's lovely." He kissed my hand.

"She's an anthropologist, and I am hoping will be my next subject. Basil is a musician. He's a charmer . . . plays the guitar. . . . Is that Giselle?" Derek asked, with that *just got caught* look on his face.

Basil grinned, "And she's been asking where you are." I turned to glance in the direction that they were looking.

A woman approached us, rising up on her tiptoes and waving, and calling Derek's name. When she was within a foot or two of us, she threw herself into Derek's arms and wrapped her legs around his waist like they were quite comfortable there.

"I've been waiting! Alex said you would be here soon." She was tall, dark, and coppery, and her hair was in a long ponytail that brushed her behind as she danced in his arms with her legs locked around him. "Giselle, this is Jocelyn," Derek said as he pried her off and placed her on the floor. She turned and eyed me, scanning slowly from my head to my toes, and then back up again. She tossed her head as if she casted off concern and planted an open-mouthed kiss on his lips.

"Did I hear Derek introduce you, Jocelyn? I'm Alex. Holding down the fort a bit." She was another long and lanky woman, with tanned olive skin, wearing red short shorts, with a red shirt tied up under her rather large bust, which spilled out over the top button. She leaned into my ear and whispered, "Not to worry about Giselle. They are long over." She raised her voice, "Giselle your glass is empty, and Jocelyn, you do not yet have one. What would you like?"

"Do you have any rum punch?"

"Are you kidding? Here we are," she said, turning toward the huge crockery with a spout. She took a goblet and placed two ice cubes then turned the spigot and filled the glass with the garnet liquid. "There's more rum over here if you would like."

"No, this is quite good. Thanks."

"I will mix my own," Giselle said, who was positioning herself between Alex and me. "Take me into your studio, show me what you are working on, Derek. I'm planning a small showing to coincide with the music festival in September," Giselle added in her dulcet sultry tones.

"A little later. Saying hello to my guests." He took my hand and guided me into the living room area. All conversations ceased as the women all kissed Derek European style, on both cheeks. Most of the men gave the one-armed clinch embrace. With each new cluster of people, Derek introduced me as an anthropologist doing research here from the U.S. Invariably, the women would step back, scan the length of me, and ask how long I was staying. The men would look at me and back at Derek and share a grin of approval. We wound our way through the living room and out to the veranda. The DJ caught Derek's eye, and laughed with clenched fists, then went back to the vinyl on the turntable. People were dancing, each claiming space and enjoying the beat. A woman with broad hips and short brown hair came toward us. She was short and had gone up on her tiptoes to wave; in a split second, Derek said, "This is my friend who I wanted you to meet. Cas, Cassandra, this is Jocelyn." He kissed her on the lips and then turned to me.

"Cassandra's doing the research I mentioned, on sexual mores." She stroked his arm, then put her hand out to me. I had the distinct feeling that there was something special between Derek and this woman.

"Derek, shhh. This is a party. No work. So, Jocelyn are you enjoying Bequia?"

"It's lovely, and I have been working on something ever since I got here."

"So, it's time to relax. Have you had anything to eat?"

"No, not yet."

"Derek, you haven't fed her." She took me to the dining area. "We have fish cakes over here, some fried plantain. Some conch fritters . . . and . . ." Cassandra handed me a plate. I looked back for Derek and saw the woman, Giselle, talking to him, leaning in to hear him.

"You must try some of this bacalao. Do you like fried plantain?" As I nodded, she would spoon out a bit of salad here, something from a bowl there, or stab some tidbit with a fork and place it on my plate. I looked back again, and Derek was going into one of the other rooms with Giselle. Cassandra brought me out to the terrace near where the people were dancing. We sat at a table where she picked at the small plate she had taken for herself. The terrace opened out to a view of the bejeweled waters, and the yacht lights brightening the night air. Sea breezes caressed my cheeks.

"Giselle shows his work in London and here on the islands," Cassandra said, seeming to read my distraction. Alex sat down with us.

"They are close?" I had to focus because the rum had begun to hit me. "I mean they work closely together . . . you know what I mean."

"Well, she tries." Cassandra laughed, and Alex chimed in. "Whatever they had is now just business. I hear you are moving here from Friendship Bay."

"No. I haven't decided that."

"Derek said you want to do your research from here. . . . You do know we only have *some* electricity. It is wind and solar generated and we have to use batteries at times."

"No, I didn't know that. That might be a problem. No Wi-Fi either, I bet." I laughed, as did Cassandra. "How do you do your work?" I asked.

"The old-fashioned way. I work longhand, and I have a battery pack, and I go into town or the office here to use my computer. I also have someone transcribing my interviews," Cassandra said.

"I have a one-year timeline. That wouldn't work for me. I just wanted a little break, a distraction tonight."

"Derek will distract you. That is for sure. He's very taken with you," Alex said.

"I don't know . . ."

"I'm telling you. Alex and I were telling Giselle the other day. Derek is smitten by you. Since he got back, you're all he talks about."

My cheeks felt hot. "I am sure he's got lots of interests."

"Not now. He has done so many drawings of you," Cassandra said. "And when he does so many drawings, it means he is ready to paint. He hasn't painted in over a year."

Alex leaned in to whisper in Cassandra's ear, looking in the direction of the opening to Derek's studio. "Giselle must've insisted on seeing his work. I wonder if he put away the sketches." She smiled.

"I don't think so. I saw them earlier today, and they were all over the studio."

Cassandra stirred her drink, "Derek is a bit of a rake, but he will put her in her place . . . here she comes."

"She saw them, wouldn't you say?" Alex took a sip of her rum punch and laughed. Derek came out behind Giselle, shrugging his shoulders. She faced him, having a heated exchange, her arms flailing.

Cassandra nodded, "Oh yes. That is a certainty." She covered her mouth, muffling her laugh. Derek's face was intensely focused, and he held Giselle's arm as he spoke to her.

Cassandra pushed her plate away. "Come, let's go dance. Do you dance?"

Derek followed behind Giselle out the cavern exit. Alex spun herself around to the music, and Cassandra moved to the beat of the music from side to side, looking at me. "Don't let this bother you. He thinks of her as a necessary pain. Nothing more."

"It doesn't bother me. He is free, and I am free." My tongue was loosened by the rum.

"Be careful then," Cassandra said.

"Careful of what?"

Alex laughed out loud, "That he doesn't devour you."

"What do you mean?"

Alex and Cassandra locked eyes, sharing knowledge to which I was not privy. "Let's just say that Derek has a huge . . . appetite." Alex spun one time around to the music, and Cassandra laughed. I lost my step and tried to find it again, when I felt arms around my waist. "My three women, all dancing. How lovely!"

My body rejected his comments before I turned them around in my head.

Alex danced a spin around again, and Cassandra danced over to Derek, "Giselle left?"

"You know her . . ." Derek then kissed me on the neck. I shrugged him off and danced, now facing Cassandra.

"You have kept my Jocelyn occupied I see. I hope you haven't divulged any of my secrets."

"I only told her to be careful. She's a fellow researcher," Cassandra said.

"Forget anything they have said about me. Lies, all lies." He tried to take my hand. I pulled it away. The gleam in his eye belied his comment.

"Have they soured you on me?"

"I need another rum punch."

"So do I," Cassandra said.

"What was I drinking anyway?" Alex said, dancing toward the bar. Derek grabbed me by the arm. "Sorry about that dust up with Giselle. I didn't invite her, so I wasn't expecting . . ."

"It doesn't matter to me."

"No, it does matter. I wanted us to start out with a good time."

"Derek, forget it. I am having another drink. I want to dance some more and maybe then you can take me home."

"They *have* soured you on me. They . . ."

"No. This is a nice break, but . . ." *More alive here tonight than I felt in years,* I thought. Derek and his "his women" were enticing. Women were rapt with him.

"Stay the night. Please. You will love it here if you give the place a little time."

"I have a place . . . more suited to my needs." The trapped feelings I had earlier in the day flooded my mind.

"What have you two done? Jocelyn is cross."

"The woman has eyes, Derek," Cassandra said.

"I am not angry," I said, with feigned indifference.

"I told Jocelyn about how many drawings you have made of her. Why don't you take her inside and show them to her," Cassandra said.

"You've probably turned her against my work too."

"No, we both told her how beautiful the drawings were, and that you were no doubt close to beginning to paint," Alex said, handing him his drink.

"You do want to see them, don't you?" Alex said, tugging me by the hand. Behind me, Cassandra pulling Derek was following us.

"I don't need to have someone wrestled in to see my work."

"I am not being wrestled. I want to see."

At the entranceway, Alex pushed me in and turned back to the other room while Cassandra pushed Derek in, saying, "You have some work to do. Bringing her here with so many of your old 'interests' was not smart. We didn't do this. You did."

Though she whispered, I could intuit what she said, reading her thoughts, which came in loud and clear. I spoke directly. "She's right, you know. By the time you worked the room, I ran out of fingers counting your potential old girlfriends." He looked at me, thought for a while, trying to discern how I knew what she said.

"Can't change my past. You can't say I didn't warn you. I mentioned it to you on the plane."

"You did, didn't you. I didn't, however, picture them all still in your life."

"But you have taken up all of my thoughts the last couple of weeks. Look at my work."

Drawings were arrayed on all available wall space. More than there were the last time I was here. Pictures of me everywhere, some with me sleeping, sitting, and one with the flower I was now wearing in my hair. My hands, eyes, breasts, and hips all captured there on paper. There was a full-length nude of me lying in the bed I recognized from the yacht. My breath felt trapped in my upper chest, my face flushed, and its rising heat flooded my cheeks. "You have some imagination!" words tumbling from my lips.

"I took a little license with that one. You are so beautiful. Please stay. I need to put one more drawing on canvas and begin to paint." He came around behind me, his arms resting on my shoulders and his fingers brushing against my breasts. He kissed my neck lightly as my gaze would not leave the drawings of my nude body on the wall.

"Don't. There are people in there."

His touch held an allure I could not escape. He led me into his bedroom.

"I just want to dance."

"So, dance with me." He pulled me further into the room and held me tight against his waist as he moved to the faint sounds of soca. My body could not help but to move with him as he made love to my neck and then lifted my chin to place his lips on mine. He was so skilled that I lost my sense of self in the moment, when I regained my bearings. "What about the party, your guests?"

"What about them? Do you want me to make them go away?"

"Derek, everyone is moving up to my place. Come up later if you want." I could make out Cassandra's voice. The comment made me laugh. "You are a magician!"

"See, problem solved."

"Are your female friends always so obliging?"

"I willed them away. Frankly, Cassandra and Alexandra must know they owe me this one." The impish twinkle in his eye lasted only a few minutes before he began to stroke my arms, pressing so closely that I could feel his desire. He tugged the chain on the overhead fan, stirring a sea breeze. He turned off the kerosene lamp by the bed. The room darkened with only the light from the studio and the shimmering white glow from the terrace.

He caressed my neck and effortlessly untied my halter top, which fell and hung at my waist. So deft was he that I didn't know it had dropped until I felt his hands on my bare breasts. There was nothing I could say or do to protest his exploring fingers, nor did I want to. Then he untied the sash and unwrapped me like a present. My dress fell down around my ankles, and then he kneeled before me and kissed my thighs as he placed me on the bed. Mesmerized, I could not utter a word, nor take in a breath. A master magician, he took off my sandals, as he kissed my thighs, my calves, and then my feet. His artful touch held me spellbound as I struggled to remain conscious of his movements, but I was lost in sensation. At some point he was on top of me. He stayed there still, waiting till I accepted him. Then he began to pull away, then waited until I arched my back then curled it to meet him. Again, he pulled away, teasing me, waiting till I pushed myself onto him, taking him fully. "What are you doing to me?"

"Just curious to see how much you wanted me. You were supposed to ask, remember?"

My legs and hips became loose, and as welcoming as I had ever been. An ecstatic cry flew from my lips as I tried to cover my mouth.

His movements slowed. *I remembered this. Déjà vu.*

My body was closing in on itself, and I feared I would break, and I wanted to break. I wanted to feel. He did not stop, kissing my eyes and my palms. Trembling in waves, closing my arms around him, and holding him as tightly as I could, he slowed. I could not tell how long we were connected.

"I am going to stop. Is that all right?" As lost as I was in him, he was in total control.

Unable to speak, I nodded. Despite the time that had passed, his appetite was not satisfied. *I wondered if he stopped deliberately to study me as his subject.*

My eyes squeezed shut, fearing his expression. In my imaginings, he appeared triumphant, conquest of me in his eyes. "Do you want some water?" he said, his voice low and deep, caring. I shook my head no, surprised by his question, then nodded.

"I thought so," he said.

My eyes opened and widened when I heard his footsteps approach the open archway. His shoulders were wide, and his legs flexed with each step he took. I had been with him before. It was why I had given myself so freely. Those long muscles were familiar.

The wooden floor creaked. I closed my eyes. *There are no wooden floors in this cavern! Where am I?*

Sleep and wake were one! The floors groaned with every step he took. He was as black as the night that enveloped us, and his body glistened in the moonlight. He was holding his shirt in his hand and seemed the warrior who had just finished a spar. "You have finally opened yourself fully to me." The sound of his voice was like a bass drum that pounded my chest, coursing through me and making my body quake.

My cheeks burned. I knew it too. I just did not expect him to say it. "Come to be with me. Leave the Portugee."

"And become a second wife to you? Live with your first wife? How many other women are there, how many others do you take when the night is black, and you can enter their beds unbeknownst to them." My anger, stored up for months, spat at him.

"I did not take. You gave; I never have to take." He smiled, not taking his eyes off mine. "You forget that you left the drape open for me. Remember, I'm the one who comes when you call, when you need my touch, my love." He then strode out of the room.

"Why are you going that way . . . to the front of my house?" My voice was too loud.

"I am leaving."

"Leave through the window."

"This place is now open to me as you are. Your husband left today. He will not return for many phases of the moon. I will come and go as I please. Don't you know now, you belong to me." My breath stopped in my throat.

"The people . . . someone will see."

"You think they do not know?"

"Do not shame me so."

"Come and live with me, and then you do not have to worry about shame."

"Please."

"Jocelyn. What's the matter?"

I looked at Derek but saw only Sumadi. "Leave me alone. Don't do this to me."

"Do what? Wake up. Jocelyn!" He shook my shoulders.

My eyes widened, taking in the man above me, and my answer flew from my lips. "I was dreaming." There in the darkness and the quiet, I knew. They were one.

19

A cool breeze woke me from a filmy curtain of sleep. My eyes slowly took in the room in which I lay. First, a mosquito net hung around the bed, then a gauzy drapery billowed near the veranda; it ballooned and grew full of life, dancing to the wind's whispers. I felt suspended in a chrysalis of my own construction, pieces of myself yet to be knitted together.

Through the layers of pale blue haze, there was the sun just there, out on the stone terrace. The sheets lay lightly on me, a coverlet crumpled in a pile down by my feet, which I pulled up to cover myself. Derek's easel was by the foot of the bed, and I was certain it was not there last night. As I sat up, I could see a table and a platter covered by a silver cloche, a large pitcher of orange juice, and a silver teapot. Framed by the stone archway beyond the veranda, there was the aqua blue, then turquoise, then cobalt sea.

Gathering up the sheets and wrapping them around myself, I wandered toward the sound of movement in the studio.

"Who's there?"

"Who did you expect?"

"I don't know. Some sorcerer who sent people away, and . . ."

"And . . ." He paused waiting to hear what I might say.

"Seduced me last night . . . and why is the easel here?"

"I almost woke you this morning. You looked so delicious, and I was very hungry. I channeled my desire and decided to paint you." His impish eyes twinkled.

"You are too fresh." For the first time, I saw him in his element, wearing cut off jean shorts and a sweatshirt with its sleeves ripped off, streaked with colored pigments. He was standing in front of a large easel, his hands smeared in pale blue paint, wielding a big brush, which he was sweeping over the canvas. The muscles in his arms flexed, passing the brush up and down, and then sweeping it from side to side.

"There's breakfast on the veranda, some fruit, eggs, tea, and biscuits. You must be hungry by now."

"What time is it?"

"About two."

I winced, "This is so not me."

"Sleeping in? You never sleep in? Then I am glad you came." He paused after the comment, looked away a moment, then continued, "It's time you did." This time his gaze was lascivious, gleaming with whatever thoughts were populating his mind.

"I did get a good night's sleep."

"After the bad dream that you had."

"Sometimes I remember them and sometimes they seem to fade away." *The end of this dream shook me.*

"Last night, it seemed to wake you. I couldn't tell if you were terrified or furious. You turned it all on me." His expression was a mix of curious naïf witnessing a forbidden scene, and a devilish voyeur delighting in it.

"You know Derek . . . I'm terribly hungry." I cut him off.

"All I was going to say was, I went to get you some water, and when I came back, it was as if you didn't know me."

He kept probing, but I wasn't going to discuss it with him. Out on the veranda, it was warmer, though not in direct sunlight. There out on the sea was the yacht, deserted I thought. The cavern's ceiling and an overhang shaded its entrance. Uncovering the platter, I found tidbits from the night before—fish cakes, a few deviled eggs, tiny rolls—and my mouth began to water as I sampled the halved eggs. "Perhaps you were not being a gentleman. Like right now, telling me about things that I have absolutely no interest in." The tea was still hot, as I feared my mood would be if he didn't stop asking about my dreams.

"You are right about that. The last thing a woman wants in bed is a gentleman." I heard him, his thoughts if not his words, before. I tried to recall if it was something Sumadi had said. Between the food and the view, I marveled at the changes in my life the last few weeks. I felt alive again.

Derek left the room for a while, and when he reentered the bedroom, he was holding a towel and drying his hands, no shirt. He circled in behind me, his movements serpentine as he curled himself around me, delicately placing love pecks across my shoulders. His tongue darted out and grazed me at the crook of my neck, and the sensation penetrated me to my core. With my eyes closed, I simply felt. He sucked my flesh, imprinting a love bite on my shoulder.

"Don't," I said reflexively.

"Why not? This is what I wanted to do this morning." His voice was deep and gravelly. His hands had now found their way beneath the sheets I was clutching.

He wrapped his arms around my waist and let his fingers explore my belly and the fleshy parts of my thighs. "Don't you want to get back in bed?" he asked, as my knees, hidden beneath the table, parted and permitted his entrance.

The sunlight bathed my face.

"Come." His voice spilled into my mind and then my soul. I heard myself say, "It is daylight. Why are you here?"

"Come," he said again.

"I cannot. My husband." Trance-like, as I walked, I felt him stop in his tracks.

He seemed to be turning my words over in his head. "Forget about this husband of yours," he said, his voice annoyed at what I uttered. He took my hand and walked me into the bedroom. He held the nape of my neck. Dazed, I climbed cat-like into the bed, letting the sheet drag and rest on the floor.

"Stay there," he said, his voice now with an edge, holding my hips pulling them to him.

I stopped there on the side of the bed, on my hands and knees. His hands rested on my buttocks, then pulled me back closer to him. Memories filled my mind of my mother pointing out the dogs and horses as they mated, instruction to me for marriage. He mounted me in that manner. Surprised by the sensation, my eyes widened when he entered. I tried to look back, but couldn't see him, only moved as his hands guided. He filled me, then rested himself there against me for a while as if he was learning the depth of my insides. Meeting him, I drew him in, letting him have my body, but also my mind. He seemed to try to climb into me until I could no longer stand the sensation building inside of me, and I screamed his name. When I realized what I had done, I tried to stifle myself, covering my mouth.

"What did you say?"

Something was wrong. My mother said the heat and the passion would take me. The sounds he made behind me excited me so that I bore down on him. Feeling the sensation as he pulled me back to rest my haunches down on him. I turned trying to see him, to beg him not to stop, but he shriveled. I expected to see Sumadi's tall, muscular form, but he was not there. A man was behind me, but it was not John.

Crawling across the bed and crouching on the floor, my body trembled, as I grabbed the sheet, and pulled it in, covering my breasts and shoulders.

"What's wrong?"

As much as I took in his words and focused my gaze on his face, I did not know him.

"Jocelyn . . . what's the matter?" He came at me, and I crouched on the floor, my body shuddering.

"It's me, Derek," he said, trying to quell my fear. My eyes refocused, and my sense of recognition came back.

"Jocelyn, you said the words, 'soo ma dee.' I don't know what that means."

I hid my face behind my hands.

"What is that? Soo ma dee?"

"It's a man's name. Please don't ask me any more questions." I wrapped the sheets more tightly around me.

"You spoke of a husband. Is that your husband? Let me help you," Derek said, reaching out for my hand.

"No. Don't you touch me."

"Do you want something to drink?"

"Just leave me alone."

My senses were heightened. There was a strange dull sounding ring. The intercom.

"I need to answer. Cassandra?" he said.

"Ask her to come down here," I needed her, and she called.

"Can you come down? Jocelyn wants to talk to you. She's having some kind of hallucination, I think," he whispered. Then he said to me, "She will be right down."

The muscles in my stomach began to relax. I could not look at Derek. Shame enshrouded me as I waited for Cassandra. I needed to talk to a woman. Sumadi had invaded my dreams and taken my body. Now Derek had done the same. Both had taken control of me in my sleep, and also in my waking moments. I felt utterly vulnerable. Only another woman would understand that feeling.

"Derek, where are you?" Cassandra's voice washed over me.

"We're in the bedroom."

"What did you do to her?" she questioned Derek with the tone of an inquisitor.

"Well . . . she was dreaming . . . and she seemed to not know me . . ." Derek said, seeming perplexed. He whispered, "We were just having a shag . . . you know."

"What were you doing to her?" Cassandra seemed to be assessing the situation from her position standing at the entryway. I was still on the floor, just trying to stay clear of him.

"From behind . . . you know." Derek looked out of sorts, relieved to have Cassandra there to help.

"Derek, from behind . . . ?" she looked at him her head cocked to the side, and a grimace painted across her lips.

"No, no, not that . . . just . . . you know. Cassandra!" He seemed indignant at her suggestion.

"Did you give her anything . . . drugs of some kind?"

"No."

"Could you leave me . . . leave us alone," I said, locking eyes with Derek.

"Yes, Derek, go take a walk," Cassandra said, her eyes now fixed on me. "Can I help you up onto the bed?"

My brow and upper lip were speckled with sweat. "No. I want to sit in a chair."

"Sure," Cassandra said, seemingly trying to discern what had happened on that bed. Cassandra moved out to the veranda, brought in a rattan chair, and placed it close to me. She helped me up and then tugged the string on the overhead fan. Trying to wrap the sheets more closely around me, I sat on the edge of the chair. The female voice and the touch of her hand, all of this steadied me. A gentle breeze swept in from the veranda.

"So, what's going on?"

Searching the air, trying to figure out where to begin, this question blurted out, "Cassandra, are you familiar with past life regression?"

"Sure. Why?"

"I had one a few weeks ago. I was sure it didn't take. But since I got here, I've had these dreams . . . and they seem to be of people from a long time ago."

"You had a past life regression . . . ?"

"Yes, and these entities are inhabiting my dreams." Tears welled up in my eyes. "I can't control them. And now it seems that Derek reminds me of one of them. I recognized him in the dream."

"He looks like the person in your dream?"

"No. He doesn't look like him at all."

"I don't under . . ."

"He doesn't look like him, but there is just something about him. . . . His way of taking. . . . His way with me. I cannot resist him."

"I'm sorry, I don't quite understand."

"It's embarrassing. I. . . . It's that the guy he reminds me of is not my husband."

"You are married?"

"No. I'm not married . . . in my dream . . ."

"You are married in the past life?" Cassandra asked, nodding. She went out onto the veranda, poured a glass of orange juice, and brought it to me.

"Yes . . ." I took a few sips. "And this man comes into my home. . . . I am so confused. I think I am committing adultery."

"Do you have a sense of when this was? How far back in time did you go?"

"If I am right, and this is my great-great-grandmother, her life, in the 1860s or 70s I think."

"Why do you say you committed adultery?" Her warm brown eyes and fixed gaze showed me no reproach.

"Because the man who comes into my home is not my husband." I shifted in the chair trying to turn my face from her.

"How do you know?" Her voice was filled with curiosity, no blame.

"Because I remember my marriage. I dreamed it, and my husband's gone out to sea, and this man comes into my bedroom. I am so afraid . . . so ashamed."

"Forgive me for asking, but is it you who feels ashamed, or the person who you were back in time?"

"I don't know." My hands started to shake.

Cassandra stroked my arm. "Try and relax. I think the problem is that you are confusing the feelings you have as yourself, now, with the feelings that you have in the other life. And since you can't change the events unfolding, there is no point in feeling guilty. I hope you don't find this question too intrusive, but how do you feel about this lover being in your bed?"

"I don't know. I can't remember. But when I woke up this last time with Derek . . . I felt ashamed."

"What about when you are in the dream?"

"I am afraid it excites. . . . I think I wake myself up before I know how I feel."

"It excites you." Cassandra smiled. "Maybe you wake yourself up because you are afraid of what the past life has to teach you."

I sat silent, trying to sort out my feelings. There was something so erotic about being with Sumadi that I was afraid. I enjoyed the sensation of letting my senses take me away. I couldn't tell Cassandra that. It was hard to admit, even alone with my own thoughts.

"You know, the women in that time had to accommodate the fact that their husbands left them alone for months even years at a time."

"Why are you telling me that?"

"I am just suggesting that maybe in your past life, you enjoyed having him visit you."

"This is my great-great-grandmother, not me."

"Yes, exactly. There is no shame in being excited by a past lover."

"But I'm not."

"Maybe you were."

"Don't say that."

"Derek probably tapped into that part of you."

"Don't say that, and please don't tell him . . . I think I need to get home."

"You know the women of that time were a lot less hung up than we are."

"I have read material about the accommodations whalers and their wives made to their long absences. I know even the men . . . I really need to get home."

"I'll call Derek."

"No."

"He can have his car. . . . What's wrong? Why are you shaking?"

"I'm afraid to go home with him."

"Do you want me to go with you?"

"Would you?"

"Of course. Let me call Derek, and I'll have him call the driver. Get dressed."

Lost in my thoughts about Sumadi and Derek, I had not noticed my nakedness. Now I dressed in silence. Derek called his driver to take me home from the other room. He was a looming presence there. When I finally saw him, he seemed to look through me, and his eyes seemed to see into my soul. He had done nothing I had not welcomed. "You sure you don't want me to take you?" He placed my sandals by the chair. I wished him away.

"Cassandra will be ready in a bit."

"She was great. But I need to get . . ." I fastened my sandal. "She really helped. It's these dreams, not you . . . sorry."

"Sure," he said.

Cassandra and I climbed up the stone stairs out of the cavern and drove in silence to the house.

"I want to suggest something to you," Cassandra said. "Try letting your dream just happen. It is, after all, just a dream. Let it be. Let yourself be."

"But suppose my husband . . . I don't know what . . ."

"You don't know . . . so just be open."

"That scares the shit out of me." I watched Cassandra's expression change from reassuring to quizzical.

"Jocelyn, there's a police car outside your house, and an officer at your door."

20

A tall, dark-skinned man in a khaki-colored uniform turned from the door to face me. "Are you Dr. Jocelyn Kendall?" he asked. "Officer Nigel Walker. Good evening."

"Good evening, Officer," Cassandra offered, when I was too flustered to speak. "Dr. Cassandra Owens. I am living at Moon Hole, and Dr. Kendall was our guest there for the past day or so."

"That explains it then," he said.

"Explains it?" I asked.

"Yes, it seems folks saw you with someone, and you were going in and coming out, back and forth at the door, turning lights on and off the night before last. Then I received a call from the States from an interested party saying you could not be reached," he said.

I pulled out my cell phone to glance at it. There were, in fact, a string of missed messages. "Officer, I'm sorry. I didn't mean to alarm anyone," I said, opening the door.

"You see that the lights were left on, which fueled the notion that you were taken away in the dark of night. I came out to investigate and leave you this note. I was going to give you another twenty-four hours before we investigated further. No need now."

"I can see how this must look." I said.

"She got a little sick last night, and I don't think she checked her phone all evening," Cassandra said. "That's why I thought it best to ride home with her."

"I'd like to just give the place a walkthrough to be on the safe side."

"That's fine! I would feel better knowing . . ."

The officer walked into the dining room. Several feet behind him, Cassandra and I followed. In the bedroom, seeing the clothes on the bed, I gathered them up.

"Sorry about the mess. That's how I left it."

"I can report that everything was found as it was left?"

"I'd love this kind of attention when I get home. Do you work Moon Hole, Officer Walker? That didn't come out right," Cassandra said covering her mouth.

He did not respond. "Well, then, good evening," he said, striding out of the bedroom, down the hallway, and out of the house.

"So, who do you know in the States with that much leverage down here?" Cassandra asked boldly.

I filled the kettle. "I thought my aunt might worry, but no . . . she wouldn't call. . . . Want some tea?" I dug my phone out of my purse. "Dr. Hunter."

"Who is that?" Cassandra said, her eyes wide with interest.

"Dr. Gerald Hunter is the curator at the Whaling Museum in Massachusetts. He's a friend . . . and he suggested this house."

"He's sure keeping tabs on you." Her body language indicated she seemed torn, turning back from the door, wanting to hear more about him. "I can't really stay."

"Maybe you're right." I was enjoying chatting with a woman. I took out the Earl Grey tea.

"St. Vincent police don't check on everyone who stays out overnight."

"Maybe, because I am from the States?"

"No, tourists stay out late all the time. Nope. He's keeping tabs on you. Does Derek know about him?"

"As a matter of fact, he does know. Gerald called the day Derek brought me home from the airport."

Cassandra laughed out loud. "Well, all I have to say is, I wouldn't worry about those dreams you're having. I'd be focused on these two live real men." She laughed again. "Gotta get home."

"This is not me! I don't have men vying over me. These dreams have changed my sense of myself."

"You are really shaken, aren't you?"

"Yes."

"Maybe you're struggling against the lessons of the past. Try to simply give in to the dreams, submit. Theoretically, if you learn the lessons there, it will help make sense of what is going on here." She stood in the doorway. "I really have to go. The driver must be wondering what the hell . . . and if you have any more dreams, just let go. I would love to interview you. This life you have gone back to, your great-great-grandmother you think, seems fascinating and so in tune with my research."

"I don't know if I can do that."

"Have you ever done that trust exercise? Just let yourself fall. Give yourself over to it . . ." Cassandra seemed to pause mid-thought.

Questions filled my mind. No words were spoken. Yet I felt Cassandra answer me, *It will be revealed to you.* Her words were not audible, her thoughts were.

Suppose I cannot handle it, I thought.

Then you will learn. Cassandra's instruction reverberated in my mind. She turned and left. I sat in the quiet, trying to absorb the events of the past day. There was a tapping on the door.

"Who's there?"

"Me, Cassandra." She handed me a slip of paper with her telephone number scrawled on it. "Call me whenever you need to. Day or night." She walked down the stairs into the wet heat. There was no breeze.

My phone on the table showed five missed calls, all from the 617 area code in Boston. They were definitely from Gerald. Cassandra was right about him paying acute attention to me. I didn't know whether to be annoyed or amused.

Without thinking, I tapped my iPhone to call him back. As soon as the phone rang, the muscles in my throat tightened, fearing how he would react to me. I wanted to hang up, but couldn't.

"Jocelyn. Is that you? Are you alright?" His voice felt like balm. "Where were you?"

"I was at Moon Hole. I'm fine now. I had a bit of a stomach thing." I opened the tea wrapper and put a bag in the cup.

"At Moon Hole?" There was silence.

"I went to a party there." As I said those words, I realized I was teasing him. I wanted his full attention.

"Someone said there was an altercation at the house, an argument or something. There was some back and forth as if you didn't want to leave but were pulled away."

"No, it wasn't like that. Who told you that?" My face got hot. "Never mind, I'm fine."

"You are on a small island, Jocelyn. People see things, and they talk." There was the silence again.

"Anyway, as long as you are all right." He was quiet. His words tied me up, but his silence was even more binding. The restriction felt oddly comforting. I was corseted and felt as if my breath was trapped in my throat.

"My new friend Cassandra Owen came home with me."

"Don't know her."

"Dr. Cassandra Owen, Ph.D., a psychologist, here from England doing research on sexual mores of women in the Caribbean."

He went mute again. "By the way, I am coming down to Bequia sooner than I thought. Taking my vacation early."

"When?" I adjusted myself in the chair, to ease the spontaneous excitement that struck my center.

"That will be a surprise. I have been thinking of it a while." His voice churned my insides. "Not to worry. I will see you sometime early in the week."

"When . . . ?" But the call was over. It was already Sunday. Did he mean next week or this? I turned the kitchen light off and walked into the bedroom. The warm glow of the dimmed chandelier in the dining room made the house feel warm, as did anticipating his presence. The sky had darkened, and already the moon had painted its cool silver patina on the sea's surface. In the pool of shimmering moonlight sat a boat that seemed much like the yacht I saw the first night that Derek picked me up. I felt him there, looking at me, wondering if he watched me while I was in the kitchen speaking to Gerald. I closed the curtain and went into the bathroom.

Memories of the morning flooded around me. I wanted to hide, but when I glanced up, my image reflected in the mirror above the sink. Again, my appearance surprised me. My face had color, a bright cinnamon, and my cheeks were crimson. And my breasts felt full and taut. My eyes seemed to sparkle.

"I wonder if it is the dreams, or just being in Bequia?" I spoke the question out loud. Somehow Mariel's presence had brought more than visions. She had brought me closer to my senses and my desires, giving me life.

Cassandra's words echoed in my mind. *Submit to the dream and learn from it.* Part of me was afraid to sleep and surrender, and another part of me loved Mariel's youth, her desire. My connections to that part of me had been shamed away. I wasn't sure if it was by my mother, my grandmother, or if Paul's rejection had played a role. Maybe the answers lie in the past life that I had found. Not knowing who I would meet, my question was, who am I becoming? My heart was pounding, yet my breathing was shallow, high in my chest. Trapped between fear and anticipation and a craving to know, I was tired, but not sleepy. There, next to the medicine cabinet, was a bottle of lavender bath oil with a delicately handpainted label that beckoned me. As I poured a pool of it in the bathwater, its bouquet billowed.

Dr. Gerald Hunter is keeping his eyes on me. That voice just fills me up. "Wonder when he's coming," I said out loud. "Hope he's not angry that I went to Moon Hole. He sounded peeved." Breathing deeply, letting the bouquet fill my lungs, I took off my blouse and let it fall on the floor. My toe in, I then sank into the warm water, my head rested against the wall, and I let the vapors take me away.

"Señora?"

I startled, sat up straight, holding the sides of the large upright basin in which I sat out in the yard.

"Señora? You with child?"

Leila pointed to my belly, and I felt what she meant rather than understanding the words exactly. I shook my head no. The woman pointed to my breasts, which were full, and my abdomen swollen.

"Sr. Matos is coming soon." The woman washed my back, scrubbing it too hard, then handed me the sponge, gesturing that I was to clean my opening. The woman shook her head and went to get a cloth for me to use to dry myself, waving me to follow her. Dazed, and out of sorts, I followed.

"This child is not my master's." She put my dressing gown on me and pushed me down hard on the stool on the porch. Brushing my hair, pressing the bristles into my scalp, she spoke to me, her voice in a guttural whisper. Finally, I pulled away and went into the house to find a housedress. She grabbed my arm, and in a full-throated voice, spat the words, "Carib Negro." She pointed to the window through which Sumadi came each night. She violently waved her hands at me and at my belly, and I feared she might strike me. Shame poured into my cheeks, setting them aflame.

It was the sound of the water spilling onto the tile floor that startled me. In a haze of chaotic scrambles, I pulled myself up, turned off the faucet, and threw a towel onto the floor.

There was a knocking on the door. "Mistress Jocelyn . . ." Haynes knocked and pushed the door to the bathroom open, slamming it into the wall. The woman backtracked to the hallway and came back in carrying sheets and towels throwing them to the floor.

I stood naked looking into the woman's eyes, searching for the admonishment I expected.

No rebuke came. Haynes ran back to the closet, bringing more linens.

"I must have fallen asleep in the tub."

"Me guess you was tired, Mum."

"I didn't know you were here. But I am so glad. . . . Thank . . ."

She put up her hand, blocking my words. "Me must get a mop. Mum, me heard that Dr. Hunter is coming soon."

"How did you hear that?" I asked, wrapping the towel around my waist and tucking it in across my breasts.

"He does call me when he's coming to the island."

"Do you know when he will be getting here?"

"No, but me guess soon, 'cause he only calls a few days 'fore he gets here."

A chill coursed through my body. I didn't know if it was because of the dream or because of my feeling so exposed in front of Haynes. She knew I was out the weekend before. The woman looked right through me, or so I imagined, and through time to the events of those days. I felt she could see me naked on the bed, Derek behind me.

"Mum, let me clean this up. Why don't you sit on the veranda a bit?"

"Haynes, how did you know about the water."

"Me was in the servant's quarters downstairs . . . tending to things before Dr. Hunter gets to Bequia."

It was disquieting knowing she was there and I didn't know.

"Just rest yourself. If you does fall asleep, me will see you in the mornin'."

"Haynes, this is not like me. I don't fall. . . . I don't let things like this . . ."

"Mum, you doesn't haf to explain nothin' to me. I will wait for you to wake on your own in the mornin'. . . . Let you get your sleep."

Haynes turned off the light. I could hear her mopping the floor and wringing out the mop in the sink. From the bathroom, a swath of golden light painted the dark wooden floor amber.

"Mum, I should open the shutters so you can catch a breeze. We finally got a breeze."

"No. Please don't. Maybe just the overhead fan. Please leave them closed."

Haynes untied the mosquito net. I was afraid to close my eyes. "Give in to the dreams," Cassandra said. *My God, what will these men do to me?*

21

The house shook. The explosive howl of my name battered my mind and riveted my feet to the floor. "MARIEL, COME HERE!" Then sounding like he swallowed his voice, a guttural growl came from his gut, "Where is she? Leila, where is she hiding?"

He flung the door open, crashing it against the wall, as I scrambled under the bed to hide. My breath betrayed me, and he yanked me by my ankles. His cheeks were aflame, and his sea-green eyes were black with anger as he lifted the skirt of my dress, exposing my nakedness. Grabbing the collar, and ripping it down from my shoulders, he stopped and stared at my breasts. His eyes darted to my abdomen, and the shredded garment could not cover me, though I tugged at the pieces. The fury in his eyes made me crouch on the floor in fear, my hands covering my head. The woman, Leila, came and looked in at me, her jaw set. Her eyes accusing as she shut the door.

Then he loosened his belt as sobs escaped my lips, and my eyes implored him for mercy. He pulled me to stand, raising the strap, and brought it down on my buttocks. The sting of it made me cry out. He lifted it again, and although this time his arm hesitated, again he whipped it down. The strike felt weaker than before, and twisting around to look at him, I tried to discern the expression his eyes held. His right fist shook with bound up rage, while his left clutched the strap. His eyes darted 'round the room, stopping at the window, and rested finally on the bed. He cringed and dropped the strap. Pulling my face up to him, he brushed his hand so gently across my brow.

I felt his thoughts. He tried to touch the mixture of guilt and innocence, which I thought he saw in my eyes. *What did you expect me to do, with you gone so long?* He did not strike me again. *You do not know what you have done to me.* His thoughts transferred to my mind, as his hand clenched and then shook with unconsummated rage and anguish. He shouted something in his language, and his eyes became draped with disgrace.

"John, I am yours. Please do not be angry with me. I want only you," I said in my language, holding his leg and stroking it. His body stiffened in anger at first, then he slumped down onto the bed. As I tried to climb up on his lap, his jaw tightened, and he struck my buttocks with his hand, now limp and nearly lifeless. His eyes avoided mine, and I sensed I had strangled and smothered his spirit. His face in my hands, I climbed up on him, kissing his face and his mouth. Pressing my mouth against his braced tight lips, I searched for his tongue, which he had drawn back, keeping it from me until I found it. Then he plunged it into my mouth, filling it.

He pulled my head away to look into my eyes. "You have brought shame to my house," he said. The words he uttered were a mystery to me, but I understood their import and read defeat in his shoulders. The fault was mine.

Ride me, I thought, taking him into my hands, stroking him the way he had taught me. Even through his clothing, I could feel him want me. I opened his trousers, caressed him, and took him into my mouth, letting him grow there. His head fell back, as he supported himself on his elbows. Then his back resting on the mattress, he pulled me up onto the bed beside him. He stood up behind me, pushed my legs apart, and did not care to make me ready. He stunned me as I stretched at the searing, burning entry. Yet I felt I deserved it. I had injured the loving man who had built me a home all my people admired and my family respected.

He began to speak to me in his language. The melody of his voice entered my mind and then my body. I felt myself open and accept his strides. He was so powerful a man, yet he weakened, and lying on the bed, he pulled me atop him and made me ride there. He held my behind and slapped it as he used to do. This time his hand stung my flesh.

"Jocelyn!" There was a knocking at the door. "Jocelyn, are you there? Open up."

"Oh God," I said, my senses still filled with the pleasure and pain, and the musky scent permeating the air.

I could not tell where I was, or what time it was. The shutters blocked the sunlight out. When I shook my head to wake from the dream, I could feel a breach, though benign, that left me feeling a connection to the figure left behind. Wiping the sleep from my eyes, I sat up.

There was the thunderous banging again. The sound echoed through the house.

"Are you sleeping?" Then there was the pounding again.

When I realized I was really hearing a voice, a male voice, and that it was not part of my dream, I tried to focus, grabbing the sheet and pulling back the mosquito net. I bolted through the living room, the dining room, and then the kitchen. The gauzy curtain pushed aside, there he was. I opened the door, and he stepped up onto the last step, closing the door behind him. He shielded me from view, wrapping his arms around me, one carrying a leather satchel. He towered over me. His dark face, first lined with concern, broadened into a lascivious smile. I collapsed into his arms for a moment, feeling I belonged there and all that had been wrong in the dream was righted. Slowly becoming aware of my nakedness, I tried to gather up the sheet and wrap it around myself.

"Gerald!"

"This is more of a welcome than I had wished," he said to my bare bottom, which I strained to cover as I disappeared into the next room. His laugh filled the hallway and followed me into the bedroom.

"I was asleep. You were banging so hard on the door." I grabbed my nightshirt from the closet and threw it over my head. Sitting on the edge of the bed, I tried to compose myself and push my fingers through my hair. When I got back into the kitchen, he was lifting the leather suitcase from the landing. Heat rose in my cheeks as I feigned an aloof pose, my arms crossed and leaning against the doorframe.

"That is how I capture you, startle you from your sleep."

It was as if he knew about my dreams. Yet, as far as I could tell, his eyes held no recognition of the meaning of what he said.

"Is that what that scoundrel did the night he spirited you away?"

His words seemed to deny their meaning. He did not seem at all angry. He simply seemed poised, ready.

"I asked Haynes to leave us to our own devices. Why don't you make me breakfast? I came from the ferry . . . directly." The low tones of his bass voice crept into my ears, encircled my breasts, and inserted themselves into my center.

"I should make you breakfast?" I leaned back, taking in the sight of this strapping man. He placed his messenger bag on the counter, tapped his cell phone, and placed it carefully down. The opened collar of his toffee-colored linen shirt revealed his dark skin, which glistened with moisture.

"I bet an academic like you can't find her way around the kitchen. I want some eggs, and I like them fried. Maybe ham."

"I haven't made one meal since I got here. I don't even know where everything is."

"You are resourceful." Though the top button of his shirt was unbuttoned, he opened two more buttonholes, exposing his smooth, chiseled chest. He reached up and switched on the overhead fan; I could tell he was comfortable in this space. He pushed open the door to the veranda, and backtracked to the refrigerator, taking out a carafe of orange juice. "Let me start you off," he said, taking two stemmed glasses from the cupboard and pouring the juice, handing one to me.

I was bewildered. The breeze brushed my cheeks. "I need to go freshen up."

"No, it's just the two of us. Morning light is beautiful on you."

My cheeks warmed and reddened. An odd sensibility came over me. I wanted to make him breakfast, to serve him. "I am not the domestic type," I said to him through the open door to the veranda, where he was now standing and looking out at the sea. But as I searched the kitchen, finding the frying pan, I unearthed the eggs and the ham deep in the refrigerator.

"You're not?" he laughed. "Then make me some toast too." He laughed some more, and his lilting tones filled me up to the point of bursting.

As I watched the translucent egg white grow opaque and heard the toast pop up, I grew more and more excited. It was not like *having* to make a man breakfast, it was *wanting* to, enjoying his presence nearby.

"Let's eat inside in the dining room," he said as he returned to the kitchen. He paused, and his eyes scanned me from head to toe, taking in my breasts and moving down to my hips. Ever since Vermont, and definitely since Bequia, I had grown less and less self-conscious about my body. In fact, as I felt his eyes on me, I inhaled deeply, feeling my breasts swell. The tips, like hardened pearls, pressed against the white thin cotton nightdress, enjoying being gazed upon.

"Come and bring it to me." His voice was hypnotic. I carried the two plates and utensils and put them on the table. "I think Haynes stores the napkins in there," he gestured to the sideboard top drawer.

Indeed, they were neatly stacked there, and I handed one to him, which he took by the corner, and draped across his lap. His black mustache framed his mouth, which held my attention fixed on his lips, dark and full. I didn't remember how he got here. I wondered if I were dreaming.

He handled his cutlery in the British manner, elegantly cutting a triangle of egg white. "Delicious," he said. "Come, have some." He placed a taste of the egg with the yellow oozing to my lips. He leaned in and kissed me, parting my lips slightly with a gentle sweep of his tongue. I searched but could not find my modesty.

"How have you been enjoying the house?"

"More today than ever." The words spilled from my lips.

"That's good to hear. Some more juice?" he said, holding the glass to my lips.

The phone rang with its peculiar cadence penetrating the air.

He did not respond. "Leave it. Let it ring."

"Suppose it's . . ."

"Who?" he asked, as if he dared me to answer. His brow creased in annoyance.

"My aunt or my friend . . ." I offered.

"Your friend . . ." He lifted his chin, looking me in the eye as if he wanted me to fill in the silence he left.

"Selena . . ."

"She will call back. Let it ring." His voice was firm and unyielding. He cut a piece more of the egg.

"Cassandra, too. Left me a . . . and I . . ."

"You're right," he said, his brow knitted. He went to the phone and lifted the receiver. I put my hand to my mouth. I knew he thought it was Derek. I did too.

"Hello." He stood absolutely still, holding the phone to his ear, but his eyes were glued to me. Nervously tugging the bodice of my nightdress, I started to stand, to get the phone. He raised his hand, his palm clearly telling me not to get up.

"No. . . . No, she is occupied." He paused. "Yes. Yes. No . . . no. No problem at all." He listened intently. "I wouldn't, were I you." He smiled. He put down the receiver, his expression an enigma.

He replaced the napkin on his lap as he sat and cut another triangle of egg white. He frowned as it touched his lips. "Cold."

"I can warm it up, or make you more," I said, wanting to please him.

He pushed the plate away.

I wanted to ask if it was Derek, but I did not dare. Though he never asked, I went into the kitchen to heat the pan, and took out the eggs, and broke two into the skillet. My spine stiffened as I watched the eggs grow opaque. *I am a grown woman. I can please myself without permission.* Though there was a temporary moment of tightness in my arms, I surrendered and threw the old egg into the trash bin. As I walked into the room, carrying the plate, focused on his shoulders, I thought, *Will he strike me?* My thoughts were like sliding doors . . . jumbled. The dreams were intruding into my day.

"What did he say?"

"Who?"

"Derek. What did he say? It was him on the phone."

"He said, he wanted me to tell you he called." He wiped his lips with his napkin.

"Why didn't you?"

"His intentions are not . . ."

"And yours are?" I tried to be coquettish, but the look on his face stopped my tongue. He rose and put the napkin on the table. A look of disgust mixed with disappointment on his face.

"What's the matter?"

"He is using you." The words smacked me in the face. My cheeks stung.

"Just because he is attracted to me . . ."

"No, because that is what he does. All the women who live there with him in Moon Hole. . . . Not everyone is concerned with your best interests." He buttoned his shirt one button.

"You aren't leaving?"

"The day is ruined."

"No. Please don't go." I spoke to his back as he strode over to the kitchen door. I grabbed the amulet dangling between my breasts. It caught his eye.

"Bailey said he saw the marking there."

"Where?" I was confused.

"On the pendant you wear."

"Yes, he said it was a marking of . . ." I removed it, handing it to him, hoping to lure him back and soothe his anger at me. "The Frog Woman." He reached into his satchel and pulled out a loupe, then moved through the kitchen to the veranda into the sunlight. He drew it close to his eye.

"Look at her." His voice was deep with delight.

"It's kind of . . ."

"Explicit. Yes, the Caribs didn't have the guilt and shame some of us carry. Isn't she lovely? The symbol of fertility! That is why she is depicted, knees so fully splayed . . . receptive." He looked up. "You blush?"

I didn't know what to say. My face was warm.

"For an anthropologist you seem a little . . . prudish."

"I am trying not to let that show."

"You are in the Caribbean. We're all kind of conflicted." He smiled partly at me, and it seemed somewhat at himself. "The Carib and African freeness and cultural mores, the European rules and restrictions. We are pulled and pushed, aren't we?" My own body tensed involuntarily. My lips parted. I so wanted to feel his mouth on mine. He seemed to read my defenselessness and laughed out loud.

"Look at you." His hand reached up, and his thumb stroked my bottom lip. "This is why you need someone to protect you. She symbolizes the rainy season," gesturing with the jewel in his other hand. "It has just begun. She is vulnerable."

The sensation surged from my lips down through my body to my essence. His gaze penetrated my soul. I feared he knew what I was thinking. When I looked up at him, I could tell that he did.

"June 21, a little more than a month ago," he said, "was the beginning of the rainy season. . . . You know they say the angry god Hurican is unleashed at this time."

"I've read about Hurican, a Carib god . . ."

"Yes. Named for the devilish winds of hurricane." He put the cord back around my neck and turned back into the kitchen.

"Are you leaving?"

He picked up the phone on the wall and put it in my hand. "Call him. He wants you to call him back. His number is 651. . ."

I pushed it away. "No don't. . . . I don't . . ."

"You can call him. Are you sure you don't want to?"

"Yes." His face was a stern mask that shielded his thoughts. The image of the smile Gerald had at the end of his conversation with Derek haunted me. "But, what else did he say? I saw you smiling."

"That was between him and me." He grew silent again, seeming to be choosing his words. He reached into his pants pocket and took something out. The quiet grew in the room. "Let me make my intentions clear. I do not share." He waited for me to respond. His comment so aroused me that I could not speak. His gaze did not permit me to look away. He handed me the loupe, which he opened. "Look at her."

The magnifier held up to my eye, there she was. The Frog Woman, her knees splayed, was fully exposed. I bit my lip and looked down. The image made me uncomfortable. He lifted my chin, not letting me hide. "If you are with me, you will be revealed only for me." His voice was deep, and his words pointed and probing. Every opening in my body felt his energy push its way in. He looked into my eyes as if he saw what he had done and then paused and straightened the cord that had twisted as the amulet was replaced around my neck.

The heat that came from his body made me ripe with the anticipation of his touch. He was a powerful presence that was offering me openness with protection. I trembled at the thought of it. My vulnerability felt as if it were on display in my eye, on my lips, in the heat of my cheeks, much like the figure carved into the jewel now resting between my breasts. I wanted to be opened by him and for him. I could only hope he read my mind.

"Not to worry." He paused. "Whoever etched the front of the scrimshaw was watchful. We should head into St. Vincent tomorrow," he said, his voice in charge.

"You are leaving?"

"Wear a dress. I will be introducing you to some Kingstown officials. You are in what once was the British West Indies, and despite the fact that St. Vincent is no longer a colony, its guarded African roots and British colonialization make the government officials tend toward the conservative. I want to introduce you to someone who is in charge of birth and marriage records. I will be back here at ten. We should leave before midday."

His expression was now all business. I wanted that other version of him back. But he collected his things and was gone.

22

"Is this conservative enough for you?" Beige linen dress. My caramel-colored lipstick, applied and blotted. The landline rang as I caught sight of Gerald coming in from the veranda, so beautifully handsome, and with a look of approval in his eyes.

"Should I take the call?" *Did I really ask him permission?*

"Of course."

"But suppose it's . . ."

"It's not him," he asserted, surveying me from my head to my toes in my peekaboo high-heeled shoes, the ones I threw in my suitcase yet never expected to wear.

"How do you know?" I asked, my hand gripping the phone, but not lifting it.

"I know." He made a turning indication with his index finger. I made a twirl, looking at him over my shoulder.

A charming voice on the phone said, "Jocelyn Kendall?"

"This is she."

"Jocelyn, this is your Uncle Leland. My older sister, Grace, told me that you were visiting St. Vincent . . . and I take it you have been here a few weeks?!"

"Yes, of course. How are you?"

"I wanted to give you time to settle in and then invite you over to chat." I laughed, remembering my aunt's warning not to let him and his friends chat me up.

"You're laughing. Did I interrupt something? Do you have company?"

"I do have company, but that's not why I. . . . It's just a funny story for when I see you. Never mind. We are heading into St. Vincent actually."

"Might you stop by? I collected a few things from your grandmother's home . . ."

I looked at Gerald, a little unnerved.

"Old drawings, letters, jewelry . . . other things that we had put aside for you when she . . . when she passed. It was sudden." The call caught me off guard, but his voice felt somehow familiar, and the items he mentioned piqued my interest. "Yes, I know."

"We wanted to give them to your mother, but she came and left so quickly."

I cupped the receiver. "Gerald, my Uncle Leland has some things for me . . . asks if I might come by . . . things that were my grandmother's."

"Sure thing. May I get the address from him? I am more familiar with . . ."

"Uncle Leland, a friend is taking me into Kingstown, and he's from here and can . . ."

"Sure. No worries."

"Gerald Hunter here, I can bring Jocelyn around. . . . Yes, I am familiar with Cobblestone Inn. . . . Should take us a couple of hours to get in to see a few people in town. And with the ferry, is two or three too late?" He listened again. "Sure. Great. We'll be there." He handed me the phone, which I placed to my ear in time to hear the click.

"Oh, God. I forgot to ask what he looks like."

"We're going to his home."

"Oh, I thought you said . . . an Inn of some . . ."

"Not to worry. You are with me."

Those words rang true. From the day in his office, our meeting the day before, when he woke me, and to our exchanged smiles as he came in from the veranda, it felt as if we belonged together. I felt deeply comforted.

The road from the house was steep and circuitous; sitting in the front passenger seat was startling. I gripped the armrest and planted my right foot on the floor with each downturn.

"I thought I'd rent a car, once I felt more at home, but . . ."

"There are cars to rent in Bequia, but why should you when you can be chauffeured . . ."

"For the experience . . ." My stomach was in knots.

Gerald laughed at me with a booming, deep-throated sound. "Safer with a reliable driver. . . . Haynes gave you the name I left for you. And I understand Bailey introduced you to one."

"You knew that Bailey . . . Prof. Bailey . . ." I braced both feet as the car descended once again down the steep road. My stomach was left on the top of the hill. "Do you have everyone watching me?"

"Interesting." Gerald turned the wheel, glancing at me briefly.

"What . . . ? Keep your eyes on the road. You're making me nervous." I put one hand on the dash as the car dropped once again. Gerald seemed perfectly at ease driving this steep twisty road. "Interesting, how you worded that."

"What do you mean?"

"It's not what I mean. You *said*, 'Do I have people watching you?' Do you feel you need to be watched?"

There was a clear tone of admonition in his voice. "Why are you asking me that?"

"Just the way you asked the question." He shrugged as he said this, as if there was no other interpretation.

"How else could I have asked?"

"No, you asked what you wanted to ask." He laughed. "Maybe you might have said, "Do I have people watching *out* for you?" His smile cushioned his comment.

"You're parsing words."

"No, just trying to be more accurate."

Our conversation reminded me of our first meeting. He was brilliantly exasperating. Our eyes locked momentarily, and time seemed suspended. Then he looked back at the road. "Watch out!" he shouted, hitting the brakes. A woman was rounding the bend, carrying a huge tray on her head.

"You gonna knock me down, nuh." She planted her feet, and placed her hands on her hips, staring him and the car down.

Gerald pulled over to the side of the road, and shouted back, "You all right old woman?"

"Look what you done to me fruit." The woman glared at him, bending to collect the bananas strewn on the roadway.

"I thought you were good at this," I scolded Gerald with a grin.

"I am. She came out of nowhere."

"Me fine, but how me gonna sell me bananas, bruise like dis?"

"We'll buy them from you," I said, drawn to her, making my way over to the woman "How much for the four . . . akees? We'll take these too. How much? Let me go get my bag," I said, watching the woman as she repositioned the fruit.

"No, don't do that. If you're okay old woman, here," Gerald plucked out two bills from his billfold. "Jocelyn, get back in the car. We'll miss the ferry."

"Me fine," the old woman said, smiling as she eyed the bills, tucking them into her bosom. "T'anks." She looked at me, her black eyes boring right through me, "But you . . . you better take care this path you ride."

"I know this road well enough," Gerald said under his breath, walking toward the car.

"No, de lady," she said, her bony, gnarled forefinger pointing at me. "You better take care of she. . . . Somet'in' be chasing she from the other side," the old woman said, lifting her tray up, placing it back on her head.

"What did you say?"

The woman looked in my direction, though her eyes seemed focused on something through and past me. "You know what me talkin' 'bout." She put her hand up to steady the tray on her head and continued up the road.

"Fruit Lady, here! Fresh bananas, ripe mangos, and akees!" she called out as she walked.

Gerald opened the car door for me, hurrying me into the car. "The old folks still walk this road like there are no cars on it." He got in and began to descend the next hill.

"Did you hear what she said to me?"

"Wouldn't worry about it if I were you."

"But it sounded as if . . ."

"No. She said I should take care of you, and I am here, aren't I? There's the ferry terminal . . . people are boarding. We're headed to St. Vincent. No worries."

But that's what I had now, worries. The old woman worried me. The playful banter I had with Gerald and his sense of protection felt broken. *It's my mother. She's doing this.* Whenever I felt something for a man, she put up roadblocks.

Gerald glanced at his watch as he pulled into the parking spot and grabbed my hand.

There were only about twenty or so people on the upper deck where we sat, shaded by the overhang. The locals took what seemed their favorite places and leaned back to rest their heads. A Rasta man moved past Gerald and sat to his left, his wool-capped head piled high and full of dreadlocks. The ferry's motor rumbled; then the boat glided over the water and the sound faded away. Two tourists taking selfies chattered at the front of the boat. Several people had their eyes closed for naps while the heavy-set woman next to me laughed at some secret shared in a whisper by her friend. "What's good for the goose is good for the gander. And the other way 'round." She laughed, covering her mouth.

"You're deep in thought." His voice seeped into my consciousness.

"Actually, I was wondering where we are headed exactly and asking myself why I didn't ask you that before." Somehow being in his presence made me rely on him in a way that was surprising, unfamiliar.

"You knew you didn't have to. We are headed to the St. Vincent Registry here. The Hall of Records, where birth and marriage documents are kept. I have a friend, Janice Barclay, and she will talk to you about the records kept there in Kingstown. They are in two or three places, the courthouse and the archives, and she's the expert on what to find where. Then we head to your Uncle Leland's house, not that far away."

"That woman upset me with her comment." I do feel like I am being pursued. Thoughts of her began to press on me.

"Don't let that nonsense scare you."

"I think I am getting a headache."

"Rest your head," he said, tapping his shoulder.

Leaning my head against him, I tried not to doze. I did not know how much time had passed, when I thought I heard him say, "We are just arriving at Kingstown. . . . Let's try and get off before. . . . Come."

He reached back for my hand, and as the people filled in around and behind me, I latched on to him, feeling the need to be anchored in this time, this place.

There were snickers. My abdomen was swollen. One woman pointed at me and cupped her mouth as she whispered to the woman next to her. He squeezed my hand and yanked my arm, that felt like it might come out of its socket. There at the longhouse was my father. My mother came running from the other direction. Her face was painted with disgust.

"Mariel, what have you done?" she asked in her tongue. John pushed my hand at her. When I resisted, he threw me to the ground.

"Take her back," he shouted.

"This disgrace was in *your* house," my father said, standing his ground. John screamed something in his language that I did not understand, then grabbed my hand again. My mother's face was lined in pain, while my sister's wore a smirk. The women turned their backs and walked back into the longhouse. John pulled me up, then along the road, back to the house. I thought, *He is taking me back home. He will beat me and then it will be over.* My feet hurt, and my legs were scratched as I walked through the shrubs, my husband not taking the more beaten path. I held my belly, which now ached, fearing the life would drop out of me, and I would crush it with my feet. When we got to the stairs of the veranda, he tossed my hand aside, leaving me to climb the rest of the steps behind him. He turned, his eyes on fire, and slammed the big wooden door in my face. The child balled itself up in my belly, and I felt a sharp pain under my breast.

"John!"

"Are you all right?"

I shook my head and held his arm trying to steady myself.

"What's wrong? Motion sick?" Gerald's face was etched in fear. "Do you want to lie down?" I crouched down on the floor, and a woman began fanning me. "What wrong wit' she?"

"I don't know." Gerald looked anxious, helpless.

". . . feel dizzy and nauseous."

"Bet she pregnant," the woman said, her dark face and dark brown eyes seeming more meddlesome than she should have been of my well-being.

"Jocelyn what's the matter?" Gerald asked. "And who's John?"

23

"Janice Barclay, meet Dr. Jocelyn Kendall," Gerald said.

I guessed she was about forty, dressed conservatively in a navy-blue linen short-sleeved suit. Her hair was straightened and combed in a simple pageboy framing her dark skin. She had a pleasant enough face, but she looked at me askance.

"Hello, Janice, thanks for meeting me."

"Dr. Kendall," her tone dismissive. "Gerald said you needed to find some information . . . you're a researcher. How can I help you?"

"I am trying to find out some information on my family initially."

"What are you looking for, specifically?" Her tone now turned officious, with an unmistakable air of superiority.

"My great-great-grandfather's name was John Matos. He was a whaler. I'd like to learn as much as I can about him. When did he come here? Maybe see crew lists, and then any information you might find about his wife, Maria." Behind the archivist were shelves filled to the ceiling with large leather-bound black binders. This room of the library had a musty odor, and there were people seated at tables, in pairs or individually, poring through large ledger-type books. There was air conditioning, not very strong, but the overhead fan moved the air, keeping the room bearable.

"I am also interested in my great-grandmother. Her name was Estela Matos. I would like to see if you have a marriage record and divorce record for my great-great-grandfather and mother, John and Maria Matos, and a birth record for Estela. And any marriage record for her?"

"Just idle curiosity, then?" she said, scrawling names on the small pad she had in front of her. "I am trying to understand the purpose of the search, so that I will be able to get you the records you want." She glanced up at me, then back at Gerald. I detected a sense of ownership in her eye when she looked at him.

"Well, it is curiosity in a way. My professional work is on families who are connected here and to the U.S., and Boston in particular. But my family history has always interested me."

"Boston?" she looked at Gerald, this time not hiding her designs. He seemed oblivious.

"So, I thought maybe you could help me find out about my own family first, then . . . maybe records where I could . . ."

She cut me off. "When did your family leave the islands for the U.S.?" She rolled her eyes and seemed irritated that I wasn't getting to the point. She looked to Gerald as if to say, *Help me out here.*

"Well, that's the other thing. My grandmother died . . . under circumstances . . . she died here."

"What is her name? She is the most recent and I would guess the easiest record to find. And she died here in St Vincent or in Bequia?"

"Luz . . ."

"What are you saying?"

"Oh, I was just remembering . . . saying her name was Luz. It was when I was a little girl."

"So, you are looking for the date for your family tree or some such."

A man in a tan suit came over to Janice, tapped her on the shoulder, and then whispered something in her ear. "Give me five more minutes here, Dennis," she said.

"I need your input," he said, then nodded at Gerald, and glanced at me.

"I am looking to find the circumstances of her death."

Gerald looked down at me, shocked that this was my interest. "Jocelyn, I don't know if you can find that out here," he said.

"I don't understand," Janice said this time, the irritation punctuating each word.

"What are you saying, Jocelyn? Janice, I had no idea she was searching for something like this," Gerald said in an apologetic tone.

"Well, my mother never said how she died. I never got the whole story."

"Is that what you are asking me? Her last name, please."

"Gonsalves. That's her maiden name. My great-grandfather's surname. I don't know much about him. He's from Mustique, I think."

"Portuguese?"

"No, Cape Verdean I think. I am not sure."

"Do you know the approximate date of her death?"

"I believe it was 1974 or 75. I remember I was about five, maybe six, I can't recall exactly. I forgot to mention, Oliver was her married name. Can't you just look up her name and find it that way?"

"It's not so simple, the records are indexed . . . Never mind." Janice Barclay seemed peeved and looked at Gerald. Now her eyes widened with exasperation.

"Jocelyn, are you looking for your grandmother or your great-grandfather?" Gerald seemed flummoxed, and slightly embarrassed.

"Both . . . I guess."

"It sounds as if you have the whole family tree identified. Are you just looking for dates of when people were born and married? I don't understand." Janice shook her head.

"And my great-great-grandfather, the Portugee. I am trying to put it all together. Something just doesn't feel right about . . ." I began to tremble, and my knees began to buckle. Gerald grabbed my arm and put his arm around my waist to catch me. I knew I was rambling, but I felt unwell.

"She just fainted a while ago at the ferry. She's not feeling well. I think she needs to eat something."

I knew I wasn't presenting myself clearly, but my head was swimming. I felt like I was sitting in the box of a jigsaw puzzle, and there were too many pieces. "There are just a few names I am looking for; can you hand me a piece of paper? I'll write them down."

Gerald supported me as I moved toward the nearest library table. The couple, which was looking at a folder nearest to us, moved over to let me sit.

I wrote as I spoke. "John Matos, whaler. Born in Portugal. Shipping records and whaling records would be helpful. Maria Matos, his wife's marriage records. I am looking for Estela Matos-Gonsalves, and her husband's marriage records. And I am also looking for my grandmother Luz Gonsalves, Gonsalves-Oliver, including the circumstances of her death."

Janice came from behind the counter and stood over me. "I will do my best to find whatever records I can on these people. It may take a week or so."

"Janice, I want to get her something to eat and get something cold to drink."

"Is my uncle's far?"

"Not really. Janice, do you have any cold water."

"I have a bottled water. Should I call you a car?"

"Maybe we should head home. Jocelyn, are you up to this?"

Janice brought two bottles of water. Gerald took one and rested it on the nape of my neck. Janice disappeared again.

"I want to go today. Maybe if I eat something . . ."

Janice reappeared carrying a box and pulled it open. "Some saltines? . . . And take plenty of water. You may be dehydrated. She probably is not accustomed to our heat," she turned to Gerald. "The humidity is high today, and it feels close. They say there is a storm brewing to the east. Might whip into a hurricane and travel this direction by Thursday or Friday. . . . Are you staying in St. Vincent tonight or back to Bequia?"

"That feels good," I said, as Gerald held one of the bottles of water against my forehead.

"We are going to catch the evening ferry," Gerald said.

"By the way, did you hear, they caught a whale this morning off Bequia. They are on island, and will be giving it out in Bequia, Thursday, if the weather isn't too bad. Jocelyn, have you ever tasted whale meat?"

"They are still catching and killing whales?" I shuddered at the thought but felt conflicted.

"There's a limit on what they can catch. As the great-great-granddaughter of a whaler, maybe you should at least give it a taste," Janice said.

"Maybe, but I think with the whale being hunted to extinction now . . . just a little upsetting to me." I knew that the people of Bequia did not hunt whales for sport. They hunted them as an indigenous people, who ate them for their survival, and used the products in their culture. But it still bothered me. My upset stomach couldn't tolerate even the thought of it. "I don't think I can."

"It's an acquired taste," Gerald said.

The phone rang. "Your car is outside," she said. "Keep the box of crackers. I will give you a call, Gerald, when I have located any information for her."

She leaned in and whispered. "I think she is a bit muddled. I will do the best I can."

I heard her thoughts, and wanted to say something, but held my tongue.

"That's my fault, she didn't prepare. I didn't tell her specifically where we were going till this morning. I decided it last minute. Just wanted to get her started learning the records that were here in town and focus her a bit."

"Ring me up for a chat." She said, looking up longingly at him. "You know I'll do the best I can for you."

Reading their whispers, I did not openly respond. But their conversation set off a storm of familiar feelings brewing in my chest. I had no right to jealousy. Gerald was not mine. Mute, I struggled to take ownership of my passions.

24

"Joy!" Leland was a strikingly handsome man with a shock of gray curly hair. He had square shoulders and his skin was smooth, no wrinkles, though he was supposed to be well past sixty. The twinkle in his eye seemed that of a man in his twenties. "Your face is the same," he said. He stood on the veranda and reached out to take my two hands.

I leaned back, not quite pulling away. "Have we met?"

"When you were four."

"I don't remem . . ."

"No, I wouldn't think that you would, Joy. Do come in," his attention turned to Gerald.

"This is Dr. Gerald Hunter. Joy . . . ? You keep calling me Joy."

He shook Gerald's hand. "Doctor Hunter . . ."

"Gerald, please."

"Gerald. I guess your mother didn't let my pet name for you stick. Jocelyn was not you at all. You were a joy, all smiles, and sunshine when you came here. Joy."

"I like that for you, Joy," Gerald said. "I hope you don't feel I am being rude, but Jocelyn fainted earlier, and I think she needs a little something to eat."

The house was comfortable, with cane and basket weave furniture with red thick cushions, a huge conch shell, starfish, and sea dollar on the coffee table with a beautiful white corral branch. All seemed somehow reminiscent of a familiar time long ago. Leland saw me studying the room, "You remember these things. Yes, yes, these were your grandmother's. Your mother left them . . . never answered my calls or letters. Anything you want is yours." A strange sensation of home came over me, standing cloaked in a room of my grandmother's things. A memory drifted in of her holding a conch shell to my ear, and imagining what she called "the endless sea" trapped inside, a whisper just for me.

"Come. My friend baked some bread and made some fish cakes and bakes. Juanita, folks are hungry out here. I will pour you some coconut water, Joy. That should fix you up."

An attractive older woman peeked out from the kitchen, nodded her head and said, "How d'ya do?" Her eyes barely rose, except when she looked at Leland.

She cleared the bowl of mangoes, oranges, and bananas from the dining room table and pulled out straw-woven placemats from the breakfront drawer, placing one in front of Leland, then me and Gerald, none for herself.

"Juanita, stay and join us. This is my grandniece," Leland said with no further explanation.

She quietly turned back to the breakfront and pulled out another mat. She then disappeared into the kitchen. "Bring the coconut water, nuh," Leland said in a commanding tone. She came back bringing a ceramic pitcher on a tray with three glasses. She poured the first glass and handed it to me, then the next, for Gerald. "None for me," Leland said. "Give me that rum punch I made this morning. Rum, Gerald? This punch is made with cream, rum, and sugar. Someone from the States told me it's like your eggnog."

"Thanks. I know it well. I am from St. Vincent originally. Sure, I'll have some."

"You know they call coconut water liquid plasma. Drink it down, Joy. There's plenty. You look as if you could use it." Leland looked through and past me. "There you are!" He got up abruptly and pulled a small picture frame off the wall behind me and laughed as he handed it to me. "See those sunglasses, I bought them for you." This photo of me as a child, my arms extended like a tightrope walker, walking on this low limestone wall, made me smile. "I've never seen this picture."

"That's the Joy I remember," Leland said, gesturing with the pitcher toward the image of me. "She was full of mischief when she arrived," he laughed. "She would hide behind the chaise and jump out." He laughed again.

"When I came?"

"Yes, well your grandmother was not accustomed to having small children around." His eyes grew somber. "She would dress you up like a little china doll . . . No kids to play with. They'd call me the 'imp' because I would play hide and go seek with you when I'd come by. I made ice cream with you with the ice cream churn. Remember that?"

I started to answer, beginning to shake my head no. He laughed again.

"By the time you left, your grandmother had turned you into a little old woman like herself. *You* once told *me* to stop my foolishness. That's what you said, 'Stop your foolishness!' I had to laugh."

The same words I said to my mother. Juanita brought out a platter of codfish cakes and bakes, and then a smaller plate with sliced banana bread. "You liked those as a kid," Leland said, pointing the platter toward me, offering me one, then turning the end of the platter to Gerald.

"Real taste of home," Gerald laughed.

"She was real serious, your grand. Opposite of her mudder."

Next, the woman brought a tray with a stack of plates, cloth napkins, and the clear glass pitcher, rum punch.

"You mean my great-grandmother?"

"Yes her too. Estela. She was a . . . well let's just say she didn't follow any rules."

"You started to say . . ."

"A real rebel. They say she and her mother butted heads all the time. Too much alike."

"Did you know her? You couldn't have known her."

"No, but I heard all the stories." He laughed. "They would talk when they thought I wasn't listening. Too young they thought to understand. Seems your great-great-grand had a past."

"Auntie Grace said her husband tried to tame her."

"She was right about that. But Grace was married and moved to Boston. Either she don't know or she don't remember a t'ing what I'm talking about. You want to know the family secrets, come to Uncle Leland. He tried to tame her, but she tamed him." He laughed, throwing his head back and tipping his chair back on two legs. "Thought you said she was hungry," he said, turning to include Gerald.

"I am," I said, reaching for a bake and biting into it, "Delicious, Juanita." The woman smiled.

"According to her grandnieces, Maria had him smitten from day one. And it took her a while, but she made him come home from sea every six months or so. Seems when your great-great-grandfather was out to sea, she threatened him with leaving him for her lover. She insisted he come home to keep her happy." Gerald and Leland exchanged glances and smiled as if they shared a secret. A reflexive blush warmed my cheeks and made me want to turn away, but the story fixed my gaze on his face as he spoke.

"I don't believe it." *Why did I say this? It was the matter-of-fact way he said it.*

"No seriously, she was a force to be reckoned with. She began little businesses, selling stuff, fruit from her fruit trees, and she grew cotton and cassava, which she sold. She helped them make enough money so he could spend more time at home. She told her grandnieces they should always have their own money. And she told John, he better come home, or she might forget about him. So he hightailed it back every six months, or so they say."

"How do they know she took a lover?" I asked, now drawn to how he saw her.

"Seems it was common knowledge. All the nieces talked about him. Total opposite of John! John was olive-complected, light eyes. Her lover, black as the night."

"No, I don't believe it." My tone was defensive, an obligation to defend my great-great-grandmother blurting from me spontaneously. I remembered how Sumadi broke into her bedroom and took her by force. But I could feel his fingers on my breast as I spoke and realized it wasn't force at all. My feelings were complicated and tainted by desire.

"Look at you. You look like you are trying to protect her, relax," Gerald said.

"I just think this is a lot of gossip, and we don't know what really happened."

"It's an historical fact that many whaling wives had lovers," Gerald said. "You don't have to protect her virtue. I'm sure her husband had lovers too."

Leland spoke up again. "You know, I have something for you. I had saved it for your mother, but when she was here last, she said give it to you. You had more of an interest than she."

"What is it?"

"A trunk full of stuff left by your great-great grandmother. She had left it to Estela, but like I said, the two didn't get on. Then your grand, Luz, she had it. Though I hear she took care to preserve it and pack it up, they say she never opened it again, but who knows. John always brought Mariel beautiful things."

"What kind of things?"

"Things he brought from Portugal mostly, and America. Keepsakes." Leland paused. "A few things, you know things that ladies keep. I didn't look too closely," Leland said, taking a swig of his rum punch. "A friend washed the things, and just folded it up again for you. Didn't want to throw it out till someone looked through it."

"I didn't bring my car on the ferry. Is it heavy?" Gerald asked.

"You see it there." He pointed to the adjoining living room and on the floor was a worn brown leather valise with metal corners. It was about two feet long, and a foot deep. "Not too."

Gerald got up and lifted the leather handle, and though it seemed to have some heft, he was able to lift it with ease.

"It's light enough. I can manage it if you are on your two feet this time. How are you feeling?"

The suitcase transfixed me, and hearing the truth of my great-great-grandmother's affair spoken openly made me fearful that there was something in the trunk that betrayed her secrets. "She was young when she married."

"They say in her late teens. John was in his thirties and away six months or more, a year at a time. . . . Cold bed that long," Leland said.

Gerald took a fish cake and washed it down with rum punch. He and Leland exchanged glances again and laughed out loud.

For a moment I could see the image of Sumadi standing over me, his silhouette walking out the front door. I could feel the glares of the women in the village boring holes in my chest.

"Don't judge her," I said before I could edit myself.

Leland looked at me with a curious glint in his eye, and his head tilted. He seemed to recognize he had touched a nerve.

"I think you are the one judging her," Gerald remarked checking his watch. "This was very common. I think we need to be getting a car to get to the ferry. For an anthropologist, you seem very touchy . . . so sensitive," Gerald admonished.

"It's her great-great-grand . . . she may feel a connection . . . need to protect her virtue . . . no worries. She lived a very long time ago, and t'ings were different, and she and your great-great-grandfather, had a long passionate marriage . . . twenty-five years . . . right up 'til Estela married."

"What happened?" I bit into another bake.

"Nobody know. Maria didn't want it. And she ruled John till this falling out 'tween dem, 'cause she wouldn't go to Estela's wedding." He continued before I could ask. "Why? Nobody know. She na like she husband. Some of the town folk say because he was dark skinned. But me no believe that. Like I said, she lover was black as the night. Nobody never figured it out."

"We have to go or we'll miss the ferry," Gerald said.

"Look at the time . . . I'll drive you. Juanita, pack up some bakes and fish cakes."

She opened a napkin and tied some in it. She handed the sack to me and smiled saying, "Glad you enjoy dem."

Leland opened the trunk, and Gerald put in the valise, got into the car, and looked at me in the rearview mirror. "Me sisters say I don't know when to shut up. Hope I didn't tell you too many secrets. You gotta know it's the islands . . . and the olden days." He looked at Gerald and sucked his teeth. "People haven't changed much, right bredder. They still have their passion. Maria no different."

"What'd you say?" I pretended not to hear him. But his words settled there in my chest. The laughter Leland and Gerald shared when talking about my great-great-grandmother, was lighthearted, not critical. Gerald was right, it was me who was judging her, not them. They accepted her. I had placed so many restrictions on myself as a woman, it was hard to reconcile Mariel's desire. It felt illicit. *My mother's rules.* I had to cast them off.

25

"**M**y phone has four calls. It's Selena."

"Jocelyn where the hell are you? I called a day or so ago, last night, and earlier today. Now I am getting worried."

I hadn't listened to my voicemail for a few days. There was her voice, as full as if she were in the room with us. She barely took a breath and then said, "You need that cute curator guy with the deep bass voice to come take care of you so I can stop worrying." Gerald's eyes focused on the phone, and a huge smile widened on his lips as he pushed the door closed. He looked at me as if he were seeing through me to my soul. I went to silence the phone, but couldn't do it before she said, ". . . And leave that bad boy alone!"

Gerald laughed out loud, "I like her. Who is she?"

"My best friend, Selena."

"Smart woman. She's right, you know."

"That wasn't for your ears," Selena's pet phrase in my head.

"Aren't you going to listen to the rest of the messages?" Gerald asked. "Maybe there's more about the cute curator guy." He tugged at the string that turned on the overhead fan and opened the door to the veranda. A breeze swept through the kitchen.

"No. Don't want you to get a swelled head."

"Then I guess I will head home. I need to close things up . . . with the hurricane warning for tomorrow."

"Already? I thought you'd stay while I opened the valise."

"Tomorrow."

"Yes, but . . ."

"I thought I'd take you out to dinner tomorrow. Given the weather, I think we should stay in. I will come in the afternoon to secure things here. We need to have the dinner you didn't grant me in Boston."

"I thought . . . maybe you'd stay tonight." I didn't know where those words came from. All day I could feel him next to me. I tried to read his expression, but he was an enigma.

"We'll do it my way. Dinner tomorrow."

I wanted to argue but found that there was something hot about his resolve. I could not manipulate him. He took his own direction. It made me want him more.

"Okay, but I thought you would at least stay while I opened the valise, and I surely can't wait till tomorrow. Put it on the table for me. Please."

He must have known I was trying to get him to stay. As I opened it, layers of tissue paper were covering something cream colored and tinged in pink. The rustling sound of the paper did not draw him back; he was already at the door.

"See you tomorrow."

"Please don't." Immediately I knew this belonged to my great-great-grandmother. *Was it the one worn on her wedding day in the dream I had on the first day in Bequia?* It could be a different one, but it was hers.

Maybe it was something in my silence that made him stop. "Is that a corset . . . from the eighteen hundreds? It is so well preserved," he said, as he doubled back. Gently taking the garment in his hands, he closely inspected the weave and the fabric. Then he noted a piece of boning that had risen up and protruded from the top of the corset. He pulled at it.

"What are you doing?"

"Taking this stay out. Seems to be whalebone, no, actually, baleen. This is amazing." Gerald carefully pulled a long stay out of the ribbing of the corset.

"That drawing on it is beautiful."

"Your family took good care of this. It is so perfectly intact," he said.

There was an etching of a woman, bare-breasted and wearing only a cloth across her loins, and then words in a language akin to Spanish. "Do you know what this says? Looks like love . . . *amor* that's love I know, and *sempre,* must be forever like *siempre* in Spanish.

"'*Meu amor, tu será minha para sempre.*' Yes, it's Portuguese," Gerald said. "My love, you will be mine forever. There's another one here." He pulled out another stay on the other side of the corset parallel to the first. "This one would lay under the left breast where her, your great-great-grandmother's heart would have been."

"*Tu é obrigado a mim para sempre,*" I read aloud, phonetically.

"*Obrigado?*"

"You are bound to me forever more," Gerald translated. "He was a passionate man. This is your great-grandfather."

"Yes, my great-great . . . John Matos."

"The John you called out earlier today?"

"Yes, I told you that I was having dreams . . . dreams since I got here . . . it's hard to explain."

"I have to get home to close up that place before the storm. He held up the corset in front of me. Looks like it would fit . . . a bit snug. But they are supposed to be snug, aren't they?" He grinned.

"Should I wear it tomorrow?" The words tumbled from my lips, and I felt myself grow warm from the thought.

"Yes." He turned the garment around.

"I was just kidding. Don't know why I said that." I blushed.

"I was totally serious, actually," he said, turning the garment around. "Looks like you might need some help with this . . . lacing it up. Wait till I get here, and then we'll put it on you and tie it up. You know the intent of corsets, don't you?"

"To cinch the waist."

"It was really about arousal."

"For the man."

"Well, yes, exciting to see the waist cinched in and breasts lifted and exposed . . ." his nostrils flared. "Let's just leave that thought right there.

See you tomorrow at about four. I need to get some sleep. Tomorrow, I want to secure the storm shutters before the storm hits. They say it should arrive around midnight tomorrow. When I finish, we will lace you up." He leaned down to kiss me.

I was miffed at his leaving and turned my head, eluding his lips. "You don't mean that. Do you?" he said.

He glanced down, the corset still held there against me. His eyes seemed to say that he saw me in it. I stood there, mouth open. He smiled, seeming to enjoy making me wait. The interaction felt familiar, yet also brand new. I had always been more reserved, a "good girl," partially because of my upbringing, and because my mother cautioned me away from involvement. Something in me was definitely changing.

He lifted my chin and kissed my parted lips. Then he was gone. Tucked in the corner of the valise, I discovered a small box. It took some forcing to open. An ornate gold ring with a hinged chamber was inside. The latch was too tight to pry open but appeared to be a sculpted house. It was beautiful! Inside the shank there was an inscription in Portuguese. "*Ligados por meu amor.*" *Ligados?* I have to ask Gerald about this tomorrow, I thought. I put the ring back in the box, hid it in the corner of the valise, and reached for the light switch, when there was a knock on the door. *He changed his mind.* My heart began to flutter as I ran-walked to the door. "Who is it?" I said out of habit.

"You know who." I heard the voice and turned the lock at the same time, before I fully registered who it was. It wasn't Gerald.

26

"What are you doing here?" The air felt heavy on my skin.

"Here to give you a present."

"At this hour?"

"Waiting for . . . *him* to leave . . . *I* wouldn't have left you."

"You've been here since . . ."

"Don't be angry with me." He shot a smile at me, his eyes with a charming glint, the same expression from the last night I spent at Moon Hole. Outside behind him, it was pitch black.

"You don't want your present?"

"What present?" He reached down and picked up a large rectangular package on the top step, leaning against the house.

"The portrait I did of you."

The weekend I had spent with him was a blur of images. I searched my mind. No portrait. "I don't remember sitting for . . ."

"Well, it is more of a recline," he said playfully, moving into the kitchen and placing the canvas on top of the valise. It was covered in brown paper and tied with twine that was fastened in a bow. My cheeks flushed.

"A recline?" Memories of his hands on my hips drawing me to him filled my mind. Blending with Sumadi, their images swept in like the sea.

"Derek, you have to go."

"Aren't you going to open it? Maybe I will take it back . . . considering putting it in a show this fall anyway."

"Don't you dare!"

"You haven't seen it yet. It's lovely. Here," he untied the bow and pulled the cord away. Fearing seeing an image of myself exposed, I was unable to move.

He pulled the brown paper away and there he had captured my image, nude, in his bed. Draped in russet sheets, I was leaning against pillows in the bed on his yacht. My breasts were revealed. The heart shaped beauty mark on my left breast was clearly depicted. The look in my eyes was hypnotic. It was as if he captured who I was becoming, what I was feeling inside. No longer the person who left New York, I was becoming someone else. He captured the fire.

I covered the canvas up with the brown paper. "You can't exhibit this."

"Why not?"

Unable to pull my words together, I became aware of my thighs, which grew warm. My bra now seemed to strap me in.

"You said it was a gift." I turned the painting toward the wall. "Derek, get out of here."

"You liked it, didn't you?" He smiled.

"Just get out now, or I will call . . ."

"Your suitor? He's not right for you. You know that. And he has other interests."

"No, I'll call the police. . . . What other interests?"

He laughed. "Call them. They will want to know why you let me in. This is an island remember? And as for his other interests, you'll see." His laughter filled the room this time. "I will go. Why don't you come with me? I am sailing to Barbados to ride the storm out there."

"Just go, Derek."

"You just call when you want me to come get you."

"I won't . . ."

". . . You will. Wait till he goes back to Boston, you will call."

"I will not."

"A cold bed, and you will remember my touch."

"What did you say?"

"You heard me." His eyes now had no glint but were as dark as the black night into which he stepped. Gone. He said *a cold bed.* The same words Leland used about Mariel. Derek's tone reverberated through me, making me shudder.

As I pulled back the curtains to the kitchen window, the lights on his yacht drew my gaze out to sea and down on the beach, I could make him out, wading into the surf, then climbing into the small boat. The motor sounded like a murmur that disappeared into the darkness. There was no moon.

Though it was warm in the house, a chill ran through my body. "Gerald must not know about this." I tied a knot in the twine and searched my mind for a place to hide it. But as I carried it to the bedroom and reached to turn on the lamp, I had this powerful urge to see it one more time. Struggling with the knot, my fingertips burned from the rough cord that fell to the bed. I parted the paper.

There I was. Derek was right. I was lovely. My breasts were beautiful. My left calf was exposed, stretched out from beneath the sheet. Transfixed, I wanted to lift the sheet draped across my thighs, to see more. He captured something in my expression that was at once at peace, and yet on fire. Aroused, I looked away, and then back at the painting. It was as if all of my defenses were stripped away. In the bottom right-hand corner, there was some writing. His signature I thought. I took off my distance glasses and leaned closer to see it better. It was not his name, it said, "Ravished."

I covered the painting with the brown paper, and this time I tied the knot and pulled it tight. I pushed it into the closet, against the wall behind my clothes.

"Gerald can't see this. How could I explain it to him?" My thoughts spilled from my mouth. The closet door was shut tight as I sat on the edge of the bed. It was the first time since I got to Bequia that my waking thoughts felt more frightening than my dreams. The sound of warning haunted and shook me. Derek's words and Sumadi's voice: "You will remember my touch."

27

I slept with no dreams. Slate clouds filled the sky, and the wind had begun to pick up, buffeting the coconut and palm trees, now bent and bowed in surrender. Pieces of debris lifted up and spun about as if possessed.

Gerald hadn't called, and I feared he had changed his mind about coming. I sensed his change of heart. Though I did not yet trust my ability to read his thoughts, yesterday I experienced a connection to him that felt tranquil. Curious and open. Now I picked up a disquieting feeling.

Searching the house for sources of light that were portable, I found flashlights and several kerosene lamps on the pantry floor. I made some tea, which seemed better than coffee for my nerves, and I scrounged the fridge for some cheese and Haynes's bread. While eating, I was setting the lamps on tables in the bedroom and dining room; I charged my phone and laptop. The crank on the louvered window in the bedroom needed some forcing, but I leaned my weight into it, closing it, and finished shutting all of the windows and storm shutters. It felt good to make the house safe on my own.

The valise in the dining room called to me each time I passed it. Gerald's voice played in my mind, telling me he wanted to see me in the corset. I took it out and placed it on the bed. I ran a lavender bath to calm myself. When I got out of the bath, I reached for the phone to call Gerald but stopped. Instead, I willed him to come. My great aunt had called it "using the craft." I called it an energy that I had, along with the eaves-dropping on people's thoughts. Sometimes, just sometimes, I could will them to do things, or just wished something to be, and it was. It didn't always serve me well. Sometimes, at very important junctures in my life, I had no power to make anything happen no matter how I wished things to be different. But I wanted him, and I could not contain that thought.

As I waited for the kettle to whistle, and watched the waves in the sea swell, there was a stillness in the house, an unsettling calm.

Pounding on the door ruptured the silence. It was Gerald, I knew without looking. While holding the opened door, so happy to see him, my stomach tensed. He stood there almost a full minute just looking at my face before coming inside. He was wearing a black T-shirt, and jeans. It was the first time I saw him so casually dressed. But though his outer body appeared relaxed, he seemed to hold a storm within him. Compared to me in my bare feet, he was so tall, and his shoulders and chest so broad, the sight of him stopped my breath. His arms bulged as he lifted the shopping bag he was carrying into the air and onto the counter. His face was lined with what appeared to be contained rage.

"Is everything all right?" I asked, trying to discern what the cryptic expression on his face meant.

"I don't know, is it?" he said, talking first to the air in front of him, then boring a hole in me with his glare.

"I guess . . . found some flashlights, and I was able to close the windows and the shutters."

"You are quite capable on your own, aren't you?" he said, moving around me and looking past me into the dining room.

"What's the matter?"

He backtracked to the kitchen and opened the cabinet, grabbing a platter. "Nothing."

"What can I offer you? Something to drink?"

"Get some . . . two plates, a Coke, and the rum in the liquor cabinet in the dining room, glasses over here . . . some ice." He barked the list at me.

I reached for the shopping bag. "What's in here? It smells good." He pulled it away.

"Just make me a drink first, okay?"

"Gerald, what's the matter?"

"Nothing. Let's get this food out before it gets cold. I don't like eating cold food."

"I could heat it up."

"No." His eyes flashed as he tore the bag. He opened the drawer for the utensils. I had just gotten the glasses from the cabinet when he went into the dining room and grabbed the bottle of rum, poured two fingers high of it, and drank a swig. He poured Coke into the rest of his drink and sat down at the table. His jaw pulsed. I brought in serving spoons and the napkins and sat down adjacent to him. I wanted to touch him, make contact.

He stabbed the fried shrimp with his fork, moving it from the container onto his plate. "I hear you had a guest last night."

All day long, he was all I thought about, couldn't wait to finally feel his touch. I searched my mind for meaning, and for the right words to answer his question. The vise-like pain in my head engraved that relentless crease in my brow. As the cloud of tension cleared, my mind focused. He was talking about Derek.

"Did he stay the night?" He scooped out some rice and peas onto his plate.

"Gerald, he was here maybe ten minutes. How'd you even . . . ?"

"Why'd you let him in?"

Derek said the police would ask me that. I laughed.

"Something's funny?"

"No, I just let him in, because he said he had a gift for me."

"A gift?"

The comment about the painting just slipped out, and now it was too late to divert his attention from it. There was a crack of thunder and the light over the table flickered. My hand shook. "There are some candles in the cabinet behind you," he said.

The candlesticks were right behind the silver candle holders. My hands were trembling, and the candles wouldn't stay in. He took them from me and forced each of the six sticks into the taper cups.

"Are you planning on telling me what the gift was?"

"No!" As soon as I said it, my jaw tightened.

"No?" he laughed, then looked bemused. "Bring me the gift. I want to see it."

"It is a painting, a bad one."

"Go and get it and bring it here."

In the bedroom, seeing the corset set out on the bed sent a heat through me. I pulled out the painting, realizing I wanted him to see it, to know that another man wanted me. Defiantly, I stood it up near the table. He pushed his chair back, lifted up the canvas placing it on the table, and gazed at it.

"He said this was a gift . . . for you?"

"Yes," I said, a mix of sass and shame in my voice.

"He lied."

"I . . . that's what he . . ."

"This painting was a message to me. He was telling me he had you first."

I could not speak.

He was silent a long time. I sat down, this time next to him on the other side of the table. I had lived this before. Maybe not these words, but these feelings, memories.

"It's time to get this out of the way," his words were pointed.

He put up his hand to stop me when I started to respond.

"The past doesn't matter to me. What matters is where you are now, and the future."

"All I can think about is you."

"I do not share. I will not be part of this game he is playing. I will deal with him in due time."

What he meant by that remark was a mystery, but I had to let him know how I longed for him. "I wanted you to stay with me last night. I wanted you in Boston, but I was too afraid. Since you got to Bequia, here the other day, I can't think of anything but you." My desires dripped from my mouth.

A rumble of thunder shook the house.

"Where's the corset?"

"On my bed."

"Go, put it on."

His eyes pierced deep into my soul, setting me on fire. The heat between my thighs was explosive. As I got to the bedroom, the lights began to flicker. I took off my blouse and bra letting my breasts fall free. I loosened the lacings and began to step into the corset, stopped and took off my panties and left them on the floor. I lost my balance and sat down to steady myself. *What is happening to me?* There was a peal of thunder, and the lights went out. A scream was trapped in my chest.

Candlelight entered and warmed the room. Gerald placed the candleholder he carried on the bureau across the room. Now that he was there, I felt exposed. The corset supported my breasts, and my behind was bare.

"Come here," he said, and pulled me to him, then tugged at the lacing that tightened the garment 'round my waist. As it hugged my torso, my breasts grew fuller, yearning for his touch. His hands cupped my bosom, and still behind me, he kissed my shoulders. He swept his hand over the coverlet and patted the bed for me to sit. That quick gesture felt familiar. He pulled his T-shirt up and off, then took off his shorts. In the glow of the candlelight, I could see his chest broad and smoothly hewn. Transfixed by finally seeing his chest and his arms, I did not search the darkness, which hid the rest of him as he moved to the other side of the bed. He stood there gazing at me for a full minute or two, finally taking off his watch and placing it on the night table. He was fully focused on me.

As I lay there waiting for his touch, I could feel my arms tense, and I had turned my thumb into the palm of my hand, which I clenched tightly closed. He took my hand into his, and kissed my clenched fingers, and then released my thumb, "Never clench your thumb like that. It is a sign of fear. Certainly, don't show that to your enemies. But you don't need ever to be afraid of me." His gentle touch made my hand open, gain strength, and as it blossomed, he kissed my opened palms.

He stroked beneath the mound of my breast, leaving the tips to rise in anticipation of his touch, which he did not yet give. The very peaks, hungry for his caress, were now hardened pearls plump with desire. His forefinger traced softly down to my navel and then lower to where my craving was secreted.

He drew me in, knowing me intimately. "Do you know how long I have wanted you?"

Unable to bear my longing, I reached out for him and stroked him as he had taught me, remembering the ways he made me want him. These feelings had been tucked away a long time ago. *They were surely from my dreams. Then, not now.*

Seeing him in the shadows, straddling me, and craving him, I placed him so that he could fill the emptiness. And he delved into me, taking care not to hurt me. By now, all I felt was the need of him, and he knew. I groaned, and he entered me again, and then slowly began to stride. He was like a beautiful stallion, riding, his strides were long and lingering. He filled me into my belly.

As we both learned each other's rhythms, he rode me, and I rode him. I felt that each time he entered me, he sought out a new space that he might seize. My legs wrapped around his waist, and I let him take me on a pounding ride. The thunder sounded, my body quaking.

"I have you," he said.

"Don't leave me."

He slowed his stride, looked into my eyes.

"You are angry with me," I whispered, remembering his expression when he saw my swollen belly.

"*Nao importante,*" he said, pulling my face to him as he kissed my eyes.

"Just don't leave me alone so long. John, I can't be alone so long." I pulled back to look at him, and his green eyes loved me despite the hurt I caused him.

"Remember me," he said, beginning the ride again.

"*Te amo.*" I spoke to him in his language, as my body opened, receiving him. The tears fell and streamed down the sides of my face and rested in my ears. He held my shoulders and probed deeper each time. "Feel me when I am gone."

"Hold me here inside you when I am afar." He rode past joy, to that place where pain and pleasure intertwine. He pierced me deeply, taking possession of my soul.

A scream flew from my chest.

"Jocelyn . . . are you alright?" Gerald's voice entered my consciousness. His dark face above me was no longer angry. He wore a puzzled look. I had gone back in time.

"It has taken so long for you to come back to me," my thoughts took on sound.

I felt he understood. "I won't leave you again." The storm raged outside, and he never tired, claiming the recesses within me, taking full possession of me until my body contracted on him. In one engulfing moment, my body feasted on him in pleasure. Then his head reared back and he exploded into me, filling me with himself; hues of violet, magenta, and turquoise swirled about as stars exploded in my mind. I took him in and squeezed him into my joy.

It was Gerald, not John. But it was as if an orgasm that began so many lifetimes ago had culminated in this beautiful light show within me.

We lay together quietly. The sound of the rain outside filled the room as the waves in me subsided.

"I feel like I have waited for you forever," he said, his voice now echoing my thoughts.

28

A warm veil of sunshine rested on my cheek as my eyelids fluttered open. There was tugging at my back.

"Are you finally getting up?" That magical deep voice continued my awakening.

"What are you doing?" I giggled.

"Trying to loosen this corset and get it off of you . . . for now." He laughed, seemingly at himself, then said, "I don't know if it was my anger yesterday, but that garment seemed to place me back in time. . . . I mean I'd seen them in the museum many times, but it was a turn on. . . . I loosened the lacings some while you were sleeping, but I didn't want to wake you."

His kisses warmed me, and a flush of recalled openness filled my mind. "You felt it too?"

"Sit up, so I can get this off . . ." he said. Then he pulled the lacings loose, one by one. He sucked the flesh on my neck, and then, as I stood up, the garment fall to the floor. My comfort in his touch was as if we had been together for all time.

He pulled me to lie down, and took my right breast into his mouth, holding the left in his cupped hand. My body was so quickly heated by him that I wanted to relive the night before.

The phone rang, jarring us both.

"Shit! Should I get it?" I asked, hoping he would say no, his teeth now teasing my left nipple.

"It's mine," he said, reaching out for the cell phone and glancing at it. "I have to take this."

I wondered who it could be. It was well past noon.

"Not bad. No real damage here. What about there?" He listened.

"You did? . . . How? No, I know." He got up and walked out of the bedroom. He was wearing cutoffs. Although they were so different in stature, John sturdy and barrel-chested, Gerald's body was long and lean. When I looked at Gerald, I sensed John.

"Where?" he whispered, and then he walked into the kitchen, where I could no longer hear him.

Having ended the call, he came back. His eyes searched the air in front of him. I tried to read his thoughts, but it was as if he had lowered a curtain, blocking my senses. My curiosity quickly transformed into suspicion. He looked at me quizzically. Having conjured a female figure, another "sexual interest" as Derek put it, I read his expression as distance. "So, who was that?" Feigning nonchalance, I got out of bed, but my distrust betrayed me.

"Janice," he said, and then became silent again, studying my expression. Now the woman I had created had form.

"She's got a thing for you."

"We go way back . . . friends."

"No, I think she is kind of . . ." I was angry. Taking out a nightshirt, I pulled it over my head.

"Is that jealousy?" He had climbed back into bed and clasped his hands behind his head, a broad grin growing on his face.

"Why else would she be calling you but to find out if you are with me."

"Jealousy means you want someone for yourself . . . alone."

"I'm going to put up some coffee," I escaped the room and his scrutiny, past passions now roiling in my gut.

"Jocelyn, come back here."

"No."

"Do you want to hear what she found about your grandmother's death or not?" he called out behind me. His words a few steps from the doorway.

"She called about me?"

"Yes, it seems she found your grandmother's name in their records."

"What did she tell you?"

"Not much, just that when she died, there was a commotion in town when they found her."

"My mother said the town was in an uproar."

His phone had just received a message. "Janice says there are some newspaper clippings about it online if you want to look. She sent me a link."

Gerald opened all the storm shutters in the living and dining rooms, filling the house with sunshine. Everything from dinner the night before had been cleared away. The sea was calm. There were a few fronds of palm and coconut trees down in the yard, but it was almost as if the storm had never happened.

"Guess the storm wasn't too bad. Doesn't look so terrible out."

"No, the worst of it missed us completely, but did some real damage in Barbados."

"Barbados?" As I filled the coffeepot with water, my hand shook.

"They got the brunt."

He sensed my reaction. The room seemed to grow still. "What's the matter?" he asked, taking out two mugs.

"Nothing." I looked out at the horizon. Maybe he heard that the storm changed direction and decided not to go, I thought.

"He's not there." His head was in the fridge. I couldn't say for sure that I heard his voice. It was more like his thoughts, coming at me with a power I had not felt before. I took the eggs from him, miffed that he wanted me to cook. He took out the skillet.

"Small crafts have been damaged at sea. There has been some loss of life," he said. He seemed to study me, to watch my reaction. He got two plates and poured some orange juice while the sound of the sizzling skillet and frying eggs took my attention.

We ate in silence. I felt his eyes on me. "He got there," he said.

This time I was watching his lips. "How did you know . . . ?"

"Your thoughts are often . . . sometimes I am able to receive them."

"You read my thoughts."

"Not all the time. I just . . . I have always had that ability. Anyway, you are not that difficult to read. Like I said, he's okay, just had some trouble at sea."

"How do you know?"

"Because I caused it. It was a warning." His face was calm, and his jaw firmly planted. He reached for his coffee and drank it down.

"What do you mean?"

"You don't need to know. He knows what *I* mean. He and I have an understanding now." He got up from the table and picked up his plate.

"Look, I wanted us to take some time to get to know each other. Then this wouldn't be so . . . I don't know . . . so surprising," he said. "But I have always had a . . . let's call it a power to get what I want. I try not to use it. Sometimes, when I do use it, I get what I want, but I lose something. Suffice it to say, he pushed me."

"You're kidding." My hand trembled, spilling some of my coffee on the table.

"It shouldn't frighten you. You wear that amulet around your neck because a relative wanted to protect you."

He was right. Without thinking, I clutched it. It was becoming crystal clear that Gerald and Derek had some connection to which I was not privy. These men and I had met before, and this was not the first time that they had battled.

"Come inside with me," he said. He pushed his hand into his cutoff jeans and pulled out a key. And I walked ahead of him to the bedroom.

"No, into *my* room." He unlocked the room that I had passed each day.

"Your bedroom? This *is* your house?"

"Yes."

"Why didn't you tell me this was your house, not a rental?"

"Didn't think you would stay here if you knew."

"I wouldn't have."

"You see. Like I said, you are not that hard to read."

"So, what do you want now? You think you can tell me that you read my mind and have some kind of powers and then get me in bed again?" I was furious, but I did not know if it was at him or myself, because the truth was, I wanted to see his bed, be in his bed, and stay there with him. I had felt this was his home for some time.

"No, my computer is in here, and we can look up the articles Janice mentioned, but we can spend some time in bed instead if you want."

He opened the door fully. The room was pristine except for a pair of carefully folded jeans on a large chocolate-colored leather couch against the far wall. The room was twice the size of mine and seemed as if it had once been two rooms converted to one. Once inside, I saw the bed. It was a mahogany, four-poster with hand-carved columns and crown. It was wider and longer than a king-sized, with bedding the color of black coffee. The mosquito netting was drawn back on either side like a gauzy drapery.

At the far end of the room, there was a six-foot long desk, a rather large monitor and modern keyboard like the one in his office. He powered on the computer and pulled out a folding chair for me. He opened the email, and there were the words, "Here, as promised." The body of the email only held two links. He opened the first. "Death Certificate," with highlights focused on two phrases. The approximate date of her death was June 6, 1975. Suspected cause of death, "Suicide by poisoning."

For some reason, I felt nothing when I read it. Having searched for answers to what had happened to my grandmother for years, now that the mystery was solved, I had no reaction. Gerald put his hand around my waist in comfort, though I felt no need for it. I was numb. Then he opened the second link, which was to the newspaper, *The Vincentian Herald*.

Suicide Shocks Friendship Village

The death of Luz Gonsalves-Oliver disturbed the residents of Friendship Village because they had not seen their neighbor in days. The morning of June 10, the unmistakable odor of death permeated the air around her house. A neighbor called the police, and when they arrived, they searched the premises and found her body already quite decomposed on the kitchen floor. On the table was a cup with the residue of dark liquid, later found to contain the concoction made from poisonous herbs. The woman was known to be an herbalist, who was well aware of the properties of healing herbs, and neighbors speculated that she must have brewed the cocktail that took her life. Neighbors say that in the days before the woman disappeared, she had a violent outburst with several neighbors, when she shouted at them saying, "I am not who you think I am. I am not who I appear to be." She ranted at them and ripped her housedress open, exposing her breasts. The neighbors reported not knowing what she was yelling about. The only unusual thing they saw was that she was wearing two necklaces, one, which appeared to be a scrimshaw, and one heart shaped pendant. Her closest friend ran to get a sheet from her home to cover her and was asking neighbors to help restrain her. But she suddenly appeared calm, saying, "Leave me be," and entered her home quietly. They heard her singing later and thought that she had recovered. Luz Gonsalves was last seen alive on June 6, 1975.

Beneath the article was a photo of Luz. She appeared to be in her thirties. The photo was captioned, "Luz Gonzalves in better times, courtesy of her friend, V. Gomes." The photo was in black and white, but you could see that she was wearing a floral-print dress, pulled in at the waist, revealing a shapely hourglass figure and beautiful legs. Her hair was thick and wavy, and the ringlets fell on her shoulders. I was taken by seeing this picture of her, seeming so alive, and then my eye was drawn to the ornament that fell between her breasts.

I pointed to the screen and began to speak before I knew what I would say, "Is that . . . ?"

Gerald answered before I finished the thought, "I think it is . . ." then tapped a couple of keys that enlarged the photo. And there it was.

It was the pendant that hung on the cord that was draped around my neck. The thought flashed through my mind, and I couldn't help giving voice to it. "It didn't protect her." And there was the second necklace just beneath the first. This one was heart-shaped, and a glimmer of light shone from what appeared to be a crystal locket.

29

"Why did she do it?" Hours had passed and I couldn't rid myself of the image of my grandmother screaming and baring her breast. *What could have made her kill herself?* My feelings that I thought were numbed began to surface. A burgeoning anger was building in me, a rage at both of them. My grandmother and my mother. My mother sent me to live with that old woman, and after all these years of searching for an answer to what killed her, I know now that she did it to herself? My breathing grew shallow, and I looked out to the sea, searching for the serenity that I once found there. When Gerald entered the kitchen, his eyes drew me in. I did not recognize what I saw there.

"I'm still shaken." I blurted, unable to stop my thoughts from squirting out. My hand covered my mouth, not wanting the childish tantrum to display itself in me.

"I know." His voice seemed to reflect not only understanding but more. As I studied Gerald's expression, I learned its meaning. His gaze bathed me in acceptance and compassion.

"You need to let this go for a while." He had been working on the computer, and I tried busying myself, making us sandwiches, which I took out to the veranda, but I barely put the sandwich to my lips. The air grew still, as did the calm flat sea that lay before us. There seemed nothing to say.

"Let it go, babe. Let me cook for you tonight," Gerald offered, putting his arms around my waist as we came back inside.

"You cook? You're just distracting me." My feelings coalesced into a festering annoyance just beneath my skin, leaving me irritated with myself. I recognized the sensations of a child when he or she is angry and has no way to express it. I'd seen them throw their bodies on the floor. When you do not look closely, it seems like defiance. But as you study more closely, there is more. A sense that their frustration is too much to contain. As I suppressed it, I felt not only anger at both of them, but guilt. There must have been a hurt neither my mother nor my grandmother could share, leaving me with the entrails of their pain.

"You know men are the best chefs . . . and I'm from the Caribbean, of course I cook." He laughed. "Let's see what Haynes has in the freezer. Ah, kingfish steaks!" He elbowed his way into the pantry and came out with a box of rice and a bag of pigeon peas.

Gerald was at ease in this kitchen, his concentration focusing on each of his dishes in turn. He squeezed lime on his fish, seasoned it from a special tin, and put his peas to cook. His choices reminded me of the food my grandmother prepared. My mother only cooked West Indian dishes on holidays like Christmas and Thanksgiving. Then she'd bring out big pots for her peas and rice and curried chicken. From time to time, Gerald came up behind me and kissed me on the neck. It was a whole different side of him, yet a side I felt I knew. His affection warmed me to him even more.

"I need to finish something on the computer, while this cooks," he said.

My mind was on my grandmother. My aunt said the talisman was passed down by my great-great-grandmother to my grandmother, Luz. Then the other necklace caught my attention. Its significance was a conundrum: heart-shaped, like it was from a husband, but maybe it wasn't my great-great-grandmother's husband who gave the heart shaped one to her. *Could it be Mariel's lover, Sumadi? Did she think of him as a lover? Would she wear the pair of necklaces to declare her love for both of them?* The pieces of this puzzle manipulated my emotions as I pushed them about.

Where is it? Where is that necklace? I was standing over the valise my uncle gave me. pushing my fingers into its corners when I felt the box I had found yesterday. "Gerald, there was something that I wanted you to translate, and it was on a piece of jewelry that I found!" Before he got to me, I was on my phone searching for the Portuguese word "*ligados*" on the translator. Why didn't I do this yesterday? It was as though I was in a fog the day before, and as the fog lifted, I could think.

"That necklace they wrote about in the article?" he called out to me.

"No, it was a ring."

Feeling around where I thought I put it, I found a small clay bowl wrapped in tissue and then newspaper. The bowl was beautifully painted. Next I felt something a little more pliable, a basket also wrapped in tissue paper, woven in an intricate pattern of light and dark straw. The pieces were much like the artifacts in museum collections of crafts of Indians of South America. I wondered if the clay bowl and the basket were the kinds of things Mariel sold that Uncle Leland mentioned.

My fingers dug under the many packets, searching for the box that held the ring. I also felt for a box or a tissue wrapped piece of jewelry like the heart-shaped pendant. A small stack of letters was off to one corner, and I was careful not to tear the paper, some of which had grown brown and brittle with time.

I felt it! The worn velvet covered box was deep in the corner of the valise, and as soon as I removed the ring, Gerald took it from me.

"Where did they get that?"

"Isn't it extraordinary?"

"If I am correct, this dates back several hundred years." He dug into his pocket and pulled out a loupe to examine the ring, turning it to inspect the hinge and the clasp.

"I think it opens too. I didn't try it the other night. It was a little . . . hard to pry . . . open."

"The gold is so elaborately sculptured. The clasp is intact, and the hinge seems as if it. . . . Where did your family get this?"

"I don't know . . . obviously, it was my grandmother's or my great's, probably my great-great-grandmother's. That makes it almost two hundred years old."

"I think this ring dates back to the sixteenth century, maybe earlier. I could be wrong. These symbols. . . . I'm not certain . . . but I think . . ."

"I wonder if it fits."

"There's one way . . ." Gerald slipped it onto my right ring finger.

"It fits." *It probably wouldn't have a few months ago. I've lost a little weight*, I thought. "But the inscription, it's Portuguese."

"Ligados em amor para sempre." Gerald read aloud.

"Love forever. *'Ligados.'* I just found out, means bound to."

"You are taxing my abilities in Portuguese here, but I am thinking from my Latin from years gone by . . . related to ligature . . . binding . . . tying." He took out his phone and began to type into the tiny keyboard then said, ". . . Let's go inside and use the computer."

He went to the bedroom, holding my hand and tugging me along with him. The giant picture window in his bedroom framed a lovely sunset, but he hardly seemed to notice. "If it means what I think it means when I put it on your finger, we are now married for life." He smiled the broad smile to which I had now grown accustomed. He sipped his drink, a rum and coke, and raised his glass to me.

"Would you stop!"

"Seriously though, we are engaged. I think that is a betrothal ring from the fifteenth or sixteenth century . . . and . . ." He stopped talking and read, yes, ". . . bound together in love forever. The infinitive *ligar* is to join, to be bound, but where in God's name did your great-great-grandfather get this?" The intensity of his focus was exciting.

"Maybe he just bought it," I offered. "A whaler in many different marketplaces . . . around the world."

"I guess . . . but if I am right, these kinds of rings are handed down in families. Let me take a photo. I want to send this to someone at the museum, who has a specialty in this . . . if it is what I think it is."

"What do you think?"

"No, just wait, and let me send it. Don't know if he is still there, but he usually stays late." He snapped a picture of my ring finger with his phone, then opened the gabled roof-like top and took a picture of the symbols inside the bezel. He emailed the image and then began typing so fast I couldn't believe how quickly the letters appeared on the white screen.

"How fast do you type?" I asked.

"Ninety words a minute."

I just watched him and the museum images that filled the screen.

He laughed and lifted my chin to kiss my lips. His tongue brushed and parted my lips. "Gerry, did I catch you at a bad moment?" A voice came from the computer, and the image of a thirty-something-year-old young man with long hair and a beard appeared on the monitor.

"Just momentarily distracted," Gerald said to the screen, "FaceTime," he said to me, pointing to the image and the green dot on his computer, which I realized was a camera. I blushed, realizing that we were being watched.

"Do you know what this is? Where'd you find it?" the young man asked.

"Aaron . . . Aaron Steinfeld this is a friend . . . actually my wife, Dr. Jocelyn Kendall. Well, Dr. Kendall Hunter now." He laughed mischievously.

"Is this the Dr. Kendall you were talking about . . . ?"

"Yes, in Bequia." Gerald cut the young man off mid-sentence.

"And so, congratulations are in order? You got married? Nice to meet you."

My cheeks heated up. This was the most unpredictable man I ever met. He had caught me so completely off guard that I couldn't even argue with him.

"She's speechless, Aaron." He grinned. "But I may be a little premature in saying we are married. Let's just say that we are betrothed, though I haven't actually asked her yet. But is this what I think it is?" He held up my hand to the camera.

"It is. It's a Jewish betrothal ring from somewhere between the fourteenth and seventeenth century. It was probably made around the time of the Inquisition. It was usually worn on the index finger on the right hand, the finger closest to one's heart."

"And the writing . . . ?" I asked.

"That's easy. It is Hebrew. And it means good luck. How on earth did you get this?"

"A long story, and we still have some digging to do, but do me a favor, see if you find anything in our archives like this."

"Probably won't."

"Why?"

"Because the artisans usually made these specifically for a family and . . . well it's just not something that was reproduced. Each one is unique."

"Whatever you can find to date it would be good. By the way, I will be doing a conference call on Monday morning."

"You heard . . ." the man said, and then he laughed.

"I hope to get everything straightened out in a week or so."

"I certainly hope so." He laughed again. "See you then."

The screen went black. Focusing was difficult. My mind was stuck on the word Hebrew.

"Was your great-great-grandfather Jewish?" Gerald took a sip from his drink.

"No, he was Catholic."

"How do you know?"

"This is going to sound crazy, but one of my dreams . . ." I remembered the dream of the day I married John. It was the first time I wore that corset. I remembered I thought I would die because I couldn't breathe. "It was a priest who married us there in front of the house, our house. Oh, and I went to a Catholic church . . . St. Mary's here in Bequia to see some of the marriage records. No, I'm sure."

He shook his head.

"I don't understand."

"These rings were made in the fourteenth and fifteenth centuries and handed down by Jews fleeing persecution during the Inquisition in Portugal and Spain. Some of them converted . . . to Catholicism so they wouldn't be killed."

"In my dream, he was Catholic, but this was much later in the eighteen hundreds."

"But these items weren't usually sold. They were passed down. But by the time he married your great-great-grandmother, his family may have been Catholic for generations," Gerald said.

I searched my mind for clues to corroborate what he said, and there were none. And then I remembered the conversation with Ouida Barrows. "You know when I went to the church to find out about the marriages of my great-great-grandfather, and then my great-grandmother Estela, they first said they had records, but then said they didn't. This woman, Ouida, who worked there, called me. She said that the priest had found something in the private writings, which said that my great-great-grandfather and my great-great-grandmother were married twice. He had the first marriage annulled. Then they remarried and their child, my great-grandmother Estela, was christened some months after the second marriage."

"That's very strange . . ."

"She said the priest didn't want me to know, and she asked me not to ask any him questions about it."

Gerald's eyes searched the air. He turned his gaze to me, "I get it," then shook his head. "What he probably found was that the priest at the time was paid . . . you remember your history . . . Catholics paying indulgences. It went on for hundreds of years." He laughed. "So, what probably happened was he annulled his marriage, came home, impregnated her, and then remarried her. Your great-great-grandfather was a wealthy whaler, so he probably bought the priest, but that in and of itself doesn't give us any evidence that he had converted. We should look through those letters, maybe there is something there."

"Or maybe this ring is his only evidence," I asserted. I began to shiver. I remembered John pushing me away, throwing me onto the wooden porch and leaving me there. Gerald must have noticed it because he reached out for me and drew me into his chest. "What's the matter?"

It was beyond my ability to explain the guilt I felt for betraying my husband. "Nothing. Except I think you are right."

"Jocelyn, look at me."

I could not. I felt such shame. "I think I did something wrong."

"You couldn't. It wasn't you. You are here . . . now."

"It's so confusing. The feelings . . ." My belly was swollen with this second child. I had not permitted Sumadi to touch me this time. I was carrying John's child for sure. My powers had grown within me, as did the child. John had placed this seed, but he looked at me with doubt in his eyes. I could not speak his tongue well enough to let him know it was his, so I gestured—touching my belly and touching his chest. His eyes filled with water, all the months away at the sea, and sadness, maybe he felt it too. My heart sensed his trust now—and, for the first time, he seemed to be fully with me. He held my hands and took me to his bed, and all the while I felt I might not breathe. Tears filled my eyes. He bent down and pulled his trunk from beneath our bed. As he pushed things about, I feared for a moment he was looking for his belt, to beat me. I would have to fight to protect this child. I wanted to run, but I had nowhere to go.

He took my hand in his, and it rested there, clenching my thumb with fear. His touch was so gentle, loving, luring my eyes up to meet his gaze. He still loved me, despite what I had done before, the last time. He placed a gold ring on my hand. It was shaped like a house on the top and was more beautiful than anything I had ever seen. A new beginning for us was possible now. He kissed my lips and took me to his chest, resting my head there.

"So, you think we should consummate this." I was startled. Gerald held me, my head nestled on his chest. I was wearing the beautiful ring. John was gone. I wondered how I could tell Gerald how, in my mind, he and John were the same entity. He wanted to make love to me. But instead, he just held me, as if he knew that was what I needed. The comfort took me back in time to John's touch, his embrace so long ago. Today and yesterday, now so mingled, tangled.

30

When I opened my eyes fully, I found myself in Gerald's bed, much wider than mine. Finally grasping the phone on the third ring, I heard Gerald's voice.

"Good morning," he said. I cupped my hand over the mouthpiece. It was clear that Gerald had taken back his home.

"Gerry, is that you? Welcome home, man."

"Thomas, good to hear your voice."

"I met up with your friend . . . very lovely and smart, though I daresay she's a bit muddled in her work." Prof. Bailey sounded much younger as he chatted with Gerald than when I saw him.

"I took her into St. Vincent the other day to get her research going and introduced her to Janice Barclay. You remember Janice," Gerald said.

"She would be of help to her, but I don't know about putting the two together."

"No worries."

"I felt that your friend was troubled . . . about something."

"We're sorting it out."

"So, is she . . . should I say . . . going to make an honest man out of you?"

"I don't know . . . Jocelyn, *are* you going to make an honest man out of me? She is on . . . she just . . . picked up."

Embarrassment heated my face. The door to the bedroom squeaked open and Gerald came in holding the receiver to his ear with a supercilious smile on his face.

"Yes . . . hello!" I searched for my words. He gestured impishly that I should talk, his thumb and four fingers opening and closing as if inside a hand puppet. "Good morning, Prof. Bailey."

"How have you been enjoying your trip Dr. Kendall? I hope Gerry has been treating you well."

Gerald nodded and pointed to the bed. He drew back the mosquito netting, demonstrating his attentiveness. My cheeks warmed even more shamefully, and I covered my face with the sheet.

"I shared some Bequian food with her the other evening, a day in town . . . seeing relatives."

"I didn't think you had any more living relatives here, Gerry," Prof. Bailey said.

"No, not mine, hers." He gestured to me as if it was my turn to talk.

I cleared my throat. "My uncle, Leland." I sat up and propped the pillows up behind me.

"Nice. This is a good sign, Gerry. She is domesticating you." I raised my eyebrows. Gerald feigned innocence, shrugging, and then grinned, a sexy glint in his eye.

"Of course, the hurricane put a cramp in things," he walked back toward the dining room.

"Well, let me cut to the chase as they say." Professor Bailey said, "I received a message from Vivencia. You remember Vivencia, Dr. Kendall?"

"Of course. Please call me Jocelyn. I was hoping to meet her again to clarify a few . . .

He cut me off. "She sent a message to me, which is very unusual. She said she wanted to see you again. . . . Said she had something to tell you."

". . . Something to tell me . . . ? What?"

"I don't know. She didn't say what it pertained to. I would take you back, but I am off to London for a presentation. Gerry, you still there? I can't be certain, but the person who conveyed this message to me said there seemed to be urgency in her voice when she asked her to bring the message."

"Okay." Gerald handed me a mug of coffee.

"You remember where Vivencia's house is, you take her.'

"Sure."

"And stay with her."

"Of c—"

"I don't know what Vivencia has to say," he cut Gerald off. "Frankly, I don't recall her ever asking me to bring anyone to her like this. . . . Strange. Though it was the day after the hurricane."

". . . That she called?" Gerald asked.

"You know how storms stir the energy up. Anyway, go up there. Dr. Ken . . . Jocelyn, you still there?"

"Yes."

Before I got to say anything more, he cut me off yet again with a, "Cheery bye, then."

"Thomas, Thomas?"

"Yes . . . Gerry?"

"I will be headed to Boston next week. When do you get back from London?"

"Only going to be in London five days."

"Call Jocelyn when I'm away."

"Of course. I want to find out what Vivencia had to say. . . . Got to go now . . ."

"Gerald, you didn't tell me you were going to Boston."

"Just got the call this morning. Negotiations I have to do in person . . ."

"How long will you be gone?" I couldn't breathe.

"I am not sure. This ship restoration project has a lot of moving parts. . . . There are union issues . . ."

"Never mind." I cut him off. I didn't want to hear what he had to say. He was leaving me alone.

"You want to go to Vivencia's today? Before it's too hot?"

"When are you leaving exactly?"

He poured the coffee, "Sunday morning. Why?"

"Maybe I could go . . . with you to Boston."

"That's not a good idea. I will be working odd hours . . . I . . ."

"Forget it. Never mind." I felt *needy*. I was furious with myself. *This is not me*. I sipped the coffee and took a piece of cheese he had on the cutting board. The combination made me nauseous.

"What's wrong?'

"I don't know. I guess I thought you'd be here a while. I was wrong." Feeling dizzy, I sat down and rested my head in my hands. My food was in my throat about to come up.

"You don't look well, maybe we shouldn't go to Vivencia's today," he said.

"My stomach is a little upset. But I want to go."

He went into the pantry and pulled out a box of crackers. "Here, eat some of these biscuits. Leave the coffee," he said, handing me the box with one hand and taking the cup with the other.

"I am a little lightheaded."

"Same as the other day?"

"Sort of."

"We need to get you checked out. Let's get going before it gets too hot."

"I'm fine . . . I'll be fine." I headed into the bathroom to get washed up. "Why would Vivencia want to see me? Professor Bailey said it was 'highly unusual.' Isn't that what he said?" I pulled the strap of my sandal up onto my heel.

"I have always found her enlightening. You should really wear your sneakers with socks and insect repellent. She knows all the history of the island dating back I don't know how long. The Carib's maintaining an oral history is well known, but they say she's also a conduit."

"What do you mean, a *conduit*?" I bent down to look under the bed for my sneakers.

"They are in the closet. This one," Gerald said. "What I mean is just that she's like a . . . portal . . . is how we say it now. . . . She's able to see back many generations when she has the desire."

"How'd you know my sneakers were in there?" Gerald looked at me, shrugged his shoulders as if to say, that was easy.

"I am saying," he raised his voice, projecting it into my room, "people say that she can bring energy from many years ago through, and allow it to speak to us."

"Something's been bothering me since the last visit with her. Skin color . . ."

"Skin color, what?"

"She told me last time that my great-great-grandmother had two, and I think she was implying two husbands, one dark and one light. Not one Black and one White. That's what she said. Prof. Bailey heard it too, and he thought because she said it after looking at the amulet that she meant one White, my great-great-grandfather the Portugee, and the other black, a Black Carib, who he thought drew the other pictograph on the back of the amulet. After all these dreams, and since Uncle Leland's comments, I think that's what she meant."

"I don't think so." Gerald took my straw hat from the clothes rack, sprayed the brim with mosquito repellent, and put it on my head. "You're cute," he said, lifting my chin and kissing my lips. He hadn't touched me since the night with the corset, then the incident with the ring. Once we put it back in the case, he just seemed protective of me, but distant.

"Look, Bailey said so too. Some of my relatives have a thing favoring lighter skin color and so-called 'good hair.'"

"I disagree with both of you. I just don't think that Vivencia would be focused on something so mundane as skin color. I could hear her say the Portugee and the Black Carib, but not necessarily referring to them just in terms of skin color. She said white and black?" He pulled open the top drawer of his chest of drawers, took out a handkerchief, and pushed it into his back pocket. "I think she was talking about their energy. I'll ask her."

"You are going to ask her? Well, don't tell her I said that she thought that. Even Bailey was leery of upsetting her."

We drove almost all the way there in silence. *What does Vivencia want from me?* I wanted to ask her about my grandmother's suicide. What Gerald was thinking was a mystery. It was his work, I guessed, because he was on the computer, writing notes to himself before we left. He was also on the phone with his assistant about his schedule, and the agendas he had planned for several meetings. As he became more and more remote, I realized that his stay in Boston might be longer than I anticipated, despite his promise it could be only a week or so. I couldn't expect him to give up his work for me. His world was there. Planning my work should be my concern, if I could just focus without the intruding thoughts of my family.

When I heard the engine stop, I marveled. Patches of aqua, then green, had rolled past me, but I hardly noticed the steep and winding roads that had frightened me just the week or so before. It was a function of how safe I felt with Gerald. It wasn't only the sex with him that made me feel that way, although being with him was the closest I had ever felt to anyone. Although we had not had sex the last couple of nights, I still felt truly connected, just lying next to him. Being with him helped me understand Mariel, not only her fears of her husband leaving, but also the alienation from her family, and being watched.

I hadn't told Gerald about my flashbacks of John. I didn't want him to think I was crazy. I needed to know if how I felt was just a passing sensation of that evening, born of memories of my dreams, which since then seemed to have abandoned me. But I hoped that he would make love to me one more time before he left.

"You are a million miles away. I turned off the engine minutes ago and have been watching as you drifted into space." His voice, its deep bass tones, flowed into my soul.

"Sorry."

"Where were you? I can sometimes read your thoughts," he laughed, "but today, no. What are you hiding from me?"

"Lots of things." I laughed and started to open the car door, and he came around to open it for me.

He looked puzzled by what I said, then we started up the hill. A black goat kid trotted down the hill, looked at me with its odd rectangular black pupils.

"Tuck that belt in your pants, the goats will try and eat . . . there it goes." The goat bit at it. I laughed to myself, thinking Gerald had lost his magic protective powers.

"Is that Vivencia coming out to the front yard? I don't believe it. I have never seen her do that before," Gerald said under his breath.

The old woman was indeed standing in the front yard, an old bent straw hat on her head. She extended both her hands to Gerald as we reached the top of the hill. Her face, though it was still lined and hollowed out around her eyes, seemed so much brighter.

"Long, long time, Gerald. I knew when I told folks I wanted to see this girl, you'd come. I heard you was here."

As she spoke, I studied her face. When she smiled at Gerald, I realized what was different, her false teeth. She looked ten years younger. I remembered seeing her face, this face, before, but I didn't remember where.

"You could have told them you wanted to see me," Gerald said to her.

"You'd've come in your own sweet time. You men do t'ings in your own time." She winked at me. I detected a sparkle in her eye that I had not seen the last time. "You want some coconut water," she said, turning to him. "This girl always looks like she could use some coconut water." She hooked her arm in Gerald's and then he held her elbow as they went up the steps onto the porch. It was as if her persona had completely changed. She seemed younger by twenty years, flirty even.

"You have some?" Gerald asked, looking back at me with an, *I can't believe this*, look in his eye.

"I have a pitcher full for you."

"How'd you know we were coming today?"

"You know, me know t'ings."

She opened the screen door and held it for him. Gerald stopped, "You want us to come in . . . inside?" He looked back at me, shrugging slightly as if this was a totally out of the ordinary occurrence. When I entered the house, I was shocked. It had been so dark behind the screen door that I imagined it to be untidy and in a state of confusion, but it wasn't. It was small, but it was clean except for a little dust in the corners. It was a bit cluttered, but with colorful ceramic bowls on shelves and mask-like clay sculptures. There were decorative baskets hung on the walls, and baskets with handles nested together in two different corners of the living room. She handed each of us a ceramic cup and went to get the pitcher of coconut water from an old pale-green fridge, which reminded me of the one my grandmother had when I was a child—new back then. Gerald gestured to me with his hand as if he had never seen the inside of her home before. As she poured the drink in Gerald's cup, she said, "So tell me. T'ings okay up there in Boston?"

"Well, a few little problems, but I think I'll get them under control."

"Who's causin' you trouble? You know I can . . ."

"Vivencia, nothing for you to be concerned about. Don't even think. . . . But Jocelyn and I were trying to make heads or tails of something you told her last time you saw her." He was shifting the attention from himself and his problems to me. I was miffed. He knew I didn't want to say this, but she was looking at me now with renewed curiosity.

My cheeks flushed, "Well, I was telling Gerald that you said that my great-great-grandmother had two, one White and one Black . . ."

"She was wondering what you meant," Gerald said.

"You well know what I mean, Gerry, two husbands—one light and one dark, nuh. But dat too simple, it don't say it all. It not the men who was light and dark, it the energy they bound up with, those energies fightin' wit' one another cause so much confusion in what I feel, when I see her last." The old woman sat down opposite me and focused directly into my eyes.

"I thought that's what you meant," he said.

She cut him off saying, ". . . Dat day I did feel it strongly, I know this girl. I mean, I know she grandmother."

"My grandmother? Are you sure? She passed . . ."

"She name Luz. Luz Gonsalves. . . . Well, she married name is Oliver."

"Yes, that's her. How did you know her?"

"We were young girls together here in Bequia, then she go to the States a while." The sequence of events she described was correct.

"You came to visit her. You were a little chile." She took my hand in hers.

"Yes." I didn't remember Vivencia at all from my childhood. But as I looked at her, especially with her teeth in, I had a sense that I had seen her before. Not the last time I visited, but when she was younger.

"Luz was so fill with confusion. I was there the day she take she life."
Now she searched my eyes, both her bony, veined hands held mine.

"Do you know what happened?" I asked.

"No. I ask her, but she tell me it was about she parents."

"What about them?"

"She didn't say. She say she always felt like someone put a spell on
she." She drew her hands away.

"A spell? Why? She say why?"

"She say she jus' feel it, and her grandmother Mariel knew, and tried
to get her to use she magic to make it go away. I try too. Cleanse the
house. Give her herbs to cleanse she body and she mind."

The old woman's eyes searched the air in front of her as she seemed
to travel back to that time.

"In the end, it plagued her. I could not reach her. I gave she some tea to
soothe her and help her to sleep. Then she no come out two days. On the
first mornin' me think she just sleepin' sound. The second, me tell me friend
to check on she. The commotion in town with Crop Over Carnival and
t'ings . . . and me son was sick with a fever, so I forget the time. Nobody did
come till three or four days. She lying there in the heat for almost a week."

I didn't want to cut her off. She was in somewhat of a trance.

"I t'ink I know what she done . . . the tree was right dere in she yard.
She tole me when she was ready . . ." The old woman shook her head as
if she didn't want to see whatever was before her. Then she took my cup
up and poured some more coconut water into it. "She come to me the
other day and tell me about you."

As I lifted the cup, the hair on my arms began to rise up.

"She say, I must try and stop this before it hap—"

She stopped speaking. Her eyes explored the space in front of her.
And then her gaze bored through me. *You must choose the light.* I heard
her say the words, though her lips did not move.

"It start wit' Mariel. But must end with you." She looked at the amulet that hung 'round my neck.

"What must end?" I reached for the amulet. The old woman's eyes
traveled off again. This time, she seemed to search the room, but not

focus on anything in particular. Her eyes darted about in a fury, hunting for something, but finally rested on me.

She say I must go through you. I can come to the answer only through you. I heard her thoughts, but it was not clear if the thoughts were Vivencia's or someone else's.

"I am blind. I cannot see." Suddenly her eyes shut tight.

I froze. The stillness in the room was deafening. I did not know how much of what I heard was audible, and how much was spoken directly to my soul.

"Vivencia, are you alright?" Gerald broke the silence.

Come to Lowman's Church tomorrow night. Be sure to wear the amulet. Her lips did not move. *You hear me girl.*

"Me tired. Must rest meself." The woman held fast to the back of the chair to steady herself and left the room. We sat there for a few minutes, waiting for her to return. Her sudden departure startled me. Gerald nodded toward the door, indicating that we should leave. As we got into the car, he said, "I hoped she would help . . . shed light on your questions . . . but that was . . ." he paused. As he seemed to turn the events of the encounter over in his mind, searching for the right words. I, too, was searching for meaning in what had transpired. I could not find it. He then said only one word, ". . . Odd."

31

He collected papers, clipping them together and placing them in file folders. Sitting on the side of the bed, I was trying not to spill my thoughts and the tears that were right behind my eyelids. It seemed from the amount of paper he accumulated that he'd be in Boston much longer than a week. I would have laughed at my thoughts had I not been so filled with sadness.

"I'm taking the first ferry out in the morning, catching a charter plane from St. Vincent tomorrow morning. Couldn't get one from here." He looked at me for a response. I gave none. I couldn't speak. The time we spent during the last week felt as if we had always been together. At first, I wondered how much of his passion for me connected with his jealousy of Derek. But now, it was as if Derek didn't matter. Gerald had seemed a bit controlling at first, but seeing him at his work, hearing him on his phone calls to the office staff, I understood that this was his way. He noticed the details and took care to attend to them. He was attentive toward me, affectionate. So much like John in the ways he was watchful and protective of me. The thought of being without him was haunting. Vivencia's words summoning me to Lowman's Church loomed like an added specter I could not fight. Gerald didn't mention it, so I know he did not hear Vivencia's thoughts. They were meant only for me.

The printer spat out page after page of some document. Gerald carefully placed his laptop inside his attaché, then assembled the newly printed pages and placed them in a file folder and into the case. "Almost done," he said, glancing up at me. The sun had begun to set, and the sky was a turquoise blue and peach. "You hungry? Want to go out for something? We still haven't had that date."

"I'm not really hungry. . . . I don't want to go out . . ." My back was turned to him, and I swallowed not to let the melancholy in my chest touch off tears that were welling up in my eyes.

"What's wrong?"

"Nothing, just going to . . . I don't know, make a piece of toast or something . . ."

"You angry at me . . . ?" I felt his steps on the floorboards catching up with me.

". . . To busy my hands," I grabbed Haynes's coconut bread that was on the counter. The edge of the plastic wrap hid from me, and I crushed the corner of the bread searching for it. He took it from me, found the edge of plastic wrap, and peeled it back. I then dug through the drawer for the bread knife. He produced it from the wooden caddy close to the stove. My eyes finally could no longer elude his. "Slice me a piece," he said.

"Slice your own." Those words flew out of my mouth unfiltered.

"You *are* angry. Gonna miss me?" He smiled, then came up behind me and put his hands on my shoulders.

The heat between us was palpable, and it rushed in like a wave. I shrugged, trying to brush him away. "I don't know what's so funny. . . . There some woman up there in Boston? Slice it yourself." For two days, I had hoped he would make love to me, but now I needed him. I didn't remember needing anyone like this. It was primal, and I ached.

He persisted in caressing my arms with his fingertips and kissing the back of my neck, light kisses that left my flesh tingling in anticipation. His hands had now moved to cup my breasts. "There's plenty of women in Boston. None I want. My hands are occupied," he whispered, "I want you to slice it for me." He leaned against me, and I could feel his desire through his jeans.

Slicing the bread for him, my hands were visibly shaking.

"Now feed it to me," he whispered. "Turn around and give it to me," he said, his voice now taking on a gravelly, guttural tone.

I broke off the corner of the bread and put it in his mouth. His lips, framed on his top lip so beautifully by his mustache, tantalized me. I wanted to have them cover me.

"Aren't you hot . . . in these?" he said, pausing as he unsnapped my jeans. "Take them off."

"Here?"

"Yes." He reached for the string and turned out the light. The dusky sky held only the memory of a sun that now rested out of sight. He turned me back around facing the window as I stepped free of my jeans, and I could see the sea and sky that had darkened to indigo streaked with violet. He put his hands under my T-shirt and grazed my breasts, then toyed with them until I squirmed. Against the silence in the room was the sound of him unzipping his jeans, which hit the floor in the shadows. He bent down, I thought to push them away, but I felt his lips kissing my back and then moving down to caress my backside.

"Go out on the veranda." The dulcet tones of his voice, along with his warm breath in my ear, made me grip the counter holding on, unable to move. Hearing, but not understanding what he was saying, I stood there stock-still in the dark kitchen.

I said, "Go out onto the porch!"

It was dark out there, but I was only wearing my T-shirt; though it was long and down to my knees, I was bare underneath it from the waist down.

"Go out on the veranda."

"Someone might see . . ."

"It's dark enough." He rubbed himself against me, only our thin cotton shirts between us.

Outside, there was a breeze that brushed my thighs as I walked the few steps to the edge of the veranda. The darkness cloaked us, and I leaned against the railing. I bit my lip. The sky was now a deep midnight blue. Though I knew it was not yet the witching hour, the sea had turned to ink. My flesh was aflame, and my mind possessed with him.

"So, talk to me," he said.

"What do you want me to say?" I searched my mind for words.

"I want you to tell me that you want me." In his eyes, I saw desire mixed with something else, though I was not sure what it was.

"I do."

"Tell me how much. . . . After all, I am going to be gone for a few weeks."

"I want you," I whispered, looking down at the beach hoping there was no one there.

"Then say it. Tell me what you want."

I reached back to take him in my hands. He pulled away.

"To . . . to . . ."

"Yes . . ."

"To make love to me."

He laughed. "We are way past that tonight. Tell me what you really want."

He was silent.

"I want you to have me, be in me, be with me."

He pierced me, then paused.

"Is that all?"

I felt hollow inside. "No."

He began to bury himself in me, and then stopped. Yet again, I lifted myself up to accept him, but he did not move.

"I want you to fill me."

I covered my mouth, feeling I might have said it too loud. If people were down on the beach, though it was many yards away, they might have heard me. But it was as if this game he was playing, he had played with me many times before. It was familiar foreplay that we shared often when he left me. I remembered this. John wanted me to tell him that I loved him and wouldn't forget him.

"I know," he whispered. And he began to slowly probe, penetrating me little by little, more and more with every stroke until I could feel the root of him. He rested himself there for a minute. I felt I would swoon. "I am going to faint."

"I know you don't want me to stop," he said as he slowed.

"No. Don't." I had never felt so full.

He pulled away. It shocked me and left my body trembling. He held me 'round my waist, and pulled me over to him as he sat on the armchair, and gently pulled me to sit facing him, his mouth covering mine, his tongue exploring my mouth. We were still, knowing the centers of one another.

"You are so beautiful," his words whispered to my heart. My insides now shivered in waves drawing him in, encompassing him for my own. He throbbed. My eyes closed, I left him, not to feel the pain of losing him. I knew he would go, and all I would have was the longing. Withdrawing into the darkness, trying to escape the loneliness, I gave in, and I took him into my soul.

"Mi amor. Te amo." I had taken him there in the tub as I washed him and stroked him. I knew he wanted me. Easing myself down on him, I held the sides of the tub for support as I writhed on him. *"Tenho que ir."* He kept telling me he had to go, but he could not stop himself from growing inside me. He tried to lift me off, but as I bore down and took him in, he could not hold himself back. He held on to the side of the tub and stood up. He was a bear of a man, so strong that he lifted me, climbing up onto the porch and pushing through the door.

He put me on the bed, looked down at me shaking his head no and holding himself. He turned me around and pulled me to the end of the bed. My belly, swollen with Sumadi's baby, drooped under me. He drew me to him and then entered me. He was so careful. He had not touched me since he arrived home and saw that I was with child. It had been several weeks, my watching him. Cooking for him, and bathing him, and trying to entice him with my touch, but he would not give himself to me. As he finally entered me so tentatively, I begged him for more and so he gave himself to me. I wanted to feel him for all the tomorrows he would be gone. He plunged into me one last time. He emptied himself in me, and I fell onto the bed, turning to take him into my arms. I wanted him to lie with me.

"No!" he shouted at me.

He stopped as he was climbing onto the bed to be with me. My body began trembling not in fear, but of something I saw in his eyes. He bit the reddened, tightly clenched fist, trying to release what seemed was the scream trapped in his throat. Not having the words in my language tormented him, but suddenly I could read his thoughts as clearly as if he were speaking in my tongue.

He stood so still I feared that the life had drained from his body. As his voice left his lips, it seemed a mournful moan. "You do not know how much I miss you—how I long for you when I am at sea."

His thoughts shook me as they came to me in my language. I wondered, could he understand my words, my thoughts.

"John, I miss bringing you mangoes in the morning sun. I love to watch you peel each one, as you do, carefully cutting slices that look like smiles of the fruit's flesh, and feeding them to me. I miss that when you go."

He closed his eyes, not to meet my gaze, seeming to hear my thoughts with them stinging him as they penetrated his being. He tugged his shirt closed and pulled on his pants. "Mariel, this is my work. I am not a man if I have no work. I need my work to care for you."

His words churned in my belly, feeling the life that he had not mentioned, but seemed to glance at as he stuffed things down in his satchel and strained its strap shut. I could not stop myself from running behind him, wanting to press his eyes with my fingers to stop the tears from flowing from them and bathing his cheeks. Such a powerful man, this steady stream of sadness we shared, draining his soul as it did mine. I had no words to stop them, so I said, "John, my heart does not beat when you are gone. It remains still till I see your ship again."

He looked at me as if he understood. His lips like gentle petals rested on mine, feeling as if this was his last taste of me, and I him.

"*Tenho que ir*," he said, repeating he had to go.

As he opened the door to leave, I rose from the bed, throwing my nightdress over my head so that I could follow him, catch him. My bare feet bruised as I scrambled through the grass and roots of the trees. I caught him as he reached the clearing leading to the beach. There were women and children standing there waving at the whaling ship out in the water. A rowboat with two oarsmen sat waiting in the shallows. My arms clutched his neck. He pried my fingers back, and I feared he might break them. My legs no longer able to carry me, I fell to the ground, the sand, shells, and pebbles pressing into my flesh. I held his leg, and the weight of me stopped him from the next step.

"Mariel!" He shouted my name. My arms, now encircling his thigh, holding fast as he dragged me, and the sea flowed beneath me. My skin burned from the saltwater. He waded into the surf and climbed into the rowboat. He looked toward me, and I screamed, "No!" but he turned his back. "This is my work!" The boat moved out to sea. Emptiness overwhelmed me, and a wail escaped my lips.

"Jocelyn, am I hurting you?"

My eyes did not wish to open, my mind unsure of where I was.

"No, don't leave me." Gerald was there inside me and it calmed me. We were in his bedroom with its familiar shadows. John was gone.

"Are you crying?" he asked.

"How did we get in here?"

"I carried you. . . . You don't remember?"

"I don't want you to . . ." The humiliation of begging John to stay filled my chest. I could not do it again. It was useless.

"Then I'll stop."

"No. It's just that there are so many things I understand better now . . . just sad, that you are leaving."

". . . Only be gone for a week or two."

"I'll be all alone." The tears finally fell, dripping from the corners of my eyes down my temples and resting in my ears. I could feel the emptiness that Mariel had expressed.

Gerald drew himself up to look at me. "You *are* crying." He kissed the tears, drinking them from my cheeks, so that they would not fall. "Haynes will be here. Bailey will check on you. I'll call you from Boston. You won't be alone."

He did not understand my fears, or Mariel's anguish. My dreams had returned. John was gone. Sumadi would come back. As my mind filled with images of them, I could feel him probing me, still filling me.

My longing for John beckoned Sumadi, drawing him through my bedroom window. He always came when I could not wait any longer. Then Sumadi's image transformed, and standing at the bottom of my bed was Derek. "I told you that you would call me."

Gerald studied my face, and his eyes flashed in anger. He knew. "When I come back . . ." I opened my eyes. I had to see who was talking to me. Gerald gritted his teeth. "You are mine. Do you hear me?" He looked down at me and plummeted the depths of me, now seeming to want to prove his virility, his prowess. He had read my thoughts. I was sure he felt my thoughts of Sumadi and of Derek.

"Tell me that you are mine." He stopped.

"I am."

"I need to hear you say it before I leave."

"I belong to you . . . only to you." He buried himself in me. That's what I saw in his eyes earlier. He wanted me to tell him that I was his alone. I was.

I wanted to remember him, the sensation of him, the smell and feeling of being filled with him. He drew his head back and let out a sound of release, and he fastened himself, locked himself inside me.

What about me? John, are you coming back? Tell me. Tell me. Do you belong to me?

I opened my eyes and through the shadows I could see Gerald's form. The thought grew in my mind. Though I always wanted to feel that I belonged to someone, and I finally heard that from his lips, it was not enough. I wanted him to belong to me. I wanted to know that he would return to me because he was mine.

At that moment, I wished that I could have children. "Old eggs," the doctor had said. Gerald was the first man with whom I ever really wanted children. I hooked my ankles together around his waist. He was dead weight, and shrinking, but I held him between my thighs as long as I could. He finally lifted himself off and lay beside me. I listened to his breathing as sleep came. Just the feeling of him within me stayed. But I wanted more.

32

His absence awakened me. My right hand sought him out, reaching. The bedroom was filled with sunlight, and my eyes squinted at the empty bed. I called out his name, but I knew he was long gone. The digital clock said 11:07 a.m. I buried my face into his pillow to breathe him in—his citrusy, sweet musk.

The phone rang. *There he was.* "Why didn't you wake me, I would have made you breakfast." There was silence. Switched the phone to my other ear. "Gerald?"

"It's me, Derek. I would have awakened you, if I knew you needed me so soon."

My first thought was to hang up, but I hesitated.

"I wouldn't have left you alone. And when you speak to him, tell him that the trouble he whipped up for me at sea in Barbados left me unscathed."

"What are you talking about?"

"Didn't he give you the lecture on my paintings and how I *display women* as he put it? Can't believe he missed that opportunity when he saw my painting of you . . . or maybe . . . you didn't show it to him. Kept it our little secret."

"I have no secrets . . ."

"Sure, you do. We have lots of little secrets." He was spinning a web for me. "Did you tell him about our nights together?"

"Don't call here again, Derek. Nights, what do you mean nights," I said, remembering only one.

"You don't remember our first night . . . what about our last morning? Did you tell him about our morning?"

The beginning of that day flashed through my mind. I could not speak.

An absence of sound, and just a sense of his presence lurked on the line. I should have slammed the phone down, but I was drawn to the silence. For some reason, I needed to hear his voice again. He laughed. "You will call me." He was still there, breathing. Then a click.

"You will not manipulate me." My words bounced out loud around the room. "I'm not Mariel. Been alone before in my life, and this is not new to me."

I went to the bathroom to pee. I ached all over. There on the mirror was a sticky note with a message.

Do you still feel me? Love, G.

I did. Selena always talked about being love-bent. Now I knew what she meant, and I welcomed the sensations. I went to the pantry to find some tea and there was a loud knock on the door, startling me. The image of Derek standing at the door, the night he brought the painting to me, flashed through my mind. I stayed in the storeroom, not wanting him to see me through the glass in the kitchen door. A key was pushing into the door. I wondered how he got a key. The door opened then closed. There was a rustling sound, and something plopped down on the counter.

"Mistress Jocelyn. Mistress?" Her full-throated voice was at first alarming, then washed over me like a balm.

"Haynes?" The woman jumped as I emerged from the pantry.

"I was digging around in here . . . didn't know who could be there. . . . Did you knock?" I was tongue-tied, foolishly trying to explain what probably seemed unexplainable.

She looked perplexed, but said, "Sorry mistress, Dr. Hunter asked me to come and see about you. What you need. . . . You know today's

Sunday. . . . I go to church, so I just stopped to see if you want me to bring anything tomorrow morning."

"Looking for some tea."

"You want the Earl Grey, or herbal?" Haynes put down the straw pocketbook she had hooked on her arm. "The Earl Grey is on the shelf on the left of the cabinet."

"I am having some trouble with my stomach. The other day Gerald gave me something to settle it." I gave her too much information about our relationship, though I assume she knew we were sleeping together. "It was an herb for that."

"Was it mint . . . or maybe ginger?"

"Yes, mint tea. Ginger is good too. I'll try that."

"Haynes, did you say you are going to church tonight. . . . The one on Lowman's Road?"

The woman left the key in the cabinet and filled the kettle. "No Mum, went this mornin'. Just come back."

"You know what time the service is tonight?"

"Might be a meeting, no service. . . . Don't know. Why, Mum?"

"You know Vivencia?"

"Sure," Haynes said. "Everyone know Vivencia."

"She told me to meet her there tonight. She didn't mention the time."

"Knowing Vivencia," Haynes nodded, ". . . she'll know when you are getting there." She laughed out loud. "I guess, about seven. Don't go after dark 'cause you don't know the road."

She opened the refrigerator. "I'll buy some eggs tomorrow. Something for dinner? Some swordfish. . . . Dr. Hunter said that I should come by every day."

"That won't be necessary."

"He said you would say that. I see you liked my coconut bread." Memories of the bread and Gerald's kisses heated my cheeks. "I can do some baking tomorrow too," Haynes chattered on, doubling back into the closet, ". . . have some pilot crackers . . . good for your stomach, Mum."

The woman then gathered up the newspaper and put it on the table next to me. "See you in the mornin' . . . wait," she went back into the pantry and grabbed a lantern flashlight. "Take this with you tonight, Mum."

The room fell silent, and as my shoulders dropped, finally relaxing, the phone rang. Instantly, I thought of Derek and willed it to silence itself. In that moment of hesitation, my spine stiffened, and I vowed that he was not going to put me into a state of fear.

"Yes," I announced in my professorial tone, the one I used to quiet my grandest lecture halls.

"You okay, babe? Wanted to hear your voice before I board. Did you get my note?"

Gerald's voice entered my consciousness, soothing me like a warm bath.

"I did."

"So, I made a lasting impression?!" He laughed in that deep bass voice that literally made my center vibrate.

"I don't know what to say to that."

"Don't say anything. Love that you are speechless. Did Haynes come by?"

"Yes, but you told her to come every day?"

"Just want to be sure that you are . . . looked after . . . while I am away."

"That is ridiculous. I am fine on my own."

"I recall that you told me you didn't want to be alone."

"I meant without you."

"That's why I asked her to sleep downstairs in the servant's quarters a few nights this week."

"You have got to be kidding me."

"No, it's arranged."

"Gerald, I don't like being treated like a child. And I don't want to ask Haynes to sleep in the servant's quarters on my account."

"What did you s . . . ? That's the last call for boarding. Gotta run, babe. Just want to take care of you." He hung up.

His caring bound me around the middle like a girdle, and I could not breathe. I brought it on myself, though. Bound up in Mariel's sadness, I had expressed her loneliness. The veranda beckoned me, but seeing the expanse of water stretching to the horizon was now irritating, and my hands felt like restless appendages needing something to do. *That feeling of being alone and watched and closed in must have been exactly what Mariel felt.* I wondered if I enjoyed painting so much, after the past life regression, because that was what she did. As my mind focused on her, my thoughts fixed on her things in the valise. Her keepsakes might shed some light on her.

The valise was right where I left it in the dining room. I lifted it and was surprised that it was not as heavy as I thought. *How had I not even tried to lift it till now?* The past life regression was inhabiting my thoughts, coiled and knotted up in my imaginings of women's history and lack of freedom and weakness. I vowed to pay closer attention to understand the complicated truth.

In the suitcase, a small handsewn notebook caught my eye first, the paper pages browned and curled up at the edges. On the first page, there were sketches of baskets and tally lines. Twenty-three strokes. On another page, there were drawings of what looked like bread with stick-like lines beneath it. Each new page revealed other things Mariel must have sold, like pots and jugs. It was an order book, a rudimentary ledger. Here she kept track of her sales. She did in fact have a business and was careful to do record keeping. I was amazed at how she could build a business with little more than her will.

My attention was then pulled to two large envelopes and a small bundle of smaller letters—one with alternating red and blue chevron markings around the edges and tied with twine. The top one was from Estela, my great-grandmother, addressed to Luz Gonzalves, my grandmother. It was tied with ribbon. There was one in my mother's handwriting, and it was addressed to my grandmother. It was odd, but I just had not thought about my mother and my grandmother corresponding by mail. Four generations of correspondences were collected here. Mail belonging to Mariel, Estela (her daughter), and Luz (her granddaughter) all collected here. I pulled my mother's letter out and kept it next to me.

My curiosity was piqued with the large letter tied with twine . . . it was from John! I wondered how Mariel understood his correspondences and was fairly certain she could not read or write Portuguese. Then I remembered Leila, the housekeeper John had hired to look after her needs and guessed she might have been instructed to find someone to read them to Mariel, even if she could not read. A sheet of brown paper fashioned into a scroll, which was flattened, covered a wide piece of velum and wasn't a letter from John at all. It was an ink drawing of his ship, its sails ballooned, surrounded by roiling seas. There was a rendering of a whale, and a harpooner standing atop it, plunging a harpoon into its back. The detail was extraordinary. At the bottom, there were a few words that I could translate.

Meu amor, eu estarei em casa breve.

My love, I will be home soon.

Something gnawed at me as I looked back at the drawing. The next packet held a painting on a piece of thin bark. It was lovely, though the pigments were dulled with age. There was a beautiful picture of a house surrounded by palm and mango and lime trees, with a woman standing on a veranda looking out to the sea. As I looked more closely, what I first thought was shading, there on her abdomen was an image of a baby. This must have been Mariel's painting because it was totally different from the other ink rendering. John's drawing had some magnetic force, I thought, because I went back to it trying to figure out what was needling me about it, then noticed the way he made the waves in the sea. Those markings were from the amulet I wore around my neck. Placing the amulet and the drawing side by side, although the markings were images of waves, they were made of a unique rendering of the letter "s," repeated in both the drawing and the amulet's etching, as exact as a signature. Now I was certain that John had etched the amulet.

As I put the necklace back on, my eye was drawn to the letter my mother had written. It was dated June 10, 1975, on a postmark, but it was still sealed, stamped in red "Return to Sender" The date, maybe it was the year, rang a bell. I was five at the time it was sent. So I couldn't have re-membered seeing the letter. I ran to search the kitchen drawer for scis-sors and slit the envelope at its side.

My mother's handwriting was deliberate on this page, not at all as I recalled it. Her hand was always light and gently leaning to the right, as if she were attempting to draw rather than write.

June 6, 1975

Dear Mother,

I am writing you one last time. After this, I want nothing more to do with you. I asked you specifically not to have my child baptized in that church, and you went ahead and did it anyway. And I had to hear it from family members. I can only hope that my child has not been damaged by your superstitious acts. She has said nothing, so I can only hope she does not remember the incident. But it's outrageous that you try and justify it with these stories of jumbees and obeah spells and mumbo jumbo about protecting her. You want to control her like you tried to control me, and that will not happen. You ruined my marriage. You will not destroy my child's future. You will never see her again. You are dead to me.

Rosalie

P.S. You have tried to turn family against me, and my decision, even Tantie Grace. I gave her back the necklace. I certainly won't put that on my child.

The date on the letter, June 6, 1975, jumped out at me. It wasn't just the year. It was the actual date. It seemed like a small piece in a large jigsaw puzzle. There was a big picture in here somewhere, and this was one small detail for which I had to find the place. But the venom in my mother's writing was so hateful, I felt for the amulet, now suspended between my breasts. My chest felt as if a huge weight rested there, and stroking it gave me the sense of protection I felt since I put it on. Yet I could imagine my mother's anger at my grandmother going against her wishes. I did not remember a baptism. Tantie Grace never spoke of it. It was good that my grandmother never received this letter. It would have killed her to read those words. For all her faults, she loved me. Despite their differences, I felt she cared for my mother. *But what did she mean about my grandmother ruining her marriage?*

I shut the suitcase, the date, June 6, 1975, indelibly imprinted in my mind, I began searching the internet for what was happening in Bequia around the time of June in 1975. Carnival! There were posts on the "crop over," a celebration of the end of the harvest. Photos of the festivity were in black and white, lacking the color and the bacchanalian spirit of the town's people prancing through the streets. The photos were jarring, colliding with thoughts of my grandmother preparing to kill herself. Vivencia's words crept into my thoughts like a confidence shared, her voice low and raspy, "Someone put a spell on she . . . and she grandmother. Mariel knew it started with her." Vivencia's words speaking for my grandmother, as if from her grave.

Years of feeling unnerved, and it was no wonder. My passions set in motion with a swirling venom.

I had to head for Lowman's Church.

Grabbing my cell, I locked the door, then remembered the flashlight Haynes gave me. *Getting forgetful like my grandmother.* As I stood for a moment collecting my thoughts, seeing her image, I recalled where I saw that date, "June 6." Janice Barclay's email. As the print illuminated the screen of my laptop, my copy of the link opened the attachment of the newspaper article. I scrolled through it, and there it was. *"Luz Gonsalves was last seen alive on June 6, 1975."*

Part V

Confusion surrounds the path I walk, and more beings reveal themselves to me. No answers yet, only more inquiry. A glimmer of white light, a thin ray I see with the confounding bits of knowledge that I glean.

33

The last sunlight, cast by the fireball that fell into the sea, was fading. Fronds of palm and coconut trees littered the narrow road that led to Lowman's Church. The flashlight illuminated the thicket of undergrowth and decayed leaves and stems that seemed several inches deep. My eyes were trained on the ground lest my feet get caught in the tangle. With no landmarks, just trees and the bed of leaves and branches to mark my passage, it felt like an endless journey, but it may have been just about a city block that I walked. When the road turned to the left, I heard the voices singing. There was one that chanted, and the others answered. Then the drum began a throbbing rhythm that spoke in bass tones. Ahead was a clearing where a white structure, more like a house than a church, loomed. Wooden stairs led up to a porch with three benches on each side of the entryway; a kerosene lamp hung by the open front door. There was just a glow of dim light within. The music grew and enveloped me as I got closer.

Then I heard her beckon, not with her voice but with her mind. *Come child*, Vivencia summoned. As I reached the door, the sweet odor of incense wafted in the air. Inside, there were chairs against the back and sidewalls. Devotional candles in tall glasses lined a table at the rear of the room. Three women were singing, their eyes closed and their bodies rocking forward and backward to the drumbeat. The man playing the drum was small but wiry. In the corner, a shadow moved, and I jumped. There was Vivencia. She lifted up a large gourd that she shook, making it rattle, syncopating with the drumbeat. A chair sat alone in the middle of the room with the women to the back and the men and Vivencia in the front. She nodded toward the chair, indicating that I should sit. My knees began to buckle as I approached, but no one reached to help me. The drummer changed to a slower, deeper, more resonant rhythm that insinuated its way into my body.

Vivencia's eyes were now wide open. The movement of the gourd stopped. She did not look at me, but studied the space around me, her eyes tracking the movement of something that encircled me. She lifted her forefinger and pointed in its direction as it moved. She spoke in a language I did not understand, but the import of what she said came to me. She was pushing something away, telling it to stay clear of me.

"Drink the light," she said, handing me a goblet. Though I feared it, I sipped from the clay chalice she held. She moved 'round the room, giving each woman the cup, and each one in turn drank some of it and then grew quiet. Last was the drummer, who pounded the drum one last time, and then took the vessel to his lips. He, too, then fell still. Vivencia began talking to something in the corner of the room, speaking in what sounded like pidgin. I heard Spanish or Portuguese, but only in bits. Her eyes darted to the left, taking in something there. She spoke to it like she knew it well. My head turned in its direction and there was my grandmother, Luz, her hair askew and her face wracked with pain. She spoke to Vivencia, pointing to the other corner of the room where Vivencia had directed her voice. My eyes followed where she looked and there, crouching on the floor, was Mariel. Vivencia spoke Luz's name softly. "No. No. You don't want to do that." It was as if they were speaking to each other—sometimes audibly, then telepathically.

Now Luz, my grandmother, looked at me. She screamed. "Take care of the darkness. Do not go her way. Look at me."

Mariel scowled, "It not my darkness. It follow me." And her whole form darted at Vivencia, pouncing just in front of her. She looked like she would attack her, yet Vivencia did not flinch.

When Mariel spoke, I heard her thoughts. They were like crystal in the darkened room. I was taken by what she uttered. "She did this to me. I searched for her."

"You blame everyone. You blamed my mother," my grandmother said, her eyes flashing in anger.

"I never blamed my daughter, Estela. She didn't know." Mariel's body was laden with sadness. "I worked hard to make this all right, to bring John home, to hold our family togedder, to protect my children and Luz. I searched for who did this."

"You find her?" Vivencia asked, her voice calm and resolute.

"I find her here on this side. She said the spell she cast haf nothing to do wit' me. She did for she son."

"For her son?"

Now it was for her son. Luz's thoughts were filled with anger. "Look at me. You made me."

I will not talk to her. That one . . . Mariel pointed at me. *She will see. It is not so easy to stay away from the darkness. I no stay here.*

Who was he? The essence of her form seemed to dissipate. *Stay! You will not leave this place, Mariel. What is her name? Who was her son?* Vivencia shouted.

She reappeared, a trapped expression on her face. *Nereida.*

Where is she?

She is of the sea.

Summon her.

I CANNOT! LET ME GO, Mariel shrieked.

You will bring her! Your work here is not done.

Can you not see what she has done to my life, my child, my children's lives, all of the life that has come from me? Leave me in my pain. Help her! She pointed to me before she disappeared. Vivencia's eyes scanned the room. Mine did too, but I could not find her anywhere. Vivencia turned to my grandmother, who now turned her eyes toward me. "You take care. Hear me, well. She ruined me," Luz said. She pointed to where Mariel stood. I looked in her direction, but Mariel was gone, and when I looked back for my grandmother, she, too, had disappeared.

I will find her, this Nereida. Vivencia's ruminations were powerful, and they echoed in my mind. *We will find her.*

34

I could not sleep after I returned from Lowman's Church, fearing the entities had followed me. Mariel's agony plagued me all night and into the next day. As the night fell again, I was overly tired. Haynes had not come, though I would have welcomed her presence. The humidity made the air in the house heavy, and I pushed the door out to the veranda hoping for a breeze. Out on the water, there he was.

The lights on the deck of Derek's yacht dimmed and then lit up again. He saw me.

"I will not call him," I said aloud, though I was all alone.

Gerald's room, and the safe presence he offered, beckoned me. Shutting the light and closing the door to the hallway, making the room pitch black, I parted the drape slightly to peek out the window. The lights on Derek's boat dimmed again.

You can't see me. How are you doing this? The phone rang. No one from the outside could see me. It rang again.

Shit. I am not going to cower in the darkness because of you.

I picked up the phone and shouted into it, "What do you want?"

"Jocelyn, is that you? It's me, Cassandra. Cassandra Jacobs, the psychologist from Moon Hole. Is everything all right?"

"Did Derek tell you to call?"

"No, I . . . I was just thinking about you. And you must be reading my mind! I was thinking you put a real hurting on him. Frankly, I am concerned."

"Don't be. . . . I am not interested . . . in hearing anything about him."

"It's just that he's been shaken up since the hurricane. Been drinking. Hasn't painted. We're all worried."

"I am sure he will be fine as soon as he finds a new conquest. By the way, what happened during the hurricane? He mentioned it when he called the other day."

"We all went to Barbados in the yacht: Alex, me, Giselle."

"Giselle was there? I thought Derek and she had split."

"We were all consoling him, and he said we should head to Barbados to ride out the storm. It wasn't supposed to hit there. The sea was calm for most of the trip, then the waves rose up, lifted the boat into the air and spun it around. We were knocked about. We thought it would capsize."

"But he . . . all of you are fine?"

"Sort of. I still have bruises, but it was weird. Out of nowhere, the storm barreled down on us. He was really shaken. Still is."

"I don't know how shook he is. You know he is in his yacht outside my house right now."

"You're kidding."

"No, he's . . ." I looked out the window, and he was gone "Never mind. He's finally gone."

"You sure it was him?"

"I'm sure."

I searched the horizon and didn't see any sign of the boat I'd seen just minutes before.

"Okay, no more talk about Derek. How's your work coming? Last time I saw you, you were plagued by dreams . . ."

I turned on the lamp on Gerald's nightstand and sat back on the bed. "Actually, I am having trouble sleeping tonight. Went to Lowman's Church yesterday and had an encounter with Vivencia. Do you know her?"

"I know of her. She's known as the keeper of the knowledge here on the island. A shaman of sorts."

"Well, she seemed to tap into my great-great-grandmother, whose life I learned about after my past life regression."

"What do you mean?"

"I mean I saw her. She spoke to me."

"You sure you weren't imagining . . . hallucinating."

"No, I saw my great-great-grandmother." I propped Gerald's pillow up behind me. "She did give me something to drink . . . just before it happened."

"This is up at Lowman's Church?"

"Yes, everyone drank a sip . . ."

"I know the locals do use hallucinogens, but it usually just makes you open to . . ."

"Vivencia spoke to them, my great-great-grandmother and my grandmother, and I could see them and hear their responses."

"Yes, they take stuff that helps them see. . . . That's what I mean, just be careful. What I was going to say is sometimes we have too much information . . . you know, without guidance. . . . Do you understand what I mean?"

"Not really. I sense that my dreams and my grandmother's death are somehow connected."

"Your grandmother's death? You said Derek was in your dreams too. You sure you are not just projecting things from your current circumstances into these . . . dreams."

"I knew if I told anyone about this . . . they'd think I am crazy."

"I didn't say you are crazy. Projection is a natural occurrence psychologically . . ."

"But I'm fairly certain that what I am seeing in my dreams really happened in the past." The image of being with Sumadi's child came back to me. John's expression of anger as he held my dress up and glared at my belly made shame flow through me again. The painful memory flashed through my mind and fastened itself to the memory I had during my past life regression that day with Luis.

"Oh my god! I know what happened."

"What? Jocelyn, what's the matter?"

"I gave birth. I gave birth to that child, and they took it."

"What are you talking about?"

"My past life regression. I was pregnant, and this woman was talking to me. . . . I have been so focused on the feelings, and the dreams after, that I forgot the actual events that triggered them. . . . I can't remember it all, but this woman—Leila—was there when I was giving birth."

"So, what are you feeling about that?"

"Don't patronize me."

"I am not patronizing you."

"You are asking me questions as if you are my psychologist."

"I can't help it. I am a psychologist, and it just slipped out that way. Look if you don't want to speak to me about it, that's fine."

"No."

"No. Okay. Maybe you just want to get some sleep. It's almost eleven. I'm sorry . . . if. . . . Maybe have some chamomile tea, or warm milk."

"I don't want you to go. I need to talk to you."

"Are you all right?"

She could hear my fear. "I think so . . . I . . ."

"What is troubling you so?"

"What they did with my child. Where is it?"

"Jocelyn, do you want me to try and hypnotize you? Sometimes hypnosis helps to free you of any inhibitions that might block you recalling . . ."

"You can do that?"

"If you are open to it. You want to come here?"

"No, Derek is there."

"He knows better than to interfere in my work."

"No, I don't want to go there."

"If you want, I could come there. Near the end of the week . . . Thursday? I just want to remind you, Jocelyn, we can only work on your feelings and what's happening now, not then."

"I know. I just need to know. What did they do with my baby?"

35

My senses were awash with the sweet smell of baking bread and the soft serenade of the songbirds at my window. The phone rang, and I reached for it.

"Hi babe. Going into a meeting, but met a guy in a Portuguese seamen's group up here, and he says he thinks your great-great-grandfather was from a long line of whalers a couple of generations before him. He's seen the name in his research many times."

"You're kidding?"

"No, but no time to check it out. Get online, and check the shipping manifests and crew lists from the mid to late 1800s. Sent you the link. Gotta go, but babe, it seems I'm going to be here longer than planned."

I wanted to tell him about Vivencia, but he was gone. I headed into my room. Longer, how much longer?

"Good morning, Mum. . . . Sorry about yesterday," Haynes called out.

"Yes, thought you would be here. Whatever you're baking . . . smells delicious!"

"Trouble wit' da phone lines. They can't find the problem. . . . No way to call na nuthin'. Everyone t'ink it angry spirits and such after the storm. Me baked banana bread if you'd like some."

"Yes, thanks. . . . Going into my office to work. By the way, it certainly isn't necessary for you to stay overnight."

"Thank you, Mum. I'll bring a tray."

The link worked, and I was onto the website. The Boston Whaling Museum archives had different search terms: crewmen's names, whaling grounds, and whaling ships. When I typed in my great-great-grandfather's name, John Matos, his ship's name came up, *The Sea Nymph II*. The category "Rigging" next to the ship said, "Bark." I Googled "Rigging/Bark", and a picture of a three-mast ship with square sails came up. It was the ship I searched for when I was Mariel, scanning the horizon each day. The description said it usually carried a large crew. I returned to the crew list, which said John had thirty-two crewmen.

Haynes brought the tray and looked around to see what needed to be done in my room.

"Not to worry about my room today."

"Okay, Mum."

When I refocused on the screen, John's voyages listed the crewmen alphabetically, and a chart of sorts held descriptive categories. John Matos, his height, five feet ten inches; his hair, black; eye color, green; skin color, Portuguese. "So odd," I thought aloud, "African, mulatto or colored, and Portuguese all categories of 'skin color.'" These details— green eyes, dark hair—all describe him, the man in my dreams, exactly.

The phone rang. I pulled myself from the computer to get the phone. "Babe, yes, he's here . . . details about . . ."

"Hey, girl. I can hear you're immersed. Just seeing if . . ."

"Selena, Gerald just met a guy who thinks my grandfather was one of a *long line* of whalers, and sent me a link to this archive. And I found him! Selena, it's him, the man in my dreams. I am seeing his port of registry, New Bedford, Massachusetts. He's listed as the 'Captain.' Selena, he was the man who held me in his arms!"

"Jocelyn just remember that is not you."

"I know that Selena."

"Remember what Luis said."

"I know, I know that !" My irritation put an edge in my voice.

"You just sound so caught up in this. I was just calling to check on you. I'll leave you to your work . . ." Her voice faded away, and my eyes had already wandered back to the screen. My mind was on the description I read. He was the man who built me a house, and who bedded me that second night after we married. Seeing him so vividly in my mind's eye made me remember the craving I had for him when he left.

As I searched further, it said that his voyages lasted a year to two years. A year to two years! The longing for him in my dreams made so much more sense. Mariel's searching the horizon . . . for an eternity . . . left alone and wanting. A young bride, no letters, no phones, so no calls. One year to two . . . she must have thought that he might never return.

His whaling ground was the Atlantic, and the West Indies, and his port, New Bedford, and the Azores. I hadn't known that. That meant that he sailed from Bequia up to New Bedford, near Boston. To the Azores, near Portugal. Leland said he brought her beautiful things from Portugal. So he probably stopped on the mainland when he went back to the Azores, which they listed as his home. It was hard to fathom the distances that he traveled when he left. Then I saw him, as if he stood before me, when he came back and found me pregnant with Sumadi's child. I shook myself and focused on the screen and read on to take my mind off of my guilt.

Taking in the picture I now held of my great-great-grandfather, the portrait of the man, of this ship and crew, took my breath away. No longer a phantom of whom I dreamed, and whose images passed before me and then faded away. He was a man, whose presence was part of this historical record.

Gerald said there were more Matos family members who were whalers. I broke off another piece of banana bread and poured a cup of the tea. Typing the family name, two other names came up, Abrahim Matos and Joseph Matos. Joseph had a Bark that sailed in the year 1830, registered in New Bedford. Abrahim Matos had a ship, *The Sea Nymph*, *Nereida*, that sailed in 1805, also registered in New Bedford. On the crew list on Abrahim's ship, there was a crewman named Joseph Matos, a first mate.

Joseph was probably Abrahim's son, given the same last name. Perhaps Abrahim was the first of the family, then Joseph, then John. Pieces of this family puzzle were now placed almost like the edges in a large jigsaw. While my eyes darted from list to list, I realized there were no slaves! The Black men and the colored men all held crewman jobs on the ship. Relief washed over me, and my gaze was pulled out to the sea. The horizon now held part of my history that went back through the decades.

As I was about to sit down, the phone rang again. A smile painted itself across my lips, "Hi, babe," I said, ". . . that call was too short. On a break?" There was silence.

"I need to see you."

I didn't recognize his voice at first. It seemed thin and strained.

"Derek? You need?"

"You have something of mine!" he shouted. "Don't hang up on . . ."

I began to listen to his rant and thought better of it, then slammed the phone down.

"Mum, is everything all right? You don' look . . ."

I gagged, and pushed past the woman running to the toilet, but nothing came up. Then my stomach convulsed, and I brought up the banana bread and the tea. Sweat began to bead on my forehead. Haynes ran the cold water in the sink, and then dry heaves made me bend over the toilet again.

"Mum, should I call Dr. Manley to take a look at you?"

"No, I'll be fine. Just need some crackers."

"You shouldn't let that person upset you like that."

"I know. I am fine." But my stomach was in spasm, and my forehead was dripping wet.

"Mum, not to be . . . well . . . forgive me for asking, and I hope you won't be angry wit' me, but you t'ink you might be expecting."

"Expecting what?"

"Forgive me Mum, never mind."

Her words moved about in my mind and their meaning came into focus. "Absolutely not. I can't be. I cannot have children." A scowl wrinkled my brow. "Just get me the crackers."

"Sorry, Mum. Please, please excuse me for asking." The woman lowered her dark eyes, and her feet pounded the wooden floor as she walked to the kitchen. She pushed the open box of crackers toward me. I wet a washcloth and placed it on the back of my neck. "I can do that for you, Mum."

"No, I can do it for myself."

"Should I call the doctor? All kinds of things could make your stomach sick," she persisted.

"Sorry . . . can't argue with you. Call him and see if you can make an appointment for me for tomorrow. . . . Maybe in the morning . . . before it gets too hot." Haynes walked me into my bedroom and pulled back the covers. ". . . Rest yourself, Mum."

I was exhausted, drained.

"I'll call Dr. Hunter? He would want to know if . . ."

My hand closed into a fist and tightened as my anger grew. "No. Haynes. Stop it!" My body sank into the thick mattress; a cool breeze rushed over me as a stupor pulled me down.

36

The cold rag on my forehead and over my eyes felt so good. My belly weighed me down. Leila gently patted my eyelids but scowled at me. I had no words. She pointed to the window and was threatening to tell my husband about the man who was coming into my house. Her footsteps plodded out of the house, and she slammed the door. The sound of a bird called from outside my window. The chirp repeated, then I realized it was he who was signaling me, as was now his habit. Sumadi was there, climbing into the window.

"Mari, wake up," he whispered. He kissed my neck.

"A woman said she see you, and the baby drop." He ran his hand over my stomach. "Not much time. Come and live with me. Have the baby there."

"With your first wife?" I pushed his head away.

"She will help with the child. She cannot have."

"You are crazy."

"Mari, come be with me. You gave life to my child. How do you look at me with those eyes that do not trust me? Can't you see that I enjoy your eyes in the morning haze? I cannot get enough of your touch. A smile grew there on his lips, "When you turn away wit' a pout like that, it makes me hunger for your bottom lip."

He had a way with my heart.

"You know that woman, the Portugee's servant, will kill my child. You know that." He was right. This morning, the woman swept the whole house, and with every stroke of the broom, she eyed me. At any moment, I feared she would strike my belly with the broomstick.

Sumadi leaned down and took my left breast in his hand and put his lips to it, suckling it, "When you live with me, I will drink from this one. And the child can have the other." The gold flecks in his eyes gleamed impishly.

Though the feelings warmed me, I plucked the breast from his mouth. He reminded me I was a woman and desired, even though I felt unwanted, forgotten by my husband.

He pulled me up, and I threw my nightdress on. This bedroom held so many things I wished to take with me; my eyes searched the room and stopped on the large, looking glass John had bought me. It was made from fine wood, and it had carved knobs on either side of the frame. The scrimshaw John gave me hung from one side, with the etchings he made of me and our home. Lifting it to place it around my neck, he snatched it from my fingertips.

"All you need is in my house."

"You give that back to me, or I will stay and give Leila the child myself . . . to do with as she wishes." My jaw shut tight.

"You would not!" My hand caught hold of the scrimshaw, while he gripped the cord.

"You watch me."

He loosened his grasp, and I placed the cord around my neck. He turned his back to me and walked out the front door; I followed, leaving bits of myself in my home. The surf shimmered with the pale patina of moonlight. There in the water was the rowboat, the one that I had imagined him arriving in as he slipped into my bed each night. But a man, bulky in build, sat in it. Sumadi lifted me in the air as he made his way through the surf and handed me up to the other man, who stood to lift me into the boat. Sumadi climbed into the craft and the man rowed as Sumadi sat at the back and steered. Behind me, there were voices, more than one or two. Turning to see over my shoulder, we were nearing a huge ship that loomed in the darkness. The sails and outline of four oars that were hoisted in the air on the side of the boat facing me. Four more rowers were on the other side. I had not dreamed that he arrived in such a large craft, and with a crew of men rowing under his command.

A hoist was lowered down to Sumadi, who attached it to the back of our boat. The other man pushed past me and attached a second hook to the front of it. The men on the larger boat began to chant on Sumadi's signal, then heaved our boat onto the vessel. Sumadi spoke in his language, and they helped me climb out. It was not Carib. I understood none of it. Sumadi shouted something at the men, and they began to row to the cadence another man called out. I held fast to the side of the ship, and Sumadi gripped my shoulders as we lurched forward each time the oarsmen pulled in unison. My heart began to pound. We traveled for quite a long time before we reached the shore of another island, which I guessed was Mustique, where he told me he lived. So much I left behind, and my heart ached, fearing I would never see my husband again.

Sumadi pulled my arm to get me to climb back into the smaller boat, which they then lowered into the water. He and the other man rowed long strokes in what were the first glimmers of dawn until we reached the shore. He jumped into the water, then lifted me out of the boat into the surf, which was up to my thighs.

"Come," was all he said. I followed him onto the beach and into the bush, holding my swollen belly. I stopped and put my hands on my hips, my breathing now labored.

"Where are you . . ." I paused to draw a breath, "taking me?"

"Just there." He pointed a few yards more into the thick of the bush. Once we reached the thicket, we walked a good length inland until we met a large hut that reminded me of my home when I was a child. A tall, thin woman, her hair wrapped in a colorful cloth, came out. "My first wife, Efua." The woman's eyes sliced through me like a cold steel blade. She seemed an African, and was followed by a second, plump woman, who seemed Carib. Struck dumb by the reality of my surroundings, I could not breathe.

"Efua will help you birth my child and care for him. I have built you a proper hut for after the child is born."

I started toward the hut, and Sumadi turned away. "Where are you going?" I shouted at him.

"To sleep with my second wife."

I was in shock, furious. "Take me back to my home."

"This is your home for now, until my child comes. It has dropped and will come soon. Efua is listening for your call."

"You can't expect me to live here. Take me home. My husband will hunt you down . . ."

Sumadi laughed. "And when will he come back, the Portugee?"

"My brother knows where you are, and he will find you. You will never rest."

"You will love me again, when the child is birthed. You are mine now."

A place in my heart grew hard like stone. I spat my words at him. "I belong to no man. I came to spare this child's life. When it comes, let me go, or you will never trust that this child is safe."

Sumadi's smile left his lips. The first wife pulled my arm.

"Get her off of me." I felt the child ball itself up in my stomach, and the movement was visible. Sumadi saw it too. As my abdomen lifted up to one side, it brought my nightdress up with it. I felt a sharp pain and doubled over. Sumadi reached out, trying to take me in his arms and stop me from falling. The woman grabbed at my shoulder. I shrugged him off and slapped the woman's hand away. "Don't put hands on me," I said to her, our eyes now locking. I faced Sumadi, with my hands supporting the underside of my swollen belly, my voice lowered to a gravelly whisper, "I go back to my husband's house, or this child will not draw a breath."

Sumadi waved the other woman off, and she left. "I have no need of you if you do not want to be my wife."

"Nor I you. I have a husband."

"You have no idea what I have sacrificed to be with you," his voice a throaty whisper, but his eyes a complex gaze, a mixture of rage and something else.

"No more than me," I turned my back on him, entering the hut. It smelled of mud, but was cooler than outside. He grabbed my shoulder, but his grip loosened as he looked into my eyes and then down at my belly. *What did you sacrifice*, I thought. His eyes told me he knew.

"Look at me," he said. "When I leave you in the light of the morning, I want the village to know you belong to me. When I leave hiding in the darkness, I know I am a trespasser, lost forever, pleading for bits and pieces from the Portugee's table. I am the beggar for what he leaves behind. Yet I am a man. Among my people, I am a man! I am here when he leaves. I feel your emptiness. I lick your tears."

His tall straight bearing shrunk as he spoke. His face told of his sorrow.

"You think I don't know you cry for him? When I come through the window, you think I don't see the disappointment in your eyes . . . until I touch you and you remember who I am. I am the one who mends your heart. I am the father of your son. I am not your husband, but I am your hero for your lonely nights. And your hope for a new day. Then you send me away."

He left me with his thoughts. I could say nothing in argument because he was right. When I cried, he drank my tears.

The birthing hut was dark. I hated myself for coming to this place. There was a pillow of sorts on the floor, and cloth torn into strips in a pile. In my village, I had seen women squat over the birthing space and bear down. When the time came, I would do it. The touch of the jewel that my husband had given me gave me a slice of peace. My fingers traced the etchings he had drawn of our home. Though I closed my eyes, I could not sleep. The child rested. I wondered when he would decide to come, so that I could go home.

I bolted upright in Gerald's bed, shaking the sleep from my mind. *Was Abrahim's ship called*, Nereida?

37

"The heart is beating. You see it there." The doctor turned the monitor toward me and pointed to the small, white, pulsating dot in the center of the screen.

"No, that's impossible." I sat up to look for myself. My mind raced about and settled on the night I went to see Moon Hole the first time. I had had too much to drink. He said he did not touch me, but I could not trust his word. Then I thought about the night of the party. I remembered the sex, the first I had in years. Then the next day, he took me again.

Dr. Clarke seemed bewildered by my disbelief. "Well, the proof is here. The fetus appears to be about five weeks old." She took my hand as I sat up. "You can get dressed, and I will meet you in my office. I will be prescribing a prenatal vitamin, and we can talk about follow-up appointments. Are you going to be in Bequia for an extended period of time?"

"My doctors have been saying for years that it's impossible. I am forty-five years old. This can't be."

"We will talk in my office."

I remained on the examining table, trying to process what I just learned. Thoughts of Gerald filled my mind. As I wondered how I could possibly tell him, the room began to spin.

"Let me call my nurse. Just stay put for a bit."

A tall, heavyset woman with pale skin entered the examining room. She took my shoulders, leaned me against her own chest. She felt billowy, and I rested there a while.

"Dr. Kendall!" I heard my name being called as if in a tunnel. "Wake up, Dr. Kendall."

An odious, sharp smell penetrated my nostrils, and I jerked back my head back to avoid it. The harsh vapors pierced my sinuses. Reflexively, I pushed away the nurse's hand, which I saw held a small bottle of smelling salts.

"Are you awake?"

"Yes. I don't know what happened."

"Just a little faint. Let me take your pressure. Sometimes it's the heat . . ." The nurse put the cuff on my arm. "How about some water? You all right sitting up, now?"

"Yes."

"The cooler is right outside the door." She stepped out, and I looked around the room, seeing the monitor that showed me my child's beating heart. The nurse returned with a cup full of cool water. Behind her was Dr. Clarke.

"I hear you had a fainting spell. I know you have a driver, but is there anyone I can call. . . . Dr. Manley mentioned you are staying at Dr. Hunter's place . . . maybe I can give him a call."

"No. No, please. . . . He's in Boston. I'm fine."

The nurse began to squeeze the blood pressure bulb and the cuff tightened around my arm. She listened to the stethoscope and then squeezed the bulb again.

"One ten over seventy."

"That's all right," the doctor said. "Did you eat today?"

"Not really . . . been nauseous."

"Geneva, help Dr. Kendall get dressed. And give her some graham crackers. Will bring up your blood sugar. I will alert your driver."

The nurse helped me dress and patted my back. "Let me get you the crackers." She came back with the graham crackers, which I ate, and she held the door for me, pointing down the hallway to the doctor's office.

The room was pale lavender, and on the desk sat an orchid growing curiously—first to the left and then to the right. Dr. Clarke's office was stark, save the orchid that seemed as if it was carving out its space in this otherwise all-business environs.

The doctor's dark-skinned face was like an ancient African sculpture holding some secret wisdom. She revealed no emotions as she spoke, "So I take it this was a surprise. You should know that though it is unusual to have a pregnancy begin when a woman is in her forties, with proper care, there should be no problems. Here are your prenatal vitamins," she said, placing a bottle on the desk. "In the case of expectant mothers in your age range, I always suggest that you take it easy for the next few weeks, especially in this heat. Saltines should help with the nausea, and bland foods of course. No medications of any kind. No alcohol or any drugs during the pregnancy. I would like to see you in three weeks just to check on your progress, if you will be in Bequia. And I suggest that you avoid flying in the near future . . . for at least a month or so."

I watched her lips while trying to capture the sentences which flew out of Dr. Clarke's mouth in her crisp West Indian accent. But her words ran together in my brain, as yet unprocessed.

"Do you have any questions?"

I am pregnant. "How did this happen??"

Dr. Clarke's face seemed to take on an inscrutable Mona Lisa smile, not full enough to elicit a smile in return. "Did you use birth control?"

"No. I thought . . ."

"There's your answer. Should I send the results to Dr. Manley?"

"No, please. I need to . . ." I flushed, and my face felt hot.

"As a courtesy . . ." The woman's gaze seemed to slice into my consciousness, "It would be confidential, I assure you."

"No, I'd rather not."

"Fine. No problem. Geneva," she raised her voice, "call the driver, please."

I moved through the waiting room filled with women—some slender, some stout, some with rounded bellies, some not, many who looked up at me. I soon found myself outside in the car, not remembering how I got there. The car took me to the house, and Haynes opened the door to let me in.

"Is everything . . . are you all right? Mum?"

I made my way past her and through to Gerald's bedroom. "I need to rest." Images of Gerald, then Derek, then all I could see was the image of the pulsating white dot of light from the sonogram. "Could you put on the overhead fan? There is no air in here. I can't breathe. Maybe the air conditioning. I need to breathe . . . and close the shades." I pulled off my blouse and bra. I took off my sandals and tugged at my slacks.

Haynes collected my clothes and folded each piece, placing them on the couch near the desk. She handed me my nightdress, which I threw on the bed beside me. "Should I call Dr. Hunter, Mum?"

"No Haynes, please. Just do as I ask. Put on the air conditioner. Close the shades."

I pulled the sheets and coverlet down.

"I can do that for you, Mum."

"No, leave me. Leave me be."

The room grew dark around me. I pushed all the images out of my mind except one, this child now in my body. I wanted to rest.

"Mariel!" I heard the voice of my brother, Tindaro, disturbing my peace. "Mariel!"

"Don't go in there!" Sumadi shouted, from outside the hut. Vibrations shook the structure as I heard men pushing and striking each other. There were more than the two. Blows landed, and the grunts of a few men in combat moved away from the door.

"Señora Matos." Leila's commanding voice seeped into the hut. The muscles on the sides of my abdomen contracted. Fear surged through me, and I reached for the necklace, which was not there. The woman gave me her arm and pulled me up. She held a knife ready to strike as she pushed her head out, surveying the area in front of the hut. She pulled me past the men, who were striking each other with their fists and clubs, and blocking blows with bamboo-like sticks.

"She will not take the child," Sumadi said, his face bloodied and his arm cut. There it was. My necklace hung around his neck.

"Suma," his first wife shrieked, running from the rear of another hut, holding a stick with a sharp blade on its end and tossing it to him.

Sumadi snatched it from the air and clenched it, pointing it at Tindaro, who stood stock-still with only three feet separating him from the blade pointed at his chest.

I grabbed the knife from Leila. "Hurt my brother, and you will watch your child die."

Everyone froze. I held the knife like a dagger pointed downward toward my abdomen. "And give me my necklace."

My brother was the first to speak. "Mariel, no!"

"You would not," Sumadi said, his voice now lowered and his hand shaking. The first wife held her hand to her mouth. Sumadi's second wife emerged from another hut, carrying an infant. Sumadi gently dropped the weapon near his feet.

"My necklace."

"Here, have it," Sumadi said, his voice thickened with a sneer.

"I will go to my home, my husband's home." Leila snatched the necklace from his grip. My teeth were gritted, and my voice strident, "When the child comes, I will send it to you. You raise him. I have no need to see him or know of him."

"You must feed him," Sumadi said in a commanding tone.

"Let her do it." I pointed the knife to the woman with the child. Sumadi waved the woman off, and she turned and ducked her head, going back into the hut with his first wife following.

"You will not rule me." My stance hardened. "After I have this child, you will only come when I summon you."

"You, summon me?" he asked, seeming incredulous.

"Why do you think they came for me? I made them come. Do not cross me."

Tindaro heard me and did not challenge my words. I knew he had gone to my house that morning, though he did not remember why. Leila did not question me. Both came because I willed them to do so.

The path the men walked took us toward the sea. Leila walked ahead of me, and my brother behind me, pointing the weapon at Sumadi until we were in the thick bush. Once on the shore, Leila placed the necklace over my head. I craved the comforting feeling of it resting between my breasts. But the weight of the scrimshaw was off. It was just a bit askew.

A long boat sat in the water with two men holding oars. The sea was peaceful. The two men walking with us waded into the surf and climbed aboard. Tindaro leapt into the water and together they lifted me into the boat. I sat in the stern, and I twisted the cord on the scrimshaw to right its weight and feel. Maybe, I thought, it was just Sumadi's touch that I felt and that remained. With time, it would regain its feeling of safe-keeping, I thought. Leila climbed in and sat beside me. The child rested through it all.

I slept undisturbed through the night. It was the pounding on the door that woke me.

38

The thunderous blows to the door reverberated through the house. Then came the shout.

"Jocelyn, are you in there? Can you hear me?" The room was frigid and black with only slits of light that penetrated the sides of the shades. The hammering at the door began again. Then there was the sound of something pelting the shutters of the bedroom window. "Jocelyn, do you hear me?"

Was that Cassandra's voice? I pushed back the mosquito net, threw my nightdress on, and moved as quickly as I could to the door. "Coming! Cassandra?"

Cassandra stood just outside the door, sweat sheeting her forehead, and behind her there he was. He was wearing shades, hiding his eyes from me.

"What are you doing here . . . ? I told you I didn't want to see him."

"I got here almost two hours ago. I knocked, you didn't answer. The shades were drawn. I called, nothing. So, I rang him up. I was worried."

"We heard you might be . . ." he paused, as he took off his sunglasses, ". . . ill." His facial expression showed no concern, just a glint in his eye.

"Who told you that? I'm not sick."

Derek turned to Cassandra, now a grin growing on his lips. Her face turned crimson.

"Someone said they saw you at the doctor's yesterday," Cassandra said.

"Who said that? That's not your business."

"I was just worried. Can't we come inside?" Cassandra asked.

Derek stepped up behind Cassandra, his face with its usual lascivious aspect. "I understand that you have something that belongs to me."

His voice had a way of wending itself through my insides. "I don't know what you are talking about."

He leaned closer and whispered, "Sure you do. I knew it, that night, that very first night."

Our eyes locked.

It was strange how the heat of excitation and the chill of fear could take over one's body all at once. I fell back against the counter. Derek held fast to me, and Cassandra braced my fall.

"You really should reconsider coming to Moon Hole . . ."

"Derek!" Cassandra said, and then caught hold of his arm.

"So we all can look after you," he said. "How long will he be gone?"

"Get him out of here!"

Cassandra pushed him out through the kitchen doorway.

"Call me," he said.

"Sorry, I would have called. . . . Let me go make you some broth."

Cassandra and Derek's bickering outside the doorway became muffled as they moved down the stairs. *Why was Cassandra here?* My thoughts came together. It was Thursday, and I was supposed to meet with her to do the session of hypnosis. I forgot completely. Who in the doctor's office told them I was there? This island thing is really getting to me. Then I heard Derek's words, "I knew that night." *He is messing around in my head.* Can't let him do this to me. Maybe I could not change what was happening inside my body, but I could reclaim my mind. Cassandra came back in, putting up the kettle.

She hooked arms with me and walked me into the bedroom. A few minutes later, she returned, carrying a tray with coconut water and some crackers.

"So, you serious about this guy . . . the guy who owns this house?"

"Why . . . what do you mean . . . ?" She opened the shades and turned off the air conditioner.

"I don't know. You just seem so comfortable here . . . in his bedroom."

". . . If you are just fishing for information for Derek . . ."

"There's some sort of animosity between them. I never heard about it before Barbados, but then . . ." Cassandra's brown eyes holding back.

". . . in Barbados?"

Cassandra laughed.

"What did he say?" I asked.

"It's not important. I boiled water for broth. It's freezing in here."

Cassandra left, and I thought about the exchange Gerald had with Derek before the hurricane. She brought back a cup of bouillon.

"What did he say in Barbados?"

"I told you we were all knocked about when the boat was spun around. Almost immediately, the sky cleared, and he yelled out, 'That bloody bugger,' then called out his name." Cassandra laughed.

"You're kidding?"

"No, I didn't put it all together until today, when I called him to say you weren't answering. He said he'd come and take care of everything, then mumbled something about a score to settle."

I studied the air in front of me, and the events of the day came rushing back. The image of the beating heart on the sonogram. Dreams of being taken by Sumadi to live with his wives. Derek's presence in Gerald's home.

"That's not going to happen this time." The words spilled out.

"What? What is this energy between Derek and Gerald?" She paused, ". . . And you. He has a real thing for you."

"I am not a pawn in his battle with Gerald. Don't much care about the scores he would settle. And I am not coming to Moon Hole."

Cassandra looked as if she had heard too much and wanted to extricate herself. "So, you forgot our meeting this morning . . . for the hypnosis?"

"I'm sorry, I did. Was pretty tired when I got home yesterday."

Cassandra stood up with the tray and looked me in the eye. "So, are you sick, or are you pregnant?"

39

"*Um pé. Meu Deus, um pé.*" Leila's face was ashen, and her mouth dropped open. Her gaze seemed to move from my face to between my knees. I tried but could not see down beneath my belly. But all at once, I realized. "A foot," she said. "She said a foot." In my mind's eye, I saw it protruding, and a scream rose in my chest. My mother and the midwife were supposed to come, but they refused because of the shame I brought to the village. Leila had torn cloth and placed a cushion of soft bedding in the base of the tub, which sat in the yard behind the house, just next to the veranda.

Leila gently pushed the foot back in, then slowly inserted her hand. The burning pain made me pull away, and I bellowed in agony, but the woman held me still by bracing her hand on my abdomen. My feet pressed against the tub, pushing me up against the back of the basin-like structure, trying to get away from her. Despite my begging her to stop, she twisted the child around. And then she shouted at me, "*Empurre!*" A shriek escaped my mouth and lengthened into a howl. Holding the side of the tub, I bore down as hard as I could.

Leila pulled the baby's head out, and then the shoulders. I took a breath then pushed out the behind; legs and feet finally emerged. The bloody afterbirth spewed with such force that it slapped the front of the tub.

"Um menino. E um menino," Leila told me, but I knew it was a boy. I had known it for months. Leila cleaned the inside of the child's mouth with her forefinger and slapped the baby on the back; he wailed and trembled. She tried to place him on my stomach as I finally leaned back, but I pushed him away.

"Take it to him," I said, without opening my eyes. The woman angrily pushed the baby into my arms. She took the knife resting on the towel-covered stool; after tying it off with string, she cut the cord.

When Leila stood to take the child away from me, I tried not to look, but I caught a glimpse. I told her to wait as my gaze fixed on him. He was golden brown, his fingers and toes were tiny and perfectly formed, and the full head of curly hair was as black as the night. I could not stop myself from caressing his hair, so soft. His mouth was wide open, and his scream made his bottom lip tremble. I asked Leila for the knife with which she had cut the cord. She shook her head, and took the child from me, placing him in the blanket she had brought.

"Bring him here, and give me that knife," I said.

The woman looked at me, fear in her eyes, and wiped the bloodied knife on the hem of her dress. Leila held the child to her own breast. I repeated myself, and when the woman began to plead for the innocent child's life, I shouted, "His hair!" I tugged the damp strands of my hair as I shouted at her. Leila seemed poised to pull the infant back if I made any movement to strike him. Reaching out with the hand that did not hold the knife and taking hold of the hair at the nape of his neck, I spoke again, "I just want a small bit of his hair." Leila held the child's flailing arms away from the blade and held his head as I cut a curly tuft. As Leila released her protective grasp on him, the child looked up at me and grew calm. He seemed to have knowledge of me, and I him. It was strange looking into the eyes of an infant and seeing what seemed the wisdom of an old soul. I noticed a beauty mark in the shape of a teardrop just above his left chest—resting, I thought, on his heart.

As I handed the child to Leila, I immediately wished to have him back. Torn as I was, the wish was powerful and complete. *I want him to come back to me.*

Leila took the baby and wrapped him in the blanket. Tindaro appeared from behind the mango tree where he must have been waiting, watching. With the baby in his arms, my brother left. I held the lock of hair tightly in the palm of my hand. "I want to go inside." The torn bits of cloth, stained with blood, clung to my hip and thighs. Leila helped me bathe; she wiped me with a towel and held it around my waist.

It is done, I thought. His father will raise him. His father's wife will care for him. The place, the time, seemed to recede.

"When I count backward from ten, you will leave this place. You will feel calm and fully awake. Ten, nine, eight. Take deep breaths. Seven, six, five, four. You are waking, feeling refreshed. Three, two, one."

"He is going to his father," I said to Cassandra, my eyes blinking open. I was between both worlds. I closed my eyes wanting to see him again, but he was gone. Hopes of hearing him were dashed, he was no more. "He was healthy and whole. He had a good strong cry."

"Who is his father?"

As I took in my surroundings, Gerald's bed, Cassandra seated at the foot of it, and the window behind her, I tried to hold the images I was leaving behind in my memory. "What did you say?"

"I said, what was the father's name?"

"Sumadi."

"That name sounds African," Cassandra said.

"He was Black, but a Black Carib, I think. Though he had brown skin, he had golden eyes like he was a mixture." I realized I wasn't sure. "Maybe I just assumed he was a Black Carib, knowing how many Africans joined Carib villages and intermarried."

"You mentioned that it was a large ship that he came in with a large crew. Sounds like he was an accomplished man. Was the larger boat a whaling ship?"

"I believe so. It had a sail, but there were eight men rowing and it was shaped like a canoe."

"The islanders who were whalers used large canoes with sails."

"I could be wrong about him being a Black Carib. He wanted to keep me there with him, and his other wives, a Carib and an African, I thought, but they seemed to understand his language, which was not Carib. It sounded like an African language . . ."

"That makes sense because many of the African men from Ghana or Nigeria had more than one wife."

"I know."

"But you said he's the one who reminds you of Derek?"

"Yes, it's hard to explain because they don't look alike. It's more as if their personas are the same."

Cassandra sat silently for a minute. And then she seemed to have a new understanding.

"You are pregnant? And it's Derek's?" Though she posed the questions, her eyes and tone said that she knew the answers.

I wanted to hide, but I had nowhere to go. Cassandra had witnessed this regression in real time, and she knew Derek's connection to it. I nodded because I could not say the words. I was certain Cassandra could read the tangle of emotions in my eyes. She didn't know the details, but she knew that he and Sumadi and I were tied together.

"I wished for him back. Is that why this is happening to me?"

"Who? Wished for Sumadi back?"

"No, for my baby."

"That's not how it works. That was then. This is now. You cannot change anything then."

"I feel something terrible is going to happen because of my wish for him to come back to me. I could feel it as I thought it."

"What do you mean?"

"I mean, I felt as I said it to myself that I wanted him back, I had willed it so. And as I had the thought, I knew there would be terrible consequences." I looked to Cassandra for comfort, but her eyes held none. Instead, she appeared frustrated—no, disgusted.

Cassandra stood up and walked toward the window, facing the sea. When she turned to face me, I could see only her shadowy form in silhouette. I could not see her eyes because the light came from behind her. But I heard her say, "If I were you, I'd stop worrying about what is going to happen in the past and focus on what is happening now. What are you going to do?"

My eyes darted about the room, where everything reminded me of Gerald. How could I tell him what I had done, and about the life inside me that did not belong to him? My gaze moved to the window. The sky had begun to darken and rest heavily on the indigo water. There were no answers there either. The horizon had always seemed to represent promise, but now it seemed more like a wall of decisions closing in on me.

40

I awakened from a dreamless sleep, the quiet in the house closed in around me. My forehead and upper lip were draped with sweat. I went out to the veranda to catch a breeze and to hear life.

As I opened the door, the whistling whine of the crickets filled my ears. I flipped the switch, and in just seconds moths swarmed, looping and diving into the light. They darted in and out, tapping the glass globe, casting shadows as they flitted and flew. The smell of the salty water filled my nostrils. As I breathed in the odors of the night, I imagined the swirling sea creatures moving through the black water and tangle of seaweed, wriggling through the surf just yards away. My senses now jarred, my thoughts turned to the hypnotic episode earlier that day, and the sense of foreboding I felt when I wished for the child back. The muscles in my belly contorted. Something about my wish, which seemed more like a message to the universe, was wrong.

I needed to go back *there*, but I needed to be guided. I couldn't ask Cassandra again. Her interest was in Derek, and I could not have her influence the journey. Luis's warning, that I could not change anything in the past reverberated in my mind. I am trapped now in events over which I have no control.

"I need to talk to Luis," I said to myself, but the words flew from my lips into the night air. I wondered if he and Selena were home yet. I opened the screen door, which gave off a high-pitched screech. I wondered why I hadn't noticed it when I opened it to go out. I filled the kettle, and a shadow moved past my head. I searched for its source. There it was. One large moth had slipped inside. I batted at it, hitting it with the back of my hand. The feel of it made my skin crawl, and I kept my eye on it as it flew into the overhead bulb. The tapping sound it made, hitting against the globe, was unnerving. It bounced about and finally landed on a blade of the overhead fan. Its wings fluttered until it got its footing, folding its wings back and resting there. I marked where it stopped.

"I need to calm down," I said to myself. I went to the pantry to get the chamomile tea, and before I reached for the string to turn on the light, I noticed that the cabinet door on the wall was ajar. Haynes must have left it open by mistake. There on the third shelf down, alphabetically in place, was the periwinkle tea. I remembered Haynes warning that I shouldn't drink it. "I will call Luis tomorrow, just to find out if he knows about this. Maybe he can guide me from there."

Haynes will be back tomorrow, and she might lock it up again. I took out the boxes, the periwinkle and the chamomile, and spooned half a teaspoon full of the periwinkle leaves into a foil wrapper. "I wonder if this is enough," I thought out loud, and then spooned some more of the herb into it. The herbs left in the box didn't look appreciably depleted. I folded the waxed paper bag holding the tiny bits of purplish leaves and tucked it back inside the small package. The phone rang, my hand shook, spilling leaves all over the counter. Some even rained down onto the floor.

"Shit," I said, grabbing for the phone. "Who is it?"

"You must be pissed off at somebody," Selena laughed. "Caught you at a bad time? Did I interrupt . . . ?"

"No, just dropped something, trying to . . . never mind. I can't believe it. I was just thinking about you and . . . Luis."

"We are in the airport, leaving Italy."

"So much has happened. I so need to talk to you guys."

"Luis said he just got a strong feeling you were in trouble. Here . . ."

"Hey, beautiful! We are getting ready to board, but I had a sense of foreboding. You must be a sender. Got this vibe. Could swear it came from you. Did not want to wait till we got to New York and hear something bad happened. So just be careful."

"Weird. Luis, I wanted to ask you about. . . . Can you regress me when you get to New York?"

"No. I wouldn't, not long distance. You coming back . . ." His voice dropped out.

"Luis, can you hear me? What do you know about periwinkle, the herb?"

"Good for relaxation . . . careful . . . be danger . . . if you . . ."

"What did you say . . . ?"

"I said the one thing . . . and you should . . ."

"What? I can't hear you."

"We are boarding, went into . . ." His voice dropped out again. "Just don't . . . call you . . . New York." He was gone.

I brushed the herbs from the counter. I wet a piece of paper towel and wiped up the bits that were on the floor. When I sniffed the paper, the floral scent filled my nostrils, and though I was drawn to inhale it more deeply, I turned my head away.

"Periwinkle . . ." I went to my computer. "I can look . . ." The screen was black. "Didn't charge it." The cable dangled behind the desk, unplugged. In Gerald's room, I jiggled the mouse and the computer came on. The Wi-Fi icon was grayed out. When I clicked on it, the prompt asked for the password. "Damn it!" Just below my consciousness, the kettle wailed, adding to my irritation. There was a pounding on the door. The digital clock on Gerald's side of the bed said 9:34 p.m. "That better not be Derek." I went into the kitchen. "Who is there?" I heard nothing. "I said who is it?"

"Vivencia here, miss."

"Who?"

"Vivencia? Gomes!"

"Vivencia? What . . . are you all right?" I opened the door a little and then drew it back so that she could step into the kitchen. Vivencia was breathing heavily, her chest rising and falling. "What's wrong?" I asked. Her eyes searched each corner of the room, beginning with the screen door. The screaming kettle became deafening, and I, mesmerized by the old woman, stepped backward to turn off the gas. The old lady seemed not to care about the kettle at all, seemed not to even notice it. Her eyes rested on the box of periwinkle on the counter. "What dat?"

"Periwinkle . . . tea leaves. I was going to make some tea. What are you doing here? I hope I don't sound rude, but I am just surprised."

"You call me."

"No, I didn't. I didn't call any . . ."

"I hear you. I be at the church . . . and feel you call . . ."

Bewildered, I thought of the old woman's idiosyncrasies. But watching her movement triggered my memory of Cassandra's comments about the locals using periwinkle. "Maybe you can help me with this. I don't know how much periwinkle to use for a cup of tea. Just want to relax . . . you know . . ."

"Dr. Hunter haf dis here?"

"Yes."

"He no tell you . . ."Haynes told me that I shouldn't . . ."

"Then you no listen. You know you not to haf dis now."

The old woman studied me hard. She pinched some periwinkle and put it in a cup.

"What do you mean, *not have this now?*"

"You know what I mean. Mariel know the truth."

"What did you say?"

"I say, 'Mariel right.'"

"What do you mean?"

"Other night. I see you dance with the darkness." The old woman then grabbed the box and stuffed it in her big apron pocket. "I see confusion all around you. Darkness fighting light. Mariel say it Nereida. I need to find her. You haf a strainer?"

"What?"

"A strainer nuh? For da tea."

The top drawer beneath the counter held a small tea strainer as well as a tea ball. The wiry little woman put her bony hand in the drawer and stuffed a pinch of chamomile into the tea ball.

"You say you want to find you child?"

"I didn't say that. I didn't tell you that."

The old woman lifted the kettle and poured in the steaming hot water. "I hear it."

My knees weakened. I held on to the counter.

"Sit girl. Mariel come to me and say we mus' stop Nereida. She have power of light and dark, and it all in a ball of confusion. She follow . . . she here."

The woman placed the chamomile tea in front of me and began to sip from the periwinkle she had made for herself.

There was that shadow. It sliced through the amber light, and I hunted for its cause. The cup shook, spilling the yellow liquid on the table. I grabbed for a napkin to sop up the mess, but I could not stop searching the room for what was creating this darting, spiraling shadow that moved past me. The moth moved along the edge of the door and finally rested on the top right corner. Vivencia was looking at it too. Her expression was bewildering, then her jaw clenched, and she seemed to be filled with resolve.

"Hold dat girl," she said, and pointed her bony finger. "Your grandmother said you haf power you no use."

"What?" I looked in the direction of my nightdress.

"Dat," she repeated. She pointed again this time, stretching out her arm and placing her finger on the amulet that hung 'round my neck. I had grown accustomed to the feel of it resting there between my breasts. I reached for it and let my thumb and forefinger feel its etchings. Peacefulness flowed through me. The old woman sat, her eyes searching the room once more, then settling on the moth, which once again fluttered then seemed to climb holding fast to the screen. It was trying to escape, I was certain. The woman closed her eyes, but I could see her eyeballs moving behind her closed paper-thin lids. I held the amulet. I sensed I would be tested, and I hoped it would protect me.

41

"Get she 'way from me!" The raspy, guttural whisper came from someplace in the room, but I could not tell where. The old woman stood up, steadied herself against the table, and held the back of the chair. She moved to the pantry and came back out with a tall devotional candle with a charred wick. She lit it, and I noted how she knew the room and everything in it. The smell of sulphur hung in the air after she struck the match. Then Vivencia seemed to almost glide to the door, "Come and face me," she said, her voice monotone. She flicked the switch, darkening the room, save the glow of the candle and the swath of light from outside the screen door.

"My work here is long done." The whisper now grew more grating.

"What you do?" Vivencia turned and spoke out to the center of the room. Then there was that shadow that moved past my head. I ducked, looked over my shoulder, and then out to the center of the room again. Vivencia sat motionless.

"She know." The voice grew stronger, strident. This time it came from the corner of the room near the screen door, the silhouette blotting out the light from the porch. As I caught sight of it, it moved.

"What is it? What you do? Show yourself to me," Vivencia said.

The shadowy form moved in a semicircular arc back to the center of the room and took on substance. "She go back den. She go back to

Mariel." She began to laugh, pointing at me. "Too late. Now me son haf her, too."

"Why? Why you do somet'ing to this girl?"

"Me no care about she. It Mariel."

"Why you do somet'ing to Mariel?"

"Me no care 'bout Mariel. It me son."

"You cause confusion. Why you do dis?" The more Vivencia spoke, the more the dark shadowy form coalesced.

"Let me go. The light is burning me."

"I let you go when you tell me what happened to you son."

"Abrahim make me do dis. He make me promise."

"Who is Abrahim?"

I knew the name. I looked to the figure, now a looming phantom, for the answer.

"He come and lay wit' me. Promised to take me 'cross the water."

I remembered the image of the registry of the whaling ship that Gerald had sent the link to, "*The Sea Nymph, Nereida.*"

"My great-great-great-great-grandfather, Abrahim?"

The shadow reared up and pointed at me. "She did, dig, dig. She know."

"I'm just trying to understand," I shouted at the ghostly figure.

The amorphous dark specter now took on features and formed into a beautiful woman, dark skin. Her regal stature, and close-cropped hair made her seem more like a sculpture than a being with life. Yet her dark eyes glared at me. She seemed to float there in the room. Vivencia placed her bony finger on her lips. "Nereida, we need you help."

Nereida's visage softened, as she turned to the old woman. "He leave me, not come back so long. So long. So many moons."

"Who? Your son?"

"No. Abrahim."

She wore her misery not only in her face, but also in her figure, which grew bent. Melancholy filled the room like a heavy lavender perfume. I could feel it too. It was too familiar.

"He lay with me. I please him." For the first time, her words were soft and loving. "I know I please him." Her voice grew strained. The light from the candle flickered.

"I ask him if he come to take me wit' him. He say, no." She began to weep. "I beg, and he turn his back."

"I watch him ship grow small and then fall over the end of the sea. I wait and wait, and he no come back."

"You can't blame Mariel for that," I said, my words just flying out.

"Me no blame her. She just there. I grow old waiting for him." The apparition grew bent, her hair turning white, as I watched. The sadness in her eyes seemed to turn cold and bitter. "He son, Joseph, come back to find me. Tell me him dead. Tell me him gif his ship me name, Nereida."

"What you say 'bout Mariel and your son? Who your son?"

"My son tall and strong. I haf him learn to find whale, use harpoon like his father." The tall regal form now shrunken, shoulders curved in, "Abrahim and his son, Joseph, come to me in Cape Verde when he was younger, and I ask him to take my son 'cross the water. Joseph haf his own son, John. He haf eyes like the sea, like Abrahim. Black hair in ringlets like Abrahim."

"But you son. He take him or leave him dere? You son?" Vivencia asked.

"He take him 'cause I make him do it, and dat's when I . . ." Her voice was low and filled with anger.

"What? What did you do?" The ghostly form dispersed. A laugh reverberated through the room. "She know." She pointed in my direction.

"What did you do?" I yelled in the direction I thought she moved. "Don't you leave this room!"

Her form coalesced once more and came back to face Vivencia. "Why you hold me? She burn me with her light."

"What you do? I can fix now." Vivencia's voice seemed to plead with the apparition.

"You can't undo dis." Nereida shook her head, and it hung down in shame. "I try to help my son. . . . My pain hurt . . . hurt him. My hex it turned bad."

"What your son's name?" I yelled. "Who is your son?"

"You know him. He had you."

Vivencia's eyes flashed in anger. She gritted her teeth as she hissed, "Shhhh" at me.

"Wait." I shouted at Nereida. "Come back."

"You know his name." The ghostly form murmured. "Mariel know him well. . . . Sumadi."

"Just tell me how you hurt . . . how you hurt him," Vivencia called out. "What you do?"

I searched the room. "Where are you?"

"She gone," Vivencia's knitted brow was visible even in the shadowy darkness of the room.

"You speak when you should be quiet," Vivencia said, her voice growing louder as she slumped in resignation, her head resting in her hands. "We need her. I must find out what . . . who this Sumadi is . . . and connection to . . . Mariel. I feel I know it but can't say."

"Sumadi is Mariel's lover. I had his child. I wish for him back."

"Girl, you lost . . ."

"No, I told you. I wish for my child. It's Sumadi's. . . . And now Derek, I feel Derek . . . is . . ." My voice trailed off as I struggled with the pieces of the story, ashamed of what the old woman would think of me.

She looked at me. It was clear she understood. "I know now . . . but Nereida . . . Nereida mus' set dis right." Vivencia labored to walk to the switch to turn on the light. "You mus' use your will, not your voice."

The scolding stung my cheeks. I picked up her cup and saucer and placed it in the sink. "Should I blow out this candle?"

"No, leave it burn," Vivencia said.

"You haven't helped me go back. I need to get back and find out about my son."

The old woman picked up the candle and cupped her bony fingers around the brim and walked into Gerald's room. "You sleep now."

My fist clenched; frustration tightened my grip. "Are you going to help me, guide me?"

"Your power is in your will, girl. Just use your will."

42

"Cut off the head!"

The girl, Estela, took the large carving knife and cut just below the gills, pressing the blade down until she heard the bony spine crack.

"Put it in the big soup pot." The bloody guts were resting on the brown paper on the table John had sent me from Barbados. John placed it near the sink so that I could put the fish and pieces of whale meat on it. The scales flew off the fish as my daughter scraped it. Using the big shears, the girl cut off the fins and then the tail. Estela stretched herself up to look out the window, then sucked her teeth.

"What you looking at?" I asked.

"Nothin'."

The girl spoke in a patois. It was a mix of the Carib and Portuguese language we shared.

I watched this scene unfold around me, first as an observer, then fully a part of it. I was Mariel, though my body had grown old, and my breasts drooped. My shoulders bowed from leaning over, weaving my baskets and baking my breads each day. I made good money, and made John stay home with me more. My shape didn't matter much in the cotton housedresses I wore. I squeezed the corn meal and water together, forming and flattening dumplings.

My mind pulled away from the scene. "Your power is in your will. Just use your will." Vivencia's words echoed. I didn't know how to will something to happen. Things had happened when I wished them, but I always looked for the evidence that somehow there was a reason. It couldn't be my wishing or willing it to be.

As I scanned the room, the chiaroscuro of Gerald's desk, his couch, the computer—all the objects—emerged from the black background. I felt the gauzy light rest on my skin and enter my pores. When I closed my eyes, the sensation grew stronger. Beneath my eyelids, it was there too, the light. It pulled me, drew me to it. It was the light of that day, with my daughter.

The girl was taller than I was. Her hair was long and wavy, pulled back into a plait that hung down her back. The end of the braid was bound with a navy-blue ribbon tied in a bow, which sat on her behind where it shook as she worked on the fish. Estela lifted her hand to wave through the window, then used the back of her hand to brush at her brow.

"Want some green bananas for the soup? I could go outside and look for someone to pick some."

"Who's dere? Who you wavin' to?" The girl stiffened her spine and turned to fully face me. I saw her stained hands, which she held rather precariously upturned, trying not to drip the pieces of scales and bits of gut and bone onto the floor. When our eyes met, she blinked and turned away. She dipped her hands in the basin and shook them. Brushing away the debris, she grabbed the dishtowel and dried her hands, her jaw set.

"Someone I want you to meet." Her language became more formal as she squared her shoulders.

I knew that posture well. My daughter had been that way, since young. She would straighten up and make herself as tall as she could, once standing on her bed to look down at me, and then declare what she wanted. When she was little, it was amusing. I saw something of myself in that resolve. My mother would have struck me had I ever done that, but I wanted my child to be strong. I pushed the bowl with the dumplings away, folded my arms, and said, "So what is this?"

"His name is Rohan. He has a small whaling ship and hunts here in the water near Bequia."

"You fadder not like dat."

"Father met him when I went to see him at his ship, here at the docks in Bequia last month."

I picked up the bowl and slammed it down on the worktable.

"You keeping secrets wit' your fadder, 'gains' me? Clean this mess up."

"No!"

"What'd you say to me?"

"I . . . said, no."

My hand flew up and struck the girl on the face before I could stop myself. Her olive skin blossomed bright red on her cheek. She returned an angry glare and walked heavy-footed, slamming the porch door.

Outside, I watched Estela talk to a tall muscular young man, dark skin, long curly hair, who scowled in my direction. He looked away from me to her, stroked her cheek lightly with his fingertips. She nestled her head in his arms as if she had been there before.

Opening my eyes, I was still in Gerald's bed. I had willed myself back in time. It did not happen in a dream; I had *made* it happen. *This is what started the split between my daughter and me. I can fix this. It was foolish of me to slap her.* Luis said that I cannot change the past. But this was something minor, I could just apologize, make it right. I closed my eyes.

"Estela," I shouted to her, but I don't know if she heard me. John's voice called out as he climbed down from the wagon. Estela's young man turned, extending his hand to John, who shook it warmly, patting the man on the back. John pointed to the large sack resting in the back of the wagon. The young man looked down at his shirt, a white shirt. John gestured to Estela, and the young man took off his shirt and handed it to her.

"Come up," I said, as I waved to them from the veranda. "I am making some fish soup." John strode up to the porch steps. He waved the young man on. Estela stayed back, folding the shirt over her forearm. "Estela, don't you want to help make the fry fish for your guest," I said. The girl hesitated, and John said, "She makes fry fish as good as her mother." Estela seemed frozen in place. "Better than mine," I said, raising my voice so that she could hear me.

"Get my bottle of rum, woman, and pour us two glasses."

As I opened the porch door, I noticed how the young man's muscles bulged with the weight of the huge sack.

"Cassava flour from St. Vincent for your baking, should make many loaves like you said," John eyed the bottle of rum, and pulled the cork out of the bottle.

"Put the bag on the floor dere so, next to me basket," I said to the young man. "Estela made these dumplings for a fish soup."

I tried to smile at my daughter, hoping I had softened her heart with the lies about who made the dumplings. Her jaw was clenched and pulsating, and her cheek still pink from the slap.

"Mother, this is Rohan."

I wiped my hands on my apron, feeling that I had looked too long at his handsome face. His features seemed a mix of African and Carib Indian. His hair was wavy and would have fallen into his face but for the fact that it was greased just enough to hold it in place. "Where are you from . . . your family?" I asked, watching the careful way he rested the sack on the floor.

"Mustique Island," he said. "My father is a whaler. And my mother is not well."

"How many years do you have?"

"I have twenty years."

"He owns a whaling boat, and he does hunt whales all over the Caribbean. He has a crew in Bequia, Mustique, and St. Vincent. He sells his oil in St. Vincent and Barbados." Estela had stretched herself up to deliver that speech to me.

"It is good to meet you . . . Rohan," I said, extending my hand. He stood a full foot and a half above me. There on his left chest was a birthmark, shaped like a teardrop. The sight of it jarred my senses, and my memory seemed to explode in my head. I saw the baby, my baby, as I handed it to Leila. I saw its beautiful curly hair, and the birthmark, the tiny teardrop that rested on his left chest.

"NO, NO, NO!" My scream bellowed through the house. "THIS CANNOT BE!" I shouted. "Get out. Get out now. Do not come back to this house!"

The fear and pain on my face were mirrored in the face of my daughter a moment after the shock subsided. John looked stunned.

"Be quiet woman! What is wrong with you?"

"GET OUT OF HERE. DON'T YOU GO AGAINST ME JOHN! GET OUT!"

Rohan grabbed his shirt from Estela. He looked into my eyes and turned to her. The girl's body was shaking.

"I HATE YOU! YOU ARE NO LONGER MY MOTHER!" The words seemed to come from somewhere in the girl's belly. Her face was imprinted with indignation.

Rohan opened the door to the porch. Estela slammed it against the wall as she pushed past him. Rohan followed her out.

John balled his fist and banged it on the table. "Mariel, why did you do this to our daughter!"

I shook. My mouth fell open, but no sound came out. I was trapped. My husband could not know who this man, the man my daughter loved, was. Shame stifled me.

My eyes flew open again. In Gerald's room, I held my head with my fingers laced, and my palms pressing like a vise on my temples. I tried to squeeze the thoughts out. They would not leave. I had willed the child back, and he had come.

43

I had no sense of time, searching for ways to fix the mess my life had become. When the phone rang, I was afraid to answer it. It could be Derek, who I hated for trapping me with this life I carried. I could not hate the child. He was faultless. I had let it happen.

I wanted to talk to Gerald, to hear his voice, see his face. *Could I will the life within me to be his?* This twisted play that I was acting out seemed to have come from this woman Nereida, but I didn't know what she had done, or how she had used her power. There was the ring again. It was irritating, and I couldn't avoid it any longer.

"Hello!"

"Babe? . . . Did I wake you?"

"No . . . I'm up . . . just thinking . . . about . . . you."

"Your voice sounded . . ."

"Just lots on my mind."

"I am on my way home."

"What?" I sat up.

"Yes . . . finished the work with the union yesterday, got an agreement signed. Called the airline last night, they had nothing, but they called me a little while ago . . . said there was a cancellation. I have a flight, first class to Barbados. I should be home this evening."

"What?" I pushed back the mosquito net and planted my feet on the floor. There was a haze outside, as if moisture fought to cling to the air, and rain wanted to come.

"I got a clipper flight to Bequia from Barbados at 4:30 this afternoon. You don't sound . . . ?"

"I . . . I . . . am just surprised. I thought you'd tell me when you were coming."

"I am telling you. What's wrong?"

"Nothing! I just would have wanted . . . to . . . do something special . . . now there's no time."

His voice deepened, and he whispered, "I want you just the way I left you."

The night before he left, he had ravished me completely. My memories aroused me before I could stop them. But it was more than that. I felt a connection that I know went back in time so many decades. I felt that he knew it too. And it was as if my will had made him come back to me. Vivencia had helped me to find power within myself.

"Keep the change," he said.

"What?" There was a great deal of chatter in the background.

"I'm at the airport, babe. Taxi. See you tonight. . . . I missed you."

I heard a car door slam. "I . . . missed you too."

"I love you."

I wasn't sure I heard him. His words entered my ear and seemed to roll around in my mind. No man had ever said those words to me. Now I wasn't sure I heard him or if I imagined it. I felt I loved him the day he put that antique ring on my finger. There was something genuine in that gesture, even though he was being playful.

"Jocelyn . . . are you there?"

"Gerald when you get home, we . . . have to talk . . . about something." The words tumbled from my lips. His words were tangled up in my mind with the thoughts of Derek's child.

"I don't like the sound of that. I gotta catch . . ." His voice dropped out. "Gerald? . . . Gerald are you there?"

There was no answer. *I need to try and fix this before he comes.* Vivencia was right, I needed to know what I did to make this all happen. *Where are you old woman?* I was certain that Nereida made Sumadi come into my bedroom. I was certain that what happened then was echoed now, and I could fix it if I could only get to Nereida. If I cannot change it *then*, I still have a chance to fix it now, if she will only tell me what she did. *Vivencia come to me. Help me find Nereida.*

As I drew back the curtains, instead of light, the room grew noticeably dark. The sky was obscured with huge billowing thunderclouds. A rustling sound was coming from the other room. "Haynes?" I headed down the hall and stopped in the dining room. The valise with my grandmother's things was open, and Mariel's painting was on the floor. The little trinkets she had wrapped in tissue—shells, sea stars—were scattered about on the table and strewn across the floor. I had not heard from Haynes in days. She couldn't be downstairs? Surely she would have called out if she had come up. And I couldn't imagine that Haynes had opened the valise and gone through my grandmother's belongings.

In the kitchen, it was even darker, and cold. I rubbed my arms, trying to warm them from the chill. Goose bumps rose up, speckling my exposed skin.

Outside, the palm and coconut trees bowed in the wind, their broad fronds whipped into grotesque angry silhouettes like women in some crazed bacchanalian ballet. Lightning carved the sky, no warning, and I feared that the electricity might leap in at me. Thunder shook the house.

The telephone rang.

"Mum, Haynes here. Sorry I no there this week. And me can' come today. They sayin' the storm won't be long, but a lot of rain comin' in a short time, and the road not safe. Mum, are you there? Been having so much confusion here. Telephone lines not working for days now. Regular lines and the cell power on and off."

"What'd they say it was?"

"Nobody know. Electric down too. And by the way Mum, Vivencia? She gone to hospital."

"Just thinking 'bout her . . . I saw her a few days ago!"

"Dey say she be walking down the road to Lowman's Church and somethin' happen."

"What?" The rain began to beat on the roof.

"Dey say she was fightin' wit' somet'in', and she yell out."

"What? . . . What'd she say?"

"Women say dey can' make out . . . what she say."

"They hear who was she talking to?"

"No. People was in de church. She outside walking . . . coming. One woman say she hear her say, 'No Ride here.' But dat don' make no sense, cause with all the tree roots, no one can ride, no bike, na nothing dere. But when they get to her, she knocked down. Talking out of her head."

"Was she hurt . . . badly?"

"One woman say dey find her on the ground, and she just in a trance talking to a spirit. But she head was bloody. The las' t'ing she say was 'You strong, make dis right.' Den she pass out."

A peal of thunder reverberated through the house. I spoke trying to steady myself. "This is some storm." There was no response. "Hello?" I tapped the receiver button, but I heard nothing. I hung up and then listened again, no dial tone. The kitchen was darker still. Rain sheeted the window on the door.

My old self flashed before my eyes. The woman who walked out of the college offices, wanting to retire, feeling defeated. I heard my aunt saying that I should have learned the craft. I could see Gerald—tall, handsome; I saw myself wanting him but afraid to be touched. I remembered how my hands shook because I was fearful that a man like him might be interested in me. Then, that past life regression! I felt at home in my skin for the first time. Mariel with her raw desire and will to survive had become a part of me. As all those thoughts knitted together, I was stunned with understanding. *Nereida is doing this.* She attacked Vivencia. She is here somewhere in the house, and she is trying to intimidate me.

I reached for the amulet that rested on my heart, held it between my forefinger and my thumb, and ran my fingers across the back. There I felt the tiny etching of The Frog Woman. The engraving of her no longer felt like a threat that weakened me, but a gift from Sumadi, who loved me during those long stretches that John was away. No matter how I pushed him away, he came back to me.

I pulled out a chair from the table and sat down, my feet fully planted, and knees splayed so that I might stand and meet any force Nereida might throw in my direction.

Nereida. Come to me.

It was a quiet thought in the midst of the clamor of the storm. The rain pounded the roof and rattled the shutters. The sky lit up, and another booming crash of thunder shook the house. I did not flinch.

You do not frighten me with this . . . bluster. Just come and face me.

"BE CAREFUL WENCH!"

The darkness in the kitchen coalesced in the center of the room. It loomed over my head. I felt no need to stand.

Finally.

"Dat old witch try to t'reaten me." The guttural sound of her voice filled the room, as the dark shadow collected and shrunk into a bent form, barely my height in the chair upon which I sat.

No need to fear Vivencia.

"FEAR? I do not fear she. She keep calling me. She no leave me. Her light burn me."

I spoke with just my mind: *She did that for me. I need you.*

"Me done wit' you."

I know. I feel it.

"I just come to . . . find . . ."

Find what?

"Mariel haf it. Me look for it . . ."

First tell me how?

"HOW?" she shouted.

How did you do this?

"No. First, you tell me where."

Vivencia must have told you, your work here is not done!

"She want me to fix it. Me can't fix it. Can't."

First you tell me why? Why?

Why? She answered me with her mind and then spoke aloud.

"My son. Abrahim promise to take my son. His son Joseph later come to tell me he dead."

The old woman stopped talking. She looked at me. Her visage now softened, and tears ran down her face and streamed into her form below.

"I beg Abrahim and Joseph take my son, and he say yes. But . . ." Now she wrapped her arms around her chest. She whimpered. "Dey make him walk in back. IN BACK! Joseph haf his son John, and my son look just like Abrahim. He have his brow, his lips, his bearing. He also have his mind. He study the sea, and know the whale like no other man on Brava. But Joseph put his hand on John's shoulder, and they all make my son walk behind dem . . . like he a slave."

The woman grew bent in humiliation.

"He no slave. He a free man." She heaved a breath. "He can ride the whale and wield the harpoon." A deep sigh escaped her mouth. "So, I say to them, the three of dem walking, 'What you have, my son shall have.'" Her voice reverberated through the room. "Dey leave me dere." *What you be, my son shall be.* "I know I never see my son again."

She then spoke as if an incantation, and it stirred the winds and the lightning that carved and lit the sky. Her voice was low and steady, yet filled the room in which we sat, reverberating, and causing the house to quake with its echoes.

What you issue, so shall my son. John will have nothing my son will not possess. Me say it and it is done.

The primal nature of the old woman's spell resounded in my bones. The words seemed to hang in the air for a while. Then they echoed, hitting the walls and glass in the room. The elemental power of this woman had set this spell in motion more than a hundred years ago, and it had endured until today.

I addressed her in my own strong voice. "You know your son did have the riches you wished for him. He had whaling ships and a crew of many men under his watch. He had two wives and children and grandchildren who made him proud. Your power is great. But your sons are not happy . . . locked in this spell of yours."

"Me know," she said, her voice weak. "Me had to fight such evil. Dey would make him a slave, take away his freedom. I would not let that happen!"

"Your power was fierce enough to cross the sea, and undo and secure your son from slavery. But now, your sons and their sons are not free to do as they wish . . ."

"Stop speaking . . . leave me."

". . . To have whom they choose of their own will."

We each spoke using our own voices, barely raising them.

"I can't fix this. The evil of slavery has corrupted my hex. I tell Vivencia."

"Your children's spirits, and the spirits of their children, too, are locked in this prison you have willed. The brightness you willed is bringing darkness."

"Me know. I no can break it. I need my necklace. You must give it to me."

"I have it here." I showed her the amulet.

"No, the other one. She, the one they called Mariel, she made . . ."

"I don't know where that is. I have searched for it," I said.

"Then it cannot be undone. Mariel tied them to it."

"I will stop it." I peered into the dark spaces that were her eyes that seemed to go on into forever. The storm had quieted. I could feel my own power building. "The equity you willed must be more than the same. You want a world where slavery is no more."

Nereida's pain shall turn to good.

The dark will turn to light.

My thoughts now were but a whisper, yet the ghostly form pulled away in fear. She drew up her arms, her bony fingers curled, then clenched. I steadied myself, watching this frail form trying so hard to defend herself. The apparition trembled, drawing back, now hovering in the corner of the room by the door, her back to me as if she would escape through some hidden opening in the wall.

No fear from me. Only your spell's ill shall you lose.

Your sons shall live free, and love as they choose, build futures as they will, the meaning of true equity.

The mask of terror on the woman's face took on the appearance of curiosity. She listened to my thoughts, her head slightly cocked to the side, as if paying close attention to each word.

I, too, felt a sense of wonder. The thoughts came in a flow of energy from deep inside me.

They ne'er shall be slaves, nor their issue be.

But stand in their light and breathe air that is free.

The old woman's dark, gnarled form began to lengthen and straighten. Her beatific image now loomed above me. This beautiful woman, the one Vivencia and I had seen days before, was in the prime of her life. Her features were strong, and her bearing proud. Her lightness filled the room, "Tell me again," she said.

"They'll breathe free."

I must have blinked, and all that she was, was no more, leaving behind only peace.

The storm had ceased, and sunlight sliced through the clouds. A shard of light pierced the window. I had confronted Nereida and righted the wrong that breached my family's harmony. I accepted Nereida into my family—not a dark spirit, but a hurt soul fighting for a rightful place for her child, his freedom.

I stepped out onto the veranda with my bare feet, feeling the rainwater that had pooled on the polished wooden surface. The surf was murky, and seaweed had collected on the beach. My gaze was drawn out to the aquamarine sea. The further out I looked the deeper the blue became, which then was streaked with violet. A vast calm washed over me.

I decided to take tea there. Haynes had left hard-boiled eggs the other day, and there was orange juice, and I would make some Earl Grey tea, which was all I wanted. As I turned to go back inside, I caught sight of a flash of light out of the corner of my eye. The lens of his spyglass had trapped the afternoon sun somewhere behind me and transported the spark to me. The heat of it shot through my body, and I knew he was coming.

44

———

"Y ou have something that belongs to me," Derek had said. Desire for him came upon me involuntarily, but my body battled it. I pulled my nightdress off, grabbed Gerald's T-shirt, and threw it over my head. I had held it like a pillow as I slept the night before. The clean scent of him wrapped around me. But curiously, I already felt strong, powerful, protected, even before I put it on.

Through the window, I saw the speedboat heading toward the beach. I needed to stop him before he came into the house. The engine of the boat murmured and then stopped.

The air was thick and salty as if the storm had left the memory of its violation behind. I made my way to the beach and saw Derek waving to me after he dropped the anchor of the small motorboat. The shells and plant life had mucked up the beach, so I tiptoed and zigzagged my way to the water's edge, trying to avoid the knotted, brown patches of seaweed that covered a wide swath. He jumped into the water, which was waist-high.

"Such a great greeting," he shouted out to me. "I was worried about you . . . the storm seemed so . . ."

I hated myself for giving the wrong impression and searched for ways to correct it immediately. "No! Just wondered what you want."

He scowled as he moved toward me. "Is he in there?" he lowered his voice to a whisper.

I leaned back and away from him. "He's on his way home."

"I wouldn't have left you by yourself so long. Where was he, in Boston? You know he has other interests there."

"What other interests?" I spat the words out at him, hoping to back him off.

"You know what I mean . . . other interests . . ." he smiled. "He has interests in St. Vincent too."

"Get the hell back in your boat, Derek."

"Not until we talk about my little gift you have there."

"I don't consider this a gift. It is a problem that is mine to solve."

"Don't you mean ours? You can come to Moon Hole to live until it . . . Giselle will want. ."

"I know exactly what I am saying. Certainly, you do not think in this day and age you can tell me what to do with my body!"

"What about . . . him. You told him? You think he will stay with you and my child, and watch it grow and remind him of me."

"Get away from me."

"Don't think that's possible anymore . . ." he laughed. "You and I are bound together."

Speechless, I searched for the power within me to make him leave and I could not find it.

"It is my business if you are carrying my child," he called out.

My shoulders hunched as I looked toward the neighbors' houses, hoping no one heard him.

"I came here because I realized you were here alone during the storm. Why don't you pack some things and come to Moon Hole with me? Cassandra can look after you."

"I am not going to Moon Hole to . . . what . . . live with you and your women? I can look after myself." A sharp pain stabbed me in my abdomen.

Why is this still happening? I thought I broke the chains of her spell. *I cannot let him take me as Sumadi made me go with him.* Derek grabbed my arm.

"I am not going to let you jeopardize my child, staying here alone . . . being here with him." His face was a contorted angry mask.

The feelings of guilt for my indiscretion mixed with anger at myself for being here yet again. I turned away, planting my feet in the sand as best I could despite the pain that stopped me in my tracks.

"Get in the boat. I will not leave you here with my child." He pulled my arm toward him, fingers digging into my skin, but now I held firm. My steady physical resistance to his pressure filled me with power.

"You have no child." The words rushed from my throat.

He looked at me, his expression quizzical, disbelieving.

I shook his hand loose. "If you know what's good for you, you will leave me alone." The words I uttered flew from my lips. "You do not have any idea what lengths I will go to be sure that what I said is true. . . . You have no child." I whispered it this time. I felt a pain, and held my stomach. Then it went away. He seemed stunned. The heat of his glare seared my back as I walked away.

45

The words I voiced left me swimming in melancholy. I never admitted to myself that I wanted children, because I was never with a man whom I trusted. Now my only hope was to live out the hex placed by a woman so many years ago. Caught in its unintentional consequences, I tried to fix it but failed. Mariel must have carried so much pain, trying to right this too. I wondered if her secret was kept.

I am not who you think I am. I am not who I appear to be. My grandmother's words rang out in my mind. In my mind's eye, my grandmother was wearing the amulet and the other necklace, a locket of some sort. It wasn't in the valise. Where was it? The spell was tied to it.

From room to room I went, turning on the lamps trying to warm the space with light. Gerald should have been here by now. Why didn't he call at least? The landline was still dead from the storm, but my cell was perched against the sugar bowl and plugged into the wall. The lit-up screen now revealed the message, "Two Missed Calls." He must have been trying while I was outside with Derek. In the first voice mail, I heard Gerald's voice speaking over noise in the airport, "Seems there is a storm there in Bequia, babe. My flight was delayed, then cancelled. . . . So I'm taking a flight to St. Vincent in an hour if it isn't cancelled too." The second message said, "Just got a call from Janice about something to

345

take care of in St. Vincent . . . you later." His voice dropped out. ". . .
Ferry out of St Vincent tomorrow."

Janice? You got a call from Janice? You are going to St. Vincent? My face
was hot.

The more I thought about the messages, the angrier I got. Why was he
spending the night in St. Vincent? Derek's comment about Gerald's interests in Boston stirred me up again. "He has interests in St. Vincent too."

I tapped out his number, then stopped before I finished, putting the
phone down. "I'm going to sleep. I'm not going to worry about where he
is, and if he is with her, and what he is doing."

I filled the kettle and went to the pantry. The chamomile tea was not
in its proper space, but next to the periwinkle tea box, which was askew.
A pinch or two of this shouldn't hurt, and if it helps me sleep . . . maybe
I can dream. Maybe Mariel can tell me about this necklace. And why did
Luz wear both of them? Maybe being *there* will reveal the whereabouts
of the missing amulet.

I sat cross-legged in bed inhaling the vapors of the tea. The floral fragrance filled my nostrils, but it was still too hot to drink. I took a spoonful and blew on it, but it burned my bottom lip. Already I was increas-
ingly relaxed. "Placebo effect," I said out loud and laughed. The pillow
felt particularly soft and billowy. *Mariel come to me!* I was slipping away.
The darkness swept in and wrapped itself around me. When the phone
rang, I could barely summon the energy to reach it, as if it had moved far
into the corner of the room. In the darkness, I picked up the receiver.

"Hello?"

"Jocelyn?"

The voice was so distant. Was that Gerald?

"You there?"

"Don't want to talk to you."

The sound went away, and I did not follow it.

There was light on the other side, which I followed to the house, a
small house. My body had aged, and I had become Mariel once again.
Walking was painful because my knees and back ached. "Mama, thank
you for coming." The woman spoke to me in English with some Portu-

guese and Carib patois, but her speech was more refined. It was my daughter Estela, a few silver strands streaking her hair at the temples, her waist thicker and her hips broader than when I last saw her. She looked so much older than I remembered. Her hair was cropped and barely touched her shoulders. She was very beautiful, though her brow was lined. She placed a valise on the floor.

"Mother, my husband Rohan was injured at sea. His men brought him to the hospital in St. Vincent. I can't find out how bad he is unless I go. They say, I may have to stay the night or more."

Estela diverted her gaze from mine, but her eyes were filled with love for her husband and the fear for his well-being.

"Where's the child?" I said.

"Luz, come. She's not a child anymore! Sixteen years old. This is your grandmother Mariel, your avó," I said as best I could despite the pain that stopped me in my tracks.

The girl was beautiful, the color of cinnamon, a little darker than Estela, with thick long tightly curled hair pulled back into two plaits. She was much taller than Estela and me, which shocked me some, and I stepped back out of the house as I took in the full measure of her.

"Mama, come in. I have to go. Luz, go bring your grandmother some coconut water."

Steadying myself by holding on to the doorjamb, I stood there taking in the view of her kitchen, the icebox in the corner, and a large stove. It was much fancier than I had imagined. I always thought they were struggling, heard village people shunned them.

"Your fadder bring dis. He buy it and gif it to you?"

"No, Rohan bought it. His whaling boats are doing well, Mama. I have to go."

The girl put the glass of coconut water on the white enamel table. "You want to sit here?" she said.

"No, I go inside." Maybe I might know my daughter through her things, the things she had collected in that home I had never seen.

The table at the center of the dining room was large, made of a fine, highly polished mahogany wood. At the head of the table stood one chair with a high back and sturdy arms; smaller cane chairs were arranged on the sides. I saw a large living room, which had bent wood armchairs and a settee with two large cushions in the seat and along the back. There was a rocking chair with a tall back of woven cane. The rooms were tidier than my home, kept as I taught her, though I never seemed to manage myself. Rohan had provided well for Estela, and for Luz.

"Better for me back," I said holding on to the arms and easing myself into the bent cane chair. "You know me? Know who I am?"

"Yes, Vovó."

"What your mother tell you 'bout me?"

"That you an' she don' talk." The girl looked in my direction, but when our eyes met, she looked down.

"She say why?"

"Say, she don't remember, it long ago. We have your picture . . . there." She pointed to a space on the wall behind me.

I turned to look at it. It was a picture of John and me together I remember the day we sat in front of that box trying to be still as the man John called a "photographer" took it. I was about forty then, and fidgety, always having things to do. My eyes began to tear up. The years I felt that they had forgotten me, they kept me alive here in their home.

"Vovó, don't cry." Luz reached out to pat my arm. Her hands were soft, and her touch tender.

Then I seemed to retreat from that space, and I remembered seeing the photo in my aunt's home, knowing it was now mine. The space between then and now as thin as silk.

"You a healthy girl?" I took the girl's hands, turning them over to look first at the palms, then the backs of her hands. I pulled her to me and turned her around to see her back.

The girl laughed and flinched as if she were tickled by being touched around her waist. "Yes, I am fine Vovó, why?"

"You do good in school?" I eyed the girl. Her mannerisms were so much like Estela's, my eyes brimmed.

"Yes, Avó. I will go to the University when we move to U.S."

I choked on my coconut water, "What are you saying?"

"We are moving to the U.S., to Brooklyn, New York. Avô bought a house there . . ." The girl covered her mouth, and her brow furrowed. "Grandpa didn't tell you?"

"He bought a house? How long has he been planning this?"

"I don't know. I'm sorry. Avó, please . . . I didn't know it was a secret. Please . . ."

"So, John, was he moving to U.S. too?"

"I . . . I don't know, Avó." Now the tears flowed down her cheeks. "Vovó, Grandpa is coming soon. Please don't tell him I told you."

"No, let's see if he tells me." My head ached with anger. *They have been plotting behind my back since I tried to stop this marriage.* It should not have been. They are lucky this girl is not crippled, no clubfoot, no damaged brain. . . . If I did not protect them from the darkest punishment, everything would be different.

The screen door opened in the kitchen, and the girl jumped. "That's Avô! Vovó, please . . ." Luz said, pleading with her eyes.

John's hair was a white mane, his beard gray, and his cheeks were ruddy. Though he was somewhat bent, he seemed strong, and his footsteps, as he walked in from the kitchen, made the floorboards shake. His belly bulged over his belt, but his barrel chest looked as sturdy as in his youth.

"*Cade meu beijo.* You forget your Portuguese going to that English school. My kiss. Where is my kiss?" He stopped barking at the girl and turned to me. "Mariel, why are you . . . ? Why is she crying? What did you say to her? What did you do?"

"Avô, I didn't know it was a secret."

"What?" he said, his shoulders in a shrug.

"When were you going to tell me you bought a house in the U.S.?"

"Luz, go to your room." His voice bounced off the walls.

"Are you moving with them? . . . Always plotting . . ."

"Woman, just stop. You took your love from your daughter. Estela has a father and Luz has a grandfather. I care to help my family as long as I have life."

"You think me don't care."

"Why won't you accept them, their marriage, even to this day."

"I have my reasons."

Time stopped. What she said reverberated, fastening me to that moment. It was what my mother always said. To me. Had she learned it from Luz? Did Luz say it to my mother? Were these her reasons? As instantaneously as time stopped, it began again. John was shouting at me. His face was aflame.

"You can't make the rules for Estela . . . control her."

"They should not be together. They no listen to me."

"You're just a wicked old woman who wants to control everything. . . . Luz, come here."

"No, Luz, you stay in your room!" I shouted at the girl as she came to the doorway, her eyes swollen red and tears flowing.

"You did this, John. You were never there. I had to fix it. I prayed, and you see her, she is healthy and strong. I did that."

"What are you talking about?"

My hand tightened and my teeth clenched. "The girl in there is my doing, my power to make this clean. . . . Luz, come here. Here girl," I said, pulling the scrimshaw from where it rested against my bosom and lifting it over my head. The girl looked to her grandfather for his approval. "Take this, girl, and wear it always. Don't take it off."

"Is it a scrimshaw, a whale's tooth, Vovó?" The girl ran her fingers over the front etchings.

"You know about them. Yes. It will protect you. Your grandfather made it for me. Now it is for you."

"It's beautiful, Avô. Thank you, Vovó."

I held a second pendant, a crystal locket.

"What is this, Vovó? Is that hair inside?"

"It is . . . I make it clean, and. . . . Just put it on, girl. You take this too."

"Mariel. What is this?" John demanded.

"Don't get in the way, John. I need to do this."

"Girl, give me that. Go in your room." The old man snatched the pendant and flung it out the window. The girl shook as she saw the rage in his eyes but ran to her room.

"Why did you do that?" I said through gritted teeth.

"Because you acting crazy, talking 'bout protecting the girl. You scaring her."

The pendant I had prayed over so many years was gone. "You don't know what these children have done, and I have to fix."

"You are just out of your head. Now you scaring the girl. Selfish ole woman!"

"Me? You did this! You take your fault in this. You leave me alone. You leave me . . . years you leave me."

"What you talking?"

I struggled my way down the steps in front of the house. "I have to find it . . ."

"You going on about that again? I give you a house, and pretty things, and all you do is complain I leave you."

"I have no one . . . and so he take me. You leave me to him."

"What are you talking about?"

"You don't know? Sumadi. You leave me to him."

"You could have said no."

"I could not. You beat me and make me give the child to him . . . his chile, Rohan, and Estela togedder."

John slammed the screen door shut. He seemed to hear me as he turned to go look for Luz. The words must have moved about in his head, and I was watching as the thought entered. I imagined that it twisted itself up into an ugly wriggling form.

"NO!! You are not . . . saying . . ." He shouted at me through the screen door.

"Yes, they both mine." I whispered. "Me think someone put a spell on me . . . do this terrible thing to me." I began to moan as I crawled on the ground in search of the locket.

"Why didn't you say something?"

"What . . . to say? What would you do to me? I know your beating, John. The people in this village. I had to fix it. And she is beautiful, she is healthy, she is smart. I did that. I made it right. She must learn to use the power to protect herself."

John balled his fist and started down the steps. I stood up and started to run, then crouched down, waiting for the blows, feeling I deserved them and had escaped them for too long. I looked up so that I could watch them rain down on me.

Then the thought seemed to be born inside me, only a bit of life, much like when I had my children. I was energized by the thought. I placed my hands on my thighs and pushed myself up, feeling the muscles in my back tighten and my spine lengthen.

"John, take your part in this. It was not me alone in this deed. If you did not beat me, and leave me so long with that pain, this would never happen."

He was frozen in place, his stare fixed on something. There in the doorway was Luz. The girl stood stunned, her face gray, its color gone.

"Avó, stop." Her voice was calm and deliberative. "What are you saying Vovó?"

"Nothing . . . I . . ."

"Luz, your grandmother is crazy."

"No. I think she said my father is hers and my mother is hers."

"No . . . that's not what . . ." I shook with fear looking at her, not knowing what the girl understood.

"I am not stupid . . ."

"No, you are a smart girl. You should go to school . . . build something. . . . I want you to build something for yourself . . ."

"That is why the people in the town shun us, isn't it? That's why mother wants to go to U.S. And they knew this all along?" She came down the steps and stood over me.

"No, I didn't tell . . . them. They don't know," I whispered.

The girl turned away, then doubled over and vomited. John grabbed her and put his arms around her.

She shrugged him off, wiping her lips with the back of her hand, and turned to glare at me. "I fix it. You perfect."

"What am I? What do I call myself?"

I stood up, trying to reach to stroke the girl's forehead, to smooth the lines sliced into her brow. She brushed my hand away. "Luz, you are light. They named you well. You are brightness. You are the good that has come from this darkness that was my life. You are beautiful." My stomach ached from the pain I had caused.

"Where is the necklace, Avô? Where did you throw it?" Luz bent into the bushes, pushing the branches aside. The thorns from the rose bushes scratched and tore at her hands and her arms, but she pushed them aside, her bloodied hands pulling back the thorned branches.

"Luz, stop!"

"No, I must find it. Right, Vovó? I should wear it."

"Luz please," John whispered, reaching to pull the twigs away from her arms as she searched through the brambles.

"No, Avó. I will wear it." She laughed, crazed by what I had done. "It will protect me. Here it is." She stepped fully into the thicket, though the thorns tore into the flesh of her legs. She pulled the cord up and out of the tangle and studied it for a good while. Then she pulled it over her head.

"So, Vovó, is this the hair of both your children? Both my parents. What should I learn, Vovó?"

"Nothing more. You are fine."

"No, I will pray. Should I pray for forgiveness that I was born? Should I pray that my children are not idiots? Maybe, Vovó, I should pray that you did not do this to me." The girl went up into the house. "You cannot ever fix this, Vovó."

John clutched my shoulders, and shook me, digging his fingers into me.

"My . . . God." Jolted from my sleep. My eyes opened wide.

I am about to do this again if I don't stop it now. How can I make this end?

46

I covered my head to stop the blows. "Pare!"

"What? What did you say?" His voice was a beacon in the harbor, beckoning me. He shook me, and I succumbed, my head bobbing like a rag doll. As I opened my eyes, I saw his face lined with anguish.

"Are you all right? Wake up. You're dreaming. What did you say?"

I expected to see John, and he was not there. "I said, 'stop!'"

"You drank that periwinkle tea. I told you. . . . How long have you been asleep?"

I rubbed my eyes with the heels of my hands. "What time is it?"

"It's almost four in the afternoon. I called you from the Cobblestone Inn last night, and again as I was leaving. . . . Why did you hang up?" Gerald's brow was furrowed with fear.

I had slept almost the whole day. The pain in my arms and across my back radiated up into my shoulders—from the blows that pummeled me and from John clutching at me. I was tangled in a twist of time, then and now.

"Why did you do take that periwinkle tea?"

"I wanted to connect with Mariel . . . it was just a few sips, if that much . . . I am sorry. . . . I have done something unthinkable."

My mind traveled back, and shame filled my soul. I felt myself shrink in stature, and I thought, *No me mate! Don't kill me, please.*

As the light filtered through, the scene became clear. I was in the center of the village. The women surrounded me, all of them holding stones in their hands, lifting them to aim at me. I did not know all of their names, but their faces were familiar. Malevolence pinched their grotesque, hate-filled expressions. Fearing the weight of the first stone hitting me, I drew energy from the space about me, and the first stone was hurled.

It fell short.

The woman standing behind me moved, then extended her arm behind her, and pitched her rock. I knew the jagged gray missile was flung with all her force, yet it fell two feet behind me. Now all of the women, each one in turn, looked at one another, stepped closer together, making the ring tighter, and in concert lifted their stones, heaving them at me in unison. Every stone seemed to hit some wall they could not penetrate. I did not flinch, knowing that they could not touch me. The women had begun to shout "Bruxa!" as they backed away.

"Yes, I am a witch."

Your tongues are tied.
You will not say
what happened here
on this day!
My child will thrive and all my children forever nigh;
if you speak of this, yours shall die.

The women's eyes went blank. Each one walked away from that place to their home, not saying a word.

"Jocelyn, wake up. What are you mumbling? Are you hallucinating? Let me get you some coffee or tea. Some toast." Gerald shook me, trying to bring me out of the trance.

"They were going to stone me, Gerald."

"That's what you were dreaming?" He held his hand over my head, cradling it, drawing me into an embrace. The sight of those women attempting to kill me in such a brutal way had crystalized my understanding of Mariel's crushing guilt. I felt their condemnation firsthand, and it burned my soul. I understood how alone Mariel was and how she suffered. It was not only from her own personal shame, from betraying her husband; the Portuguese men and the Carib men expected obedience, and the society of women around them expected conformity. Disobedience was to be hidden in furtive conversations and hidden behind a glass of rum.

Strangely, thoughts of Mariel gave me strength. I knew where I was, but I had to fix this time and space.

"I feel woozy." I said, swinging my legs over the side of the bed.

"Stay there." Gerald headed for the kitchen. "I'll get you some orange juice. You don't listen."

"Stop scolding me. I know what I am saying. I told you how I was married . . ."

"You are talking about your dream . . ."

"It is not a dream. It is what I lived. And it's now too. Gerald, I'm pregnant."

"Okay, so is this your great-great-grandmother like you told me, and the . . . Portugee?"

"No, this is now. Me. I am pregnant."

Gerald sat down next to me and seemed lost in his own thoughts.

"You're serious?"

"Yes."

"What do you want to do?"

"What do you mean?"

"I know what I would like to do. I had this planned differently. I thought we'd have that date, but . . ." He went quiet, but I was too.

"I love you," he said. "I feel as though I have always loved you. And even though I was going to wait for the right time . . ." He reached into his pants pocket and pulled out a ring box.

"No, stop. . . . Gerald. . . . Don't . . ."

"I thought you felt . . ."

"Stop . . . it's not yours."

"What?"

The confusion and pain in his eyes pierced my heart.

"This child is not yours." I wanted no misunderstandings.

"How do you know?" he asked, then shook his head as if he knew the answer.

"The timeframe. From what the doctor said, in my last visit, I must be eight weeks by now. I have another appointment. Wait, what's today?"

"It's Monday."

"Shit, I had an appointment today at three. I have to call. . . . Give me my bag. I have her card . . ."

Gerald handed me my purse. "Did you go to Dr. Clarke?" I began digging through my things in my bag, pulling out my keys, my wallet, and papers. Gerald disappeared into the other room.

He returned, holding the open telephone book. "Here. 341-5555." I dialed the number while studying Gerald's face and his body language. He seemed to have taken a blow to the gut.

"Yes, hello, sorry this is Dr. Kendall, Jocelyn Kendall. I was supposed to have an appointment today at 3:00 and I slept . . . forgot completely. . . . Now? Vacation for how long? I don't . . . I would have to get there by 5:30," I said, looking at Gerald.

"I'll take you, come . . . you shouldn't miss . . ."

"Okay. It will take . . . I will be there by 5:30." I started into the bathroom, and his words stopped me in my tracks.

"It's Derek's, isn't it?"

His expression was bewildering, and I had no idea what he would do or say. John had lifted my dress and seen my bulging belly, struck me, and dragged me out of our house. I remembered cowering on the porch hoping no one would see me there. I had to fix this, and I had to remain here in this time with Gerald.

"Yes."

"Have you talked to him?" His voice was tentative.

"He has no say. This is my body, my choice, my decision."

"Wait. If you don't want to be with him . . . we can go to Boston, have the baby. No one . . . has . . . to know . . ." Though his brow was creased, the love in his eyes was clear. He reminded me so much of John. He always wanted to take care of me. Despite John's anger, when he let me come back into the house, he seemed broken by his love for me—but I knew he had a will of steel.

Gerald's love often felt like an overpowering force, sometimes taking away my strength. Mariel, with far fewer resources, had done her best to exercise her agency over her situation. It was now my turn to do the same for myself. I had to own my own decision, and its consequences.

I got washed and dressed, and we drove to the doctor's office in silence. *I don't want to lose you, like I lost John.* The world we lived in back then did not permit women and men to work their way through complex problems such as these.

"Babe, we're here. Your mind is a million miles away." He opened the car door for me. "Maybe you should tell the doctor about the periwinkle tea."

"Gerald, stop it. Stop! I barely had a full sip. It burned me. Stop trying to be so good to me and control my actions, I can't stand it." I shook as I shouted at him. "You squeeze the power from me, when you try and fix things for me. Let me be."

The waiting room was empty. No one was at the receptionist window. Dr. Clarke came out. "Hello Dr. Hunter. How are you? Dr. Kendall? I thought it best to see you before I go on vacation."

She paused. "Would you like to come in Dr. Hunter?" It was clear she thought Gerald was the father. "We should hear a clear heartbeat today and have some good pictures." Gerald looked at me, trying not to speak. I nodded my assent and allowed him to follow me in. We sat side by side in the office.

"So how have you been feeling?"

"Okay, I guess."

"Any spotting?"

"No."

Gerald nudged my foot with his. I was annoyed, but blurted out, "Well, last night I had some periwinkle tea, a few sips, because I couldn't sleep."

"You remember I said not to take any medicines, and herbs are in essence foreign substances like medicines. Periwinkle is actually a powerful herb that can cause reactions . . . hallucinations."

"I only had a small amount . . . a sip or two."

"Don't do that anymore. And Dr. Hunter, I will call you in a few minutes."

"No. No. NO!" I could feel myself fading away, doing as I was told.

Dr. Clarke looked shocked at my outburst. "What's the matter?"

"I want to talk with you alone."

"Of course." Cheeks flushed, Dr. Clarke seemed embarrassed to be caught in the middle of our spat.

She preceded me, handed me a gown and said, "Why don't you change, and I will take your pressure and weight. And we can chat here in the examining room. I will be back in a few minutes."

As I undressed, I could hear Dr. Clarke talking with Gerald. I could not hear their words, but I could discern the cordiality of their conversation. Then I heard the rap of Dr. Clarke's hand on the door. As she placed the blood pressure cuff on my arm, I asserted, "I wanted to ask you about my options."

"Dr. Kendall, first let me apologize. I should not have invited Dr. Hunter in with you. I just saw the two of you together and him holding your arm and . . ." She paused as if she did not want to say what she presumed, but it was clear. "Your options?" She seemed perplexed, off guard. "What do you mean your options?"

"I am forty-five years old. Should I even be having this baby? Am I likely to be able to have another? What if I . . ." I wanted to spill my thoughts out here, like the murky sea that came after the storm. I was about to ask about an abortion and thought better of it. If that were my choice, I would think it through, and have done it in the U.S.

"Slow down. I think you are raising your pressure. Take a deep breath. Let's take a look, see how you're progressing. Just lie back," she said, placing my feet in the stirrups.

Dr. Clarke positioned the sonogram machine next to the examining table. "So, nothing unusual. No cramping, spotting? Oh, how's the nausea?"

"Better, actually."

"Really, so soon? . . . And when did it seem to come under control?"

"About two weeks ago . . . maybe three weeks ago. Time has been a little confused for me lately . . . I've been having . . . dreams."

The doctor squeezed some gel onto my belly, and I flinched from the cold. She moved the probe around on my abdomen, first below and then above my belly button.

"Last time I saw that little one was right near this small fibroid down here. No . . . Could it have moved?" She moved the probe around and adjusted the screen toward her.

"That's odd . . . I don't . . . wait, here is a gestational sac. This is a very, very early pregnancy, maybe just four weeks. I can't quite hear the heartbeat, but maybe in about a week."

"Is something wrong?"

"No, just . . . well . . . it's very strange."

"What?"

"This is a much younger . . . Didn't I say you were in about the fourth or fifth week then? Now you'd be in the about the seventh or eighth week. Let me look at the chart and the measurements."

She grew quiet while studying her notes. "You are sure you didn't have any spotting, pelvic pain . . . ?"

I shook my head. "What are you seeing?"

"This fetus appears to be just about four weeks in gestation. I can't find the one I saw four weeks ago. You're positive you didn't notice any spotting?"

"No spotting. But I was upset by someone, so my stomach did react with a little cramping, but it went away quickly."

"Well, the only thing I can say is, the other fetus resorbed into the lining. That happens sometimes in early pregnancies. But the strange part is, it seems you conceived again." She turned the monitor and pointed to the screen. "See that pulsating dot there? Look, that's the fetal heart."

"I don't know what I'm looking at . . ."

"This dark space here, that's the yolk sac. It's too early to see much more yet. The heartbeat is so faint, but you see that flicker of light."

"You're saying, five weeks? Could that be . . . ? You see only this fetus?"

"Yes . . . there's simply no sign of it. I would have found it very easily at this stage, were it here. This is unusual, but we are often surprised in medicine."

"Could I have done this? The periwinkle?"

"No. A few sips yesterday? No. Nothing you could have done could have caused this. It happens. And it's a natural occurrence."

My mind travelled back to the night when Gerald and I were first together. I wished it! I wanted children for the first time.

"Can you get Gerald for me, please?"

"Of course. And were you always this fertile? This is so unusual."

When the doctor left me lying there on the table, I heard Luis say, "You can't change anything back then." I heard Cassandra repeating the same thing: "You can't change anything back then, only now." And despite what the doctor said, I wondered, *Could I have done this? With my will?*

Gerald had concern written all over his face. He seemed reluctant to speak.

"I just want the doctor to tell you what she found."

The doctor looked at me, and then at him, "Well, yes. Dr. Hunter . . . The fetus that we saw last time seems to have resorbed itself into the lining."

"Is that dangerous?"

"No, what I am saying is, it is no longer viable, a miscarriage, and holds no threat to her health. But we are lucky to find another fetus, only about four or five weeks in gestation."

"Four or five weeks?" He studied the monitor. "And it's healthy?"

"You might not be able to hear the heartbeat, because it's faint, as it should be at this stage. But that flickering light is the baby's heart."

He looked at me, tears welling up in my eyes as I nodded.

"So . . . congratulations are in order. I'll give you a moment alone." The room was so quiet. Gerald reached for my hand to lift me to a sitting position, and then brought it to his lips. His eyes locked with mine but still held a question.

"It's ours," I whispered.

47

"Stay here. Someone's in the house. The door's open." Gerald quietly closed the car door and grabbed the crowbar in the trunk. He walked slowly as he neared the base of the stairs, his head leaning to the side as if listening for any sound coming from the house.

"Haynes?"

"She doesn't usually come this late," I said, getting out of the car.

Haynes pushed her head out the door, "Good evening, mistress. Dr. Hunter, what you have in your hand? Planning to bash me head in?" she laughed. "Sorry, me didn't call, but I hope you don't mind. I come to bake some sweets for the funeral. They bringing she body this way to go to Lowman's Church soon."

"Who died?" I asked, coming up the stairs behind Gerald.

"I asked you to wait in the car. . . . I haven't told her yet," Gerald said to Haynes.

"Told me what?"

"Come in and sit down first."

"Why? Why should I sit down?"

"Jocelyn, just do as I ask for once. Please. I was going to tell you earlier, but everything . . . Vivencia."

"When did she die?"

"Day before yesterday," Gerald said.

The night of the storm. "I should have known."

"What?" Gerald looked perplexed.

"Never mind." I couldn't tell them how much Vivencia had done for me. She had strengthened me, urged me to stand up to Nereida. *Maybe she was there with me.*

"How did you know? Weren't you still in Boston?"

"Yes, but . . ."

"When did you eat last, Mum?" Haynes pulled a sweet bun from the loaf, dropping it on the saucer. "Still hot." She poured me a glass of coconut water..

Outside there was the sound of steel drums. Voices, a chorus of them, filled the air. Haynes handed a sweet bun to Gerald, "They bring the body . . . need the sweetness now to push away da bitter."

In the living room, I pushed back the drapes to better see out the window. The throng of people, singing and dancing as they followed the hearse, went on forever down the road. The procession slowed to a stop near Lowman's Road. Two men opened the back of the hearse, and four more grabbed the handles to pull the casket out. People danced in place and then turned into the narrow road toward the church.

"Me breads." Haynes sniffed the air and ran into the kitchen.

"She was here with me the day before she died," I said to Gerald.

He didn't seem surprised, just seemed to search my eyes for the breadth of my knowledge of the woman whose body had just passed in front of the house.

"How did you find out about her death?" I asked. The sound of the voices waned as the last of the people turned up Lowman's Road.

"Janice . . . called me."

My cheeks heated up with the memory of Gerald staying overnight in St. Vincent.

". . . Well, she called to tell me about this file she wanted me to see."

"A file?"

"Yes, something she found on your grandmother."

"What does that have to do with Vivencia? How did *she* find out about her dying?"

"I am trying to tell you, if you would give me a chance. She knew . . . got word in St. Vincent. Vivencia is respected as someone who knows the history here. And don't you remember Janice sent us the article online about your grandmother?"

". . . Of course."

"Well, she found something else. She said something bothered her about the newspaper account and she went looking for the file on your grandmother's death. She had some clerk digging around in storage for days and days, and they found a file with the actual newspaper article, not the microfiche. There were a letter and some other things in it."

"Me going down to the church to the service," Haynes called.

"We should go," I said, "to pay our respects."

"You sure you can handle it? It's hot out there and you know it's a bit of a walk, with all the cars lining the street. Let me finish telling . . ."

"We need to go. If we walk in after the service begins, it would be disrespectful."

"Funerals here aren't . . ."

"Gerald, I can handle it. She . . . helped me . . . I want to go."

Gerald hardly said a word as we trudged up the main road and turned up the footpath to Lowman's Road. The trees closed in above and around us, blocking the waning light from the setting sun. As we neared the church, the preacher's baritone voice blended with the sounds of weeping women. Then steel drumming and a sort of call and response chant began. Glowing torches illuminated the building. People surrounded the church, swaying and dancing. The cacophony filled the space and echoed through the trees. The casket was on a table of sorts, in front of the entrance. People encircled it, a few moving in to touch it, or to drape their bodies over it. They talked to the corpse inside and prayed, then moved off and danced nearby.

As I got closer, the throng of people nearest to me seemed to sense my presence there, because they did not look up, but just parted, making way for me to pass. The nearer we got to the coffin, little by little, all of the men and women who had been engrossed in singing and praying, simply gave us a pathway to the space next to the casket.

My thoughts flew from my chest before I could fully formulate them. *Vivencia, I don't know if you can hear me in this space with so many voices lifted in honor of you, but . . . I need to thank you for the power you gave me to . . . to undo the darkness of my past. There is more to do. I feel it is not finished.*

The preacher stopped speaking and began spinning, his feet barely touching the ground. As he turned, he pointed his finger and then stopped as he faced me.

I closed my eyes in prayer, but I could feel a coolness settle in around me. Through my closed eyelids, I felt I was bathed in a pale blue glow. Compelled to open my eyes, I saw I was, in truth, standing in a shower of blue light. No one else seemed to see it. The people were chanting and leaning in to pray. I searched for the source of the light and could not find it until I heard the voice. And as I looked up, I saw Vivencia's face and her comforting smile.

"I hear you. How could I not?"

The preacher began speaking again, but I couldn't discern the meaning of the words. And then Vivencia spoke again.

"But you are wrong child, you have always been bathed in light."

Though I heard her voice, I responded with my thoughts. The preacher seemed to hear my thoughts too, because as I spoke to Vivencia, he looked at me. And when Vivencia spoke, he looked in her direction and cocked his head to the side, taking in her words.

The terrible wrong of my great-great-grandmother, the abomination of my great-grandmother and father, and the suicide of my grandmother . . . How do I set all this right?

"You bear no blame. Mariel fought to survive the spell cast on her. She stood tall against those who would have shunned her and stoned her. Your great-grandmother Estela knew only the love she felt for her husband, and he for her. Your grandmother, Luz, did not know the protection and love Mariel held for her—and her own shame killed her."

But my mother's letter, keeping me from my grandmother Luz? I think it killed her.

"Your mother wished only to protect you. I taught you of light and dark, and now you know that lightness is all about you. All who came before you have blessed you and protected you. You have cast away the darkness. Cast away the shame. Nereida wanted only to protect her son from the darkness of being enslaved. Her power had to cross the seas and cloak her son in a perilous world she could only imagine. Equity must be built by us all. Move forward. Your name is Joy. Live its meaning."

I stood in the light and felt its energy. Mariel's strength and will to survive filled me to brimming, a gift from my travel back in time. This knowledge was a powerful gift. Now shame transformed into compassion for the women who came before me.

I looked at Gerald, whose gaze was now upon me, and gestured that I wanted to leave. The throng of people, who I hadn't noticed for some time, were singing and surrounding me. Once again, they parted to make way. The sky had turned azure.

We walked home in silence, Gerald pointing out fronds and roots that might cause a stumble. We went onto the veranda and looked out onto the sea. The sky had now darkened to indigo. Though I felt a sense of peace I had never before felt in my life, I could sense a discomfort from Gerald.

"Is there something wrong?"

"I was telling you about the newspaper article before we left."

"I am so sorry. Please, tell me, continue now."

"I just wanted to tell you that Vivencia knew your grandmother very well. They were close friends. She was the V. Gomes in the article we saw, and she's the one who told the reporters what happened. Janice said, 'She collected all the things that were given to your Uncle Leland.' I saw the list. They found both their names in the records. But the interesting thing is . . . Wait, I have to go get it."

"Get what?"

"Janice said it was probably left in the property room by mistake all these years. But they are sure Vivencia left it. An artifact of the time that I have seen before in collections . . . a mourning pendant."

"What?"

He pulled out a woven cord attached to a clear crystal like covering, and in it was hair. Sure enough, when I looked closely, there were two locks of hair, one ringlet lighter in color, and one tuft of tightly curled black hair. I took the locket into my hand and caressed it with my fingertips.

"I know this."

"You do?"

"Yes, I saw it in my dreams."

I pulled the cord over my head. The pendant from my great-great-grandmother rested between my breasts, a few inches above the scrimshaw carved by my great-great-grandfather, both conveying the enduring love and protection given to my grandmother, and now to me. It is no longer lost, as Nereida wished.

"There is one more thing. It seems when Vivencia was in the hospital, she gave this message to one of the nurses. The nurse said, they thought of what she said as the utterances of someone who is overcome with facing death all alone."

He dug in the pocket of the satchel to pull out an envelope with a scrawl of my name, "Joy."

"The nurse said she was compelled to write down her words, because Vivencia told her goodness would come to her if she did. And if she didn't write them down, the worst horror of her nightmares would be visited upon her." Gerald laughed.

"Why are you laughing, the poor woman!"

"I am laughing because they say the woman ran as fast as she could and grabbed a stack of paper from the nurses' station, knocking into the head nurse. Both ran into the room causing such commotion."

"You're kidding."

"No. When they got to the room, Vivencia laughed and said, 'Me didn't know me words haf such power.' Janice said the woman wrote down her words exactly as she said them. I don't know what she said, but she told them to give it to you. Here."

I opened the envelope and unfolded the oddly creased paper. Obviously, someone rushed to put it in the envelope. It said:

You came to me looking for answers in your past. Your grandmother, me friend, ask me to give you protection. She closed herself off from the love of her husband and your mother, Rosalie. She said, "Don't live my way, but choose love and find joy. You can choose. You have the power."

Me and she baptized you, seeing the confusion that hovered above you. We greatest sadness was your mother's hiding you from Luz after dat. So, me make her da promise to find you and shelter you from darkness. Me taught you the lessons of your will. Use them. You are stronger than you know.

And me sent you the light that stands next to you. Me sent him to you in Boston, you walked away. His love goes back through time. Accept his love and protection. Become his Joy. I sense that you already have it growing inside you.

Your Griot,

Vivencia

"What did she say?' Gerald's concern was etched into his brow.

I folded the paper and put it back in the envelope. A tear cooled my cheek. "She said so much. Suffice it to say, I think she has a thing for you."

"Me?"

"Yes, you."

I finally understood my mother and why she said the things to me about marrying. Her mother, my grandmother, had said those things to her. She did not want me to marry, and have children, fearing that they might bear the scars of their lineage. The peace that settled in around me was profound. All the pieces were assembled here now. Yet all the stories were not quite complete.

48

Each day, as I reached for the pendants that I wore around my neck, I would take time to study the hair inside. Some questions about my family history still vexed me. The past month's dreams of living Mariel's life pushed and prodded me to learn about the hair. Was it truly from both of Mariel's children? Where did Sumadi come from? And what of Nereida? Could her tale of sadness be traced to Portugal and John's grandfather, Abrahim? I remembered Nereida's words. "He come and lay wit' me. Promised to take me 'cross the water." And later her revenge, the incantation that set all of this in motion. "So, I say to them, the three of dem walking . . . *What you have, my son shall have.*" Her thoughts reverberated through the room.

Dey leave me there.

What you be, my son shall be.

I know I never see my son again.

What you issue, so shall my son.

John will have nothing my son will not possess.

Me say it and it is done.

What if Sumadi's background traced back to Portugal and this whaler called Abrahim, just as John's did? She spoke of *three of them, Joseph, Abrahim's son, John's father.* As those words came into focus, I heard the priest's voice. Fr. Silva had said on the day I visited him, "I have sorted it out. A case of two different men named Matos. A John and a Joseph, no relation . . ." *Could the priest be wrong? Or maybe hiding the truth? Were all these people really connected by blood as revealed in my dreams and in my encounter with Nereida?* The shame I carried was not mine to bear. Vivencia was right. It was not mine, and I knew now that it was not Mariel's.

Searching online I found a company that analyzes DNA. Their procedures entailed gathering cheek swabs and submitting them for genetic analysis, which would reveal the geographic origins of the source. I could do that to analyze my background, and I would. But I called them and asked if they could also analyze the hair samples. I explained we were leaving Bequia in a week, so the company overnighted the kit to me, agreeing to send a hard copy of the results back to me in Boston in about six weeks.

The next few days, I spent time down on the beach with Gerald, and we went out to eat. He made wonderful love to me, and I felt filled with him, his child, and our shared happiness. We made wedding plans for the fall in Boston. If I had my way, it would just be us at City Hall, and maybe Luis and Selena, and Aunt Grace if she were up to it. Gerald wanted to invite his sister, and his brother, and colleagues and friends from the museum. All of those, he said, who couldn't believe he was finally marrying. Gerald taught me about celebration and jubilance.

We had dinner with Uncle Leland before we began packing up the house to leave Bequia. Leland had a package all wrapped in colored paper. I took it as an early wedding gift because we told him we were marrying on the phone. When I opened the wrapping, my breath got caught in my throat. Inside was the music box my great-great-grandfather gave Mariel. The wood was chipped, and the hinge on the door had come off. "It doesn't make music anymore, but I thought you'd like to have it," Leland said. "I forgot that I had taken it out of the valise for safe keeping."

I could not speak as I touched it.

"Guessing it was your grandmother's," he said.

I started to tell him the story of John and Mariel but thought better of it. When sharing my dreams, I always felt as if people who listened were humoring me, thinking me either a little delusional or naïve. I could tell they did not perceive them as real. They had not lived it as I did. Another time to remember silence.

"I know this artisan at the museum who might be able to fix it," Gerald said.

The calm I felt inside was complete. My uncle had reconnected me with the pure joy of childhood, the memories of the sounds of the music box. My joy and Mariel's held a connection to my body and to my senses.

Now, just two weeks before we were going to leave, I was looking out to sea, and a large ship glided off into the horizon. Derek came into my mind. I hadn't heard from him. The air was dense with humidity, no breeze. The trees out on the veranda were still, and there were no birds or insects or even lizards out and about. We had received an invitation to the art show from the gallery a few weeks earlier. Gerald didn't mention him, and I couldn't tell if Gerald knew that I was wondering about him.

Cassandra called the week before the show, leaving a message about it. Gerald said he had no desire to go. I didn't want to go without him. But at this moment, the energy that had settled around me began to vibrate. And the phone rang, disturbing the drape of stillness and moist heat that hung about me. I walked into the kitchen, then my office, tugging the chains from the overhead fans as I went.

Lately, all I had to do was think about someone or something and it came to me. On the phone was Cassandra.

"I called you a few days ago. Are you coming to the show?" There was an urgency in her voice, a plea laden with desperation.

"I don't think so. We are supposed to leave in a couple of weeks," I said, trying to think about how to bring up Derek without sounding too interested. "Been thinking, putting Gerald and Derek together might not be a good thing." I hadn't seen Derek since that day on the beach.

"The show runs through Saturday. Derek hung it almost three weeks ago and left space for a painting, then disappeared."

Through the window, it was as if the boats were frozen in time. "What do you mean, *disappeared?*"

"I mean he wasn't at the opening. I haven't heard from him. The space on the wall for the painting is still there. A writer in the local newspaper said he might be doing this for publicity, but I don't think so."

"Knowing him, he's probably on his yacht, sipping a drink with some beautiful woman."

"No, the boat is here . . . been moored since he disappeared. Jocelyn, can you meet me somewhere? I need to talk with you . . . something he said before he left . . . I really need to talk . . ."

"Sure, you want to come here? I can make us something for lunch."

"No. Gerald's there, right?"

"Actually, he's in town at . . ."

"No. If I can pick you up, maybe we can . . . I will think of some-place . . . I just need to talk to you."

"You sound upset. When do you wa—"

"I could be there in an hour."

"Okay. Sure."

"And Jocelyn, please don't say anything to Gerald."

Cassandra hung up. The air was soupy, thick and wet, stagnant, but I got ready. I turned on the fan to just move the air. I freshened up a bit, and before I fully escaped the disquiet I felt in her voice, the horn tooted.

"Have you heard from Derek?" Cassandra asked the minute I got into the car. Her face was pale, and there were dark circles under her eyes.

"I would have told you earlier if I had. . . . What is wrong?"

"I have to ask you something. I know . . . it might be too private . . . but . . ."

"What?"

"Did you abort Derek's baby?"

The question felt like ice water flung in my face. "No . . . no, I didn't. But . . . it's gone." The words tumbled out, unfiltered. I thought about how I had willed the child away, thoughts I would not share. My owner-ship of my body and my agency over it *and* my decisions about it, had been actualized. I knew it.

"Gone?"

"Yes. The doctor said it was a natural occurence in an early preg-nancy. . . . I guess like an early miscarriage."

"He knew . . . somehow he knew . . ." Cassandra put the car in re-verse and pulled out of the driveway.

"He knew? What are you talking about?"

"Derek knew. About two weeks ago he was making up the mailing list for the show. He gets to your name, and he begins to pace. He had hung the show, all except the one painting he said he hadn't finished. Then he doubles over and begins to howl . . . like a mad man."

"Was that unfinished painting of me?"

"I asked him that. He said, no. He said he hated you. Couldn't bear to think of you."

I was mute, hearing his words hurled at me.

"I fixed us a pitcher of rum punch," Cassandra said, "figured it would calm him down. It did mellow him out a bit, but only for a while. It made him amorous. We always flirted with each other, but he would always say, 'Cassandra, you are my best friend. Can't fuck you. I'll lose you.' It was fine with me, because I felt the same way. He had his women, but we were friends. But that night it was different."

Cassandra seemed mesmerized by the road and her thoughts. "We had a few drinks, and he took out his charcoals and sketched me. It made me self-conscious. He asked me to take off my top. I laughed and said I couldn't. He asked why, and I said, because you are making me hot."

Cassandra giggled nervously, then covered her mouth. I laughed in response. She grew silent. She drove on for what seemed like an eternity, then pulled onto a beachside road and parked.

"I was afraid if he saw my breasts, he'd know how turned on I was. He calmly said, 'I know. I want to draw you now, at the beginning.'"

I tried to be coy and asked, ". . . The beginning of what?"

Cassandra's brown eyes tried to conceal the feelings she held inside. But the lust was unmistakable.

"Us. He said, us. Just like that. And then he stroked my cheek and kissed me. I thought to myself, he's going to make love to me and everything will change. But I couldn't stop myself. I tried to make him wait a bit and asked him to put on a . . . you know. . . . But he said he wanted to feel me, inside. At first, he was gentle and loving, and then it changed. He seemed angry, not at me, but at the gods, or fate, or something. I can't say he hurt me, he's quite a skilled lover. He didn't stop—I don't know for how long. I finally stopped him because I was exhausted, but he was still . . . you know. I asked him if he had taken something, Viagra or something. He said no, said he had wanted me so long."

I felt a bit embarrassed. "What happened after that? You said on the phone he disappeared."

"I don't know. He made love to me the next morning. I left his place because I felt if there was some space between us, I could sort out what had happened. That evening he came up and wanted me again. I couldn't resist him. It was as if I were possessed or something. I finally said to him, 'What's going on?' I figured it was some kind of rebound thing, or something related to his outburst the day before."

"What did he say?"

"He said that he had to get away. He left my place and went downstairs. I was supposed to go with him to hang the painting the next day. I called him that night to make plans and he didn't answer. Nowhere to be found. Frankly, when I called you last week, I thought he had said something to you before he left."

"No. Nothing."

Her mood plummeted, and her eyes overflowed with tears. "Do me a favor, would you tell me if he does . . . contact you?"

"When did this all happen?"

"Last week. . . . No. More like two weeks ago."

"We are leaving in a couple of weeks. I promise, if I hear anything, I'll let you know."

Cassandra swallowed hard and wiped her eyes, then turned the key in the ignition. "Are you headed back to New York?"

"For a while. Then we're on to Boston. Gerald and I are getting married."

Cassandra's face showed no reaction to my news. "Will you come to the show?"

"I don't think so."

She drove, not saying anything for a while, her eyes trained on the road. It was as if our thoughts hung in the wet hot air.

"Can we keep in touch?"

I was transfixed by Cassandra's sad profile. There was a plea there, but also something else. To me, it seemed there was desperation. Cassandra pulled into the driveway of Gerald's home and turned off the car. "I hope you come to the show. Maybe Derek will show up with the painting, and all this will be solved."

"You know Gerald was not . . . fond of Derek. I doubt . . . I don't know."

"There you are!" Gerald called from the front door. "I was worried."

Cassandra's eyes flashed as she looked up to the door. When she looked back at me, her gaze was mystifying. "I am not sure if I am staying here in Bequia at Moon Hole. You have my cell. I need a . . ."

"You coming in, Jocelyn?" Gerald called.

"I'm sorry. What did you say, Cassandra?"

"Nothing . . . just safe journey."

49

The next week, I felt wistful, reflective. Gerald spent days working, teleconferencing with people at his office. One afternoon, he said he was going into town to ship some signed documents, contracts, and paperwork to Boston. I decided to go with him, to stop at the library in Kingstown to peruse some of the newspapers of the early 1900s, to give me a sense of how St. Vincent and Bequia had changed over time. Privately, I wondered if I might find out any more about Sumadi. My ruminations placed me right back in the mindset of Mariel; I had become her again, but just in my unresolved feelings.

Sitting in front of my computer, I went back to the original site where I read the crew list including Abrahim, Joseph, and John. Abrahim was the captain of his ship *The Sea Nymph Nereida*. Reading through the crew list, I found Sumadi's name, showing that he boarded the ship on the island of Brava. I scanned trips that had Abrahim and Joseph and John listed, but found no further trips by Sumadi with them, returning to Cape Verde once he came to Bequia.

"I'm ready if you are," Gerald said, startling me out of my reverie.

We were both silent in the car, all the way to the ferry and onto the ramp. Standing on the upper level, the ferry's movement toward St. Vincent, gave us a nice breeze, and I found myself gazing at the shore with the realization that there would be only a few more crossings before we were headed to the States.

"We'll be back. Don't worry," Gerald said, his mellifluous deep voice flowing into my ear, still warming me as it had the first time I heard it.

"What are you doing hanging around in my mind?" I asked, laughing at how commonplace that was now becoming, but feeling exposed by his secret presence there. I had been thinking of Sumadi. That musing was hidden in the midst of a montage of memories of Bequia now filling my mind. I didn't want Gerald to misread my intentions. These thoughts simply matured my understanding of who I was.

In town, Gerald dropped me off, kissed me on the lips, and said, "I love you. You know that, don't you?"

"I do. I love you too."

The librarian in Saint Vincent, who Gerald had introduced me to weeks earlier, was a woman in her sixties and a no-nonsense Bajan. She mostly wore a serious expression, except for her momentary smile, acknowledging my return. "Dr. Kendall, I believe I found something of interest to you, but I need to retrieve it."

I proceeded to write out the call slip for the microfilm that I wanted to view, and gave it to the young assistant librarian, who disappeared into the back and brought me the reel. The *St. Vincent Herald* issues confirmed the scholarly articles I had read, describing Bequia, despite its small size, as a major center for whaling in the Caribbean. ". . . second only to Barbados." As I scrolled through the newspaper looking at photos and headlines, Ms. Bell, the head librarian, came up behind me. "Pardon me, Dr. Kendall. I found this article, which was published in America, in our collection on whaling and women. It was written by an American woman from New Bedford, Massachusetts, but it was about a woman who was the wife of a whaler here in Bequia. The article seemed very much in the area you outlined as within your interest."

It was a photocopy of the original article, which had a formal looking photo of Mrs. Mary Charles. She had traveled on her husband's whaling ship to Bequia. She cited her previous articles in the *New*

Bedford Monitor about the women of New Bedford and their business enterprises, when the husbands were on their long whaling trips.

She then mentioned the similarity of activities she found in a woman living on Bequia, Mrs. Maria Matos. *Mariel?* My arms first stiffened, then went slack and numb. A chill ran through my body. The hair raised up on my arms. Mary Charles had interviewed Mariel, describing her clay pots, bowls and plates, and her baskets. The article told of Mariel's hammock weaving, as well as her pottery and basket business, and showed a picture of her advertisement in the St. Vincent newspaper. It mentioned a trading company that was beginning to take her crafts to Barbados for sale, then on to New Bedford. This article spoke of her husband as a successful whaler who traveled the world, but it focused on her businesses as a source of income for her family and a pastime for her during his long trips. "Maria" even harvested cassava and baked bread, which sailors bought and ate.

> It is more than a pastime. It is my work when my husband, Sr. John Matos, is away at sea. A woman has to have her work. My husband once told me he has to have his work. Chasing whales around the world was his. Making things and selling them, which has become my business, is mine.
>
> I tell my nieces, my daughter, and my grandchild now, I tell her, make something for yourself.

Tears filled my eyes. Proof of what I knew to be true! I remembered the first argument I had with Gerald. He said, "I would have taken you for a feminist." Mariel didn't sit idly by, paralyzed by guilt. She built a business to allow her husband to be at home and keep her family together.

At the same time, the article brought back memories of tall and handsome Sumadi. My mind fixed on him. I printed the pages that held the article on Mariel but looked back at the *St. Vincent Herald* that I had selected and scrolled through. The issue was from January 1905. And there it was, as if I had willed it there.

Soloman S. Gonzalvez, Hauls in the First Whale Catch of the Year! Soloman S. Gonzalves, hailing from Cape Verde the island of Brava, has been a native whaler in the Grenadines for more than twenty years. Soloman Sumadi Gonsalvez has homes in Mustique and Canouan and has struck the first whale of the year . . .

Sumadi! My hand reached up to my mouth when a gasp left my lips.

One of Bequia's own, he is known for his keen eye. He spotted the whale from the island of Bequia, a high watchpost. He and his team made chase, beating Portuguese, British, and Yankee whalers, who were also in pursuit. His large canoe was swift, and his crew skilled. Two of his sons joined him on this catch. Old timers said that in his younger days, the British tried to capture him, unsuccessfully, as his canoes crisscrossed the waters of the Grenadines.

I remembered how he said that I didn't know what he sacrificed to be with me.

"Dr. Kendall, was that article of interest to you?" Ms. Bell's voice filtered through the thick library air, laden with the dust and bits and pieces of time. Rich mixtures of time gone by—and they were all there. Mariel, her husband John, and Sumadi.

"Yes, thank you, Ms. Bell. I love librarians!"

She seemed bewildered by my statement. Too much to explain. Time to be quiet and treasure my keepsakes of Bequia.

My gaze drew me out to the road at the side of the library. Images of Kingstown and St. Vincent from so long ago blurred my vision and then it refocused. The last time I saw him, I—Mariel—was standing in front of the library, which was not here back then. A man was walking across the road, and I sensed something familiar in his stride. Our eyes met at that moment, and my lips smiled wholly on their own. He stood where he was, waiting, it seemed, to see if I would come toward him. I couldn't stop myself.

Our children were set on marrying. We had not seen each other to talk, until now. Yet this meeting was happenstance.

"Did you speak to him?" I said.

"Yes, but he will not listen. His eyes are filled with love for Estela, as my eyes were with you." He said what we had avoided for a lifetime— that he did love me.

"You know this should not be."

"I know we must stay silent," he said, "so no one but us knows the truth. These self-righteous people would kill them."

"I am using all my powers to 'will' them a good future."

"He seems set on chasing whales. His eye is sharp, and he is aggressive. My second wife gave me two sons and one daughter. I have three grandchildren." His chest swelled, and he stood taller. "My sons are all chasing whales with me. They are good salesmen, and the whale oil gets a good price. . . . I have seen your hammocks and weavings in Florida."

His eyes did love me once, I thought. *The remnants of that love still glimmers there.*

"You are still swift." I laughed. "They write about you."

He shrugged his shoulders, then squared them and grinned. I could not stop loving him, even though I was committed to John and knew I could never betray my husband again. John had finally stayed in Bequia, sacrificing his love for the sea and long voyages, as I asked. Our love was bound together with the long stretches in time that we were apart and the times when we came back together, missing each other. We had made peace with our past.

"You look beautiful," Sumadi said. "Time has kissed your face." The words spilled from his lips as if he had no will to stop them. "It was not all the passion of our youth. *It was more.*" His words and thoughts flew to me.

The impact of our encounter caught me off guard. A townswoman walked by. Sumadi nodded in my direction and turned, as if we were two passing acquaintances. That too seemed sudden, unexpected. There was nothing more to say out loud, though there were so many words left trapped in my chest. He turned to walk away, his stride still powerful, though time had slowed his gait. He did not look back. Our paths had now been set. I was headed to the photographer, where John was waiting. The man would capture our image in a box and put it on paper.

50

We finally had that date at the Seafood Shack. It was wonderful to see Gerald in his element. The chef came out to chat when he heard that he was there, and he made us a delicious lobster and crab feast celebration dinner, which I had learned was a traditional Carib wedding feast. The waitresses were so attentive, and hung on Gerald's every word, though he was spellbound by me.

The last day of the art show came and went. Gerald didn't want to go. I wondered if Derek had come back. There was no time away from Gerald to call Cassandra, so I felt the fates militated against me having the closure that I thought I wanted. I didn't know what I would have said to Derek, but somehow, I imagined that I wanted to see that he was happy and moving on. My memories of Mariel's encounter with Sumadi comforted me, and I hoped for such an encounter with Derek, though we were grounded in this time and place. What I learned from the past life regression and my travels back in time were not his lessons. They were mine.

The day before we left for the States, we finished packing up the house. Haynes came over to empty the refrigerator and to take out sheets to cover the furniture. She would not let me lift anything heavy—or anything light, for that matter. I packed my carry-on with toiletries and brought it into the dining room; she admonished me, saying, "Mum why didn't you call me to do that?" I would miss her.

We flew to New York first. I kept my place for two months to move stuff out, vested my pension, but I knew I wasn't going back to the college. Though I was saying good-bye to my apartment, my life there had been empty for some time, and I did not miss it. Gerald's place in Boston was a townhouse apartment and big by most standards. One of the bedrooms became my office. We began looking for a bigger space: Gerald wanted a house to accommodate the baby and to put down roots.

My four-month appointment went fine. The sonogram pictures of the baby were so clear that I felt I knew him. Gerald seemed entranced by the image. He lifted my hand to his mouth and kissed my open palm. When we got home, Gerald stopped to get the mail. There it was.

"It came," I said, taking the big manila envelope from him.

"What?"

"I sent the hair . . . you know, from the pendant, to be analyzed and . . ." I sat at the kitchen table, silently reading the documents.

Dear Dr. Kendall,

We have analyzed the specimens that you sent and have some interesting findings. Both hair specimens are of the same mother. She seems to be of mainly Amerindian ethnicity, and one specimen is of Amerindian and Iberian European and Middle Eastern ancestry. The other is of Amerindian and Iberian European and North African and West African ancestry and Middle Eastern origins. The percentages vary, and you will see that it suggests that one specimen has more ties genetically to North Africa, and West Africa, in percent of blood lineage. Our guess would be that the area of North Africa that he comes from, we determined the gender to be male, is Cape Verde because of the Iberian European mix there. You will find the pie charts and map of ethnicities enclosed. There is an interesting tool online, and we have also sent this material to you via email and zip file so that you can see the migration maps that likely explain the lineage we found for the samples.

The third sample you gave of saliva was also analyzed. Interestingly, that has a genetic lineage that includes West African, Amerindian, Western European, North African, Iberian, and Middle Eastern descent

as well. The more detailed analysis is attached. If you should have any
questions, please don't hesitate to call.
    Sincerely,
    J. Viera

The letter, which documented my ancestral roots, had a powerful effect on me. For the first time since I left for Bequia, I felt grounded. I stroked my belly, feeling that my child, too, had a history that dated back many generations and included many cultures. I chattered at Gerald about some of the connections between my great-great-great-grandparents and the hair in the locket. I pieced together some of the evidence from the dreams about John and Sumadi. At some point, he seemed as if this knowledge was not new to him. I worried that all these genetic connections might cause him concerns about the child growing inside of me. He had none.

"You have to know, by now," he said, "how many cousins and family mixes there have been in history."

I loved him for his intelligence and his caring for me. It was like a reawakening each time he said something that made me rediscover his love.

So, there it was. I felt whole in the knowledge that my dreams were confirmed. I didn't know why the report mattered. I always believed the things I saw in my dreams when I traveled back in time—I never ever doubted them. My encounter with Nereida rang true. Nereida's spell may have bound Mariel, John, and Sumadi together; her intent was not to do harm, but to protect her son's future, and in that she was successful. I was able to embrace her as a matriarch of the family. The history I learned as my dreams unfolded transformed me, and made me less judgmental, more accepting and loving.

My cell phone rang.
    "Jocelyn, it's me, Cassandra. Can you talk?"
    "Sure. What's wrong?"
    "I'm pregnant. Have you heard from Derek?" Cassandra asked.

"No. If I had, I would have called you."

"I am moving to Toronto with my sister until the baby's born." She was silent, then added, ". . . And he *was* here."

"Who? Derek?"

"Yes. His yacht is gone. And I never saw him . . . never even came to speak to me."

"I am so sorry."

"You all right?" Gerald asked.

I nodded and then took the phone to my office. Cassandra was silent for a long while. Then she said, "You had all those dreams. Did you learn anything?"

"Yes. I learned so much . . ." I reflected on the past few months as I sat in the room with Mariel's paintings and my own, now framed on the walls of my new space. "Strength. I guess I learned that I had power that I never knew."

I was quiet for a while taking in the view of Boston Harbor. "Cassandra, you would understand this as a woman and a psychologist. I needed to embrace Mariel's connection to her body. I learned that Mariel's desire is what kept her alive, not buried in loneliness. She stayed connected to her needs, her passions. Do you understand me?"

"I think I do," Cassandra said.

"For so long I buried my needs, my passions. Mariel gave herself permission to have desires. I had to accept that in her and in myself."

"I think my needs just get me in trouble," Cassandra laughed.

I laughed with her. "Mariel's desire kept her interested in the world and was the source of her creativity. It was the source of her drive that helped her survive."

We were both quiet for a long while.

"Men never question their desires and drive," I said.

"Nope, they never do." She laughed again.

"They see it as part of their strength, their manhood. As women, we always do . . . question our. . . . I think we need to own our sexual energy, not punish it with . . . shame. Our sexual energy is part of our life force."

I felt a flutter inside, like I had swallowed a butterfly. It was the baby . . . the first time I felt him move.

"I also learned that Jocelyn doesn't suit me anymore. I am changing my name to . . . Joy. My uncle gave me that name. And lately that's how I feel, full of joy."

"It suits you now. You've changed since we first met. I feel so weak, so scared. The guy . . . your friend . . . who regressed you, did your past life regression?"

"Luis? Yes."

". . . Think he can do that for me? I have so many questions. Why did I let this happen?"

I didn't know what to make of the question. I felt it was better to be quiet, a lesson Vivencia taught me.

"Maybe you can be there . . . you know, with me?"

"I don't know . . . I . . ." I didn't know what to say.

"I need your good energy. . . . I saw it that last day we were together. Through all of this, you weren't afraid. I need that too."

"I'll ask Luis . . . but I can't promise . . . and I can't possibly guess how I can help by being there."

"I don't know . . . I just feel maybe you can . . . I need your courage. I gotta go."

Gerald was in his office at the computer when I ended the call. I wanted to hold him, to touch him. Cassandra sounded so alone. I came up behind him, putting my arms around his chest and resting my head on his back.

"Babe, I have to make plans to go to Canada for a week's stay at the end of the month. I have to authenticate some artifacts for a private collector. He's going to meet me at a conference. A little mysterious! He didn't give me a list of the artifacts . . . says I should be familiar with the main object when I see it. But . . . figured since he was offering a hefty fee, I'd do it all in one trip."

"That's odd. I was just talking to Cassandra and she's going to Canada. Don't tell me you're going to Toronto."

"No. I'm headed to Nova Scotia. Why don't you come with me? The conference should be interesting, 'Whaling Families in Nova Scotia' is the broad theme. You can network in case you want to do some consulting . . . or maybe just see the city of Halifax. Have you ever been? Beautiful town."

"Networking . . . if I knew what I wanted to be when I grow up . . ." I laughed. ". . . By the way, the conversation with Cassandra, it seems she's pregnant." Gerald continued typing on the computer.

"That's the psychologist who lives on Moon Hole . . . friend of . . ." his voice trailed off as if he didn't want to voice his name.

"Derek, yes. Well, it's his child."

"You have become part of the island culture, haven't you? Knowing all the secrets."

"My girlfriend Selena would call it *bochinche*, the gossip. I have to call her and Luis. But that's not why I told you. She asked me to have Luis do a past life regression on her."

Gerald looked up from the computer. "Why?"

"She feels she made a mistake. I guess she thinks the past life regression might give her some answers from past lives about why she did this, and . . . she said that maybe I could help guide her with Luis."

"Why would you get involved in that? Knowing that she's involved with Derek . . . we're finally free of him.

"He's gone . . . nowhere to be found."

Gerald looked up and then back down at the screen. "If you learned nothing else from Vivencia, you should have learned about how complicated . . ."

"I did. I also learned about my strength, and my ability to see into the past, to be there, and to learn there. My dreams revealed so many truths to me. The report on the DNA I got about the hair my great-great-grandmother saved, told me that the things I learned are all true."

"You were not always unharmed in those dreams," Gerald said. "Look, I would never try and stop you from pursuing . . ."

"That's good because you can't!" I said, laughing. "How far is it from Nova Scotia to Toronto?"

Gerald shook his head, smiling. "Too far."

"Want to take a side trip?"

Fall's cool kiss began the confetti of color, gold, ruby, and russet leaves diving, drifting, and dancing in celebration of our wedding. As a wondrous surprise, Uncle Leland flew in, so he and Auntie Grace—my only living Bequian family members—were both present to witness and rejoice in our marriage. Auntie Grace said she had been waiting for that day too long to miss it. Gerald placed the Jewish betrothal ring, which belonged to my great-great-great-great-grandfather Abrahim, on my hand. And at that moment, I felt an even more physical connection to a lineage that I had not known before Bequia, but which I now fully embraced. Abrahim and John left me a gift that had been guarded through generations—even through the Inquisition. Mariel left me my great-great-grandfather John's scrimshaw, along with her own Carib people's prayers over the locket of hair of my great-grandparents. Nereida left me the gift of knowing the power of my will. Her will crossed the sea from Cape Verde with defiance and transcended time—keeping her son, Sumadi, free from enslavement. Through his presence, I knew the feeling of being desired and fully alive. The events of the weeks in Bequia brought together so many pieces of my past, and also reawakened my excitement about the future. I hadn't dreamed in months. I didn't know if the gift for seeing and living in the past was now a closed chapter in my life, but I hoped not.

The End

Acknowledgments

Writing is a solitary endeavor, but never lonely. My characters and I are in a dance, and sometimes I don't know who is leading. But friends, family, and readers spur and energize my work. I do not believe I could have finished this book without them.

My husband, Karl Friedman—my best friend and muse, to whom I dedicated this book—was the inspiration for my writing from the beginning. In 1970, when Karl and I first met, he discovered my fiction on scraps of paper and in unlabeled notebooks. He suggested I collect my scribbled jottings of poetry and snatches of narratives to save and complete them. When I strayed too long from writing fiction, he would remind me that I should be finishing my novel. In the beginning, it was *Wildflowers* that he pushed me to complete, then *Tangled Dreams*. He never let me forget that writing fiction was my first love, and my calling.

My heart is full of love and gratitude for my son Ian, a software engineer, who always replaced or fixed any piece of technology that I used so that my writing was never hindered by technical difficulties. No matter what time of the day or night, he would come to my aid. His memories and his words of encouragement throughout the years, were rich and sprinkled with love. During the darker days, the past few years since we lost Karl, Ian was my reminder of happier times, the times the three of us shared. He has been my rock, the person upon whom I leaned to get through the tough times.

Although *Tangled Dreams* is pure fiction, I did spend my early years in the West Indies with my grandparents, as did the main character. Writing this book and the reflection that came with it, brought me gratitude and grace for my time spent in Barbados with my grandparents, and my parents' decisions to send me. They did their best with difficult circumstances, and my memories dance about in my thoughts from time to time, and come alive in my writing. That time was my beginning as a writer, giving me my introduction to aloneness, solitude, and creativity. I keep the brave little girl, who travelled by herself to a strange place, with me always.

I am eternally grateful for my editor, Elizabeth Rosner, who has become a good friend. She is an author of award-winning books, essays, and poetry, and a sought-after speaker on the topic of trauma. She brought a wellspring of knowledge and wisdom about writing, and she was a welcomed ear whenever I needed to talk about the difficult choices writing sometimes holds. Liz Rosner also suggested the copy editor, Elizabeth Block, who did the first copy edit of *Tangled Dreams*. She was an excellent copy editor, but my characters were not finished speaking.

The Mayfly Design Services team completed the publishing services for the manuscript. Julie Scheife and her design team, Jess LaGreca, did the finishing touches on this book for publication. My special thanks to Sean Strain, an extraordinary proofreader, whose research of granular detail of the historical references surprised and delighted me.

Karl and I visited the New Bedford Whaling Museum at the beginning of my research for this book. The New Bedford Whaling Museum's online exhibitions, photographs, and historical essays on whaling kept me in contact with the stories of the people who chased whales. The historical figures and the artifacts and documents of the museum all informed my understanding of this rich, diverse community of people who make up the whaling community. *Tangled Dreams* is a purely fictional work, but the ethos of the whaling women and men, Black and White, all remained alive for me through the updated images from the museum. The African, Portuguese, and Cape Verdean men and women who searched for whales became my guiding stars.

I am thankful and grateful to my beta readers. I passed my initial ideas for *Tangled Dreams* by my friend Nancy Mintz, an avid reader, and she encouraged me to write it. Rose Ranieri Crosby, M.S., a dear childhood friend and a voracious reader, would read *Tangled Dreams* right after my husband Karl, my alpha reader. Donna Laurin, a trusted reader, and my friends Myrna Rivera, M.S., CIMA, Entrepreneur, and Philanthropist; Fern Khan, M.S.W., Dean Emerita, Bank Street College; Rosemary A. Bova, M.S.; M.S.W., and Kiesia Messado Anderson, Ph.D., each spurred my writing by their comments about the characters and the book's pacing, plot, and spirit.

Thank you to the creatives who shared their gifts to present this book to the reading public. Their generosity helped me realize my vision of *Tangled Dreams*. Lisette Brodey, an author and friend, suggested The Cover Collection, which designed my book's cover. The Cover Collection, Inc. was a pleasure to work with. Thank you to Walter Uhrman for his artistic eye. My photographer, R.J. Lewis, who did my photo for my first novel, *Wildflowers*, also did my photo for *Tangled Dreams*. He's a talented photographer, whose head shots for actors are works of art. And my gratitude goes to my gynecologist, Dr. Joan Haselkorn, M.D., who answered my calls when I needed clarifications on the reproductive process. Lastly, thank you to the writing community and the authors who shared their expertise and information with me, that kept me focused this past few difficult years: the Kauai Online Writing Conference, faculty, the Winning Writers Team, Carolyn Howard-Johnson, and Jendi Reiter.

My warmest gratitude I send to my beta readers and the rest of my family and friends, who have always asked about my writing and my novel, despite my grief after the loss of my husband. Their calls, chats, and visits kept me alive, and focused on making *Tangled Dreams* a reality. My dear friends and family—Keith Figgs, Ed. D.; Carolyn Lowe, Shana Molt, Maggie Kirscher, Stanley and Harriet Kratenstein, Marlene Pannell, M.S., Cheryl Boyd Gross, M.S. M.A.; Iris Plafker, Christine Pollice, M.S.; Barbara Dodick, M.S.; Linda Larisch, Lou Ann Norelli, Alexis De Persia Granger and Chris Granger, Gerrie Summers, and Hyacinth Brown—you didn't let me wither for lack of warmth. You called and wrote and pulled me out into the sunshine. I am so very appreciative. You reminded me, as Karl did, that writing is my calling.

About the Author

Delores Lowe Friedman began her writing career in nonfiction authoring a monthly education column for *Essence Magazine*, while teaching in the New York City public schools. An advocate for parental involvement, she authored the book, *Education Handbook for Black Families*, published by Anchor Press/Doubleday. Earning a doctorate from Teachers College, Columbia University, she began a twenty-one-year career as a professor in the City University of New York, while authoring scholarly articles on equity in promoting the teaching of Science, Technology Engineering and Mathematics (STEM) to girls and children of color. Her early fiction writings were children's books published in the educational market by Houghton-Mifflin. She shared stories about the Caribbean American, and African American families in *Ian's Pet*, *Trevor from Trinidad*, *Jenny's Faraway Family*, *The Math Bee*, and *Journey to a Free Town*.

Once retired, she focused on her first love, writing adult fiction. *Tangled Dreams* is Delores Lowe Friedman's second novel. Her debut novel,

Wildflowers, won the 2021 North Street Book Prize for Hybrid Published and Self-Published Books in Literary Fiction/Mainstream Fiction. The review by Jendi Reiter said, "Delores Lowe Friedman's *Wildflowers* is an emotionally rich and intimate novel that follows a decades-long friendship among three Black women in New York City . . . This story celebrates the power of women's bonds, . . . The writing was eloquent . . . *Wildflowers* would be an excellent book club read. Kirkus called *Wildflowers*, "A solid historical novel with engaging characters." When she is not writing, she loves to draw, paint, go to the theater, and cook.

www.ingramcontent.com/pod-product-compliance
Lightning Source LLC
Chambersburg PA
CBHW020652110726
47901CB00001B/160